SLY MONGOOSE

TOBIAS S. BUCKELL

TOR®

A TOM DOHERTY ASSOCIATES BOOK
NEW YORK

SLY MONGOOSE

A Tor Book
Published by Tom Doherty Associates, LLC
175 Fifth Avenue
New York, NY 10010

www.tor-forge.com

Tor® is a registered trademark of Tom Doherty Associates, LLC.

ISBN 978-0-7653-5872-1

First Edition: August 2008
First Mass Market Edition: April 2012

Printed in the United States of America

0 9 8 7 6 5 4 3 2 1

For Geoff Landis: Thanks for Chilo . . .

SLY MONGOOSE

PART ONE

CHAPTER ONE

Pepper lay strapped to a blunt, cone-shaped heatshield with a hundred miles of Chilo's atmosphere to fall through yet. The edges of the 2,000-degree fireball created by the shock wave of his reentry licked and danced at the edges of his vision. A small taste of hell, he thought, as the contraption under his back wobbled and threatened to overturn.

When the roaring abated, Pepper cracked free of the crude heatshield and ran his spacesuit through a self-check. Even with the protection of the ablative plastics he'd just ridden down out of orbit, the suit had become a bit toasty.

But within tolerances. Inside, Pepper only broke a gentle sweat.

He threw the blackened cone away from him and reoriented himself to face downward. Dirty brown and yellow clouds choked the world below him as far as he could see. The planet Chilo in all its glory: sulfuric acid-laced clouds, crushing pressure, no breathable atmosphere. Not somewhere most would call home.

A quick look straight below again. It really didn't feel like he was moving faster than the speed of sound.

He'd survived deorbiting in nothing more than a spacesuit and a personal heatshield. But now the tricky part approached.

A tiny buzz in Pepper's ear got his attention. He yawned, eardrums popping. His dreadlocks, bunched up inside the helmet, scraped against each other as a young-sounding male voice piped up in Pepper's helmet. The man sounded bored with a side of professional neutral. For the man behind that particular voice, this was just another shift, just another day. "Unidentified reentry vehicle, this is Eupatoria Port Authority, come in."

Air thundered past Pepper, buffeting him.

"Hello, Eupatoria," Pepper said. The spacesuit's radio still worked. That would be helpful.

"Yes, unidentified vehicle, your transponder seems to be down."

Pepper threw out his arms to maximize drag. "I don't have a transponder."

"That's a finable offense," the voice replied. "What are you deorbiting in? We're having trouble tracking you."

Pepper explained the situation in brief while scanning the horizon.

There was a long pause on the other end. Then a polite cough. "You deorbited with a handmade heatshield and an armored spacesuit?"

"The situation was complicated. Can you do me a favor? I need you to provide me with coordinates. Where I am, where I'm headed, and where I might be able to land." Eventually this slowing parabola would end.

A brief off-mic murmur drifted by. "Unidentified . . . just please hold."

He wasn't going anywhere. Pepper caught the glint of a far-off structure: a tiny thread reaching up from the clouds into the dark depth of space. Shame that hadn't been an option. A lot less excitement to just take an elevator down to one of Chilo's floating cities. At the bottom of that thread might even be Eupatoria and the somewhat surprised Port Authority officials who'd started the day out thinking today would be a day like any other.

"Sir?"

"Still here," Pepper said.

"What's your name, sir?"

"Juan Smith." Pepper's last alias. Over the last few decades working as assassin, spy, and general all-around human weapon, he'd gotten used to a regular rotation of false names. In the centuries before that, he could dimly remember even more identities and names.

A crisp, older, and quite officious woman joined the discussion. "Mr. Smith, voice identification has been confirmed. Mr. Smith, you are aware that you are wanted for the murder of the entire crew of the *Sheikh Professional.*"

"Ah." Pepper nodded. That would come up.

"Well, Mr. Smith, this is quite an unorthodox methodology for deorbiting yourself, and you must realize that even if you survive you'll still be a wanted criminal. We are scrambling recovery vehicles for you right now. When you pop your parachute we will pick you up. But I am being asked to explain your rights before you are picked up. In the event that the pickup is not successful, would you like to enter a plea for prosperity and name legal counsel to continue your defense in the event that you are not present for your trial?"

"No need for all that crap," Pepper sniffed. "I did it."

"Your confession may not stand up due to the peculiar circumstances. Can you elaborate?"

The never-ending carpet of dreary clouds visibly rose to meet him. Not a lot of time left for details. "About that rescue effort: one little problem," he said. "I don't have a parachute."

Silence from Eupatoria filled his helmet as they

digested that. "You don't have a parachute?" The original male voice sounded shocked.

"Are you committing suicide?" the woman asked just after him.

"Spaceships don't routinely include parachutes in their manifest," Pepper muttered. "Particularly ones where no one expected anyone from the ship to ever dip into the orbital well."

The clouds rose faster, gaining definition. He could see lumpy clumps, and long whisps scattered behind those larger formations.

"So here is what I need," Pepper said. "You need to tell me where the nearest city is."

"But without a chute . . ."

"Terminal velocity at city height is a hundred twenty miles an hour. As some aboard the *Sheikh* found out, I'm not easily breakable. You help me hit a city, you either get to pick up my body, or come arrest me."

"You'll endanger others, you're a projectile."

"I'll hit one of the farm levels," Pepper promised. "Besides, you'll want to hear my side of the story."

More off-the-mic chatter between the two people watching over him. Then they returned. "What *did* happen there? We still need more details."

"I didn't start it," Pepper said. "I just replied . . . in kind."

Several minutes later he angled himself toward a glint in the clouds. He'd slowed down over the long minutes to just over a hundred miles an hour.

It was still going to hurt.

"Eupatoria." The glint grew into a round silvery shape just above the puffy yellow and orange clouds. Pepper felt he might as well tie things up, just in case he didn't make it. "I'm sending you a prerecorded burst. It explains everything."

If Eupatoria, or any other of Chilo's floating cities, paid attention to his warning, they all might live.

But Pepper doubted it. The invasion of Chilo would begin soon enough, in fits and starts. If he survived the impact, he might be able to help rouse its populace to defend itself.

A round silver city hurtled toward Pepper.

They said one should relax before major impacts, but at this speed Pepper really didn't think it mattered what he did, it was going to hurt either way.

With just one last-second adjustment to aim himself at the green band of the farm section of the giant floating city, Pepper tensed before he hit.

CHAPTER TWO

The day Timas and his friend Cen saw the alien, everything changed.

Outside the spherical floating city of Yatapek, a hundred thousand feet over the ground, the winds had died. The forecast from the Aeolian cities, with their satellites and computers, gave Yatapek a seven-hour window. The city could anchor over the ground safely.

"Timas, it's time," his mother had said gently as she woke him that morning. He'd heard the old phone ring, and he knew what it heralded as he blinked sleep from his eyes. Time to descend into hell again.

Timas had donned his cumbersome pressure suit with the help of a mechanic as the doctor Amoxtli watched. The mechanic checked over every seal and joint, making sure Timas stood ready to get dropped into the ninety-times-normal pressure of Chilo's surface.

"For the city," the mechanic said as he slapped the helmet into place.

"For our people," Timas murmured.

Then the city's elevator had lowered Timas and a similarly suited-up partner down to the ground, swaying and jerking them about inside. It dug in with its screws when it hit bottom, holding itself and the city steady as the incredibly strong nanofilament wire quivered all the way back up to the city's docks.

Every week, weather permitting, boys like Timas checked over the mining machine their city depended on: the cuatetl. It hunted for the precious metals Yatapek needed to survive. This week it had radioed a panic failure code.

Despite the calm a hundred thousand feet above him, Timas strained his way forward through the hurricane-like winds here. He'd first come to the surface on his thirteenth birthday. In the following two years he'd never seen a calm day. He heard from older boys that it happened, but he'd believe it when he saw it.

Timas stood on smooth rock, melted and flattened out by hundreds of years of sulfuric rain and howling winds. He watched as the giant conical drilling nose of the cuatetl breached the surface upwind of him, vomiting debris. Most of the giant worm of a machine, hundreds of feet long, lay hidden under the ground right now.

Grit and pebbles smacked Timas, pinging off the acid-polished shine of his groundsuit. They left tiny dents and pits.

"Damnit." Timas had expected the cuatetl to appear on the surface to his right. Standing downwind of the cuatetl could leave him with a cracked suit. If that happened the insane pressure of Chilo's atmosphere at ground level would crush him instantly.

If the heat didn't kill him first, all 800 degrees of it. Hot enough that the horizon constantly rippled.

Timas watched the thousands of counter-rotating disc cutters on the cuatatl's head finish spinning down. They still kicked more dirt into the air as he moved upwind. He winced as each loud pop and ping reverberated inside his protective armor.

Each step took its toll. The groundsuit weighed over fifty pounds, despite being made of special lightweight alloys. It was manufactured by some distant city on Chilo, since Yatapek didn't have the means to make anything like the groundsuit.

The pelting stopped. Timas sweated and panted, wishing to the shady underworld that he'd picked a better spot to stand.

The silver figure of his companion loomed out of the oppressive gloom of the surface in a cumbersome, gleaming, buglike suit. Winglike vanes stuck out of the back of the older suit dumping excess heat out above it in ripples. Timas sighed. Cenyoatl, Cen for short, had certainly gotten lucky today. He stood well upwind of the recall buoy they'd triggered. The cuatetl hadn't popped up to the left of it, as Timas programmed the buoy to tell it.

Cen would probably say, "I told you so." His family could drive someone off an edge like that. Always perfect, always stepping to the beat of tradition, always following the rules handed down.

Timas and Cen were xocoyotzin: young, thin, and small enough to fit inside the groundsuits designed to fit svelte outsiders, not adults from his city. Timas lumbered toward his fellow xocoyotzin. They touched their oversize helmets together to speak.

"I told you so." Cen's voice buzzed, sounding like it came through a tin can a room away, even though his smirking face stared right at Timas. "If the cuatetl isn't working properly, what makes you think it's going to follow the recall code correctly?"

"I know," Timas replied. Every time he touched helmets just to talk he wondered what it would be like to have the luxury of working radios in every suit. His father's father once told him that they'd all had working radios when *he'd* been a xocoyotzin, fifty years ago when the city had been built in Chilo's upper atmosphere. Now just a handful of radios worked, used by the city to call other cities or help airships dock. And the one on the mining machine, of course. "You're right, upwind is safer."

"We're also right on the edge of the debris field, you know we're supposed to tell the cuatetl to move farther upwind of the elevator. Just in case."

"It's right on the edge. It'll be okay. Come on, let's get to work." Besides, if something had failed Timas didn't want to have to haul equipment much farther than this.

The cuatetl's stilled nose dripped detritus, stuck in the air at a forty-five degree angle. It loomed into the sky, dwarfing them. The two boys walked in between a large gap in the segment between the cutter head and the main body.

Timas clanked on, avoiding slurry dripping down from twenty feet over his head. He clambered onto a small alcove, no-slip surface crunching underfoot. The machine's angle meant that Timas had to brace himself as he leaned forward. Cen stayed back, worried about knocking his heat vanes on something in the tight quarters and boiling himself to death.

Cen lived in terror of mistakes. His entire family depended on him to provide for them. But even more than that, Cen's family thrived on the status of being one of the twenty xocoyotzin families.

Lights blinked at Timas, advertising the interface panel he needed to check.

The entire cuatetl stretched six hundred feet down a slope under him. He hoped the problem was in the drill head. It usually was. Timas and Cen had been lowered with three new disc cutters.

If something else had failed, the next couple hours would drag on.

Timas didn't want to have to go tromping around through the whole machine. Last year he'd been working with an older xocoyotzin when one of the ore processors to the rear broke down. It had taken weeks of hard work by all thirty of the xocoyotzin to get a whole new processor winched down to the surface and swapped in.

Timas checked the diagram on the panel. It indicated a broken disc cutter.

Good.

Now he and Cen just had to get outside and lug a fifty-pound piece of equipment back and swap it out.

Timas glanced at his wrist. He he had three hours of air left. He didn't bother looking at the pressure or heat dials. Thinking about either just got one jumpy.

Three hours of air. It would take an hour to get winched back up to Yatapek. You couldn't swap out a new air bottle on Chilo's surface.

He backed out of the alcove and bumped helmets with Cen.

"It's a disc cutter," Timas said. And even luckier, the cuatetl had rotated the failed unit down toward the ground for them to access.

"Great." Cen grinned on the other side of his slightly warped visor. "We can get one dragged over and changed in time. No second trip tomorrow."

Even duty-conscious Cen, proud of his family and his

role, didn't want to return to the hellish surface tomorrow. Once a week to service the mining machine was enough.

When the Azteca of New Anegada left aboard ships bound for other planets, trying to escape their history there, had they ever imagined ending up on a world like this? Timas doubted it. His ancestors may have been tricked into believing things borrowed from a lost culture on a distant Earth by cruelly manipulative aliens. They may have warred with the Ragamuffins who lived on New Anegada and lost, but this he would never have wished on his worst enemy. He didn't imagine his own great grandparents had willingly wished this on him.

"Okay, let's do it."

Cen took the lead and Timas followed him. One of Cen's heat vanes had a slight bend. Even upwind some of the debris had hit Cen's suit. Timas reminded himself to tell the mechanics when they were winched back up.

Out from the shadow of the cuatetl Timas checked the markers they'd left drilled into the ground. The red blinking lights, powered by the fierce wind, led the two boys deep into the murky orange gloom away from the cuatetl.

Timas fell into a pattern. Step, step, rest, mouthful of stale, recycled air. The smell of three generations of sweaty xocoyotzin before him filled the suit. Step, step, rest, breathe.

Cen pulled well ahead of Timas. Timas stopped, panting and watching his visor fog, and noticed something move out of the corner of his eye.

Shadows. Here on the surface, in the brown muck and low visibility with the heat rippling and wind kicking, it wasn't unusual to imagine things moving about.

But no, he did see something.

Timas turned and saw a hazy figure on all fours run at him through the edges of the muck. Cen moved on, oblivious, as Timas squinted at the metallic tentacles that draped from the front of the creature. It wore a formfitting suit, more advanced and flexible than his.

It veered away. Timas struggled to catch up to Cen so that he could bang the back of Cen's suit and point. Both boys stared, amazed as the alien moved farther away until it faded into the brown haze.

They pushed helmets together. "Did you see that?" Timas shouted. "Something else is on the surface with us. It doesn't look human."

"That can't be." Cen's brown eyes widened.

"It's an alien!"

"That's heresy," Cen said. "Forget we saw it, let's go."

Timas looked back, trying to spot the creature. What did he care about heresy? His grandparents had Reformed and left Aztlan back on New Anegada years ago during the DMZ wars. Their fears of aliens trying to rule Timas's people again didn't mean anything anymore. True, some believed that god-aliens had followed their exodus to this city and still looked over them. A crazy belief. Aliens were just . . . other kinds of creatures.

And apparently at least one of them walked Chilo's surface.

"We should follow it," Timas said. "If there are aliens here, on the surface, don't you think people would be interested in knowing that?"

"It's too dangerous." Cen shook his head. "It's too deep in the debris zone."

Cen and the rules. Yatapek floated far overhead. Downwind of the city lay the debris zone, a dangerous place to stand still. But Yatapek didn't drop things.

Not unless some airship collided with it by accident, driven into the city by a gust of wind. And airships from other cities visited Yatapek less and less each year. The city just didn't have much to offer the others.

Timas made up his mind. "I'm going. Come or not, Cen. You don't have to share the honor of the greatest discovery Yatapek has ever made. Can you imagine the visitors from the other cities that will come if we are the ones who find aliens hiding on Chilo's surface?" Most human worlds didn't welcome aliens, so it wasn't surprising that they'd hidden. "Maybe they'd even trade with us, or if we swear to keep the fact that they're hiding on Chilo secret, maybe they'll pay our city."

That got Cen's attention. Both of them knew that being down here helped the city, and that they were responsible for its health. The idea that aliens could help got Cen to follow Timas as he lumbered downwind.

Both boys moved as fast as they could through the thick air, trying to find the alien. The sense of getting away with something illicit deep in the debris zone made Timas smile.

Then something hit the ground in front of him. It looked like a shard of plastic, melted and contorted. As he watched, it bubbled and melted away.

He leaned back and peered up into the gloom.

Something much larger hit the ground. He felt the thud through his feet, but didn't see anything. But Timas knew what that meant. This was bad, this was really bad. He'd screwed up.

"Cen! Debris!"

The shouting served nothing, it was just a reflex. They couldn't hear each other at all. Timas ran at Cen.

He had to force himself up into the wind, legs pushing hard. His thighs burned and sweat dripped from his forehead, stinging his eyes, as he overtook Cen and bumped into his side.

Their bulky groundsuits clanked as they almost both hopped off balance for a second.

Timas grabbed Cen's helmet and yanked them both face to face. "Debris!"

Cen paled. "The cuatetl!"

Their training told them to separate and hunker down near any depression or hole they could find. But everywhere Timas looked the ground stretched out smooth and even.

"Run." They both scrambled, running back toward the barely visible silhouette of the mining machine through the murk.

It cleared as they got closer. Timas slowed just as something hit the top of the cuatetl's cutter head. He threw his hands up and dropped to the ground as metal shards pelted him.

He waited for the inevitable with his eyes closed, raising his hands and praying to the gods to at least make it a quick and painless death.

Fifteen years, two as xocoyotzin, an honored position in the city and for his family. It had been a good life.

But nothing hit. The debris had stopped.

Timas opened his eyes. A jagged rip in the cuatetl's side billowed smoke. A bad sign. Yatapek could not afford to replace an entire cutter head.

He turned around to check on Cen: his friend lay facedown on the ground. Timas walked over to tap helmets, but Cen didn't stir when he rapped on the back of the large metal suit.

Two of Cen's radiators had broken off. The suit was overheating.

Gods. Timas got on the ground, pushing Cen carefully onto his side so he could look into his visor. He could see nothing but fog clouding it.

They had to get off the surface.

Timas rolled Cen back onto his face. He couldn't lift the old extra-bulky hundred pound suit. But he could pull it along the smooth surface.

The helmet wouldn't crack, he kept telling himself. If he damaged the suit's vanes by dragging him any other way, Cen certainly wouldn't survive. The groundsuit slid slowly over the surface.

It took almost fifteen minutes to get Cen along the wind beacons to the large metal sphere of the elevator. A slim ribbon of material stretched from the elevator's roof up into the gloom above, disappearing into the sky.

Another few minutes fell away as he pulled Cen carefully in among the three massive disc cutters inside.

The elevator's large portholes shattered four years ago, leaving it open to Chilo's boiling depths. Yatapek couldn't repair the damage. Everything seemed to break down these days. Timas held on to the empty airlock's door frame. He slapped the green switch wired on the outside to give the haul-up signal.

Then Timas sat next to his facedown companion, blinking away sweat and watching the condensation from his own exertions run down the inside of his visor in little rivulets.

What had happened up there, a hundred thousand feet over his head? There shouldn't have been any debris. Not like that.

There might have been tears of frustration and not

sweat in his eyes, but he wasn't sure as the elevator jerked. The groundscrews buried into the rock underneath disengaged and folded up into the elevator. They bounced along the ground, and then rose into the air over the rippling heat waves of the orange-tinted surface.

The higher they got the cooler it would get. Timas bit his lip as they ascended into the sulfuric gloom of his world.

"You can make it, Cen," he whispered.

He sat there and stared at the dials on his wrist. The heat dropped down from 850 degrees into the high 700s, PSI began dropping.

But would it be enough?

A gust of wind slammed into them, pushing the elevator out at an angle from underneath the city. His groundsuit creaked, metal joints and ribs popping as the immense pressure decreased.

Timas put his hand on Cen's helmet and urged the elevator to *move* as he promised every god he could think of offerings at the family altar if they could just get winched back up to Yatapek in time.

CHAPTER THREE

The elevator slammed down to a slower speed on the final approach to Yatapek's city docks. Timas waited as the massive lower airlocks engulfed the small elevator and sealed themselves shut. Through the ruined portholes the lower curve of the city dominated the sky above, and in the distant gloom clusters of maintenance blimps floated, ready to intervene in case anything went wrong for this final stage of the winching up.

Pumps whirred as clean air flooded into the chamber. He looked out of the doorway into the lock and banged his armored fists against the side of the elevator to get attention.

Heutzin, one of the mechanics, ran in, pulling a large heat-safe glove onto his right hand. He popped the seals on Timas's helmet and Timas took a gasp of fresh, unsweaty air.

"You're back early."

Amoxtli, the doctor, stepped in next.

"What happened?" Heutzin looked him over and wiped his grease-stained hands on his chest. "I told them something had been knocked loose. There was debris. Doctor!"

Heutzin had been a xocoyotzin in his young teens, now his belly spilled out of his shirt. No groundsuits for him. But he knew exactly what the panicked look on Timas's face meant.

"The debris got him," Timas said. He kneeled down next to Cen and started to try and crack the groundsuit, but with his hands still in armored gloves he fumbled with the clasps and catches.

Heutzin pulled Timas up to his feet by his one heat-safe gloved hand. "Was his suit holed?"

"I think it was the heat vanes." Timas turned back toward the elevator, but Heutzin turned him right back around and pushed him forward.

"Keep moving," he snapped.

Behind them Amoxtli cracked the suit. Timas could hear steam whistle out. An odd smell drifted through the chamber.

Burnt flesh.

Timas gagged, and Heutzin kept pushing him toward the airlock out of the chamber. "Just keep walking."

"What happened up here?" Timas asked.

"Something hit the city." Heutzin rubbed the few hairs on his upper lip, leaving a long streak of grit.

"An airship?" Timas screamed. Why right then?

"No. A person fell out of one of the clouds. Hit some solar collectors lashed near the farms, knocked them off. I thought I saw debris headed your way, but the doctor and others were too busy to notice. They were running around, holing up the patch in the city and trying to save the guy who hit us." Heutzin helped Timas sit on a bench near the showers. He hit the chest clasps with his gloved hand, and then unbolted the cumbersome wrist joints.

Timas flexed his hands until they felt like they would crack. He said what came right to mind, what scared him. "I don't think Cen's alive. I think I killed him." He did kill him. He should never have asked Cen to go into the debris field.

He should have followed the rules, just as carefully as Cen.

Should. Should. Timas grabbed Heutzin. "We saw something. We saw an alien. We tried to go see it. And I think it's my fault Cen's dead."

"You let the gods and Amoxtli decide that." Heutzin lifted the chest shield up on its hinge. Timas crawled carefully up out of the steaming hot groundsuit. "Now stop talking."

By itself with the top hinged back, the suit looked like a monster from the deep. A soulless, bug-eyed alien.

Timas didn't have anything left in him. He leaned forward and rested his head in his sweat-wrinkled fingers.

Heutzin grabbed his shoulder and squeezed. Timas swallowed nervousness as Amoxtli stooped through into the shower room, a grim look on his face.

He shook his head.

All three of them stood surrounded by the giant unmoving groundsuits. Somewhere on the far end of the room, behind the lockers, water spattered as a shower turned on.

"I'm going to go tell Cen's father." Amoxtli snapped the black bag he carried with him shut with a sharp click.

"I'll stay with Timas," Heutzin said.

Amoxtli walked over and put a hand on Timas's neck. "Lay something at your family's altar tonight, will you?"

It felt a little late for prayers and incense, Timas thought.

Timas walked alongside Heutzin in a daze, stumbling as the docks shifted and swung in the wind. Large clamps for airships, gantrys, and walkways, all spider-webbed and dangled from underneath the city like scraggly vines. They acted as a counterweight to the floating globe of Yatapek above.

"Breathers." Heutzin handed Timas a breathing mask as they dodged the hoses and electrical lines snaked around the grated floors. He held it to his face to make a seal.

The rickety cage elevator took Timas and Heutzin up through a chaotic free-swinging structure. The docks hung like wind chimes, downward facing cylinders of girders, with large tubes spiked out in random directions away from each other for airships to dock at. Random pockets of enclosed and air-filled workspaces, corridors, and storage facilities clung wherever.

It all passed them by as they rose toward the very bottom of Yatapek proper: the curve of the city's south pole swallowed the cage up with another set of locks.

They left the bottled air and masks, cycled through the doors, and both stepped into Yatapek's lower streets. Dim lights from the top of the fifty-foot ceiling flickered, struggling to penetrate the haze of overworked air scrubbers.

"You're damned lucky to be walking the streets now," Heutzin said.

"Lucky," Timas mumbled. He grabbed Heutzin's arm. "Lucky! It hit the cuatetl! Cen died!"

Heutzin sighed. "It's been damaged before. We'll barter for replacement parts."

Timas shook his head. "That doesn't make it lucky." He didn't know why he was arguing about this. He just didn't want to feel like something good happened today. "I shouldn't have gone for the alien. I wish I'd never seen it."

Heutzin stopped and grabbed his shoulder. "Shut up about aliens. Don't repeat that ever again. It's heresy. We see shadows, nothing more. And some have died running off into the muck to chase those shadows. Besides, you'll lose the honor of being xocoyotzin if you keep saying that. So trust me, Timas, you must shut up!"

Timas stared down at old, scuffed plastic sidewalk. "I'm sorry."

"We'll talk to the pipiltin tonight. It is their duty to run the city, not yours," Heutzin said. "They'll probably decide to send xocoyotzin down tomorrow to assess the damage. But likely, the city will be focusing on Cen, and on the damage done to the city. Stop blaming yourself."

Timas wanted to go home now and crawl into his

room. He felt like a ghost following Heutzin around the street.

Here at the bottom of the globe, the lowest layer of the city housed the heavy factories. Timas could taste the smoke and fire in the air as they walked down the industrial street toward the city's core.

"Heutzin?" Flickering streetlights cast a shadowy hue over the thick-armed workers going about their business.

"Yes."

"You know any xocoyotzin who died? When you worked the surface?" Timas looked at the man. Heutzin didn't look like he'd once worked on the surface: his stomach alone would have trouble fitting in the largest of the groundsuits.

They stopped at the Atrium, the cored-out center of the city. Heutzin looked up. The layers of the city dwindled away overhead, and elevators constantly crawled their way up and down the inner sides of the shaft, filled with tiny groups of people going about their business.

Yatapek floated above the clouds, where the sun filled the atrium with cheerful orange light. It felt like a different world after going on the surface.

"Heutzin?" Timas prompted.

"Yes. It isn't exactly a safe thing to do, going down there. You'll lose many more friends before you give up your groundsuit." A distant groan from a large shifting deck plate filled the air around them.

"I wouldn't do it if the family didn't depend on me," Timas said. "It feels like I'm holding them all up on my shoulders."

"And it doesn't feel fair, does it?"

Timas shook his head. "No."

Heutzin led them both into an elevator along with a

small crowd. Timas stared at a boy who looked his age, but far more muscular, who carried a bag with papers sticking out over the top.

As Timas watched the boy rubbed his forehead, pushing aside a fringe of flat black hair. "What you looking at?"

"Nothing."

Heutzin grunted. "You shouldn't talk to xocoyotzin like that." He stepped forward, menacing, and the other boy shrank back into his peers. They all stared up at the dirty mechanic as he leaned over them. "In my day even little runts had some respect for those risking their lives on the surface."

"It's okay." Timas put his palm to the glass of the elevator, looking down as it rose farther up the massive atrium shaft.

The elevator stopped, and the boy and several of his friends shoved their way into a crowded street. They were middle layer. Not top. Not like Timas and his family.

Neon signs blinked just past the elevator doors, and garish track lighting bathed this layer in a blue glow. The houses jammed together, reaching from the floor to the ceiling: warrens. Many of them looked unsuited to stand, strung between wires reaching from the bottom of one layer down to the next. Timas wondered if the city's Balance Commission fined them for illegal weight distribution, and if they ever paid. Tight alleyways, dirty and filled with litter, disappeared behind the doors as they shut. The smell of body odor and frying oil hit Timas.

As the elevator continued up, more and more people got off, until just Heutzin and Timas stood with each other. They glided to the dizzying top, where the parks and farms basked under the sun's warmth, protected by the city's globe above them.

Here the crowded underlayers and streets of Yatapek fell away.

A cool mist hung over the gardens just outside the elevator entrance. A noble elderman with his hair tied up in a jade clip and wearing a deep red tunic nodded as he passed them and took their place in the elevator.

"Do you want me to walk home with you, or are you okay?" Heutzin asked. He took a deep breath of the misty air and looked around at a low hedge of hibiscus bushes.

"I . . ." Timas almost said he would be fine, but Heutzin had a mournful look to him. Timas suddenly realized how long it must have been since Heutzin lived among the upper layer as a xocoyotzin. The gardens, the clean air, the constant sunlight: all this he would remember as he toiled in the lower layers of the city. Heutzin, even though escorting a grieving friend, now had a brief chance to relive those days.

A small point of anger flared as Timas wondered if Heutzin had so quickly helped him below just to get back to the upper layer. But Timas quelled that thought. That wasn't fair to Heutzin. Heutzin always checked his groundsuit twice over and listened to him when he thought he'd heard odd creaks or whistles while below in the murk and pressure.

Timas felt a sudden surge of hatred for the generation that came to Yatapek. Seduced by pills and technological tweaks to keep their bodies svelte and elfin, they'd never assumed their great grandchildren would fall into near poverty and that only their children would fit in the groundsuits they'd purchased for the city.

Yatapek couldn't afford to replace the aging suits. Choices made long ago now made Heutzin a low man, using tricks to visit a part of his own city. And those same choices made Timas responsible for his own family, if not the entire city.

Sometimes at night it felt like the hulking ground-suits sat on his chest, the pressure crushing his lungs to the point he could hardly breathe.

"Yes," Timas said. "Please, come with me."

He could use Heutzin's support to face his mother anyway.

But when they arrived Itotia didn't get upset. She waited by doors to the courtyard. Her hair lay flat. Her simple white cotton dress stood out against the brown brick of their house. No warrens in the lower layer, but a solid house with a straw roof over the metal rafters. A haven for Timas and his lucky family.

"Heutzin." Itotia nodded at the mechanic. "Thanks for bringing him up. One of the dock workers used the telephone to tell me what happened."

"It was no problem." Heutzin looked down at the ground. "I know what it's like. The ride back up is long after you lose someone down there."

"Mom." Timas wanted to run up and hug her. But not in front of Heutzin.

"Come." She turned and led them into the courtyard where several pitchers and wooden jicara bowls sat on a table. Timas took off his shoes at the threshold as he followed them across the cool courtyard flagstones.

Itotia poured him a bowl of pulque. Mango flavored, orange, yellow, and thick, the alcoholic afterbite stung when Timas sipped it. Warmth dribbled down into his core. He relaxed.

"The servants have a meal ready for you in your

room. I'll come in when you're finished," his mom said. "I want to talk to Heutzin for a moment."

"Okay." Timas felt his stomach twist slightly from the pulque. Normally she didn't let him have it, even when his dad drank it and offered him a sip.

Timas walked across the courtyard into one of the many interconnected rooms. He closed the wooden door behind him, but then stayed by the crack to spy on them.

"He's safe, he's okay," Heutzin told her. Timas watched through the crack as his mother's shoulders slumped and her head drooped.

"Every time he goes down, I burn something on the altar for the gods. Was I too stingy this time? Should I have burned something more?"

Heutzin shifted from foot to foot. "He came home safe. You did right by the gods. But then, who knows what the gods want? In this case, it seems to have been Cen."

"Tomorrow it could be Timas." Itotia pushed her hair back and paced, her voice getting shrill. "Their suits get older every year. Already we've lost one xocoyotzin, and the year is just begun. Last year we lost five. *Five*. When you were xocoyotzin how many did the surface take?"

"Not as many," Heutzin admitted. He made a face as he did so.

"Is it worth it?" She stared at him as she yelled. "Really, is it worth our children's lives?"

Heutzin looked around the courtyard, and Timas pulled back from the crack for a second, then peeked back out again. "You seem to enjoy the fruits. Of all the things I miss the most," Heutzin took a deep breath, "it's the freshly filtered air, not the dank must that falls down to the lower levels."

Itotia looked him up and down and said, with a small amount of scorn, "There is no age limit on xocoyotzin. All you have to do is fit in the groundsuit."

Heutzin winced and pulled himself out of a slump. He held his hand over his stomach, as if shielding it. "That's true." And even though he stood up straight, it looked to Timas like the man had deflated slightly at the reference to his weight.

His mom must have realized how deep the barb she'd thrown sank. She spread her hands. "I'm sorry, I'm angry. That was crude of me. Tell me about the cuatetl, I will have to tell Ollin what I know when I visit him."

"Timas says it's very badly damaged. I believe him." Heutzin's pained grin displayed his worn and acid-damaged teeth. More indication that Heutzin had once been xocoyotzin. A badge of pride. "They'll send older xocoyotzin down to check and take pictures for the elders and senior mechanics to look at."

"You'll be there."

"Be sure of it. No cuatetl, no city."

A voiced fear. Timas shuddered. The city, his way of life, his family: it would all disappear if the cuatetl fell apart.

"We'd be on our hands and knees begging for handouts from the Aeolian cities then," Itotia said. "Disreputable."

Heutzin shrugged. "We'll do what we have to do." He turned to leave the courtyard. Realizing how long he'd eavesdropped, Timas turned and padded quickly for his room. If his dad caught him listening he'd get a solid hiding, no doubt, even despite the day's events.

His stomach growled as he ran down the corridor and turned into his room. Before a surface drop he drank nothing but water and ate vegetables to make sure that he would fit in the slim groundsuits.

The post-surface meal usually featured a family celebration, where his mother and father congratulated him on doing his job as xocoyotzin well.

Now he picked over the tray. He gobbled the three still-steaming tamales and then the bowls of sliced fruit.

By the time Itotia reached the room Timas had finished.

"Where's Dad?" He wanted to talk to Ollin about what happened on the surface today.

"He can't come." His mom sat by him on the bed. The ropes under the mattress creaked. "Did you hear about the impact on the city's shell?"

"A body hit the city. That caused the debris, right?"

"Yes. Your dad went to help seal the dome; if you climb to our roof you might be able see the patch from here. The person who crashed through, he's still alive. Ollin is with him in quarantine."

"Quarantine?" Timas had never heard of anything like that before.

"The person insisted. Two days quarantine. The pipiltin decided to do it."

"So I can't see Dad?"

"No."

They sat and drew comfort from each other's presence. Then Itotia stood up. "It's been long enough."

Timas got up and followed her to the bathroom.

"Do you need help?" Itotia asked.

"No." He wanted to be alone now.

Timas planted one hand on the edge of the flat, square sink with the oversize drain. A small polished wooden dowel stuck out of a ceremonial cup on the right edge.

Timas picked it up and steadied himself.

Then he slowly pointed it down his throat until it

touched the back. He gagged, convulsed, and then whipped the rod out as he vomited.

The sink caught most of it. The door squealed open as he shivered and held himself over the sink. Itotia wet a rag and held it over his head.

"Was that everything?" she asked.

He nodded as he ran the tap and splashed water to clean the sink off. "Enough."

"Enough?" Itotia leaned over to whisper in his ear. "You don't want to end up like Heutzin before your time, do you? He left early, you know."

Acid burned Timas's throat and the back of his teeth. He rinsed his mouth and spat into the drain.

He raised his shirt. "You look," he said. "Do you see a shred of fat?"

Itotia leaned over and pinched the side of his stomach. She squeezed approvingly. "I know you've had a terrible day, but if the cuatetl is damaged, we'll need all the xocoyotzin. We depend on you, Timas."

He felt so weary. "I know. I know." He let her guide him back to his bed. The room still smelled of fresh tamales. It made his stomach twitch, nauseous again.

Itotia set a candle to burn by his bed as Timas crawled in. He lay still and listened to the city flex as turbulence bubbled past it, shaking it just enough to get its parts to tense against each other: harmless constant metallic earthquakes that ran along the fault lines of Yatapek's seams.

Later that night the word arrived that the weather remained good and the next shift of xocoyotzin had gone down and returned. Even despite the tough job of assessing damage in the night on the surface they had come to the same conclusion as Timas.

The cuatetl had been badly damaged. Yatapek did not have the resources to fix it.

Neighbors drifted in and out of the courtyard. Worried adult voices discussed what the news meant for their futures, for the xocoyotzin, and for each other.

Itotia sounded calm and measured, but Timas heard the worry in her voice.

Later into the night, once most people had left and the electric lights dimmed throughout the courtyard, scraping and squeaking noises drifted into Timas's room through the street-side window.

He poured himself a cup of warm water from the pitcher by his bedside and stood up to look out the window.

Cen's older brother, Luc, pulled a large wooden cart along the road. Bundles of clothing, furniture, and chests hastily stacked on it swayed about, threatening to fall out.

Chantico, Luc's wife, walked slowly alongside her husband. Behind her: Luc and Cen's mother.

No longer the family of xocoyotzin, they moved now to the lower levels, looking for jobs where the city crowded on top of itself, where little light reached the buildings, and the alleys smelled of humanity, industry, and badly recycled air.

For a moment Luc paused and looked over at the window. Timas wanted to duck, but instead he nodded at Luc and raised a hand.

Luc didn't respond. He put his head down, repositioned his grip on the cart's handles, and kept pulling.

If the cuatetl did not get fixed, all the xocoyotzin would make that journey toward the elevators. The city's future sat on a knife's edge.

CHAPTER FOUR

When Ollin returned two days later he snagged Timas's arm and pulled him along through the courtyard away from the watered-down pulque.

Ollin didn't tower over Timas, but his bulk and presence could intimidate. Ollin made him feel like a child again. Ollin's wrinkled tunic and unkempt hair were the only signs that he'd been out of the house for two days.

"I know we don't talk often, now." Ollin's words cracked out quickly. Precise, businesslike. "But you're grown now, you've seen one of the worse things a man faces, here on Yatapek, and I should treat you as one."

Timas stumbled behind his dad into the cool shade. "I tried to bring him up in time . . ."

"There was nothing you could have done. I talked to Heutzin." The chair creaked as Ollin sat. "Itotia!"

Timas's mother appeared in the door frame with a tentative smile. "You're back."

Ollin didn't smile back. He raised his hand. "I invited the pipiltin over for a lunch. We have little time, and a crisis to move on before everyone in the city begins to offer advice and rumors to cloud our thoughts."

"I'll get the courtyard ready." Itotia hesitated for a moment, looked at Timas, then backed away.

Ollin leaned over the table and peered at Timas over clasped hands. "Would you believe that the man who fell out of the sky and hit us is still alive?"

"Mom told me," Timas said. "If he is still alive, can we hold him accountable? Is he from the Aeolian cities?" If so, he might be rich enough to fix the damage he'd done. Unlike on Yatapek, the Aeolians came from worlds where humans had lots of contact with aliens and their advanced technologies. The Aeolians had faced oppression as minorities among those alien worlds. But now they called Chilo their own, using the tools and technologies they'd wrested away from other races. How could Yatapek compete with that?

"We don't know." Ollin shrugged. "But he will pay one way or another for what he did. He's delirious, he keeps talking about zombies and invasions. We think he may have spent time here before." People nicknamed Aeolian ambassadors "zombies" due to their awkward pauses and blank looks.

Timas felt a chill at the idea of an Aeolian invasion. His city could do little to ward them off.

"And the cuatetl," Timas whispered. "What do we do about that while we wait?"

"We'll talk about it tonight. I know many will say we have to go on our knees and beg the Aeolians to give us a loan." His father looked disgusted with the thought.

"What other choice do we have?" The almost mile-wide city needed raw resources to survive. The Aeolian cities floated high, some of them even had cables that reached out into space. They got their ores and materials from asteroids. Few got them from the surface with old mining equipment like Yatapek. One of Timas's great grandmothers had helped purchase the machine. He doubted she anticipated that they would still be using it.

"The pipiltin will figure them out tonight." Ollin stood up and rubbed his face. His eyes were red from weariness, Timas noticed.

"And you will be there to help them." Timas also got up and walked toward his room. Everyone knew about his dad's desire to become one of the guiding leaders of the city.

"That is why I invited them to council here. Where are you going?" Ollin stood in his doorway.

"Back to sleep." The pulque sat heavy in Timas's stomach and made him feel weary.

"Sleep? Is that what you've been doing all this time?" Ollin entered the room and grabbed Timas's shoulder. "You at least went running, didn't you?"

Timas didn't try to lie. "What's the point right now? I won't be needed for a while, and if the cuatetl gets fixed, it will be by the Aeolians."

Ollin shoved him away. "You are *xocoyotzin*," he hissed. "You will keep your shape. You will not fall apart on me."

The anger in his dad's eyes didn't shake Timas. He gritted his teeth. "Like Heutzin?" His father mercilessly hounded him about being primed for the role of xocoyotzin.

"Heutzin," Ollin said slowly in a neutral voice. "He paid his dues, saw friends die, and risked his life for almost ten years."

Without children, though, Heutzin remained just another once-xocoyotzin. Timas left the thought in the air.

Ollin shook his head. "You need something to keep your mind off Cen. You keep your schedule, you run every morning and night, and you watch your food. And I think I have something to help you find some direction. It will keep you from circling around yourself."

"What's that?"

Ollin lowered his voice to a whisper. "There's a delegate from one of the Aeolian cities here sniffing around already, dropped off by airship an hour ago. I was going to have your mother take her around the city, but I think now you're going to do that."

His father's voice had that "no options" edge to it. Timas would spend the day playing babysitter to some snooty outsider tourist. He knew they liked to fly out to Yatapek to enjoy the large and open upper layer for vacations. No wide-open spaces in their packed cities. Handmade crafts from the lower level markets also attracted them. For the Aeolians the price of a flight here cost little, even though most on Yatapek couldn't afford to leave.

"Great," he muttered. Another of Ollin and Itotia's schemes to get involved with running the city. They'd climbed up from the filth and darkness of the lower layers thanks to him. Yet still they schemed as if the grime lay lurking just behind them.

Ollin ignored that. "Listen to me." He slapped his hands together, but still kept his voice low. "You will tell her nothing about the man who hit the city, except that we have his body. Do not tell her he lives. You understand me?"

Timas understood. "I understand."

"Right." Ollin smiled. "We want to know what we can get out of all this before we volunteer information." Yatapek had few powerful friends in the other cities. Again, Timas reminded himself to think about the dying cuatetl. His city needed the resources to fix it. His city needed him.

"Take me to the delegate, I'll give them the tour," Timas said.

Ollin pulled his brass pocketwatch from inside a tunic pocket. The city bumped at them from underfoot. Ollin swayed and Timas followed suit. Neither of them paid close attention to the unconscious reaction. "She should be waiting outside. Her name is Katerina Volga."

Timas walked around his dad and into the corridor where he could see the courtyard gates that led to the street. The girl who stood in front of them wore a silvery shirt and trousers, had her hair cut short to her ears, and her left eye glinted in the morning light.

"She's my age," Timas said. "I thought you said she was a delegate from the cities."

"She is." Ollin walked alongside Timas as he left the corridor for the courtyard. "You know the young and inexperienced of theirs can wield a lot of power. You've seen the tourists. Even the children are rich."

"She has one of those metal eyes." Timas had seen Aeolians with them before. "She's like a robot?"

"Something like that. I'm sure she'll tell you all about it, it's hard to get them to shut up about themselves." Timas looked over at his dad as they crossed the courtyard together. Ollin didn't often reveal personal opinions about the Aeolians. "Be back by lunch. The elders will want to talk to her."

"Okay."

Ollin opened the gates. "Welcome, Katerina, to my home. This is Timas, my son. I've asked him to personally take you on a tour of our city."

Katerina had wide eyes, one of them green and the other, her right eye, silver. She had brown skin like Timas's. Usually the Aeolians were black or pale, it surprised Timas to see someone that looked more like him. Maybe that was why she'd been sent, she could almost blend into Yatapek. Except for her hair. Yatapek's citizens had straight, black hair. Katerina's hair was frizzy.

"Good morning," she said. "I'm pleased to meet your son, and thank you for the hospitality."

She looked both of them up and down, very slowly, her silver eye taking them both in. It had tiny metallic veins that spidered off the corner of her eye socket and eyelids.

It was eerie. Heutzin once told him that all Aeolians could see anything any other Aeolian with silvered eyes could see. A creepy thought.

Ollin left them both at the gate.

"So where do you want to start?" Timas asked. He couldn't avoid staring at the silver eye.

Katerina waited for Ollin to walk back into the house. "We've seen Yatapek, we don't need the tour. But I haven't eaten yet since I left home this morning."

They way she used *we* and *I* differently made Timas pause. He looked at the silver eye. If Heutzin told the truth, people all throughout the Aeolian cities looked at him right now through that silver eye of hers. Through their more advanced technology.

He shivered.

"Am I making you uncomfortable?" Katerina asked.

Timas considered lying for a moment. "Yes. A little bit. Knowing that other people see what you see, back in all the other Aeolian cities. It's unusual." And a little creepy.

"We're all sorry." She blinked and held her eye closed. It looked like a normal eyelid, except for the metallic veins. She grabbed his arm. "We can keep the eye closed, if it bothers you that much. But you'll have to help me walk around if I'm doing it with one eye closed. It messes with my depth perception."

Timas stepped back. "It's okay, you can use your eye."

"You realize we can hear you." Katerina tapped her right ear.

"It isn't metal," Timas said.

"They don't have to be. The eye is a marker, a choice, by us, to let outsiders know."

"Are all Aeolians part robot?"

Katerina sighed and rolled her eyes. "Oh come on!" She bit her lip, paused, and then tilted her head. "We're not robots, Timas. We're people, like you."

Timas considered it. "You're all connected to each other, using your devices and transmitters? Do you all have similar things in your head like that eye?" He also thought: If they ever chose to invade, they would swarm around Yatapek's warriors, who had few or no radios to plan their defense. Yes, the Aeolians could invade easily enough.

"In a manner of speaking, yes."

"Then you're not anything like me." Timas felt nervous around her as he contemplated the thought of hundreds of Aeolians with silver eyes taking over his city. "Are you?"

"I'm hungry, Timas. Can we go eat?"

Happy to change the subject, Timas nodded and led Katerina down the street. Along with several other roads it radiated out from the atrium like spokes in a wheel.

Timas walked them toward the outer edge of the city. The clusters of buildings that stood near the atrium petered out into the city's farms and gardens. They made the bulk of the topmost layer, the dome curving up over all the greenery. A tiny mist of rain trickled down from the sprinklers in the dome top far overhead.

The oldest citizens of Yatapek said that the topmost layer felt the most like being back on the world they came from, New Anegada. The Aeolians said that as well. Tourists often stayed in rooms near the edge of the upper layer's fields and gardens.

"Is that a harvester?" Katerina pointed at a rusted machine that sat in the center of the wheat section on their left, with several clusters of farmers standing around it.

"*The* harvester," Timas said. It had broken down again. He kept her walking along, the harvester broke down more than it worked. Nothing unusual there.

"Where are we going?" Katerina asked. "Your maps don't show any elevators on the inside of the city wall."

"I'm taking you to the mezzanine gardens."

Even this sophisticated delegate should appreciate the food and view there.

At the edge of the dome the land gave way to tree-tops.

"Oh, I've heard of this," Katerina said. "Neat effect."

They took the steep stone stairs down the wall and descended into the trees and shrubs of the gardens that all carefully framed the clouds just outside the city. It made one aware of the fact that the whole city floated. They lived a hundred thousand feet in the air, follow-ing the currents near Chilo's great storm in a regular circular pattern, far enough above it that they were not affected. The dirty brown spiral of the storm domi-nated the landscape before them today.

At the bottom of the stairs Timas turned around and let her look out into Yatapek's second layer.

"This is the real view," Timas said.

The mezzanine he'd taken her to hung underneath the topmost layer. From here they looked out over the farms and edge gardens of the second layer. And where the sun failed to reach at the edges, the layer's streets, houses, and structures began.

"Very neat," Katerina said. Weblike towers criss-crossed the inner area, and this high up you could see that the layer resembled a three-dimensional map. A diorama laid out for just them, with the edges of it receding into gloomy murkiness.

The city lights hung from long cables connected to the underside of the top layer. They vibrated and swung whenever the city trembled from super-gusts.

"But where's the food?"

Very neat, that was all she had to say about the mezzanine? Timas led her along the path by the large windows.

"Here." A small booth with little tables and chairs scattered around flagstones hid behind a series of overlarge hedges. Timas snagged a paper menu from the booth.

"So do you have anything like this in your city?" Timas asked.

Katerina looked over her menu. "Well, no, not anymore. Eupatoria's edges are filled with developments now. Everyone wants an apartment 'on the edge' so that they have sky in their living room."

"Then how do you grow food?" The edges of the layers and the top layer got all the sunlight.

"Hydroponic gardens, we keep them around the core of the city. Or vats." More technological tricks up their sleeves, Timas thought as she tapped on the menu. "No beef, just chicken?"

"Meat, even for xocoyotzin, is not very plentiful," Timas said. "We don't have the land for grazing."

"Grazing . . . animals." Katerina looked upset for a second. "I'll have beans and rice."

Timas felt like he'd failed some test with her. She had this look on her face like his mother did when she'd had to visit one of her cousins in the lower layers, deep in the city near the recycling plains.

Katerina felt Yatapek was dirty and uncivilized, and Timas by extension, too, no doubt.

Timas walked up to the kitchen booth and ordered extra beans and rice, with chicken.

"Go sit with the young lady," the tall cook winked, "I'll bring it right out, xocoyotzin." The cook's teeth glinted with cheap metal caps when he smiled.

When Timas returned Katerina looked up. "You said 'xocoyotzin,' didn't you? You work on the surface?"

Excited that some measure of respect had arrived, Timas sat up straighter. "Yes. I am xocoyotzin."

She leaned forward, eager. "We would like to ask if you were on the surface when the debris hit your mining machine?"

"You say 'we' again." Timas did not feel comfortable talking about the cuatetl. He didn't want to say anything that the elders or his dad wouldn't want him to. They might need to bargain or beg with this girl, and the people behind her silver eye, for the repairs.

"*We* is what we say when we are engaging you. When I use '*I*' it's just me talking."

"Just you?"

"Katerina." She smiled.

"How can you both be a robot and yourself?" Timas asked. "It's weird."

Katerina sighed. "You go to school, right?"

"My schooling is very technical." Timas tapped the edge of the table. "I can continue school after I no longer function as xocoyotzin." Die like Cen, grow fat like his father and Heutzin, or just grow old and not able to quite fit. He prayed for the last.

"We know you should know what a democracy is, yes? You have, what, forty thousand people living in

Yatapek? In Eupatoria it's more like a quarter of a million, and our city is the same size. The Aeolian Consensus uses techno-democracy to handle self-governance. We're a little different than you. And there are dozens of Aeolian cities."

"But you're still controlled by that." Timas pointed at her eye. He'd seen a silver-eyed Aeolian once, visiting his dad. That happened back before the Aeolians forced Yatapek to install a large communications bubble on top of the city. Back then, the man who'd visited had taken forever to answer the easiest questions. He'd had to wait on every diplomatic phrase to get vetted and then a response voted on and beamed back to him to speak out loud. Without advanced and fast technology, it had taken forever to get through dinner.

"Damn zombies," Ollin had muttered late that night, apparently tired of the two-minute pauses.

"If you volunteer to be on a sports team of some sort, are you controlled by your team?" Katerina asked. "Or are you still you, but just within the team?"

"You're still you. . . ."

"I'm on a very big team." Katerina hunched forward. "There are three hundred thousand people from a random variety of Aeolian cities, live, voting on my every word because I'm their avatar, emissary, diplomat, or whatever you would like to call me. I agreed to this when I became a citizen. Three days ago I was studying for finals when I got the message that I'd been randomly selected for citizen's duty. And here I am, representing Eupatoria's interests."

So when she said *we* the masses behind that silver eye spoke through her. And when she said '*I*' it was only Katerina. "It takes getting used to," Timas said.

"Try having all this sitting behind your skull,"

Katerina said. "A public face of the citizenry is never an easy task. Fail to do your job properly and you get fined, or exiled and stripped of your citizenship."

The cook interrupted them, staring openly at Katerina's silver eye as he set their plates down and grinned at Timas.

Timas waited for her to start eating.

"Timas, we're not here as tourists. We have an offer for your city." Katerina pushed her plate aside. "An offer we want you to deliver to your city's leaders later tonight."

She wasn't eating. Timas rolled up a corn tortilla and scooped rice and chicken up with it. Before biting into it he responded: "To the pipiltin? Why would you want me to do that? You should speak to them directly, or maybe even my father."

He bit into overheated rice. He breathed around it and realized he was awkwardly eating in front of hundreds of thousands of people.

Timas felt horribly aware of his gangly elbows, loud chewing, and uncomfortable posture.

"We feel . . ." Katerina looked down at the table with a slight smile. "We feel that the pipiltin would be more willing to listen to someone from their own city. The voting is running two-to-one in favor of this theory. We feel that if we, with our reputation for being robotic and arrogant, stand in front of your leaders and give terms, that some will refuse on general principle."

Timas snorted. That sounded about right. He put the rice-filled tortilla down. "And what are you offering?"

"We're offering complete repair services on your mining machine. We know how desperate your situation is. Your city will founder without it."

"In exchange?" Timas was curious.

"We want the man who hit your city," Katerina said. "And we want to talk to him. Tonight. It's very important. He has given our cities information about a possible threat to them. We need more information."

Timas sat and looked at her. "What, you think the man lived through that?"

"Judging by your lack of surprise, and analysis of your body language, pupil dilation, we think you know he did. You just confirmed the suspicion for us. Let's not lie, Timas." She turned cold and expressionless. Timas felt out of his depth. He couldn't bargain about Yatapek's future! The pipiltin negotiated those things. Not xocoyotzin. "He lives and we want to see him. Your people would be foolish to turn down what we offer. What is one stranger to you?"

Apparently one stranger equaled at least a repaired mining machine. At least. Timas looked at his plate. "You're all so very sure of yourselves, aren't you?"

Katerina nodded. "The votes are decisive."

"And if they weren't?"

"I'd be eating and making polite small talk while the debate went on," Katerina said.

"I'm not going to finish my meal here, am I?" Timas asked.

"No." Katerina laughed. "I think we're about done."

Timas pushed his plate away. "I have no idea whether this man exists or not, but I don't see what your hurry is."

"The hurry is that he is, at the least, an incredibly dangerous man, we think, and the sooner we investigate, the sooner we know for sure. He might also be an early warning. Either way, we need to get him into our custody. Then we will decide what to do next."

Timas stood up and left enough money on the table

to cover the food. Katerina picked up one of the bills. "Paper money?"

"Yeah."

"Cool!" She rubbed it between her fingers. "Very cool. Can I keep it?"

"No." Timas shook his head, slightly annoyed. "That pays for our meal. If you want more I'm sure your city can provide some."

Katerina dropped the bill back down on the table, looking disappointed. "Okay."

"And Katerina," Timas added as they left, "please don't mention that I ate anything to my parents."

"Okay." She didn't ask why, thank goodness. Timas didn't feel like explaining more about the nature of being xocoyotzin. Although he imagined there would be more trouble for him in revealing that the man who'd hit the city still lived, even if unintentionally, than in anyone finding out he'd eaten too much for the day.

Timas had the feeling that a lot of yelling at him lay ahead.

CHAPTER FIVE

Y ou told her *what*?" No one shouted at Timas quite like his dad. Right now Ollin had hit a new level of fury.

Timas kept his shoulders back and bit his lip to concentrate. From behind him Katerina spoke up. "He couldn't have hid what he knew from me, we can spot the physiological responses to lies."

That didn't help as much as Katerina might have thought. Timas wondered if the statement came from her and not the people behind her. He winced as Ollin completely ignored her and pointed at him. "You disappoint me."

One of the pipiltin, Camaxtli, raised his hand to shake Ollin's shoulder. "Ollin, go easy, the girl is right. You can't take their envoys at face value. She looks like a girl, but you know she embodies their whole city, and is more than she appears. Your son was mismatched."

Ollin shrugged the hand off. "That's true. I should know better." The five pipiltin nodded, except Tenoch. His face remained sour and he hovered near the back of the group.

Timas frowned. His dad gave that up too easily. His anger blew right over before the pipiltin, when normally Ollin held on to a point like a snapwrench. It wasn't an act, was it? Had his dad purposefully used him to reveal to the Aeolians that the strange man was alive and here?

The pipiltin gathered around Ollin, Timas, and Katerina.

Ollin stepped back into the elders, as if his voice was one of theirs. "My son brings an interesting offer from the Aeolians, however. A refit of the cuatetl, and all we have to do is give up this man."

Ollin *had* been playing a game, Timas realized. He'd used his own son to leak the information.

"But who is the man?" Camaxtli asked. The oldest at eighty years he took the lead naturally, but with careful, slow words. "The Aeolians are looking for him, but that doesn't mean we should give him up so easily. He does have rights."

Katerina stepped into the center of everyone's focus. "He does have rights. We intend to ensure he gets a fair trial for the crimes he committed, but we are very serious about his return to one of the Aeolian cities. He has information about a threat to Chilo's cities. We need it verified."

"We knuckle under to the Aeolians again," Necalli grunted from the back. "Is there anything new here?"

The conversation began, the old men debating whether to give in. Necalli's anger at being forced around was joined by Tenoch and a tentative-sounding Eztli. Only Ohtli seemed to imitate Camaxtli's calm. But Timas felt that he watched a predetermined debate, whether with angry or calm words. The cuatetl needed to be fixed. They had a chance to fix it.

Yet they also had Yatapek pride and a desire to keep independent of demands handed to them by outsiders. Timas saw Camaxtli acknowledge that, defusing some of Necalli's sharp words.

Ollin cleared his throat. "The man in question expects the Aeolians to come talk to him in person. He's hoping to explain what happened."

"You could have said from the start." Camaxtli shook his head. "Ollin, quit playing games."

"Games?" Ollin spread his arms. Timas marveled at his dad's easy acting. "Games? I was quarantined with the man. He said they would come for him."

"You let us babble on long enough," Camaxtli said.

Ollin smiled. "I am no pipiltin, it's not my place to decide these things."

Another game, Timas thought. Ollin had used the long argument to see what the various pipiltin thought before he revealed all his information. Always gears within gears, his dad, like a machine. Timas thought Ollin would probably do better as an Aeolian than here on Yatapek.

"The man's in a secure location." Camaxtli stared at

Ollin. "You'll be revealing that to *her* and the Aeolians watching through her?"

"Blindfold her," Ollin said.

Katerina looked around the group. "If you're going to do that, then I'd like you to bring Ollin and his son along."

"I've been, there's no need for me to return." Ollin moved toward the back of the group, as if using them for a shield.

"The vote is up." Katerina ran a hand through her hair, adjusted her collar, and then focused on them all again. "The majority of us model that you will be less likely to cause trouble with a valued family member with you."

"We can be trusted without a semi-hostage." Camax-tli's usually calm manner disintegrated for a moment as he snapped the words out. Even he felt annoyed at being handed orders by the outsiders.

"Just the same." Katerina folded her arms. Her silver eye glinted in the dome-filtered early sunlight. "We'll have one."

Several of the elders walked out of the courtyard, grumbling in disgust.

But in the end, what else could they do? Camaxtli led the way. Katerina followed after Timas wrapped a long piece of cloth carefully around her head and over her eyes, and then took her hand. It felt smooth and dry, and she squeezed it as he pulled her along with him out through the courtyard, whispering to her to let her know of obstacles coming up.

The group drifted its way away from the atrium and down the roads into the heart of the farm areas.

They had the man imprisoned in a belowground grain silo. Several Jaguar scouts, ex-xocoyotzin who served as the city's defenders and police, stood outside guarding the doors. They raised long steel macuahuitl with razored spikes, more formal than functional, as they had guns strapped to holsters on their waists. They lowered their weapons when they realized who approached.

"Go on through."

Down the dimly lit steps and into the central storage room more guards stepped forward, then lowered their macuahuitl and nodded them through.

The man they all sought lay on a cot. Long dreadlocks lay on the pillow. His dark brown face matched the dark blankets.

Timas let go of Katerina's hand and unwrapped the long piece of cloth that blindfolded her. "Here we are."

Katerina cocked her head. "Juan Smith?"

The man stirred under blankets. "Yes?" Juan opened his gray eyes and looked at them all. Scarred cheeks crinkled as he grimaced.

He pulled the blanket down with his left hand, revealing his whole other arm to be a recently amputated stump.

"Shit." Katerina put a hand over her mouth as the word popped out. "Couldn't his arm be saved?"

"We don't have the same medical facilities you take for granted." Camaxtli helped the man sit up. Timas realized that he was missing a leg as well.

The man saw his stare. "What do you expect? I punched through the dome and lived to tell about it. No one had time to move me to a better hospital. I've survived worse."

"Yes, sorry." Timas looked politely downward. This man before him seemed to be some sort of a proud warrior, like Timas's own great forefathers from New Anegada.

Juan looked around the room and smiled at Katerina. "A big welcome to the Aeolian crowd. I take it you dragged your sorry ass all the way down here just for me."

Katerina frowned at the mild insult. "You are wanted for the murders aboard the *Sheikh Professional,* and endangering cities in the form of a deorbiting projectile. We also want further information about the . . . threat you discussed while deorbiting."

The pipiltin murmured.

Juan and Katerina faced off against each other in the crowded and warming room. Then the man chuckled. "Fair enough, I should elaborate. I did send only the compressed, quick version."

"Thank you. Meanwhile, since we've identified you, the airship I came in on is being readied for the return trip to Eupatoria. There we'll bring you to trial. Understand that while you don't have any formal legal counsel, this isn't a trial right now, and you are under no obligation to say anything at all."

"I understand."

"So, is your name Juan Smith, of Rydr's World?" Katerina leaned forward, presumably to look at his eyes the same way she had at Timas's when he slipped up to reveal what he knew about the man.

"No."

Katerina looked flustered. "No?"

"As I said, no." The man used his one good arm to move himself around so that his one leg touched the ground. He sat ramrod straight, like an emperor receiving his subjects.

"If that isn't your name, what is?"

"Pepper." The man reached out and shook her hand.

Katerina let her arm swing slowly back to her side when he finished. "Pepper. We're running queries on that."

"You do that. Look under *mongoose-men*. New Anegada's mongoose-men. I'm a Ragamuffin." Pepper rested his hand on his remaining right thigh with a grimace.

Timas looked over at Ollin. If Pepper was one of the planet New Anegada's elite military men, the mongoose-men, then something strange was going on. New Anegada allied itself with all the cities in Chilo's atmosphere; the planet's peoples had settled Chilo initially. All the cities here depended on the New Anegadans to protect the planet.

Trying this man could complicate a much-needed relationship. Timas saw one of Ollin's hands curl into a frustrated fist.

"This is an extraordinary claim for us to hear," Katerina said. "Pepper is someone who goes back a long way."

Pepper shrugged. "I have no reason to lie."

"We're working on voiceprints."

"I can change those, but you should get some decent matches from all I've said so far," Pepper said. "And I'm going to explain some more things, because I need to catch you all up pretty quickly before some real shit hits the fan."

Shit hitting the fan. Timas would have to remember that phrase, if nothing else, when he left the room.

Pepper looked around at all of them. "I was coming back from a mission, on the *Sheikh Professional*. They'd picked me up, and two days in, that's when the zombies attacked."

Ollin cleared his throat. "That's the second time

you've said that. We've kept the Aeolians at a distance from you, you seem agitated about them."

"What?" Pepper looked at Katerina. "Aeolians are fine, what the hell are you talking about?"

"Zombies," Ollin repeated. Everyone in the room glanced around with an uncomfortable pause. Hundreds of thousands of Aeolians would be seeing this right now. "We call the Aeolian representatives that visit us 'zombies,' you know, because they take orders and move slowly around and take forever to answer questions because they have to vote on it."

Pepper shook his head. "Hell no, son, that's not what I'm talking about. What I'm talking about is groaning, stumbling, dumb-as-fuck, old-school zombies."

PART TWO

CHAPTER SIX

The shell of the tiny, black vacuumball Pepper sat in hissed and cracked. Only an eggshell's width lay between him and whatever lay outside. The ball had flown a million miles in three days, with Pepper curled up and festering inside by himself. In a device made only for emergency escapes from destroyed ships.

A welcome sound, the cracking. But it came two days too soon. Pepper tensed as the shell split open with a wet, sticky rip.

"Welcome aboard the *Sheikh*." The woman on the other side had her hair pulled back in cornrows and tied off in tight braids. After skulking about the other side of the DMZ, Pepper had to admit he enjoyed hearing a New Anegadan accent again. He relaxed as he heard more New Anegadan voices behind her.

The people aboard the *Sheikh* came from a piece of the Caribbean that had picked itself up from the mother planet and held together for centuries now. They had made the exodus light-years away to New Anegada, where the members of the Black Starliner Corporation once hoped to silently create a world of their own. But as the BSC faded away into the loose-knit community of Carribean descendants known as Ragamuffins, they found themselves growing into larger players in the greater game.

"We snagged you up to save the original pickup fuel," the woman said. "The Ragamuffin Dread Council go pay us beaucoup digits for altering course and snagging you instead of them sending a whole ship out just for you."

The ad hoc representative democracy of the Dread Council guided Ragamuffin security, and they'd sent a safe ship for Pepper. Since humanity rose up against the alien races that once dominated the Forty-Eight worlds they'd gotten more involved in things like this, with Pepper eagerly offering himself up as one of their nastiest tools.

He looked at the woman. "Glad you picked me up. I once got trapped in one of those balls for longer than I'd care to talk about."

Pepper pushed past the broken pieces of the vacuumball and took her offered hand. His long trench coat brushed against the edges.

"I heard about that story," she said. "I'd have gone insane."

He had. For part of that. Before landing on New Anegada and rededicating himself to action: any action, as long as there was movement and things didn't get in his way. It was why he volunteered over and over again to pass through the DMZ and get into the League worlds. If he ever slowed down, he would face himself again like he had in that pod, once. Even this last taste of being trapped in one again had pushed him too close to the edge. He had too much blood, too many sins, and too long a history to sit down and consider it. Men like him needed to stay one step ahead of themselves.

Hopefully there would be things to do soon. Upstream among the League worlds ships disappeared, gathering somewhere Pepper couldn't find, no matter how many heads he cracked. And many of his most reliable informants had also gone to ground.

The last time the League got that organized they'd tried to invade New Anegada and unify the free human race.

Fifty years ago. Craters still dotted New Anegada from that struggle. A lot of leading League officials lay dead by Pepper's hands as well. A reminder to them that the cost of invading New Anegada wasn't worth it.

Pepper had a gut feeling that the League needed reminding again as he stepped into the confines of a cargo hold. Typically a tight area, after three days in a vacuumball, it felt like the inside of a cathedral. This cargo hold was a traditional pie-shaped segment of the ship's cylinder. Number fifteen, according to the large numbers painted on the walls.

It felt like he stood on the bottom of a wide curve, which meant that the ship spun to provide some light gravity for its passengers. If this ship resembled most Ragamuffin higgler ships, from the outside it looked like a giant pen with its end jammed into a larger cylinder of the thrust unit.

"Thank you." Pepper brushed shell fragments off his forearms. He winced as he walked: a three-day-old bullet wound to the calf. Thanks to his over-mechanized and designed body it was healing up nicely but it still stung.

The woman touched her ear and listened to something. "Cargo all safely retrieved," she said, responding to a prompt whispered into her ear by someone elsewhere in the ship. She grabbed Pepper's hand and shook it. "Grenada LeFevre, we all please to meet you. Captain Canden say welcome up in she ship, but not to ever talk or go near her."

Pepper looked up toward the narrow top of the room and the rows of catwalks with cargo lashed in on the sides. Four men with rifles, well spaced out, all sighted in on him with an unwavering patience that Pepper appreciated.

"Thanks for the hospitality." Pepper stepped forward, but Grenada moved in front of him.

She held up a hand. "Listen, in order for you leave the hold, we need to get something straight."

"I'm listening."

"You name's Juan Smith." A slight smirk from her meant she'd probably selected the name from the list of his assumed identies that the Dreads gave her.

"Really?"

"However you want play that, up to you." She shrugged. "Second, you have to hand over all them weapon underneath that coat."

Pepper nodded. Fair enough. He slowly reached in. An automatic pistol under the left armpit. The half-size mini-grenade launcher on his right thigh, the shotgun on his left. Explosives strapped to the small of his back. Extra ammunition clips on his chest and ribs.

Two combat daggers, one on a quick-release gel strap on his right wrist, another on his left ankle. Each piece hit the metal grid work under their feet with a *clang* that echoed through the hold.

"There you are," he said.

"That last dagger, strap up on you back," Grenada said.

Pepper reached back. Somewhere between a short sword and a knife with compensation issues, he'd become slightly attached to the piece. "It's a gift. Not a weapon."

He kept it for special assignments. Only the most important of the Ragamuffin's enemies saw the sword just before dying.

"Don't look like nothing I got hang up on *my* wall."

Grenada reached out a hand. "I see all that blood near the hilt, right?"

Good eyesight. Almost as good as his. No one else would notice the faint discoloration: Pepper had cleaned it up on the way downstream to the DMZ.

Pepper handed it over. "If anything happens to it I would be quite disturbed."

Grenada took it and laid it on the pile between their feet. "I take it for you, look after it real good."

"Thanks."

"Third, we telling peeps you been hole up in you cabin because you in bad health." She looked him over. "I see you already done and gone get that memo."

Pepper's body had cannibalized fat and muscle during the escape and ensuing journey, burning through immense amounts of energy in a short amount of time. He remained not much more than a tent pole that the overlarge trenchcoat draped over. His clothing covered the scarring and wounding.

The price of doing business sometimes.

"I'll be eating extra meals for the next few days. High-quality proteins appreciated."

"I feed you extra, if you tell me how it was all up in a vacuumball getting catapult out from wormhole to wormhole until you got to the DMZ."

Pepper snorted. "Maybe. I was supposed to get picked up later. Why the change?"

"Well, that there's a whole mess." Grenada shook her head.

"Thing is"—Grenada bounced in the lighter gravity of her cubbyhole of a room, closer toward the hub of the ship—"you wasn't the only one out past the DMZ. The Dread Council got a message. From some League high-ups."

The council kept a relay system going for open communications between the two. Mostly diplomatic static, but occasionally something useful snuck through. "So they bit?"

"Yeah," Grenada said. "And they send me and the captain in. Captain say she could turn a nice profit on a run past the DMZ, pick up some rich refugees on the low who want out the League. Add that to big bonuses up on taking diplomats over, at a time when antimatter fuel running higher and higher . . . hard to turn down."

She opened up a small cupboard, tossed a few packets over her shoulder at Pepper, who caught them out of the air. Emergency meals, high in protein. Just what he needed. "Thanks."

"Yeah, ship-wide dinner coming up in two or three, but that should hold you up."

Pepper tore the packaging open and listened to the meal sizzle as it warmed up. A full-course meal's worth of savory smells filled the room. Orange chicken and rice balls. He pulled the pair of telescoping chopsticks out of the package sides. "What did the League want?"

Any information to add to his suspicions was helpful. He knew that, based on his suspicions, heavily armed Ragamuffin ships waited around the wormhole leading to New Anegada. They also lurked in orbit around New Anegada. All on high alert.

"Another try to get New Anegada to join the League." Grenada pulled off her jacket. Pepper noticed the handgun, combat knife, and explosives that lined it.

"They don't stop," Pepper said through a mouthful of orange chicken.

Grenada wore an armless T-shirt. Her left arm sported a grinning cartoon mongoose, black ink on her brown skin. She straddled a chair. "Yeah, but this time they was a bit more convincing."

Pepper nodded at her arm. "You're a mongoose-man."

"Well, yeah, mongoose, but don't be calling me 'man.'"

"Where you been?"

"Got tatted up after the Tangent Run." Grenada leaned forward. "Nothing like the trouble you been around for, though."

No, but it meant she'd served ten years as part of the elite that protected New Anegada. If she volunteered for the near-suicide raid at Tangent Run, deep into League territory, then Pepper could give credit where it was due. The Dread Council trusted her with this ship's protection. She'd do.

Pepper crushed the remains of the foil wrapper in his hand. Scarfing the meal that quickly: not exactly high manners. But they were soldiers swapping info, not diplomats at a fancy table.

Grenada leaned forward over the chair's back. "You went out to watch the League kill the last Satrap, didn't you? That's the word around the mongoose, that's what they saying."

There'd been a lot more than that, but that had been one of Pepper's little missions. "Yeah. Wasn't much we could do to stop it." From rulers of the Forty-Eight worlds to extinct. A long way to fall for the alien Satraps. The revolutionary League of Human Affairs sent out video footage of the execution that took place on Midhaven, the League's heart, everywhere. For them, proof that humanity had thrown the last traces of Satrap rule off its back, seventy-five years after first taking up arms in the revolution against them.

"Not even you. But why go if you couldn't do nothing?"

"Because the universe is a fucking hostile place, and I need more usable data," Pepper said. "For example, you know the Satraps were religious?"

"They believe in gods?"

"Not as such. Those big worms, they lay in their webs of power, they may have ruled us all and the other races in the Forty Eight, but they claimed they were created by another race far away from here. They were created to act as a biological throttle on any developing intelligent creatures that evolved in this area."

"You believe that shit?" Grenada folded her arms.

Pepper shrugged. "According to the creature that I watched die, who really had no reason to lie, the last several hundred years of struggle, our bondage to the Satraps, that was just a distant race's form of preventative pest control."

"A ghost story, just trying to spook the little human."

"Maybe." Pepper leaned against the stacked bunks, already getting hungry again. "Think about this, though: on Earth we were just one of a handful of species that developed intelligence as a survival mechanism. Not a lot of competition, back there. But on the galactic level, we're on the edges of an ecosystem with a multitude of competing intelligences no doubt honed out of a stew of survival of the smartest and most dangerous. What gets culled out of that?"

Grenada slapped her tattoo. "Nothing the mongoose can't handle yet."

She was too young to remember when Ragamuffin ships hid in the depths of space, skulking around the edges of the Satrapy. Too young to remember New Anegada as a preindustrial world on the edge of destruction.

"We're ants," Pepper said. "Living on the edge of a park near a city and congratulating ourselves for figur-

ing out how to cross a road. We don't even know how
the wormholes we use to skip around the Forty-Eight
worlds were made, or why they're here." And with the
League constantly trying to consolidate humanity under one banner, everyone paid more attention to small
fights in the DMZ than trying to invest in pure research.

"We go get there. We tough."

"True, living in the cracks nothing has noticed us yet.
But at some point, something nastier than the Satraps
will notice we're here, and it'll have to make a decision
about us. I bet it might not be a decision we like."

"We have to be like them fire ants," Grenada said.
"Swarm them."

"We're going to have to get our shit together," Pepper said. "Right now we're squabbling with the League.
Humans arguing over competing ideas. These are just
distractions. We need to start getting ready for the next
wave. Or we'll get burned bad."

That penetrated. Grenada sat up. "Burned. Yeah. Just
like the League diplomat: you spinning the same story."

Pepper looked at her. "What do you mean?"

"The League, their little attempt to get us into the
fold. They made the same argument you just did. Only,
a little more dramatic."

"Tell me."

"Ain't pass me report back to the Dread Council, but
you privy to all that." Grenada stood up. "After dinner
I show you some pretty pictures. Gotta go prep now,
provide security."

"For dinner?"

"Lot of refugees from all the League areas we pass
through, in the mix with a few politicians from New
Anegada, and some freak with a silver eye from Chilo,
and some sightseeing idiots. Don't need to find out that

some refugee we taking to Chilo really an assassin. You coming?"

It sounded exhausting. "No. Bring me back some food, I think I'll rest up."

"You bunks you rest, I be back." Grenada slipped her vest back on and checked its contents.

Pepper pulled himself up into the bunk and clipped the webbing over it that would hold him in place if the ship had to suddenly adjust course. "What'd you see out there, Grenada?"

"The League think they seen what them boogeyman you worried about done." She smiled and backed up to the door panel, which slid aside as it sensed her approach.

"Which was?" A transit warning sounded. The *Sheikh* was about to pass through one of the many wormholes on the way to Chilo.

"Someone burn a whole planet up, man," she muttered, and stepped out of the room.

CHAPTER SEVEN

Pepper's feet hit the cold metal floor as the door screeched from being forced open.

"You up?" Grenada's voice sounded strained.

He grabbed his coat and looked around while pulling it on, getting oriented. A full eighteen hours had ticked away. In the two days since being picked up he'd mainly spent his time hiding out in her cabin, not in the mood to talk to other passengers. She brought him back hot meals, and he'd been trying to undo the damage done recently to his body, letting the tiny machines and souped-up biological systems in him layer muscle and bone density back on.

"I'm up." He felt heavy and tired. Each dreadlock seemed to pull at the roots of his scalp, not something he ever noticed usually.

The room pitched at a completely different angle. He stood with his feet on what had previously been one of the walls.

Grenada forced the door the rest of the way open and tumbled in. "Emergency power only." She turned around and pulled a green duffel bag into the room, which she tossed at Pepper. Outside, shadows grew and flickered as tiny red lights flashed on and off.

"What's going on?" The zipper stuck, and the fabric tore as Pepper continued to pull it open. The duffel contained all his confiscated gear.

"We going end over end."

The heavy feeling: increased gravity, the force of them being jammed down against the floor at twice a regular gee.

"Wobbling, too," Pepper said after a second of studying the varying feelings of force as he massaged his holsters into place.

Grenada cocked her head and put a hand over her ear. "Canden. She say we been infiltrate."

"League agents, a hijacking?" Pepper finished arming himself. "I'm not going to be optimal, I'm still recovering." Low bone density, a leaner body, deep scarring in the left bicep and both thighs.

"We do what do with what we got," Grenada said.

"The League got someone aboard while you were on your little daytrip?" Pepper shook his trench coat out and let it settle.

"I don't think so." Grenada flipped her mattress up to reveal an arsenal of her own strapped to the bedsprings.

"Not with me breathing down every lock, everyone on or off the ship."

Pepper looked out of their room. The once vertical bulkhead near the room had turned into a floor down "under" the door. "Maybe," he said to himself.

"We near the tip, most the passengers back near hull central. Even like this we got just enough gravity to keep them from being sick, and not enough for them to hurt themself."

He looked up. Rungs and rails ran along the corridor. They looked strange when the ship spun for gravity, but if the ship wasn't spinning and instead was being pushed, their orientation made sense. Yet using rails and runs at twice a gee, that would be exhausting in a hurry. "We joining the passengers?"

"We look like passengers?" Grenada clambered over the door and dropped to the bulkhead ten feet below.

"End over end going to flush out our infiltrator?"

"Slow him down, force the passengers up into central for the head count." She bit her lip and listened to the distant voice again. "My boys looking for the final few passengers. Once they fully round up, then you and me, we make we move."

"Thanks for rearming me."

"You want in?" Grenada tapped her ear.

Pepper shook his head. He had no capacity to network in. Yes Grenada and her friends, as well as any given passenger or crew on this ship could share and see information laid over the world, but a chipped optic nerve with a network connection could be hacked.

"You remain pure." Grenada smiled. "No accessing the Ragalamina for you."

"Satraps ruined that for me." Pepper smiled back. Accessing the reams of data that could be laid over the world around him always tempted him, but Pepper didn't trust it. Satrapic lamina was riddled with back doors that let the Satraps hack into human beings and use them as neural puppets.

Even though Ragalamina protocols were human made—custom-rolled, open-sourced, and of fine pedigree—Pepper really, really, did not like allowing anything like that under his defenses.

"Fair enough," Grenada said. "Even heavy encryption like battle Ragalamina could get break."

"Your problem then." He just hoped that if that did happen it wouldn't become his problem in a hurry.

"Fair enough."

"So what now?"

Grenada sighed. "Marsden?" She shook her head, frustrated. "Two passengers yet. Marsden ain't responding."

"He might be hurt," Pepper said. "You shouldn't have sent him alone."

When she looked at him he regretted it. Here on a tiny ship, with four others sworn to protect the ship, they would be close, a tight brotherhood. "We going."

Grenada grabbed a rung and pulled herself up.

Pepper followed. "We'll be walking toward the infiltrator, on their terms."

She looked back down at him. "You think?"

They climbed four levels up. Pepper could feel sweat collecting in the small of his back. Not a whole lot of effort to climb this, usually, but he remained weaker than normal.

Grenada glanced over the edge, then rolled over it. "Clear."

Pepper dropped down to the bulkhead with her, peering down into the dark. He pulled out the grenade launcher.

Grenada looked over. "That thing?"

He put a finger to his lips. Something shuffled a hundred feet below them in the dark. A scrape, a step, then a scrape, and then another step.

Grenada leaned over quickly with a UV penlight and painted the area as Pepper tensed. "It's Marsden. We good."

Pepper glanced.

One of the men he'd seen back at the cargo bay pulled a limp body behind him by the feet, struggling with the heavy weight. He looked up and signaled. All good.

They clambered down and dropped to the next bulkhead.

"I off the battle lamina." Marsden looked relieved to see Grenada. "Just like you had train us."

Pepper raised an eyebrow. "You don't trust lamina?"

Grenada cleared her throat. "Fifteen years ago, you once had speak in Capitol City and I went and listen. You said if we was using lamina, cut it off when stuff getting real strange. I train them the same."

Marsden grunted and dropped the body by their feet. "You want strange: the man attack me."

The heavy man still wore expensive silk pants. But a fleshy structure grew out of the neck and shoulder line: a series of black spikes.

Pepper reached out and tapped the growth with a boot. It disintegrated, bits falling through the grate and flaking off into the air.

Strange. The man's body had started reshaping parts of itself.

"Don't touch that." Marsden moved up away from the body. He kept his distance from both Pepper and Grenada as well.

"Captain. That all the passengers, all the crew," Grenada said. "Stand down."

A rumbling rippled through the *Sheikh* as thrusters fired to cancel the spin. A defensive measure worked out between Grenada and the captain to make it hard for an infiltrator to move throughout the ship.

Very solid.

The heavy feeling of gravity lessened, and then lifted completely away.

"Okay. We bringing the body to medical." Grenada grabbed the rail and hauled it up into the air between them.

"What about contamination?" Marsden still kept his distance.

"Whatever on its back all in the air now." She kicked off down the rail with body in tow. "If the League want to kill this whole ship, they already done it. They trying for something else. This man, the specialist: first one off the ship. Now he dead. But why go through all that just to poison we all when they could have just blow the ship up?"

They moved into the ship's hub: an empty core that the elevators ran "up" and "down" when under acceleration. Right now it looked like a half-mile-long tunnel with subway cars, lit by patches of emergency lights, that ran through the ship's center. It depended on orientation and perception, and what the ship was doing.

No matter which way it felt, with a dead body it became a gloomy traverse. The three of them coasted down its center with the strange corpse.

Halfway through their journey the full complement of lights returned and one of the track cars zipped down the tube and matched their speed. Grenada pulled herself aboard through sliding doors. "Get in."

The tunnel at the heart of the ship narrowed and they entered the drive cylinder: the engine and command center of the ship. They eventually got out, transferred to a spoke of a corridor, and floated their way down past a series of utility rooms.

Captain Canden met them in the sick bay, sterile lights gleaming off her shaved skull and large dark eyes that matched her skin. After studying Pepper she looked at Grenada. "He got armed."

"We was infiltrated, and there ain't none better. Better he packing than not."

"Don't like no stranger packing no gun on me ship," Canden snapped. "Strip his ass down."

"You just had to ask politely, that's all." Pepper pulled everything out, letting the weapons hang in the air in front of him.

Canden twitched and moved closer. She pushed the grenade launcher out of the way to stare him in the eye. "You a passenger to me, same as the diplomats. This a higgler ship, not some tool of the Dread Council. We independent, you hear? Don't want no hassle."

Pepper held his hands up. "No hassle." On Canden's turf, fair enough. He would go back to the passengers.

A good meal would put this behind him. The issue was dead, literally dead in the air behind him in the form of a corpse. Not his problem. Canden's. And she had enough stress without some other variable.

He could behave.

"Good." Canden smiled. They understood each other and she liked that. "Grenada, get him down to the hub, we keeping passengers there until we hit Chilo. Everyone in observation in case anything else funny happen. I ain't jeopardizing that bonus the Dread Council offering."

Grenada gave a curt nod.

Outside, skimming away from the sick bay, Grenada turned in midair. "She stress. Sorry."

"It's no problem," Pepper said. "Her ship, her rules.

I can abide." Canden sounded like she'd made one too many wormhole transits out into dangerous League territory and back to Ragamuffin safety.

They hit the central area. Crew floated outside the doors, and they opened them for Pepper and Grenada.

He floated through—she hit the door frame and stopped in place. She handed him a small wrist bracelet. "Sorry," she said as they shut the door on him. "Just a temporary thing."

Outside the sounds of the door getting dogged shut clanged throughout the room. The wheel spun down and clicked on the outside.

"Welcome to lockdown," said a man in an expensive silk dashiki nearby. His graying dreadlocks hovered in place by his cheeks. "The captain figures if anyone else is running around the ship, the sensors won't be confused by us wandering around. I know you, see you at the Council meetings. Pepper, right? Mongoose command?"

"Yeah, but here, I'm Juan Smith." Fifty other passengers clumped in various groups, many around the bar on the far side.

"Juan Smith?"

"Yeah. No one special or particular." He sighed and kicked off toward the bar.

Fifty potential problems floated around in here with him. He had none of his favorite weapons. He just had to relax here. While Canden watched to see what would happen.

CHAPTER EIGHT

Pepper remembered the man in the silk dashiki with the orange and white arabesque patterns as Audley Sinclair, a minor member of the Dread Council. He hailed from an old line of higgler ships. Pepper remembered the call to prayer, the families bowing to the walls of the ship's hull.

And no alcohol anywhere on his ship. Pepper distinctly remembered that.

Audley recognized Pepper and introduced him to the rest of the group that had tripped out through the DMZ to listen to the League's pitch.

Deon, Milton, and Edburt all introduced themselves over drinks. They took over a table close to the bar once Canden had ratcheted the ship's spin back up, as well as speed. Pepper could feel the dull background tremble through his feet as gravity returned.

Pepper had them bring him over a full dinner and a cheese platter. He ate and listened.

"Can't believe that woman," Sinclair groused. "Locking us all up in here."

"Damn straight. As if we regular passengers." Milton supplemented his grumbling with sips of rum.

"Council go hear about this, for sure." Milton folded his arms and sniffed. "Next time we take some military, show some muscle to the League. And then we ain't go put up with no higgler ship captain pushing we all around."

Milton, Edburt, and Sinclair all agreed, and Deon just smiled. "You all full of it. Ain't no gunship going out the DMZ and you know it. We don't need provocation."

"Damn League needs to know we aren't pushovers," Edburt said as Pepper ripped through a steak with a plastic knife on the constant edge of almost breaking. He had to saw and saw to cut pieces of steak off.

Deon sighed. "They know it. Or they wouldn't have call us up to go see that planet."

They all looked at Pepper, who froze with a large chunk of cheese halfway to his mouth. Sinclair nodded. "He in the Dread Council, he go hear about it."

Pepper looked at Sinclair like the man was a bug. But then, this would be a way to hear more about the planet. "Keep that to yourselves: to everyone else but you all in here, I'm Juan Smith."

Sitting near someone going incognito, but powerful within in the council, made the others sit up. No doubt seeing ways they might be able to get into his graces and work their way up the hallways of power in the council.

League or Ragamuffin, Pepper hated politicians.

He picked up the steak, ripped a piece off, and started chewing. They all stared until Deon cleared his throat.

Pepper swallowed. "So what'd you see out there?" He ripped off another piece.

Sinclair took the lead. "League found something off in a side loop on the wormhole network. Huge archeological find: whole new race and civilization never seen."

"Wiped out," Milton added. "It was this whole planet knocked completely off its orbit. By moonlets thrown at it from a gas giant, asteroids from a nearby belt. Possibly even some nuclear hits to round out the destruction on the surface. Complete xenocide. The surface now is stripped clean, airless, and completely cratered."

"But that's not the coup de grâce," Deon said. "The

final killing blow? All that energy kicked the planet out close enough to pass near the sun, where a solar flare scorched the surface clean for emphasis. That the League even noticed anything had once existed on the planet was a miracle."

"Talk about salting the fields after destroying someone," Edburt said.

"And this was recent, maybe five hundred years ago," Milton added. "Whoever was able to do all that, they probably still exist. It wasn't the Satrapy, even they didn't have that kind of destructive power. And none of the other aliens around the Forty-Eight worlds could do it either."

Pepper looked at the plate he held. "You eating that sandwich?"

Milton looked distressed that Pepper hadn't shown enough awe. He frowned, but pushed the plate over. "You're pretty hungry."

Pepper shrugged. "So the League asks us out?"

"They're freaked out and invite us in because they think, maybe if they show us troublesome New Anegadans how dangerous the universe is we'll agree to joining the League."

"They put an offer on the table?" Pepper asked, before finishing the last of the cheese and then scarfing Milton's sandwich.

"Hand over any aliens we're protecting, any wormhole manipulation technology and research, and we could be federalized under their charter with some self rule. We would hand over any military ships to them, but keep our police forces. Same bullshit deal they always want."

Deon nodded. "But looking down on that planet, knowing what could be out there, you think twice."

They didn't disagree, but looked down at their drinks. "Scorched by a sun," Milton said. "Never seen nothing like it."

"Makes the League sound rational." Pepper licked his fingers.

They all stared at him. "That's almost traitorous."

"Thinking out loud is traitorous now?" Pepper shrugged. "Say what you will, if there is something out there more dangerous than the Satraps were out there, something that can scour a planet clean, then you have to wonder if humans arguing with humans makes any sense. We may have shut down the wormhole leading out into the rest of the galaxy downstream of New Anegada, but don't forget there are still other places things can lurk."

That made them uncomfortable. And they had nothing more to offer Pepper.

"So we give up all we fight for. Give up sovereignty and freedom to the League because some boogeymen might be out there?"

"I never said that," Pepper said. "But if either the League or New Anegada starts fighting each other, all we do is weaken the both for whatever comes next. So someone better be committed to taking that all the way through if they start it up."

With that he got up, aiming toward some comfortable couches on the far side of the highly arched and overdecorated space. He stopped only in front of a pair of chairs. The fronts were fastened under the tables, but the backs had nice metal legs. He stopped to bend one until it snapped off, using his coat to cover the quick action.

He lay down on the couch and looked up at the ceiling. Nothing he could crawl through. Too bad.

He closed his eyes, drifting off inside himself to run through the notes he'd give when debriefed about the trip through the DMZ.

He dozed for the next five hours, listening to people around him get drunker and more annoyed until the captain notified the room via hidden speakers that all the diplomats needed to head for the rear kitchen doors. The crew waited for them there. Her disembodied voice sounded tired.

An interesting development. Pepper listened to them crowd the door, muttering and eager to give the captain a piece of their mind about being cooped up against their will. The tiny bracelet Grenada had given him buzzed. Her face appeared on the gold surface. "The crew and them diplomat been check over by the League. Medical safety, they said."

"So the captain is isolating anyone who had direct contact with the League?"

"Yeah. Getting those with contact out the room, making sure you all safe."

She left, leaving Pepper alone with his thoughts.

Pepper grabbed the man by the throat before he could stop himself. "Wake me up from a distance, don't ever get that close again." He let go, put the metal chair leg back in his coat, and blinked sleep from his eyes. Another nice eight hours of sleep, hopefully the last long stretch he needed. He should be caught up now. "Who are you?"

People sprawled around the great room on chairs and couches, many even using the floor and pillows.

The man, a silk suit–wearing refugee who could afford the price of a ride to New Anegada out of the League territories, coughed and staggered backward. "Gerald. My name's Gerald. Come here."

They threaded through clumps of passengers standing around Audley, who lay on a couch near one of the doors. The man's colorful robe dripped sweat and he tossed and turned in the grip of a deep fever.

"He's boiling up." Pepper's eyes gauged Audley's temperature. "He'll be brain dead within the hour at this rate." The wet cloth on Audley's forehead was a useless gesture.

"He needs help. The crew isn't answering. One of them was banging on the door, but he's gone now. Captain isn't saying anything to us either."

Everyone watched him. No doubt word had spread that he was a mongoose-man, at least. The diplomats must have blathered something to someone before they left.

Pepper stalked over to the nearest door and listened. The crew standing guard had left, but he could faintly hear what sounded like scratching on the other side. "Why is Audley here, didn't they all leave?"

Gerald smiled. "He was drunk out of his mind. Hiding underneath the bar, he must have been sampling all the time."

Pepper moved across the circular wall to the next door. The scratching got louder. He tapped the bracelet, but Grenada didn't reply to the request for a chat.

"Shame the door don't have no window," Gerald said.

The repetitive and faint scratching paused, then continued, but with more purpose now. Pepper looked back at Gerald. "There's only one problem with your theory about Audley being drunk."

Maybe he and Grenada had been wrong earlier. Maybe the League had gotten some infection, a disease, on the ship. One that they wanted to go critical on some sort of delay. Maybe one that they'd hoped would escape out into a larger population when the crew docked.

"And that is?"

Pepper stalked over to the bar. He opened the area where Audley supposedly hid. "You see any bottles in here?"

Gerald shook his head. "He didn't drink?"

"No." Pepper slouched on a chair nearby. "He was a devout Muslim. His entire ship and family. He wouldn't have been drinking under that bar, not from what I remember about him. But hiding from the captain, that he may well have been doing."

"Hiding from the captain?" Gerald looked shocked.

"Yes." Pepper got up and approached the bar.

"But why?"

"I don't know. General principle? Or maybe he suspected that he was already infected and scared that she might throw him out the airlock. I'm not sure."

"What are you doing?"

"Making a drink. I'm not devout." Tongs floated inside a bucket of ice water, the cubes long since melted. Pepper found a clean shot glass and poured a nice whiskey.

"In the middle of all this?"

"Unless you can open one of those doors, there's nothing we can do." Pepper knocked back the shot and cleared his throat. "Isn't that correct, Captain Canden?"

No reply. Pepper spread his arms.

The scratching stopped. A latch outside clanked. The wheel at the center of the door slowly spun, catching the light with its well-polished steel.

Gerald looked over. "Excellent. Now maybe we'll get answers."

People surged toward the door. Pepper watched Gerald force his way to the front as the door swung open. Milton, ashy-faced, eyes bugged out, staggered through the door with a moan. Several crewmen followed behind him. Large fans of flesh, translucent and filled with pulsing dark blood, poked up out of his shoulders.

Milton's eye sockets looked thicker, Pepper thought, as he watched the shoulder fans twitch, constantly moving about, occasionally reaching backward to touch the crew member behind him.

Milton grabbed Gerald and bit his neck. Blood instantly stained Gerald's collar.

"Shut the door!" Pepper leaped over the bar as Gerald screamed and kicked Milton back. Another crew member stumbled through the door and bit one of the passengers. Then it dragged another passenger out past the door into the corridor.

Pepper shoved the panicked and shouting people aside. "Shut the goddamned door. Don't let any more in!"

A crewman looked at Pepper. Yellow, unoxygenated eyes fixed on him. Pepper could see more crew outside, stumbling quickly forward toward the doorway. All had strange growths on their shoulders. They moved together like fronds in the wind.

Pepper kicked the man back out into the corridor. Ribs cracked from the impact and the man's head bounced hard on the grating. He didn't seem dazed. He sat up slowly and started crawling back toward them.

Gerald punched and kicked Milton back to the doorway. He screamed and cursed at the diplomat, who bit Gerald on the forearm. Pepper swiveled and kicked Milton out with one booted foot and then shut the door. He dogged it shut.

Fists hammered on the outside as Pepper turned to face the crowd, keeping a hand on the wheel as it twitched. "I vote we lock doors from the inside."

No one disagreed.

Pepper inserted the chair leg in the wheel, pushing it

hard against the frame to prevent the wheel from being spun and opened.

As passengers got Gerald over to a couch, covering
his bite wounds with a hastily donated jacket, Pepper
walked around the chairs. He broke off legs and used
them to secure the five doors.

"What the fuck just happened?" Gerald shouted.
"That was Milton."

"I don't know." Pepper finished his circuit of the room.
He walked back with a spare chair leg and pointed it at
Audley. "But I'll bet he's going to be next to freak out
and start biting people like they just did. He was part of
that group that left this ship to talk to the League. At the
very least, you need to tie him up very, very securely."

"Yeah." Gerald wiped blood off his chin. "Very securely."

CHAPTER NINE

Grenada pinged after a long hour of everyone sitting
and staring at Audley. "Don't let anyone through
the doors. We got a problem with people . . . they infected. We ain't sure what with. They biting others."

Pepper looked down at the bracelet and Grenada's
small face on its screen. "You're a bit late." And why
didn't Canden and Grenada know exactly what was
going on? The captain could see everything in the ship.

Unless she'd lost that capability.

"But everyone okay?" Grenada asked.

"Passenger named Gerald got bit. Everyone else is okay.
You need to tell the captain to get her ship together and

get Audley out of here. I'm not sure who got exposed and when."

"Pepper, here the captain." Grenada's face wavered, and then Canden's appeared. Blood streaked her cheeks.

"You got attacked?" Pepper asked.

"Anyone who got one of the League's damn 'medical exams' going crazy," Canden said. "The crew, they stormed the bridge. Tried to kill us. Grenada took care of it, secured the cockpit. Which means you right about Audley, he was the last of the diplomats."

"But what the hell is happening to them?" Pepper unstrapped the bracelet and held it in the palm of his hand.

"I don't know. I got two of the diplomats in sick bay, so I have some remote monitoring. But my doctor dead now, so this stuff don't mean shit to me. Before he died, he did do a brain scan on one of the infected: they ain't themselves. Their brain function strip out, as good as dead. He was about to say more, but three infected crew storm the bridge and started to bite everyone up. I think they was aiming for me and Grenada in particular. They tried to kill us, but bite the others. They did a good job."

"They were coordinated?"

"Grenada thinks so. She say you seen something like this before?"

"Satraps can take control of your mind via lamina. Tunneling through neural implants to gain motor control." Some eerie shit, seeing hordes of human beings moving and acting as one, just puppets of some malevolent intelligence. But there was no Satrap here.

"This looks similar, except one thing," Canden said.

"Yeah?"

"Not all crew use lamina. Why use something that

the League could manipulate when I travel out past the DMZ?"

"Well." That torpedoed that.

"I have to assume they a threat. Whatever happening to them, I don't know. But when they get infected, they trying to kill me. I have a locked door, I won't be opening it."

"Smart, we need you to keep control of the ship."

"So we have a problem." Canden wiped blood off her face with a rag. "Grenada thinks Audley's hiding in the great room there, with the other passengers."

"We found him, he's strapped down on one of the couches." They'd used decorative curtains and ripped them into strips for restraints.

Canden sighed. "Then we need a favor."

Pepper didn't give her any indication he knew what came next.

"I need you to kill Audley," she continued. "Remove the threat to the other passengers. Pepper, I will not come into dock with them all dead, understand me? We hold our shit together for twenty more hours and we in orbit around Chilo. At Chilo, we can call in the mongoose-men, we can talk to Raga central. We home free in twenty. So you'll damn well protect those people in there with you."

"And what the hell am I supposed to kill Audley with? You took all my weapons."

"You have no idea how much I regret that right now," Canden said. "But we all play what we get dealt, understand? I was just piloting my ship, heading upstream and downstream, playing out my profits, moving people, minding my own business. But I don't have that luxury anymore, do I?"

Pepper nodded. "I'll take care of it, Captain."

She looked relieved, and yet sick to have said the words. She'd hoped, no doubt, that he would suggest that solution.

But any higgler ship captain would have seen enough of the worlds to keep their composure for now. Particularly if she ever got caught in any hot spots out among the Forty-Eight worlds where the League was still pacifying alien populations, and the aliens were fighting back. Canden was holding up okay. And now she had given him the nod to do what needed to be done.

Grenada appeared again as Pepper looked over at one of the doors. Scratching had turned to banging. On two of the doors now. "I'm going to leave the cockpit now," she said. "Fight my way out the door."

"Taking care of the crew?"

She nodded, a tiny motion on the bracelet, and then her face faded away.

A grim task, that, Pepper thought. Killing all your friends, the people you were supposed to protect.

Gerald had his arm up in a sling and bound with the sleeves of some shirts donated by others. He'd watched Pepper from a distance. "What's going on? Is the captain okay?"

"Doing okay." Pepper walked toward Audley. "Let's take a look at him."

Audley strained at the braided curtains. His eyes had faded to the same unoxygenated yellow. His skin looked dusty.

When he spotted Pepper his neck muscles strained and he groaned, trying to reach for him.

Pepper used a chair leg to poke at Audley's shoulders and rip the top of his robe away. People muttered when they saw the fleshy growth by the ridge of the diplomat's shoulders.

"What is that?" Gerald looked horrified. "That growth."

"I don't know. But it does tell us one thing."

"Which is?"

"Audley's infected with whatever they were." Pepper pointed at the clanging doors.

"What do we do?"

"The captain wants us to kill him, remove the threat."

Gerald raised his hands and stepped between Pepper and Audley. "No, no no no. We can't do that."

Pepper lowered the chair leg. "And why would that be?"

"Listen, I didn't drag myself out of a hell zone of League war to end up here getting blood on my hands again." Gerald looked earnestly at Pepper. "I can't do this anymore, I have to sleep with myself at night."

"You're not doing it, I am."

"But I will have stood by. We don't know what these people are infected with. Or what the League may have done to them. They might be able to be cured. This might be a temporary state." Gerald refused to budge. "We need medical attention, not triage on a trigger finger."

One of the women stepped next to Gerald. "Gerald has a point. We can't just start killing each other left and right, we're in the room, we're safe, and he's tied down."

Pepper raised his hands. "I won't kill him." For now.

He walked back over to his chair near the bar, doing his best to ignore the sounds of the former crew members throwing themselves at the door.

The steady thumping now made some of the passengers flinch.

Someone on the far end of the room stumbled and fainted. Their head slapped a table on the way down. Pepper trotted over, trench coat billowing out behind him.

"Step aside." He squatted by the passed-out man. He was running a fever.

Pepper peeled back a set of bandages wrapped around the man's calf and looked at the human bite marks. He tapped the bracelet. Canden looked up at him from it.

"Is it done?" Her voice quavered.

"When the first diplomat went nuts, did he bite any passengers nearby?"

"Yes. Tomathy, I think the name was, and a couple others."

"That was about four hours ago, right?"

"Roughly, yes."

Pepper nodded. "It's not just the diplomats and your crew. It's spreading: one of the passengers just dropped."

Canden stared at him. "Are you . . . absolutely sure?"

"Same fever, bite marks on his calf. I think it's transmitted in the blood. That's why the biting."

After a long pause Canden raised her forearm up and unwrapped the bandage on it.

Pepper stared at the deep bite mark on it. "Although, I could be wrong."

Canden's picture flickered off. Audio only, she didn't want to look at him. "We'll find out when Grenada finds Marsden. He got bitten as well. Isolate the sick passengers. I need to think."

Isolate them? Pepper didn't want to create a miniature revolt. But he was keeping track of everyone who looked sick or tired.

Another passenger dropped to her knees and then

fell forward onto her face. A woman in short trousers and a fluffed-out silvery shirt. The man next to her dropped to his knees. "Agnes!"

As Pepper stood up a fourth person fell over.

Gerald looked over at him. He held up all five fingers. Five infected, including Audley.

"What the hell is it?" Gerald hissed as Pepper helped drag one of the comatose passengers over near Audley.

"They zombies," one of the other passengers said. "Just like in the stories. Shuffling around and biting you and spreading."

Gerald looked at Pepper, who couldn't disagree. Zombies it was. "Zombies."

"Zombies?"

"The League must have found something useful to use against us." Pepper looked around for more curtains to use as restraints. "It looks like an infection. These passengers should have been arriving planetside according to your original schedule. They wanted a larger population." Had the *Sheikh* not stopped for Pepper, going well out of its way and adding time onto its journey, it would have been docked in an orbital habitat somewhere over Chilo at this point. "The ship should have been docked already."

The bad news: these passengers wouldn't be locked in a room with infected people if it weren't for Pepper.

But if it weren't for Pepper, this would have been unleashed on a much larger group of people. Small consolation, true, but at least it was something.

"We should kill the five of them now," Gerald said. "Before they try and infect us." Pepper ripped down another huge swathe of decorative curtain, golden sheets with red ace-of-spade markings.

"Hell no," someone in the crowd shouted. "These are friends, family. We're not murderers."

"Quit arguing," Pepper hissed as he tore long strips off, "and tie them all down."

Protesting was half-hearted as Gerald did so, and Pepper pinged the captain. "How long before we make Chilo?"

Canden responded with just tinny audio from the bracelet. "I'm speeding us up. We'll transit the worm-hole in ten hours. Then I get the *Sheikh* into orbit and send out distress signals."

"You aren't doing that now?" Pepper snapped.

"Long range comms all down, I can use lasers, but I need line of sight with something besides wormhole buoys, they don't pass that on. We going to have to be in Chilo orbit to talk to anyone."

"The infected crew did that sabotage, didn't they?"

"Yes," Canden said. "I think they smarter than they look."

Pepper glanced over at the doors. "That's a problem." He turned the bracelet off.

When it was just a mindless infection that altered their behavior they faced, that was one problem. But Pepper wouldn't sit in a locked room waiting for an outside threat to slowly gain control of the ship. If some sort of intelligence was involved he wanted the free-dom to move and pick his fights.

The sound of tearing cloth filled his ears. Pepper turned and watched Audly rip free of his restraints. He groaned, and the raspy sound was quickly picked up and echoed by the other infected. Audley's thighs bunched, gathering strength for a leap right at Pepper.

Before anyone could even object, Pepper closed the distance between them, whipped out the metal leg from under his coat, and drove it deep into Audley's chest.

Audley paused. Then he pushed forward, ichor dripping from around the wound. He stared at Pepper, slowly reaching to try and grab him.

Pepper yanked the leg free, batted Audley's hands aside, and stabbed the man in the stomach.

Audley didn't appear fazed. So Pepper pulled the improvised weapon out again, and speared the man in the eye socket with a sickening crack and pop.

Pepper finished the job with two more quick jabs to the face as people nearby screamed.

Pepper pushed skull fragments aside, frowning at the black bile that trickled out toward the floor instead of blood. A rotten smell filled the air.

"Oh God," Gerald said.

Pepper turned to a man with a well-trimmed mustache and short hair with his hands and feet tied up.

"Oh no, oh no," the woman next to him moaned. "Oh please no."

Passengers intervened. They forced their way in front of Pepper and tried to lock their arms. He understood. This was murder. Who wanted to kill another human being?

It was a hard task, even for those trained to do it. And here were regular people, just travelers, in a wildly unfortunate situation.

Pepper threw them aside and brained the passenger while ignoring the screams around him.

When that was done, he turned toward the next of the infected, but the passengers had formed a ring around the three remaining victims. They made a colorful wall of determined people, unwilling to allow what he wanted next.

Behind them the three infected moaned, full into their strange transformations. Their shirts ripped in the back as their shoulders grew the strange fans out of the flesh on their shoulders.

"We can't let you do this." The passengers had linked arms. They looked serious.

Pepper shook his head. "This is suicide. They're trying to harm us."

"You can't kill them," Gerald said. "Neither you nor the captain can kill them. We'll keep them contained until we get to Chilo, and then we'll get help."

Pepper took a deep breath, planning his route, as all three infected stood up. With feet and hands tied they barely managed to stumble forward, but the first two fell and bit the ankles of the nearest passengers.

The ring realized what had happened. Passengers screamed and stomped back, the group's unity dissolving as it realized the threat really came from behind.

Pepper shoved his way through to the third infected man. This one stumbled on his way toward the nearest door.

As he reached out to undog it Pepper smacked the back of the passenger's head with the metal leg. The impact splattered brain against the steel doors.

Pepper turned around. Even though there was no tapping on this door, he'd bet anything a large number of the zombified crew lurked on the other side.

Passengers had subdued the other two, taking them down and hog-tying them again. But not without numerous bites and scratches. Pepper walked across the room in the opposite direction, stopping only to briefly wipe his metal chair leg clean on a piece of drapery left lying on the floor.

"What are you doing?" Captain Canden's voice asked

via the bracelet as Pepper continued. Apparently it wasn't just Grenada keeping tabs on him via the device. He'd gotten too close to the door for too long for her comfort.

"Going away." Pepper stopped in front of the door and put his ear to it, straining hard to listen for any scuffling through the door.

"You can't leave them here."

"The hell I can." Pepper couldn't hear anything.

Gerald spotted him and ran over. Good, someone needed to redog after Pepper stepped outside.

"What are you hoping to do?"

"Captain, they're starting to really mess with the ship; it's only a matter of time before you become one of them as well. And you're in the damn cockpit. I'm not going to sit in a room and wait to die. Not like that."

"Damnit, we need to bring those passengers in safely!"

"I don't think that's a realistic scenario anymore. Five or six more have been bitten and the passengers are reluctant to start killing each other off. And I can't blame them."

He threw the metal leg at Gerald, who looked down at it. "What do I do with this?"

"I'm stepping out," Pepper said. "Going to see what I can do outside there. You want to come?"

Gerald shook his head. "Safer here."

Pepper choose not to disagree. "Captain's listening in. Gerald, tie up anyone with cuts and scrapes. Kill everyone with cuts and scrapes and infection, and some might live."

"I know." Gerald looked down at his own bites.

"Good luck." Pepper turned his back on the man.

Pepper spun the lock and threw the door open to an empty corridor.

"Pepper, don't do this," Canden said. "I order you. You need to stay in that room. If you do what has to be done, they might live."

Gerald shut the door behind him.

"Too late," he whispered to Canden.

Grenada stepped out of the shadows near the end of the corridor with a gun aimed at Pepper, face and arms streaked with blood.

CHAPTER TEN

Grenada kept her sidearm trained on him. "She think you a threat, Pepper."

"The captain?"

"You dangerous, man: a frigging wild card all up in a fucked-up situation."

"And what do *you* think I am?" Pepper stepped forward.

"Don't matter what I think." She flicked the safety off. "But you have to get back in."

"Captain's orders?"

Grenada looked tired. "Captain orders."

Pepper snapped forward, left hand up and reaching for the gun as she fired three times. She was just as quick as he was. Pepper felt each bullet bite: one through the hand, another his side, and the third dead into his thigh.

He slammed into her and took the gun. He hit her forehead with the butt hard enough to daze her and leave a bloodied gash. A second time to knock her out as they both slumped to the grating.

Pepper leaned his back against the wall as he felt for Grenada's pulse and pulled her onto his lap.

His body burned as its hyper-engineered defenses sprang into action and accelerated healing began.

"You kill her?" Canden asked.

Something clanged down at the end of the long corridor. Pepper took a long, gasping breath. He was too weak. The bullets had taken their toll, and even with downtime he had risked a lot to assume Grenada wouldn't take a kill shot in that split-second attack. She'd tried to disable him first.

"The problem is that she idolizes you, you know?" Canden said via the bracelet. "And in the end, she didn't aim true, right? A lesson to we all."

"You manipulate people when all you had to do was ask nicely." Pepper squinted. Something definitely lurked in the shadows out there. A shabbily dressed crewman lurched his way toward them. Step by step.

"I doing what I got to to bring those people back. If you get infected, you very dangerous, and uncontained. I have me a duty here."

"I'll blow my own brains out before I fall to the infection," Pepper promised as he looked Grenada's gun over. "And I doubt it will come to that."

"I can't be taking that risk."

"I know. I wouldn't take it if I were you, either."

Another shambling figure. The two infected crewmen picked up speed. They looked like marionette dolls, their disjointed puppetlike motion the result of some lost brain function.

Lurch, shuffle, lurch, shuffle.

The shadows slipped over them, and then the deck lighting revealed ashen faces and vacant eyes. They walked in sync as they inched closer. The strange growths on their shoulders twitched and caressed each other. Did they pass on information?

Pepper crushed the bracelet in his left fist and cut off

the start of Canden's next sentence. The two zombies moved closer, and Pepper raised the gun.

They both stopped.

"Ah. So you know what this is?"

They stared at him, swaying in sync. Waiting. Pepper pulled the trigger twice.

As he'd discovered inside, they still used the brain. Destroy it and the zombie stopped. Even these refashioned things that were once human needed a CPU. Take that away and they dropped.

A third infected stood in the shadows. But it didn't approach.

Pepper pushed Grenada off and stood up. She rubbed her forehead and groaned, wiping the blood off with the back of her hand. Pepper spotted a deep bite mark on her wrist. He stared at it as more shuffling echoed down toward them from the end of the corridor.

He yanked her up to her feet. "Come on, we have to move."

"We didn't commit suicide," Grenada murmured.

Pepper looked down at the knife she had near his ribs. "You trying to get yourself killed?"

"I already dead. You see the bite mark. A few hours, I shuffling after you just like them. And no one go know everyone in this ship didn't commit suicide."

"I will." Pepper kept them moving slowly forward at the third zombie, the two of them in a staring contest.

"The captain given up on living, true. The passengers getting infected, the crew done lost. But someone got to survive and tell everyone what had happen here."

This was why she didn't kill him. "So what are you going to do?"

"Keep you alive. So you can tell everyone what happen."

Pepper shot the third zombie, and the fourth and

fifth he found lurking in the shadows around the bulk-head. Between the two of them they'd emptied the clip. He handed Grenada the gun. "Not doing much for me right now."

"But I can get you more. From the galley."

Grenada and Pepper followed the tunnels alongside the ship's core. Every door had a manual lock that could open it. They'd all been dogged automatically from the cockpit, an attempt to slow down the infected crew, but Pepper could still make his way around the ship. Safety features were on their side.

Within thirty minutes Grenada guided him to the galley. She tapped a quick combination into a wall safe behind a hand-painted picture of the pencil-like *Sheikh* hanging off a station dock over a red-clouded planet.

The safe housed his short sword, as well as a variety of ship's weapons. Pepper picked a shotgun, his sword, and more ammo for Grenada's handgun.

They both limped into the freezer and shut the solid doors behind them. "Until we both heal," Grenada said. "Then we begin killing the zombies. Once they dead, then I take care of myself. You call for help as the ship coasts."

Adjusting his core body temperature to compensate for the cold and huddling deep into his trench coat, Pepper set out to wait.

His breath formed a cloud in front of him as he leaned his back up against a large crate of frozen dinners.

Pepper could feel his thigh kneading a bullet slowly back out of the wound. A familiar post-battle dull ache. The other two shots were clean, the ragged holes closing up as his hyperactive body did its thing.

"I'm getting tired of being shot," Pepper said.

"I don't think you ever go stop getting shot at."

"Nature of the business."

Grenada laughed and wrapped her arms around herself. "I work hard, to undo it. Both my parents lived station-side near the DMZ. Border clash between the League had flare up one day, and they attack us. My parents rushed me into a pod, shot me out into the dark for a week. That's how long it take before the autobeacon trigger and someone came looking.

"But they wasn't there when I came home. There was no home."

Pepper looked at her huddle tighter than the cold should have made her. "They destroyed the station?"

"Claim it an accident."

Pepper watched his breath form crystals in the air in front of him. "What about Canden?"

"She go understand. You give her grief." Grenada looked down at her feet. "But she's solid, down deep. This trip pushed her close to being able to leave the ship."

"A captain leaving their ship?"

"She never wanted it. Inherited it with massive debt overhead. Struggling to pay maintenance, struggling to pay fuel. Resenting getting order by the Raga council to ship troops she can't afford to just to help save all of we, while she getting ruined. She tired of bankruptcy, she tired of this ship, the same corridor, same tight spaces. Swore she'd leave them when she was young, and now she struggling to get it paid enough that she could sell the *Sheikh* and get out."

"And you by her side."

"Who else would take me? I was in an orphanage.

After I had see you speak on Nanagada once, I had
decide that's what I want. Joined the Mongoose, trained
up and joined the Tangent Run mission, strike back at
the League in they own territory. Revenge.

"Never figured on coming back. Getting assigned to
some merchant ship in charge of my own unit. I wanted
to die out there, taking them with me. I was a cold child,
Pepper." She looked at him with even colder eyes. A
soldier of desperation.

"Canden adopted you."

"Was me and her, my men and her crew. Raga council can't afford to train up new fighters like us. Always
promising a rotation, never able to afford it or getting
the men. League always pressing at the border, trying
to search and grab we ships for dumb reasons. It goes
on and on, never stopping. Now they get us. And I don't
want to disappear, a name on a roster on a distant ship
fighting to keep the border between us and them."

She looked away from Pepper, too exposed and no
doubt unsure how to handle it.

The decades of dealing with the permanent revolution out past the DMZ had left refugees everywhere.
Human beings struggling to take control of their own
destiny in the throes of throwing off their shackles.
And failing.

"They'll know what you did." Pepper grabbed her
shoulder. "Trust me."

"Thank you." She cradled her face in her hands.
"But now we have a whole other problem."

"What's that?"

Grenada looked up, head cocked, listening to something in her inner ear. "Canden just decided to plunge
the *Sheikh* into Chilo's sun. The infection spreading
too quick. One sure way of ending this."

CHAPTER ELEVEN

The *Sheikh* shuddered its way through the new course corrections that would plunge them into the cleansing nuclear fires of Chilo's sun. Grenada and Pepper made their way through the maze of corridors, bulkhead by dogged bulkhead. The ship had transited the wormhole leading into Chilo and continued a heavy bout of acceleration, forcing them to anchor themselves on walls that flipped into angled floors due to acceleration.

"She using up all the fuel. She given up," Grenada said. "No sense conserving antimatter when you know you all dead."

"Point." Pepper dropped off a ladder to the bulkhead's surface, the thrum of the *Sheikh* passing through his heels. They moved at double-time: two gees acceleration.

They would whip right past Chilo, with Pepper stuck on the doomed ship.

"There are emergency pods. We get you launch early, you should live to get pick up."

"What about the passengers in the great room?"

"Canden say you don't want go there."

They moved together in silence, Grenada taking point as a human shield of sorts, but one armed with a shotgun and with pistols dripping off her waist.

The first attack came from the front. Like any past encounter Grenada pushed forward, closing the distance and firing a burst with the shotgun that obliterated the zombie's head in a spray of blood and brain tissue.

But the second attack came from under the floor panels behind them.

Pepper whirled as the heavy grates clanked and dropped to the side. Three zombies clambered up, unsteady on their feet, but moving quickly to surround him.

He shot the one to his left in the head, decapitated the one on the right by sword, and kicked the one in front of him backward into the uncovered pit under the floor.

Grenada stepped forward and fired the shotgun down at the top of its skull.

The loud echo rolled throughout the ship.

"That was a trap," Pepper said.

"They getting smarter." Grenada cracked the shotgun open and shoved more rounds in. She snapped it back closed. "We need to think of them as different than zombies."

The stumbling, biting, and moronic behavior of the infected people in the great room had faded away. Now the zombies still moved slowly, but they had gained intelligence of some sort.

"Move." Grenada pushed him forward. "They go be coming after that gunshot sound something serious."

Pepper resisted the push. He walked back over to the bodies and poked his boot at the crumbling spikes growing out of the body's shoulders. "What are these?"

Grenada looked at him. "Do I look like a biologist to you, man?"

Pepper drew the sword and walked over to the decapitated zombie. He sliced the throat open and pushed aside petals of flesh. "Vocal cords look like they work, but I haven't seen any of them do anything but groan. How are they coordinating?"

"Fucking telepathy? Who knows, who cares?"

"I do." He poked at the spikes again. "Ask Canden to scan all the wavelengths. Ask her if she's detecting anything."

"You think they growing antenna?"

Pepper sheathed his sword again. "Maybe. Or maybe all that synchronized touching is how they talk and plan. It's a question someone needs to ask. If they can coordinate, that's a problem for us."

"Still don't explain why they getting smarter. Even if they could talk, the early ones was dumb."

"I don't have an answer." Many feet moved with purpose toward them in the distance, shuffling footsteps echoing down to their ears.

"Let's move." Grenada raised the shotgun. "I don't have much time before the fever coming for me." Beads of sweat stood out on her forehead.

"And Canden?"

"She ain't hearing nothing. Now move."

Pepper looked down at the corpse. "Okay."

Ten minutes later they stopped. Both bulkheads ahead filled with shuffling bodies waiting for them to try and step through.

"All they want do is bite you once," Grenada said.

"Maybe." Pepper walked forward. "But they didn't circle around behind us. They didn't even try and spring a trap like back there."

"They learn better?"

"Or they really, really don't want us coming this way. Any other places we can reach a pod?"

Grenada shook her head. "Low budget. Keep them in the cargo hold. Can't afford to retrofit the ship out with passenger pods all throughout."

"Lucky for us," Pepper muttered. The nightmare continued. Then a horrible thought occurred to him. "They're escaping the ship."

Grenada looked down at the waiting shadows. "Canden say she ain't detect any launch. Yet."

Pepper turned and started walking away. "We don't have long-range communications. These things got smart quick. They're going for the pods." He was going to have to find another way off the ship.

But Grenada stood still behind him. "If that's true, we have to take them all down, secure the hold with the pods in it."

"And it looks like most of the infected crew is standing between us and the pods." Pepper wouldn't make it through without a bite.

"You want this shit unleashed in Chilo? Traveling back to New Anegada? I know you got friends there, I know you have strong connections, and you go turn you back up on them just like that. You that selfish?"

Pepper stopped. "There's no guarantee we can stop them."

"Giving up without a fight? Now that's something I never thought I would see from you. All that legendary shit-kicking just that, legend?"

He turned around. "You dewey-eyed innocents and your freaking stories. I don't save lives, I don't join causes, I'm no hero, I play to be paid. Paid well. There's got to be another way off this damn ship."

"What were you doing past the DMZ watching a Satrap die?"

"I like seeing my enemies suffer." Pepper stalked forward and stared down at her. Fuck her. He'd gone because he was missing something, and he wanted to watch the creature suffer to see if it would fix that rage inside.

But it hadn't made him whole again. He was still the same person, still casting about for something he hadn't found yet. Lost memories, lost friends, lost worlds.

"That's it?" Grenada smiled. "Just a field trip?"

"It's easier to go where they ask you, do what they tell you. Then the mistakes, they aren't your fault. I need that, I need that after all the things that I helped happen."

"You helped found the free worlds here. New Anegada wouldn't exist without you. We all in your debt."

"Stop that. Please. No one is in my damn debt."

And Grenada laughed. "Is responsibility you scared of."

Pepper pushed her aside. "No, that's not it."

It was her. Her and the hundreds of others he'd attached himself to. Close friends, colleagues, brothers in arms. All dead. "The alien machinery inside me, the hundreds of years I've lived as a result. Everyone dies around me. And I'm tired of trying."

"You're muddling through some damn crisis. Pepper, I'm dying!" She grabbed his shirt. "There is no other fucking way off this ship but through them unless you want jump out in nothing more than a spacesuit, which will land you in the sun with us, only you'll be a couple hundred miles over that way."

"No other way."

"You need a pod. We need stop them. And I want you to tell them we saved them. You understand? I never asked them for much, other than a chance at revenge, and I know what you saying. After Tangent Run I had nothing, until I came here. This is my family, and they're dead, and I want everyone to know why. Can you just do that little thing for me?"

Pepper looked back down at the zombies. If that

was the only way off the ship . . . "How many crew were there on the ship?"

"I would imagine that's the rest of them there, waiting to stop us."

Really.

"I need more ammunition. Then we come back this way." Pepper said that out loud. Then he turned his back on the crowd waiting for them.

She'd said he couldn't get away from the ship unless he jumped off in a spacesuit. A good idea, that.

He walked back up through the ship, Grenada behind him.

"Where are the spacesuits?" Pepper asked.

"Service airlock. Few hundred feet ahead. You ain't going for more ammunition?"

"The dumbest thing you can do in a battle is play on the enemy's chosen field. Running through a corridor surrounded by those things. I'd have been bitten." And maybe she knew that and had tried to use him to help stop them by dangling the promise of getting away alive in front of him.

"You want to EVA?"

"You think there'll be zombies in spacesuits outside trying to stop us?"

"That or Canden will have a surprise for me."

"Whatever you think Canden's about, you wrong." Grenada paused in front of the airlock.

"You reading my mind now?" Pepper folded his arms.

"Ain't reading no one's mind." Grenada shook her head. "Just you actions."

"Then you have just the tiniest fraction of the picture. I understand what she's doing. I'd do the same in her spot."

Grenada looked surprised and unsure. "For true?"

"She's just trying to keep control. We going in there?" Pepper tapped on the thick porthole looking into the airlock.

"Yeah, okay." Grenada tapped in a code. The door creaked open. "Canden don't like it."

"Of course not." Pepper grinned and walked in between the pair of plastic benches. Grenada squeezed in past him to stand in front of the suit locker.

It opened with her fingerprint on the thick lock. Four bright red deflated spacesuits hung inside the racks, snugged in between acceleration gel to protect them against sudden movement.

Pepper pulled the top one out and shook it. The fabric responded by loosening up.

"What's in, what's out?" Grenada held up her belt of handguns.

"They should fire in a vacuum." Bullet casings held everything they needed to explode. "Just watch out for jamming."

"It's more a case of what we're going to fire coming in to the storage bay."

"Keep your shotgun out, then. But don't fire it while skipping around outside. It'll blow you clean off the ship."

Grenada belted herself back up, and pulled the baggy suit up over it all. Pepper helped her with the fishbowl helmet, sealing it around the neck ring. Grenada tapped the small wrist readout and gave a thumbs-up. Another tap and the suit constricted, shrinking itself down like a tight second skin, bulging around her weapons and clothes.

"You keeping your trench coat on?"

"It comes in handy in situations like this." Like reactive

bulletproof underlayers. One didn't throw away a friend like that.

Pepper pulled the extremely baggy spacsuit on over the trench coat without too much fiddling about to make it work, and pulled his dreadlocks back into a ponytail. Grenada helped set the helmet down over them, and then pushed it down on his head. The seal connected and Grenada twisted the helmet in.

Text scrolled across the inside of the clear bowl as the suit booted up and scanned itself.

Everything was go.

The tiny oxygen tank was no larger than a hip flask with an hour of air. The scrubbers in the suit would reclaim everything else, presumably it would be a while before he'd even have to dip into the tank.

"Hear me?" Grenada asked.

"Yep."

Pepper picked up his sword off the plastic bench as his spacesuit shrunk to snug itself, bunching the tails of his trenchcoat to the back of his legs.

He belted the sword outside the suit. "Tell Canden to spin the ship down, then let's go."

"You think she'll do that?"

"I think Canden understands what we trying for."

The ship shook, shoving them against the benches as Canden decelerated it out of its spin. "Did you think she wouldn't?" Pepper leaned against the wall to let Grenada past.

Grenada's voice echoed in the helmet slightly. It crackled a bit at first, but as the two suits agreed on frequencies and protocols it cleared. "I think you both all twist up, so much you understand each other."

"Maybe."

"No maybe about it." She tapped the airlock code

and stepped in. Pepper followed. A minute later the outer door opened, blowing out air and moisture crystals.

Pepper looked out into the vacuum, and then clambered out around the edge. His entire perspective shifted. From climbing out into the dark, to crouching on a massive, grooved metal field. The hull's outer plating was pitted and cratered and stripped clean of paint from the constant abrasion of space dust and tiny rock impacts. The larger ones sealed with putty and gel. "Let's move."

With a powerful kick, his hands cupping the ladder's rail that ran the length of the ship, Pepper traversed the ship's hull.

Every twenty feet he let go, nothing holding him to the ship, to dodge spots where the ladder was welded to the hull.

"Canden just jettisoned the pods," Grenada said. "You ain't getting off."

Pepper clenched the ladder and came to a stop. Grenada caught herself before slamming into him. "What?"

"I saw red."

"Spacesuit red?"

Pepper hooked his foot under a rung and pushed himself up for a better view. There: a form hunkered down behind a mass of three communications dishes.

The zombies *did* knock out the communications, by getting out in spacesuits. He wasn't particularly surprised to find them out here.

Grenada snorted. "Whoever make them regulation for fire-engine red on the suits deserve a thank-you card."

"That and whoever designed my eyes." Pepper looked over as Grenada pulled a handgun free. Pepper grabbed her wrist. "No. Don't blow yourself off the hull."

"I can brace myself."

"Save your strength." Pepper floated free as he pulled his sword out. "They're in spacesuits, so am I, they can't bite me."

"That why you have a sword?"

"I like a variety of weapons." He kicked off toward the cluster of dishes, skimming over the pitted surface, sword held out wide.

"I'll warn Canden not to make any course corrections."

"Appreciated." Pepper closed in on the base of the three dishes.

And here they came. Four red spacesuits linked by hands flying toward him like a human net.

CHAPTER TWELVE

No holding back now, no watching out for bites. Pepper slammed into the spacesuits and cracked visors with the hilt of the sword, watching faces pinch as the vacuum sucked at them.

He snapped the sword at exposed limbs reaching for him with clumsy, grasping hands, and spun around to follow up on the cracked visors. The infected bodies spun down the hull.

Pepper wrapped his legs around the torso of the nearest, raised the sword high, and beheaded the infected crewman.

Within a mental thirty-second count four heads spun free of the *Sheikh*, their bodies limp in the air near him. A cloud of crystallized fluids slowly spread out away from him.

"Watch out!" Grenada's voice crackled.

Seven red suits swirled out the nearby airlock. "Shit." The net of four had been a feint to drag him closer and then overwhelm him.

Pepper kicked off the body he had latched on to as the cluster of new suits slammed into him.

"Too many of them," Grenada said. He couldn't see her. The entire world spun with red suits, inky space, and flashes of pitted hull. Pepper sliced off arms, legs, and smashed in more faceplates.

The next batch to slam into him impaled themselves on his sword, hands grabbing for the hilt.

He had to be careful not to throw them away and toss himself into space. Instead, Pepper twisted his sword free and shoved off at the airlock. "I'm going in."

"You think that smart?"

"How many crew did you think we have left?"

"Sixteen, now. Ten dead out here, twenty-six total."

"Sixteen's doable." Pepper hit the rim of the airlock and rolled inside. Three inside waited to stop him from getting in. Sixteen crew to kill, then head back for the passengers. If he could kill everything aboard the ship and make a distress call maybe he could still get picked up.

The waiting infected held large wrenches. Another new habit. Pepper got ready for the attack. But they stepped back as he moved forward.

This was new.

Grenada clambered in after him. The outer door shut and the lock repressurized.

He moved again, and as one, the infected retreated through the inner door. Pepper and Grenada stepped out into the bay, surrounded by yellow-eyed, silent crew members.

But no more attacking.

The three nearest removed their helmets and cautiously stumbled forward. The fans on their backs strained against the red suits, which had forced the structures to fold down. They still twitched under the fabric.

"We," said the first one.

"Can," said the second.

"Now."

"Talk."

"Our."

"Numbers."

"High enough."

Pepper stared. He stepped forward, and all around, the infected shrank back again. They had decided they couldn't afford to attack him.

"What are you?" he asked.

The group touched hands, the fans on their shoulders writhed, and waves of motion ran throughout the wave of bodies like wind through grass.

"I."

"Perhaps we."

"Are."

"The Swarm."

"I've never heard of you," Pepper said.

The words that followed ran down the lines of emotionless voices.

"Your failings."

"Do not."

"Concern the Swarm."

Pepper felt annoyance unwind inside him. "What do you want?"

"The Swarm seeks."

"A truce with you."

Pepper walked forward again, and they all moved back to the walls. "A truce? Am I that dangerous?"

"Currently."

"Yes."

"Too dangerous."

"To attack."

"Could miss."

"New objective."

"What is your objective?" Grenada asked.

All heads turned to regard her. The words moved from voices right to left this time. "Expand."

"Seek."

"Seek what?" Pepper asked.

"Cannot."

"Tell."

Four of the infected ran into the airlock and shut it before Grenada and Pepper could move.

"What are they doing?" Pepper moved to the airlock, sword still in hand.

"Leaving," the Swarm said as a whole. Another set of four ran for the airlock, but Pepper and Grenada moved to get in the way.

"Leaving, how?"

Grenada dodged another grouping of four. "Look, there."

She pointed at a large cocoon where one of the infected crew wearing a spacesuit lay strapped down. Two hung over the contraption; they'd been moving it toward the airlock.

"How many already left this way?" Pepper asked.

The Swarm didn't answer. Pairs of empty eyes regarded them.

"They can't survive more than a couple hours in a spacesuit," Grenada said. "Let them die out there."

"That's a handmade heat shield," Pepper said. "That beanbag-looking thing. It's a blunt cone." They had taken a fireproof polyurethane foam from the ship's damage-control kits and made ablative heat shields. It was almost suicidal, but it worked. In theory.

"A heat shield?"

"How many infected have already left the ship?" Pepper asked as the Swarm just stared at him. "We're moving too quickly for them to just jump off the ship and hope to get picked up, so if they're going to aerobrake and parachute down to Chilo, they must be trying to spread there."

"But why wouldn't the League try for New Anegada, why Chilo?"

"Why Chilo is a good question." Pepper wanted to know that as well.

The Swarm spoke again. "Have you."

"Ever."

"Had a compulsion?"

"Like breathing?"

"Built in."

"Deep."

"Is ours."

"Spread."

"Reduce, use the sentients."

"And now our newest compulsion."

The entire Swarm rushed them. Pepper slapped his helmet back on to avoid bites. But instead of attacking him, or Grenada, they pushed past him.

He stabbed several, got one's head lopped clean off, but they rushed their last infected into the airlock, strapped to the personal heat shield. They were all just trying to move around him.

Even the Swarm not in spacesuits clustered into the airlock now. They waited for it to cycle out, dying in the vacuum. But even as that happened, they pushed the heat shield out of the lock.

Pepper sheathed his sword and looked around the empty bay. "Canden's idea that she's killing this off isn't a hundred percent. I'm going to go out after them. This infection, the group mind, it's very hostile to us on general principle. And now they're getting off your ship."

Grenada shoved over to the airlock and opened one of the lockers. She grabbed a pair of large hand rockets and tossed them at Pepper. "You need them for maneuvering."

Sword at his side, Pepper got into the airlock. Dead infected bumped around, eyes frozen open, mouths wide.

Several minutes later the large doors swung open, revealing the vacuum. As the air blew out, so did Pepper, falling away from the immense hull of the ship.

"Good luck," Canden's voice whispered.

"You've been listening in all along, but not talking to me?" Pepper used the rocket guns to push himself away from the long, tubular form of the Shiek.

"I did what I could. I done my duty."

Pepper watched as the ship grew smaller, and twisted himself around. Chilo dominated his field of vision. A lot of people would be surprised as the *Sheikh* blew right past its stop, leaving Chilo's orbit to head down the sun's gravity well.

"Pepper. Just make sure you do what you promise Grenada. Let them know how it ended." Pepper listened, still and unmoving, as the sound of a round being chambered echoed inside his helmet. "Don't have much time left, seen?"

"I will let them know. Do *me* a favor?"

"Yes." Canden sounded tired.

"Where are the bulk of these things headed? If their trajectories hold true and planet weather doesn't do strange things?"

A long silence passed. Then, "They're like Swarm spores, yes. They're all grouping, if they make it, for the far side of the planet from Chilo's Great Storm. They'll scatter some, they can't make it alive for the most part, but they'll be trying for it. I really doubt any of them, or you, can make it."

"Thank you," Pepper said. He set about using the spacesuit's rudimentary navigation systems to compute an orbit that put him on the opposite side of the planet from the Swarm. That would give him time to recover and figure out what they were up to if he made it. He didn't trust Canden enough to ask her for help. She might give him a trajectory that burned him up in the atmosphere.

"One last thing, Pepper. Tell me once more, promise me, you don't have no bite, no infection on you. I just need to know. I need to hear you say it."

"I swear to you," Pepper's voice was calm and emphatic. "I am not infected." Already the *Sheikh* was little more than a tiny needle glinting in the sunlight. The glow of its main engines suddenly lit up the darkness with actinic light for a full minute.

Pepper shielded his eyes until it faded.

"Thank you." Canden's voice sounded fuzzy with static as they fell farther apart. "Final vector laid in. We clearing Chilo now, with an extra boost. That thing, that infection, will burn up with us when we eventually spiral into the sun, and with them when they hit Chilo's atmosphere. If they make it to Chilo, well, I did everything I could. . . ."

Pepper flinched at the sound of the gunshot.

She died before turning into one of the infected. She'd secured the cockpit. The *Sheikh* was hopefully headed out of harm's way.

Now he had to catch up to that last member of the

Swarm and take its heat shield away. Then follow the spacesuit's solutions to deorbit.

After he killed the escaping Swarm member and sliced it free of the heat shield, Pepper found, much to his consternation, that the Swarm had not provided its spore with a parachute.

PART THREE

CHAPTER THIRTEEN

The phone on the wall rang, startling everyone in the room, including Timas. Ohtli leaned in to answer it. He turned back to the room. "Aeolian soldiers are on the outside shell."

Angry words filled the room. "Who the hell do they think they are?" Tenoch spat.

When Timas turned to Katerina she shrugged. "Yes, they're coming for him."

Despite his stories about fighting in space, Timas couldn't think of the one-legged, one-armed man in the bed as particularly dangerous.

"And how long did you know?" Timas asked Katerina.

Out of the corner of his eye he saw her shift uncomfortably. "Halfway through his story the vote started. Citizens demanded that we retrieve him. No further negotiating. They want better debriefing facilities."

Necalli shook his head. "You were going to torture him to see if he kept to his story?"

Katerina looked disgusted. "Torture, no. But detailed scans of his brain and physiology, testing to determine he is who he says he is, yes."

"And you couldn't just, you know, ask us formally to hand him over." Timas's dad also looked disgusted. "You're all arrogant, you know. To just assume that you can walk into our homes and take what you want."

"One," Katerina said. "The citizenry voted that you

were likely not to turn him over based on past interaction. True, it's a small margin, but it was enough to trigger an action request that then passed by a large margin. Two, he's a criminal; why do you care?"

"And what did you vote?" Timas looked into her other eye, not the silvered one.

"Oh, that's none of your business!" Katerina stepped forward into the center of the room. The one light in the ceiling acted as a spotlight on her. "And quite rude of you to ask."

"Well, it's not your courtyard soldiers are dropping in on, little girl, is it?" Ollin folded his arms and glared.

"Little girl?" For a moment Katerina looked ready to rip Ollin in two. Timas wagered she might have enough outrage to try.

The phone rang again. Ohtli lifted the handset. "The guards outside ask if they're to fight back when the Aeolians come."

Camaxtli shook his head. His raspy voice cracked. "What can we do against them? It would be a waste of lives. They're coming in. We will pick our fights, and this is not a good one."

Ollin unfolded his arms and looked down at the ground. Timas sighed. He knew that posture of regret, weariness, and anger held in check.

"I'm very sorry about this," Katerina mumbled to Timas. "You have to understand, I'm the will of my people, I didn't choose it this way, I promise."

Footsteps got louder outside.

"So you believe him?" Timas asked.

"Enough of us are intrigued. Yes. And going back over tracking logs shows that several other organic objects the rough size of a human body deorbited during the same period. We have to check this out."

The doors burst open.

The three Aeolians wore large flanged helmets. The cross-shaped blank space in the front glittered. Reflected back on the Aeolians' eyes was shifting text and other information: objectives, maps, tactical details. Their protective gear had reshaped itself into cloaks that could absorb any shots or thrusts.

"We carry no weapons in our hands," the one on the left said.

Yeah, but no doubt dangerous guns and explosives in various forms lay under those flowing cloaks. The last time Timas saw them during the Octavia tourist incident they'd thronged through the city in pairs hunting the murderer, unwilling to wait for the city to bring the perpetrator of that crime to justice.

"Just hand him over," Katerina said. "Then you won't have to deal with us anymore."

Timas bit his lip and turned around. This would be over soon. And then he could talk to the elders about the more pressing thing on his chest: what he'd seen on the surface. Surely the criminal from space was the least important of the two.

Pepper lay on the bed, sweat beading his forehead.

He didn't look worried, just very serious as he sat up using one arm. "I can't walk. Someone will have to help me here."

The soldier on the left stepped forward, his cloak swirling to become a second skin that flowed over his insanely muscular body. He almost dwarfed Pepper. "Don't try anything stupid."

"I'm not a fan of stupid." Pepper grabbed hold of the man's shoulder. He hopped up, and Timas realized that Pepper stood almost as tall as the regal and faceless Aeolian he leaned against. His dreadlocks cascaded down around his shoulders as he struggled forward.

"We'll have someone bring a cart up," the Aeolian said. Then he spoke to some unseen voice. "Yes. We have custody."

Katerina turned to walk out the room.

As she did, drawing attention with her movement, Pepper cracked the Aeolian's helmet in the crook of his arm and twisted the man's neck.

Even before the Aeolian's body hit the ground Pepper leaped, not for the other soldier, who had already whipped a wicked-looking gun free, but for Katerina.

She screamed as he hit her and spun so that his back hit the ground. He held her like a human shield with his one good arm.

"I'll snap her neck." Pepper still looked calm and unworried. He'd moved so damn fast Timas hadn't even taken a breath.

"I still have a shot." The remaining soldier's cloak had become a second skin of mobile armor.

"Yeah, but she'll be dead. And while you'll accept the loss of a professional soldier, this innocent civilian avatar is a child that your citizenry would howl to see die."

The Aeolian lowered his gun. "What now?"

Pepper used his one leg to push himself up to the wall. He sat back against it. "I won't harm her."

"This is unacceptable."

"The moment you chose not to try and take the shot you had you were no longer in control of the situation, so shut up." Pepper frowned as Katerina tensed. Maybe trying to pull away from him. She stopped trying after a second, and then Pepper took a deep breath and continued. "Take off the armored cape and helmet. Drop the weapon as well. I like the look of it."

Timas thought the Aeolian wanted to protest, but then cocked his head as someone gave him orders. "Okay."

Underneath the helmet was a green-eyed man with scarred cheeks and tight, curly hair cut close to the scalp with a lightning bolt pattern on the left side.

He dropped the cape and helmet, eyes narrowed with the frustration of a soldier unable to act.

Pepper smiled and looked over at Camaxtli. "Don't worry, if the Aeolians refuse to pay you whatever they offered, I'll match."

Necalli moved closer to Pepper, his head cocked, thinking. Camaxtli cleared his throat. "You promise a lot, but even if what you say is possible for one man, what happens after you leave and we still have to face the Aeolians?"

"I'm not asking you to directly help me, I'm just reminding you that I'm also your friend."

Ohtli shook his head. "And if we take your offer, what about the next criminal who flies in here who happens to be rich? Do we shelter them as well? That's not who we are."

Necalli folded his arms. "So again, we lean back and let the Aeolians tell us how to run our own city, do what they want. Why not just ask for a silvered eye of your own, Ohtli?"

Ohtli looked startled at the vehemence, and Timas wondered where that had come from. Necalli harbored a lot more rage at the bossy Aeolians than anyone else in the room, it seemed.

Ollin, Timas saw, scanned the elders, taking in who wanted to show the Aeolians up, and who wanted to keep their course. His dad, the gears in his head always twirling.

"This's all beside the point," Pepper said. "I have the girl hostage, so for right now, the Aeolians are doing what I ask them. Who else will you ever entertain that can face them down?"

He had a point.

"Besides, we need to get Raga involved now."

A few seconds passed, and then Katerina raised her hand. Pepper still held her in a close grip. "I'm sorry, but we feel that would be a violation of Chilo's charter between New Anegada and the cities of Chilo." She raised an eyebrow. "In fact, we feel that overwhelmingly."

"The charter can be revoked in case of war," Pepper said. "And if you'd been paying attention to what I told you happened aboard the *Sheikh Professional* you know the entire DMZ is going up for grabs. The League unleashed this Swarm on us. That's war."

"These are just stories by you so far." Eztli spoke up from a long period of silence. "We have heard of no attack by mind-dead people, nor has the avatar there seen or heard of any such attack."

"So far, correct, no reports," Katerina said.

"None the less. We're all going to move to a nice location. A house out in the open. The avatar comes with us, my hostage. The rest of you as well." Pepper looked at the Aeolian soldier. "How many outside?"

"I'm sorry?"

Pepper shook his head, the long locks slapping his wide shoulders. "Don't play games."

"Fifteen."

"Good. They'll come with us." Timas found that a surprising twist from Pepper. "We'll need protection within a few days here. You sending more our way?"

Katerina nodded.

"Good. And now, the final demand: I want a nice house, in a nice large civilian area, somewhere the Aeolians will not want to drop a large bomb on or use unnecessary force."

Ollin stepped forward. "My house, I'll offer my house."

The elders were taken aback. "Ollin, you put your family in danger." Camaxtli grabbed Timas's father by the shoulder.

"No more danger than we face any day with our only son on the surface." Ollin returned the gesture.

Of course Ollin would do this, Timas realized, looking at Camaxtli. How many more years would Camaxtli remain an elder? Five at best.

And then there would be Ollin to take his place.

Even if it meant risking his family by bringing all these people into their courtyard.

Pepper insisted they bring one last item. A long bundle, wrapped in crinkly tarp.

"What's in there?" Timas asked as they all prepared to leave.

"His limbs," said Ohtli. "He insisted."

CHAPTER FOURTEEN

Timas finally got Ollin alone. "I need to tell you something. Something the elders will need to know about." The intimidating Aeolian soldiers, servants, and even a few neighbors who had wandered to the lip of the courtyard gates remained just out of earshot.

"Speak." Ollin folded his arms and looked out over his piece of the world, their home, with a faint smile.

"Not here." Timas shook his head.

"Then where? This is as good a place as any." Ollin walked over to the table at the center and poured himself a cup of pulque.

"On the surface." Timas lowered his voice. "Cen and I saw something . . . important."

Ollin sighed and leaned close. The bitter smell of his breath filled the air between them. "Heutzin told me you came up babbling about aliens." Ollin lowered his voice as well. "You shut up about those things."

"But we both saw things on the surface. We saw something, in a suit like ours but smaller, running into the murk."

"Gods, son, everyone sees things in the mist down there. It's the heat, the exhaustion, the loneliness. It doesn't mean they're real."

Timas fought anger. "It *was* real. If I can go back down I can get you proof."

"Don't say these things, Timas. You know our history, what our people have done and have been through. People may think our gods are really physical and can appear to us, but that is *heresy* now, and people who think ancient gods or aliens hide in the mist down below, waiting for the faithful, are troublemakers. You understand me?"

Timas swallowed and looked around. The pallet Pepper lay on creaked. The dreadlocked man stared at them both. Could he be listening from that far away?

Ollin shook Timas by the shoulder. "Do you understand?" he repeated.

Timas's great-great-grandfather had been a high priest. On New Anegada he had taken out the hearts of living people, sacrificing them to serve the alien beings who claimed they were gods to the Azteca who lived there, the aliens who had birthed Timas's ancestors to that land many centuries ago.

But the aliens hadn't been gods. Other families had similar stains on their histories, and some in the lower decks of the city still believed that aliens were gods and would return to save them all and raise them up to their proper place as rulers.

"I know what I saw." Timas didn't believe in godly aliens, he'd seen something else. But he knew he'd seen *something*.

"Yes, you and half the other jumpy xocoyotzin from lower families. Pull yourself together, Timas." When Ollin was disappointed he called Timas by name. "There are far, far larger things at stake here than shadows that spooked you down on the surface."

"Send me down and I'll come back with proof."

Ollin shoved Timas hard enough that Timas stumbled over the raised edge of a flagstone. "Enough!"

People stared. Timas kept his face serious and straight as he turned and walked into the house. He gripped a doorjamb inside and hit his forehead against it. He would have struck his dad, if he'd felt he had any strength.

Ollin would have belted him good for that.

Itotia grabbed his arm. "What else did you expect him to say, he was out in public?"

"I told him it was important, and private," Timas protested.

"In private or out loud, don't talk about superstitions like that. Our city will not drag itself down into madness like our ancestors. You will offer something to the family altar tonight, you will honor the real gods, not the false ones that tricked us in Aztlan."

But he'd seen it.

Timas pulled away from his mom. "I will be quiet. I won't upset anyone." But he knew what he'd seen. And he knew he'd be back down on the surface some time in the future once the situation passed. Zombies in outer space notwithstanding, what did any of that have to do with Yatapek, their poor little city circling the edge of the Great Storm, limping along as best it could?

He'd bring back proof.

Then they'd all listen to him.

CHAPTER FIFTEEN

Pepper watched Ollin lumber into the room and sit heavily on a wicker chair near the crude bed, that used ropes instead of springs. Katerina sat in the corner of the room, tired and annoyed. Pepper had demanded that she remain within two feet of him, and he kept the gun he'd taken from the Aeolian soldier pointed at her as he politely listened to Ollin.

His skin still tingled. When he'd grabbed Katerina she'd shocked him, some sort of personal defense mechanism designed to stun a potential attacker.

It had been annoying, at the time.

"Is there anything you need?" the soldier asked Pepper.

"The food I asked for." Pepper had burned a lot of muscle and fat in the last few days, wasting even more when grabbing Katerina. He could see his bones lurking under his now sallow and gray skin.

Nothing like Katerina's healthy brown, or Ollin's.

A woman in bright floral-printed linen robes swept through the door with a large platter of grilled meats and cheeses.

"This is my wife, Itotia." Ollin stood up to introduce her.

She nodded at Pepper and set the platter down. "This is as much meat as we could get."

The room filled with the smell of rabbit and chicken. Pepper's mouth watered, his body seemed to vibrate in anticipation of refueling and rebuilding all the muscle mass he'd burned off for speed and strength.

He'd found a good place to recuperate. The infected had landed mainly on the other side of the planet. He had time to plan getting out and away from here if needed. The medical facilities weren't much, but he was alive and he had time.

"Thanks." Pepper set the gun down and ripped into the platter. Bones cracked as he ate quickly.

At least, until he looked up and realized Itotia and Ollin were staring at him.

Ollin cleared his throat and looked away. "The bathroom is just two doors down. We'll be right back for the platter." They left a crutch by his bed that strapped to his forearm with a pair of buckled leather strips.

Pepper didn't respond, but stared back at Ollin until he grew uncomfortable enough to back out of the room with Itotia.

And Katerina was staring at him, too.

At least that was part of her job.

When he'd finished the last of the platter he leaned back on the pillows. That felt better. A meal in the stomach made their impending Armageddon easier to contemplate.

"Have your constituents gotten back to you with any word about me?" Pepper smiled.

"There is a great deal of uncertainty about you. At first popular votes ran for getting you captured and returned, but now people are wondering. We seem to be swinging to thinking that, if we can get confirmation, you are indeed what you claim to be and need to be listened to and possibly left alone."

"That's a relief." Pepper looked around the room: it was simply constructed with faux wood and thick metal beams overhead for the roof.

"We're waiting for the Ragamuffin Dread Council to verify your credentials, but they're worried about verifying details about one of their agents to a larger public like the Aeolian citizenry."

"My Aeolian friends, pass this piece of video on to the council: Fellow Dreads, stop messing round. We know my cover is blown. Get over it and get moving."

Katerina cocked her head. "I'm being voted to tell you that there are two Ragamuffin ships being mobilized and on their way to Chilo."

Ollin returned, peering around the doorjamb. "You're done?"

"Yes, thanks." Pepper pushed the platter toward the foot of the bed. "I will repay you."

"You will." Ollin took the platter. "We will bring you to Cen's funeral tomorrow morning."

Pepper raised an eyebrow. Ollin had crossed over from being a meddlesome player, obviously maneuvering to become a part of the city's leadership, into a true annoyance. "I don't like funerals."

"Cen died as a result of your actions. Not purposefully, but you still owe us this for all that we're risking by dealing with you."

"Owe you?" Pepper shook his locks. "I owe you nothing. And when this is done, you'll owe me everything."

Ollin's eyebrows furrowed. "That makes you no better than the Aeolians, pushing us around and demanding what you want, taking what you need."

"Get over yourself. Go back to insinuating yourself into the circle of the pipiltin. You've already got me under your roof, you've got your leverage. Leave me be."

Pepper's words hit close. Ollin spun and stalked out of the room without saying anything else.

Pepper grinned at Katerina. He flicked the gun's safety on and set it on the edge of the cloth. She'd been through enough, he figured. "I'm sorry about all this."

"You're letting me go?"

"It was a demonstration. If any of your soldiers tries sneaking up on me, or taking me into custody, there will be a large price paid with lives. Understand, I am willing to work with you all, but if you get in my way I will be more than just a problem."

He waited for that to sink in and be relayed back to the millions of watchers.

But Katerina didn't move. She sighed. "We think it is in our best interests to keep a close eye on you. I'll remain in the room."

Whatever. Pepper leaned back and closed his eyes while his stomach rumbled.

Later she woke him up, returning to the room with a large, heavy chair that Itotia helped her pull in. A pillow and several blankets later, Katerina lay asleep in the corner of the room.

The silvered eye was closed, but long slivers of metal glinted on her eyelids.

He was still being watched.

Katerina shook herself awake in the gloom. "Can you access lamina, Pepper? We have something a significant minority would like you to see."

Pepper twisted around so she could see him better, and shook his head. "No. No lamina."

"Okay." She walked over and sat on the side of the bed. As she leaned in close the silver eye glistened, then lit up. Laser light played across Pepper's eyeballs and the dim room disappeared.

One of the Swarm lurched at Pepper. Someone stumbled around near his peripheral vision clutching a bloody arm, mouth open wide in a soundless scream. This member of the Swarm looked heavier, with thicker and bonier facial features.

"Same as what you encountered before?" Katerina reappeared as the projection snapped off.

"Where was that?"

"Felucida: a small city on the other side of the planet. Opinion is scattered among us, it could be a psychotic rampage. Or any number of other things."

"What do the citizens there think?"

Katerina got up off the bed. It creaked a little. "They aren't reporting in. The city's communications died an hour ago. The relay dropped."

"And you think that's a coincidence?"

She shook her head. "I personally don't know what to think. Polling indicates twenty-three percent of the general population thinks you are somehow right. That's up from nineteen percent an hour ago. . . ."

"Polling, funerals. You're all dicking around." Pepper sat on the edge of the bed.

"You don't approve of the Consensus?"

Pepper realized that he stood before quite a large audience now, via her silvered eye. "Voting each governmental action? Nothing will ever get done."

"What do you call sex without consent, Pepper?" She leaned forward like a large cat.

"Rape," Pepper said evenly.

An invisible trap was sprung. She smiled, reciting a script that came easily to her. Pepper imagined it being taught in schools to Aeolians all around Chilo. "Indeed.

Rape. It is the consent that is the key. What is the act of governing without consent?"

"Getting shit done." Pepper didn't like getting lectured at by little girls, even if they embodied the will of millions.

She ignored his irritated reply. "Think of government as a marriage, Pepper. You've entered into a bond, but it does not mean that the right to do certain things is guaranteed. A wife who doesn't consent can still be raped, as an elected government can still run over its people. Better to make sure that permission is asked for each act, every time. Better yet to make the government vanish: run by monthly volunteers and automated frameworks. For a month you've been chosen to be a judge, study hard. Next year you'll be a filing clerk for a month. We all serve. We all vote. We're the government."

"That crap's nice until you have a threat breathing down your neck," Pepper growled. "Even the Athenians you adore so much turned quickly toward strong leaders when it came time to face invaders. Our time on Chilo is countable in days. You will need leaders, not town meetings."

She recoiled from the intensity with which he hissed out the last word. He noticed that she had bags under her eyes. It was late into the night, and she was just a tired, stressed-out teenager. "Well," she whispered. "It did turn out rather well for the Athenians, throwing away freedom for a good defense, didn't it? After centuries under the boot of the Satraps, I would have thought dying free would beat living safe."

Had that been the Aeolians speaking, or just her? Grabbing her as hostage might backfire: either the will of the Aeolian people had just run circles around his argument or the girl had. Either way, Pepper needed to watch out around her.

"If your people don't take care of the Swarm and it arrives, you'll be a lot more interested in surviving any way you can," Pepper said. And then, acknowledging her point, he continued, "Sometimes being alive leads to some strange personal concessions."

She looked up, he knew she was about to ask the question: What concessions had Pepper made?

Something stopped her. Not Aeolian commands, but the look on Pepper's face. Their chat had finished.

The faint sound of someone throwing up in a nearby bathroom got his attention. Pepper grabbed his crutch, got up, and negotiated himself out of the room through the hallway to the source.

A long slit of light from an open door illuminated a framed picture of an older man with a faint resemblance to Ollin, but standing in front of a massive pyramid. A photo taken somewhere in Tenochtitlome. Pepper thought he recognized the temple, he'd spent a lot of time in the jungles of Aztlan back on New Anegada.

He peered inside the bathroom. Timas turned back, wiping his mouth.

"You okay?" Pepper used the crutch to shove the door open farther, damning his injuries as he did so.

The kid looked startled. Pepper's eyes shifted into infrared, taking his temperature. No fever there.

Pepper relaxed, then grabbed Timas's chin and forced his mouth open. "You do this a lot?" Acid from frequent throwing up had worn the enamel off his teeth. He could detect a slight arrhythmia in his chest.

The room reeked of bile.

Timas turned back around and turned on the tap, cleaning up after himself.

"You do this a lot?" Pepper repeated.

"You all can take pills, technology, to force you into thinness, change your bodies. Look at Katerina in there, I bet she doesn't even have to think anymore about what she eats, does she? But I have a duty." Timas leaned against the basin. "I have to fit inside my groundsuit. If I can't fit in my groundsuit, my family loses its position. I am no longer one of the xocoyotzin."

"Groundsuits?"

"Our founding fathers purchased them to work on the surface. They used to be powered, and talk back to the city. Now they are failing, and patched by spare parts we are offered from Aeolian junkyards."

"And your ancestors, with more access to technology, used to be thin," Pepper said, understanding. "Now you all starve yourselves or use teenage boys to fit in the suits."

"We are the ones who bear the city on our backs," Timas said.

This was useful. "How many suits are there?"

"Three dozen."

A course of action, one not dependent on getting the Ragamuffins to come assist him, presented itself.

"Get Ollin in here."

There would be no sleep tonight. Pepper wanted a groundsuit.

CHAPTER SIXTEEN

The shouting lasted all night. Timas lay up, staring at the ceiling, as pipiltin moved furtively in and out of the rooms to argue with each other and with Ollin, but mostly with Pepper.

For a man recovering from almost mortal wounds, Pepper sounded full of fury. But the pipiltin wouldn't relent. Pepper would not get his hands on any of the groundsuits. Their lives depended on them, even if they weren't currently using them.

That was that.

Pepper argued that their lives depended on figuring out how to stop the threat he knew would eventually spill over the entire planet.

The pipiltin replied that it was better to let the Aeolians handle their own threats and dangers. Yatapek would be the last thing on any invader's list.

Nothing Pepper could say changed that reality: Yatapek was a tiny grain, a worthless outpost, a dead-end city in the scheme of things.

That hurt almost more than anything, to hear the pipiltin making the point that they were nonentities.

It sounded like Pepper threw his crutch at one of them. It clattered against the wall. The floor shivered, and then a deathly calm settled over the house.

Timas wondered if everything Pepper claimed was coming soon. Would the soulless hordes land an airship and stream up from the docks?

Death had always been hot, or full of pressure and choking. Now Timas considered a death that came from something invading his mind.

Better, he finally decided, on the verge of sleep, to step off the edge of the city and surrender. Sometimes, he thought, his mind circling around that idea, that stepping off an edge sounded appealing. Everything depended on him, and he controlled nothing.

A final choice was appealing.

Three hours later, as the sun hit his window, Itotia woke him up.

She looked as tired as anyone else in the house, her

eyes reddened and puffy. She laid a set of pants and a newly cleaned shirt over the back of the chair by his bed.

Timas sat up, blinking his scratchy eyes. "Mom?"

"Another city fell quiet an hour ago: Chaco." Timas felt his throat dry out as she told him this.

They had distant cousins there. Chaco suffered more than Yatapek. A sister city far on the other side of Chilo, they kept their city even wider open and less populated to make room for fields and agriculture. And they raised large exotic animals for Aoelians to ride, or butcher for the rare taste of "authentic" meat. All their radio traffic just . . . ceased.

"I just wanted to let you know before you came out," Itotia murmured. "Now come. It's time to get ready."

He took a deep breath and looked down at the tiled floor. "I don't know if I can go." Pepper's Swarm approached, it had probably taken Chaco, and Cen had died, and now he was going to look Cen's family in the face. It all crushed him.

"I don't want to ask you to do these things." Itotia sat next to him. "You're my one child. And every time they drop you down below the clouds I lock myself into the ancestor room and light candles until Heutzin calls and says you've returned."

Timas looked over at her. She pulled the rumpled edges of her blue dress over her lap.

"I'm sorry," was all he could think to say to her.

She shook her head. "It's not your fault, Timas, or your place to apologize to me. I apologize to you. And to Cen's family." Itotia stood up, and in a low voice, continued, "Though I'll never tell them to their face, I was relieved when Heutzin called."

"Relieved?" Timas blinked.

"Relieved because it wasn't you. At least Cen's mother has more than one son. I do not."

Timas grabbed her elbow. "How can you say that?"

"I don't forgive myself, but I can't lie to myself either, Timas." She kissed him on the forehead and left him standing in the doorway, leaning against the doorjamb, his stomach churning.

Pepper hobbled his way over and leaned close to Timas. "Who do you know who knows the docks and the suits well?"

Timas looked up at him, scared to answer and be drawn into some plan the man was spinning that would no doubt get him into trouble.

"Tell me and I can help you," Pepper said.

"Help me with what?"

"Your problem."

"I don't have a problem," Timas hissed. "I have a duty."

"I can make holding to your duty as easy as it is for Katerina."

Timas gave Pepper Heutzin's name, and instructions on how to contact him. "You should come to the funeral, he'll be there."

"I'm not going to any damn funeral." Pepper turned around.

They left Pepper with Katerina and a host of the city's Jaguar scouts who had arrived late in the night now lining the walls like brightly colored decorative statues against the house.

They walked to the atrium. The massive throat of the city sang its mélange of echoes, shouts, and combined hubbub of its people. Behind that the clanking metal on metal thud of the city's sturdy and simple machines bubbled up. The elevators plunged the family down the levels to the bottom of the city and the docks.

The docks seemed eerily unfamiliar and dreamlike, Timas thought. Here the industrial stench of foundries, oiled lubricants, and acid seemed at odds with the growing river of white-clad mourners.

Boots and shoes scraped gridded iron, and the cries of swaddled and upset children echoed throughout the looming gantries of steel overhead.

The priest stood up on his altar, carried down and assembled by a pair of acolytes that now stood behind him. Behind him lay Cen's body, wrapped in red and yellow cloth.

A single ray of light pierced through the windows, dust motes dancing across it, as the priest raised his hands to the gods to begin the ceremony. Timas shuffled forward with the crowd to lay down their remembrance gifts.

For Timas it was a box of wooden blocks Cen and he had played with as little kids. He set it next to flowers, money, fresh fruits, and other offerings from families.

Up close, the pile looked large and colorful. A testament to Cen and the people who loved him.

From a distance, it was a small pile of odds and ends in front of the large altar.

Luc walked up to the offerings, but he didn't place anything down. Timas frowned at the insult to his friend's memory, but it was not his place to say anything.

And anyway, back on the planet of New Anegada, their cousins would have heaped the altar even higher with offerings. This was what they had, what they could spare. Who was he to judge Luc? Their family faced hardship now that they were not the family of xocoy-otzin. They would be working in the lower levels.

The priest picked up a tiny wooden box and opened it. A bird fluttered in his hands.

He used a long jade blade to kill it, scattering the blood over the altar. "Our gifts will help Cen's soul find favor, but it is blood that the gods respect most. With this offering, we plead for them to look to him with kindness.

"But even as we do this, remember that the gods look with disdain and hatred upon those who seek to shed human blood." The priest looked angrily out at them all. "For that is the worse sacrifice, and not one that should ever be given."

Timas was sure that his people would never make that mistake again. It had not been long since the people on Yatapek had flown to space with the other New Anegada peoples and fought the dangerous aliens around Chilo and New Anegada.

They had changed, the Azteca who had done that. They had chosen to settle here, start a new life. They put all the horrors behind them that they had perpetrated and done in the name of the false gods, the aliens who claimed to be gods on New Anegada and demanded human blood.

Yatapek steered its own course, worshipped true gods, ones that didn't appear in physical form.

Here they were pure.

Several acolytes walked out and removed the altar. The priest stepped off into the crowd.

He gave the command. Off in the distance Heutzin, barely fitting in his own white mourning garments, pulled a long lever with a loud grunt.

The floor underneath Cen and the offerings swung open. Cen's body fell down toward the angry red clouds beneath, a rain of bounty following him toward the very environment that killed him.

A burning mist rose up from the exposed hole. The air in the city wouldn't be rushing out because both city and the outside had the same pressure at this height. But some of the toxic, unbreathable outside was seeping in with the strong wind.

Timas stepped back for a more air-rich breath. A large hand clapped him on the shoulder.

He turned to see Luc, face twisted in rage and his other hand curled into a fist.

The first punch left Timas stunned. As Luc forced him forward, Timas realized what Luc was trying to do.

Luc was going to throw him down into the clouds after his brother.

And unlike the idea of falling gracefully from the city, making that final choice, he found that fear and anger spurred him to desire life. Not the long fall.

CHAPTER SEVENTEEN

Timas scrabbled, grabbing at Luc, but Cen's brother was no xocoyotzin. He dominated Timas, his arms roped with muscle. He pushed Timas forward easily.

Already the air bit with acid and made Timas's eyes water.

All he could do was grab for Luc's forearm, hoping to hang on as hard as he could.

Luc hit him again and again with his other fist, trying to force him to let go.

The priest and Heutzin tackled Luc.

"What do you think you're doing?" Heutzin shouted

into Luc's face. "You dishonor your brother's memory."

Luc struggled, but while he'd been that much larger than Luc, Heutzin had worked the docks for decades now. He pinned Luc to the grating as the priest rolled on the floor, gasping for air.

Everyone gathered looked on, shocked, and moving slowly. From the ground where he'd fallen, Timas stared at the forest of their shifting legs.

"He killed him," Luc screamed from underneath Heutzin. "That little shit killed Cen. And you all know it."

"You shut up," Heutzin hissed. He pressed down on Luc hard enough that Luc coughed.

"Don't you hurt him," Chantico yelled, running to her husband's side. She grabbed Luc's hand. "Don't hurt him."

Ollin pushed people aside, his face ashen. He looked down at Luc like one would look down at a patch of mold, then stooped next to Timas.

He pulled Timas back from the edge. Three more feet and Timas would have fallen the long fall. He rolled onto his knees, head bowed and quite shaken.

"He killed Cen. He made him go out with him, out of the safe zone and into the debris field." Luc struggled once more to break free from Heutzin with no success.

Timas dropped his head to the foor. The tears weren't from the biting air, but from thinking of Luc's anguish. Luc was right. None of this would have happened if Timas hadn't convinced Cen to walk deeper into the debris zone. Somehow Luc knew.

"Come." Ollin pulled him to his feet. "Dry your face. Keep your head straight."

Heutzin nodded at Timas as they walked past, and then Timas walked into the crowd in a daze with his dad at his side. Itotia joined them, looking just as dazed as Timas.

"What will happen to Luc?" he asked in the elevator on the way back up.

Itotia grabbed Timas by the hand. "He's a grown man who tried to commit murder. The judges will not be easy on him. They should jail him forever. He threatened a xocoyotzin."

"He tried to kill my son. He will pay for that." Ollin brooded.

"I don't want anything to happen to him," Timas said.

"What?"

"Because what he says is true."

Ollin grabbed his shoulder. "Don't ever repeat that."

Timas looked out at the levels sliding by them and didn't answer.

Cen's death had to mean something. He couldn't throw it away by pretending they hadn't seen anything down there on the surface.

But speaking that truth out loud led both his mother and father to fall silent and distant. Disappointed.

Itotia looked over his bruises and got ice for him when he returned to his room in the house.

"We have to go speak to the pipiltin about this outrage," Ollin said, and he disappeared.

"I'm following. You will be alone with the stranger, but there are Jaguar scouts all throughout the house and around his room," Itotia said.

And then he was left alone in his room, looking at the beams overhead and wondering how he'd been born so unlucky. He turned off the light and lay in the dark wondering why they refused to listen to him. When had he ever lied? Or shirked his duties? *He* put his life into the hands of the gods whenever he was dropped down to the surface. And yet he was the one punished with silence and disappointed faces.

He wanted to feel more self-pity, but considering that Cen had lost his life, he couldn't feel *that* sorry for himself. It would have been far too petty.

Instead, he just simmered with frustration. The man who killed Cen and dragged this down on him also lay under their roof.

Timas wondered how much longer he could just hold things in. He needed to push back, not just endure. The glimmer of a plan floated by.

"Timas?" Katerina knocked on the door.

"Yes. I'm here. Let her in," he told the guard.

"Can I ask you to do a favor?" She shut the door behind her.

"Sure."

She moved closer and held out a hand. "Touch my hand."

Timas frowned. Maybe he should turn on the lights; he could get into trouble if someone walked in and assumed the wrong thing. He reached out and took her hand.

The moment they touched it sparked. Timas leaped back against his bed, stung, the palm of his hand throbbing. "What was that for?" he yelled at her.

She blinked when he turned on the light by his bed and held her hand up. "I'm sorry. I just needed to check."

"Check what?"

"I'm not defenseless. When they send us into foreign environments, kidnapping is a risk. I'm electrified. That was a test shock. The dose I gave Pepper should have killed him. He barely even noticed it. I was worried it didn't work."

Timas's fingers still tingled. "I think it works."

"And I did feel it," Pepper said. Both of them jumped

at the sound of his voice. So much for being insulated from him; even crippled he had snuck around the house, evading the guards all around that were supposed to keep him in his room.

The guard lay asleep on the ground by the open door. Timas wondered how Pepper had done that.

Pepper's crutch tip hit the ground outside the door, and he hopped out from the shadows. He smiled as he leaned against the inside of the door.

"You didn't show it." Katerina stood up.

"It's nice that they sent you out here with some protection." Pepper cocked his head. "Ah, Heutzin's here."

That was what he'd been doing out. Waiting.

Timas got out of bed and followed him. He had a question of his own for Heutzin anyway.

The edge of Pepper's crutch struck him in the chest. "Where do you think you're going?"

Timas looked at Pepper. "I need to talk to Heutzin."

"You've had a chance to talk to Heutzin your entire life. I need to talk to him now." The crutch lowered to the ground. Pepper had balanced on one leg easily enough. It didn't seem to hamper him as much as it should.

"I need to know how Luc found out that I led Cen into the debris field." Timas paused. As an outsider, Pepper shouldn't get as upset about what came up next as his parents did. "I need to talk to him about what I saw on the surface."

"Which was?"

"Aliens," Timas whispered.

Pepper looked at him like Timas might look at recycling scum. "Your father seems to think you were stressed, jumping at shadows."

"I saw something," Timas said.

"In tight situations, the mind gets overactive," Pepper said. "You can't trust it."

"Yes, you're right." Another person who didn't believe him. Timas let it go for now. He'd prove them wrong, somehow, someday soon, when he got back to the surface. "But please, just ask Heutzin why Luc knew what happened."

"Only if you tell that guard when he wakes up not to panic, that I'm in the courtyard. There'll be others I drugged. I prefer that my conversation with Heutzin be private for now."

"Sure," Timas mumbled. He'd shirk whatever duty required on the next visit to find the alien.

He'd get proof, even if it cost him his life.

He owed Cen that. He owed Cen a lot that he needed to fix. Including the fact that Cen's killer wandered around Timas's house at will.

CHAPTER EIGHTEEN

Heutzin looked like he knew groundsuits, Pepper thought. Greasy, burly, obviously used to working with heavy equipment. "The men outside knew I was coming," he said.

"The Jaguar scouts, yes." Pepper first encountered the warriors back in their country of Aztlan on New Anegada. Ressurected by aliens posing as gods, the so-called Azteca had certainly come far in their journey, taking to space and settling on Chilo, as well as habitats in orbit around New Anegada and Chilo. Many of them did their best to leave the memories of their ancestors' vastly inhumane wars on New Anegada far behind.

Pepper had rather expected that the destruction of their alien gods at the hands of the Ragamuffins would've destroyed their culture. Instead they declared the aliens false gods, made the divine more abstract, and proved to be the Ragamuffins' close allies against the League. Pepper would take allies that believed anything: from God, to gods, to Allah, to nothing. So long as they stood out of his way. "I told the scouts to expect you." Pepper had left Katerina behind, no need for the Aeolians to hear about this.

Heutzin looked suspicious, and nervous. "What is it you had me called here for?"

Pepper leaned in on his crutch. "I need groundsuits."

"Ollin and the pipiltin have already told us you are to get nothing."

"Let me modify my request"—Pepper dropped his voice down so that he sounded soothing, but confident—"I want your junked suits and any spare parts I can buy. In return, I'll give you several gold discs and an encrypted chip with enough of a credit line on it that you will be able to get all new spare parts, as well as whatever else you need to keep those few dozen suits you have left running."

Pepper thought it an overly generous offer. The chit was reserved for bigger emergencies than this, the sort of thing Pepper could use to access a vast line of credit set up many years ago.

"Where is the chit?" Heutzin asked. He would know, like anyone else in the city, how important securing guaranteed usability out of their groundsuits was. Pepper knew they could hardly afford to turn him down.

So why hadn't he asked the pipiltin about this new offer of his?

Politicians. That's what the pipiltin really were. And he didn't trust them not to shoot themselves in the foot over some principle. Let the men on the ground like him and Heutzin work out what was really what.

Pepper moved over to a bench and kicked it over with the crutch. He had gotten used to having one arm and one leg. He'd even remapped his neural tissue to help adapt.

It would hamper him in a fight for sure, but at least he had balance back.

"There." Pepper pointed out a long package.

Heutzin unwrapped it and then jumped back. "What is this?"

"A leg." Pepper dismissed the grim joke that leaped to mind: that he was paying an arm and a leg, or at least a leg, for Heutzin's services. "Deep in the center section of the thigh you'll find your payment."

"I can't . . ." Heutzin stepped back even farther.

Pepper slapped the crutch into the flagstone behind him. "Don't waste my time."

"You called me here."

"You came." Pepper's voice dropped, an instinctive response. But Heutzin looked harried and tired, and the whole deal was falling apart.

"What would you have a dockworker do, ignore a call from the grand house of a respected xocoyotzin?"

Pepper had to compose himself, pull in hard, and force himself to change tactics. This was not a place for action and intimidation.

He had to work people with words and deviousness.

Not something that came naturally.

"You love your city." Pepper repositioned the crutch. "I can see that in you. And you love your people. Do you want us to disappear like Chaco just did?"

Heutzin sighed. "I know your bargain is one that helps us. But that isn't all that is happening here. I know you are manipulating me: I'm a *simple* dockworker, not a stupid one. If the bargain is for our greater good, then will you mind if I tell the pipiltin your proposal?"

Pepper blinked. "I would mind. I would mind terribly."

"I thought so. So I risk what little reputation I have, my livelihood, and possibly something more, by aiding you in whatever it is you are planning."

Pepper grabbed Heutzin's oil-stained shirt and yanked the man closer. "I want to walk again. Is that so hard for you to understand?"

Heutzin stared back at him. "Is that all?"

"I'm crippled, Heutzin, and at a tremendous disadvantage. It's making me very irritable. And I'm dangerous when I'm irritable."

"Now you're making threats."

"That was no threat. I am no threat. Had I been a threat you would know." Pepper sat down next to his amputated leg. "Give me your knife."

"What knife?"

Pepper cocked his head. Heutzin could keep a straight face. He liked that. "The one in your left pocket."

Heutzin shrugged and pulled it out. Pepper opened it with a quick flick of his one hand and retrieved the chit and gold discs with several quick surgical cuts.

He dropped the bloody payment in Heutzin's hands. "You're no longer a simple dockworker now."

Pepper wiped the blade on the fabric, rewrapped the leg, and stood back up, fumbling slightly with the crutch. He watched Heutzin nod, then back away. He paused at a notch in the courtyard wall near a pair of torches and tossed one of the gold discs into the middle of rotting grapes and bananas. "Thanks to this house's gods, for their blessings."

"You are all annoyingly superstitious," Pepper said. "The boy's ramblings, your obeisance to a notch in the wall. I thought you a stronger man than that."

"Timas still refuses to change his story?" Heutzin

turned back, concerned. "He will risk his family's status."

"He believes he saw aliens in the smog," Pepper said. "He's easily spooked." He turned to hobble inside and rest. Enough intrigue for one night.

"Not spooked," Heutzin said softly.

Pepper kept ambling along by crutch.

"The boy isn't mad." Heutzin's voice rose. "Don't dismiss him like that. There *are* things down there."

Heutzin walked toward Pepper.

"Not just shadows in the mist?" Pepper said.

"I will never forget what I saw," Heutzin said. "You talk as if we're ignorant, but I worked the surface like Timas for years. I was the best. And I paid the greatest price for what I saw. So will Timas. When I returned speaking about things on the surface I was told to remain quiet. But I know what I saw. I even went out. I tried to find them. Almost died from running out of air. And they took it all from me. My suit, my life, my pride.

"Now I work on the docks, but only on the condition that I never blaspheme again. And if you say I told you this, I will lie and say it wasn't so. But you see me, Pepper, a direct man who's seen death and suffering and toil. You see me, and tell me if I don't believe I saw something real down there."

Pepper stared at him, watched his pupils dilate slightly, listened to the rhythm of his breathing. "You may believe that you saw something, that does not make it any more real."

"It was a box."

"What?"

"The creature, it just wafted out of the mist, running at me. It gave me a box, a steel box, and it pushed its helmet against mine and spoke to me. It asked me to open the box and just mail the letter inside." Heutzin's eyes were wide with his eagerness to be believed. "It said I would save many lives if I were to post that letter."

"A physical letter?"

"The pipiltin said I was addled," Heutzin spat.

"And the letter?"

"Just a random letter, someone talking about the damned weather. I didn't understand that."

Pepper blinked. The last detail sounded too jarring to be made-up. Made-up would be that the letter revealed something profound, not that it was useless. "Do you have the letter?"

"The pipiltin threw it away. But I have the box. I know it's alien, it has strange silver writing all over the sides. It's loopy, with lots of circles inside circles."

That sounded like Nesaru writing. The wrong kind of alien for the ones anyone on Yatapek would know much about.

It could be faked, but still . . . "Bring it."

Heutzin tapped his forehead. "Of course. When I come with the parts."

"Now." Pepper looked at Heutzin. "Bring it to me now."

And there was suddenly the faintest gleam of something in Heutzin's eyes.

Relief that maybe, finally, someone believed him. And Pepper thought maybe, maybe there was something to the man's story.

If true, it would mean they sat on top of one hell of a big target.

Pepper watched the dockhand leave the courtyard and then set to burying his own leg in a patch of ground, underneath a set of flowers.

He was exhausted, and for a while he lay near the flowers, looking up through the clear dome at the stars. From down here, they looked peaceful, twinkling away.

They didn't look at all like they harbored the sheer malevolence and ill will he'd come to expect of the universe.

A small dart stung him.

Pepper looked at his good thigh and pulled it out. Normally he could accelerate his metabolism and burn through the sedative, but already exhaustion from healing and moving around had set in. He'd been teetering around all day.

He spotted the Jaguar scout who'd fired the dart.

Pepper picked up a crutch to throw, but then slumped to the ground. Fast-moving feet surrounded him, and then the edges of a reactive armor cape.

A man in an Aeolian helmet looked down at him. "I'm using nanofilament to bind your hand to your neck. Struggle and you'll cut your own head off."

Another Aeolian soldier tapped his helmet. "We have him. Get the ship warmed, we're moving now before any of the locals get any bright ideas."

CHAPTER NINETEEN

The Aeolian soldiers had Pepper. They came for Katerina, and the moment Timas saw them he followed them out, Katerina just behind him.

Pepper lolled in the back of the cart with Aeolians sitting alertly on either side, their feet dangling near the ground. One of them had his gun raised up as Timas stepped into the courtyard, tracking him.

Timas ignored the barrel and walked up to Pepper. "They captured you."

Pepper straightened his head with effort, then slumped back again and groaned.

"What are you doing here, kid?" The faceless Aeolian with the gun raised it slightly. Timas stood up straight, as if standing before a large audience.

"Hey. Pepper! I wanted you to know who did this to you," he spat.

Pepper didn't turn.

"I did it. I helped them," Timas yelled. "People like you don't care about people like us, down here. But at least this once, you'll remember the name when you get dragged back out." It felt good to let this loose. Let this killer see what happened to people who didn't care about the troubles they brought on others.

"And what do you think you accomplished?" Pepper shifted, and the cart squeaked.

"There are consequences to the things you do." Timas stood triumphant in the early morning sunlight of the courtyard. He'd done something, a measure of payback. A measure of justice for what had happened to Cen. And in some small way, him.

"A butterfly flaps its wings and on the other side of the planet, a hurricane develops," Pepper grunted. "Everything everyone does has consequences, kid, not just the things that the people you're mad at do."

"You kill people." Timas pointed at him. "You killed Cen."

"And what do you think will happen to this city when I'm gone? You think you'll repel the Swarm without me? Remember this when your friends and family are screaming and dying all throughout this city of yours." Pepper leaned forward and snapped the next words out: "Remember that *you* chose to help get rid of me."

Timas flinched. "You're a bully."

Pepper shook his head, very softly. "Just hold this conversation in your head, child. Keep flapping those little butterfly wings. You're just as responsible as I am for anything that comes next."

Child? He was no child. . . . Timas started to say something, but saw Heutzin carrying a dull black box with silver circles and loops scattered all over its sides. He cradled it in his left hand, walking quickly toward them. The dockhand looked at Pepper, concerned. "What's going on?"

"Bring the box over." Pepper paid no attention to Timas now.

"Hold it." The nearest Aeolian soldier swung and aimed at Heutzin, who froze in place.

"It's just a box. An empty box."

"Not damn likely, you keep your distance. Back up." Heutzin did so. "He wanted me to show it to him."

"Move any closer and we won't fire a warning shot."

"I understand." Heutzin looked frustrated.

"Open it from there," Pepper said.

"Don't do that," the Aeolian said.

Itotia and Ollin came out. "Ma'am, stand back," another Aeolian said. A woman. Her voice sounded just as edgy as the others, Timas thought.

But Pepper ignored them all. His eyes never left the box. "Never mind, just turn it slightly this way, Heutzin."

Before the Aeolians could object, he'd done just that, though he looked ready to jump out of his skin at a moment's notice.

"Shit." For the first time Pepper looked surprised at something, though, Timas thought. Someone who fell out of the sky was probably hard to impress. And to Timas's surprise, Pepper looked right over at him. "You're right."

"I don't understand." Timas felt uncomfortable under Pepper's surprise. It felt so unnatural coming from the man.

"You're right. And so is Heutzin. There are aliens on the ground under us."

"Blasphemy," Ollin muttered.

Pepper snapped his head toward Ollin. "Oh for fuck's sake, man. Get your superstitions straight. You know aliens exist. You know one set posed as your gods once, and that they still live out there. Just because you reject the slavery they put you under on New Anegada doesn't mean you can't acknowledge some other batch might be on the surface of Chilo. That box has Nesaru writing on it."

Timas felt like he was falling, his stomach rising, rising up past his throat.

"There are those in Yatapek who'd take that as an excuse to spill blood," Itotia said. "We ran away from that after our men fought alongside the mongoosemen against the League. We helped gain your independence. We reformed our beliefs, and some of us moved away from New Anegada to leave those memories behind us. And now you say something like that again has followed us here. It's a hard pill to swallow so quickly."

Heutzin looked down at the box. "Many used shadows to jump at, wanting the return of all that because it was better when we were on top, favored by them, instead of scrabbling here in this city, in the winds of this world. Not all who moved here did it because they reformed, but because they were with families they loved."

They all looked like they were wavering. Aliens were real. Timas hadn't been crazy. He'd seen something real. Cen hadn't died for a vision.

And maybe, maybe Pepper didn't deserve Cen's death on his hands. How could he have known Cen and Timas were under the city? Was Timas dooming him for something he couldn't have helped?

One of the Aeolians almost dashed Timas's hopes when he laughed. "Anyone could buy a box with Nesaru writing on it."

Pepper leaned back against the cart and spoke into the air. "Not this box. It has a return address on it." He looked over at Katerina who stood impassively by the Aeolian soldiers. "Query it, the encryption key will prove me right. It'll verify the handwriting on the side."

She looked a bit startled to be caught up in the scene, but stepped over to Heutzin and put her palm to the box, then pulled it away as if it had burned her. "You're right. It says it comes from Hulbach Cavern, on Chilo."

Timas had helped condemn the man who just proved that what he'd seen was real, and Katerina and her millions of fellow citizens just behind her silver eye had seen it. And yet, he'd also been proved right. He looked over at his parents, who didn't say anything back. A tiny, electric moment of shock rippled through him, and then Itotia smiled sadly.

Timas dropped to his hands and knees as his stomach continued its motion, and his last meal spilled out. He kept his eyes on the cart as Ollin and Itotia rushed to him, as well as Katerina.

"What's wrong with him?" She pushed through and grabbed his shoulder.

"It's nothing." Ollin pushed her back.

Timas sat back, breathing heavily. "I was right. I did see something."

"You're too stressed. You shouldn't be involved in

things like this." Itotia pulled out a handkerchief and wiped his lips. "They should never have been brought here, Ollin."

An Aeolian pulled Timas up by his bicep. "Come on, kid. We need you to come with us."

Itotia moved between them both. "And why is that?"

"Legal maneuvers: another name has been added to the people this man is accused of killing. Cen. The accuser needs to be there. You will be witnesses."

Timas shook his head. "I take it back. I take it back."

"It doesn't work like that," Katerina said softly, still near him. "*We* all heard what you said. You made a good point, and although he's innocent until proven guilty, it is a fact that we now know Cen died because of his actions. You are right that he should at least be charged with this. You will face him."

"I don't want to anymore."

"He's just a child," Itotia protested.

Katerina looked at her. "So am I. But death is death, and Pepper is to be taken before the courts."

"Ollin, go with Timas."

Ollin stood up. "I have to stay here. The council will need . . ."

"Rot the council," Itotia snapped. "If you don't want to stand by your own son, I will."

"And meanwhile, Chilo is in danger from the Swarm," Pepper spat from over on the cart. "You're all wasting my time. We need to move, we now know why the Swarm is here, and what it's coming for. Bring Timas and his mother and let's get this pathetic show on the road. We don't have time."

The Aeolians surrounded Timas and his mother and moved them forward. Timas looked up at Itotia, and she put her arms around him. "It'll be okay."

Timas didn't think so.

As the tiny cart moved forward with its strange accompaniment, Katerina asked Pepper, "You said it won't be long now, what did you mean?"

"Before the Swarm attacks here, in strength. This is its goal. Some alien presence below us. The League unleashed this to get at that. And Yatapek will be the focus of the Swarm's entire army as a last stop on its way to this Hulbach Cavern."

PART FOUR

CHAPTER TWENTY

Aboard the Aeolian airship organized chaos reigned. Something had upset the three crewmen; they had sour looks as they dashed about.

"This shows you how cheap this operation is." Katerina leaned in close to Timas and pointed out the window. "Prop-powered airship. They must have rented it. We're not even important enough to warrant an escort, particularly now that everyone is worrying about their own airspace." She again reminded him that these Aeolians were just bounty hunters. Yatapek wasn't important enough to rate real Aeolian military, just its retirees.

From inside the docks they'd walked out along a corridor, into a gantry, and then into a long docking tube straight into the airship's car. The peek Timas had gotten from a porthole in the docking tube showed him a sleek, cigarlike ship with the teardrop-shaped section attached underneath.

The large propellers jutted out on struts, bracketing the airship's car. They started up as Timas watched.

"Why do they look so troubled?" he finally asked.

"City Lipari fell silent," Katerina said. "Just like the others."

"That's *three* entire cities," Timas hissed.

"We know. We feel it every second, their voices and votes are gone."

Twelve Aeolians filled all the remaining seats of the

tiny airship car. The floorboards up and down the aisles had been pulled up, bags of gear tossed quickly in, and the boards replaced. They squeaked as people walked over them to their seats.

A shudder rippled through the ship from the direction of the airlock in the back. Everyone bounced as the craft drifted away, passing through vortices left by the city's passage through Chilo's atmosphere. This would be a bumpier ride than just standing on the layer of one of the giant, implacable cities.

"Undocked!" someone to the rear yelled. The airship car stretched maybe twenty feet and had room for fifteen passengers and the pilot, strapped into a large chair at the front. Cables draped from the helmet over his head, a thought-control interface, but the usual assortment of panels, dials, and manual switches remained in front of him. Even a wheel and some levers.

In any other instance Timas would have been trying to look over the pilot's shoulder.

Pepper sat in the row of seats in front of them with a pair of Aeolians on either side. Timas sat between Itotia and Katerina.

The Aeolian on their left swore and smacked the seat.

"Okay," Timas said. "What was that about?"

"Upper Alucido." Katerina lowered her voice. "It's happening just like Pepper described. People are breaking out of the lower levels and attacking citizens. Alucido's fighting back, though. It's messy."

"Isn't anyone going to help these cities?" Itotia asked.

"Yes." Katerina looked out at the propellers. "While some *are* going silent, or reporting Swarm outbreaks, others are refusing to let airships dock. There's also a general referendum to move to emergency war footing."

"Then why take us?" Timas asked.

"Pepper will be safer and more secure in an Aeolian

city," one of the soldiers said. "And he may have more memories and observations that will help."

They watched from the portholes as the airship floated away. The winds buffeted it, and Yatapek's giant curved underside stretched over them. The props howled, chopping at the thick atmosphere outside, and soon Yatapek was a giant bubble in the distance, floating high over the clouds, its multiple decks visible behind its thick transparent shell.

One of the crew was so pale-skinned that Timas couldn't help staring. "Where's he from?"

Katerina glanced at him. "He's all the way from somewhere deep in the League of Human Affairs. Rydr's World."

"How do you know that?"

"It's in the lamina." Katerina tapped the side of her head. "We'll have to get you a viewer when we get to Eupatoria, you'll be able to see all the layers of info. The world won't be so . . . naked to you."

"How long will it take to get there?" Timas changed the subject away from his inability to see hidden information she saw all around her due to his poorer background. It was like being illiterate.

"Six hours. Settle in."

He found a button that let the chair slide back. Six hours. Six long hours to try and figure out how to apologize to Pepper. Six hours to try and get used to the shaking, bumping, and rattling of the airship. Thankfully, it looked like they wouldn't put Pepper to trial now, at least. So really, Timas had only himself to save, and the honor of his family.

CHAPTER TWENTY-ONE

Things, Pepper figured, weren't completely out of hand yet. They were headed back into the maw of the situation, closer to the range of the Swarm, true, but now he had more information to fight it with.

And full medical facilities lay in his immediate future. The desperate plan to rebuild the groundsuits to make up for his somewhat limbless situation could be shelved.

The girl had said the Swarm was hitting whole cities. By now his brethren throughout the Ragamuffin centers of power had to suspect that something was going down on Chilo.

But could he do anything to buy them time to arrive?

Pepper thought about the scorched planet that had so awed the crew of the *Sheikh Professional*.

It was a glimpse of Chilo's future. Each and every one of the floating cities would have to get burned out of the sky, and the planet quarantined.

A lot of human suffering.

If the other airship passengers thought he leaned back and groaned because of his injuries, that was fine, but it was really the weight of seeing what was to come.

The drone of the propellers continued on as time painfully inched by, the crew growing more and more agitated. Pepper finally looked back at Katerina. The distant sun glinted off her polished eyepiece, but both her eyes were closed. She wasn't sleeping, but reading. Her eyes flicked up and down, left and right, processing information. "They're more nervous."

Katerina opened her eyes. She snatched a cup of water and held it until a patch of turbulence passed, then let it sit by itself. "Emergency martial voting sessions all over the Aeolian Consensus. We're all trying to decide exactly what to do about the Situation."

He could hear the capitalized name in her speech. "The Situation . . ."

"Three cities, of the twelve now. No traffic, and no traffic with the citizenry." Katerina licked her lips. "We know we face some threat. A quarter of our voting public has just disappeared. It's unprecedented and we're in sort of a panic. Alliances and political action groups are springing up all over the place. Debates are everywhere."

"Democracy in inaction," Pepper said. "Everyone has an opinion on what to do, so few have action."

Katerina hit the back of his seat, annoyed. "A referendum is being called on creating an action force. We have argued once, why continue?"

"Because you're only now finally getting around to creating an army."

"Weapons are being fabbed by volunteer manufacturers on citizen pool loan groups in anticipation of an all-out assault. My recording of your story is being widely circulated as a call to action." Katerina looked out over Timas and Itotia to the porthole. "Don't underestimate us."

"I'm not." Pepper smiled. "I just don't want us to show up at the wrong city."

"Me either." Katerina looked down and closed her eyes again. "I'd like to go home, but they just shut their docks down and declared quarantines throughout the city. There are reports of infiltration by these things."

Timas had been listening in; now he jerked his head up. "Your family?"

Katerina bit her lip. "They're okay for now. But the other cities are only taking essential traffic. There's nowhere for them to run. The betting and odds pool is calling for my home to be dark city number four."

Pepper nodded. "Katerina, is there a pattern?"

She frowned. "What do you mean?"

"The cities, in which direction is the Swarm spreading?"

Katerina didn't answer for a long moment. "You suggest it is spreading toward us?"

A bit of turbulence hit. The airship rumbled and kicked against them. Timas gripped the edges of his seat, and Pepper looked around at the crew.

They were inching toward the portholes.

Looking for something visible.

Pepper sat up. "What is it?"

The airship pitched, gaining altitude in a hurry while doing a slow figure eight.

"I'm cut out!" Katerina grabbed the backs of their seats. She looked panicked. "I got dropped. I can't reach anything Aeolian outside the ship."

Pepper looked to the front. "Captain!"

An Aeolian stood up. Pepper remembered her voice from back in the courtyard. "We're being followed. The blimps won't identify themselves, so assume the worse. And we can't get anything out. You're right, we're being jammed."

The Aeolians all stood now, crowding the aircar as their cloaks shifted around. They pulled up the floorboards, unzipping their large duffel bags.

"Boarding party? Or worse?" Pepper asked. "And you're leaving me all trussed up!"

The Aeolian who'd spoke removed her helmet. Her hair had been completely shaved to let the helmet make contact with skin. Green tattoos of scimitars ran up the side of her neck and the back of her head. Outside of the helmet's protective visor her brown eyes scanned the aircar with a few blinks. "We caught you, that should speak to our abilities. The boarding party will be in for a nasty surprise."

Pepper cocked his head. "You're really going to leave me to be delivered like a wrapped gift?"

"You really are so arrogant to assume you're the only thing of value on this airship?"

"How often does this sort of thing happen out here, then?" Pepper asked.

"Not often," Itotia spoke up from behind him. "There is a lot of smuggling. The Ehactl cities like Yatapek, around the Great Storm, allow the smugglers safe harbor, we often need the goods. But outright attacks like this haven't happened in years."

"Yeah, but you still have guns mounted around the city docks."

"Rare doesn't equal none," Itotia said.

Pepper looked back at the Aeolian. She rubbed the top of her scalp and pulled her helmet back on. Green light danced over her eyes. "Tennaes, Andrew, Shella, Joquim, get up in the airbag."

They didn't respond verbally, but the four Aeolians stood up and walked over to the crew. One of them undogged a hatch at the top of the aircar and pulled the ladder down.

"After you."

The four Aeolians clambered up, pulling their bags after them. All without a word.

Pepper looked back at the woman he suspected led this small group. "Just promise me, if it gets dire, you'll let me stand for myself."

"Of course." She walked up the aisle to stand behind the captain and looked forward. No doubt she could see more information through her helmet, but that human core that wanted to see out at the situation with real eyes and real senses always overruled, Pepper knew.

"How did they find us?" Timas asked, his eyes wide.

"We're pretty high profile, all they had to do was listen carefully to public Aeolian democracy in action. A kidnap and ransom, with high stakes; whoever is planning this knows things are crazy enough right now." Katerina looked disgusted and had folded her arms. "They take advantage of us at the weakest point. As representative, I'm empowered to say that *we'll* do everything in our power to hunt them down and bring them to justice, but that we can't get any official help out to us in time."

"Everything is changing around us very quickly," Pepper said, trying to reassure her. She was feeling left out to dry, no doubt, and regretting that chance had put her here. He couldn't blame her for the emotions obvious on her face.

"You live this sort of life." Katerina looked at him like he was a bug of some sort. "And you're the valuable resource here. You'll get ransomed. Timas, Itotia, and me, we all stand a chance of getting caught in the crossfire."

Far from being the calm ambassador to the Aeolian body, she was an angry young girl right now, facing the prospect of death by herself without the protective embrace of her entire civilization.

At least she had a self-defense mechanism, Pepper knew. Timas and his mother didn't have anything, and both of them seemed calmer to him. They both faced a harder life, and Timas, every time he was dropped to the surface in some ancient, substandard groundsuit, faced dangers that most men Pepper knew couldn't handle.

He looked back at her. "You'll be fine. You're a living avatar. You'll fetch a nice ransom."

Then he realized what he'd said and glanced at Itotia, who just shook her head at him. Timas, to his credit, bit his lip and said nothing.

The captain held up his hand and looked back, goggled eyes blinking. "You'll feel some thumping and shaking. We're dropping cargo and then chaff."

"We're only an hour away from Yatapek," Timas said. "Shouldn't we be returning?"

"We are." Katerina pointed at the sun. "Part of the figure eights. Your people already scrambled a couple fighter blimps our way."

"Then why are we still climbing?" Timas's frustration filled the words.

"So that when they hit us, we'll have more time to fall," Katerina said. "They're underneath, blocking our way to the clouds in case we try and run to hide in them. The heavy metals in the cloud vapor wreaks hell with radar."

Itotia fingered a small bracelet and muttered to herself. Prayers for their survival.

Pepper chose not to castigate her. It was as productive as anything else they could do for the next fifteen minutes as they waited for their predators to rise up to them.

CHAPTER TWENTY-TWO

The airship made one particularly hard turn toward the oncoming pirates behind them. The sound of compressors filled the cabin, sucking lifting air into heavy bottles. Everything shivered as the airship props pitched down and struggled to keep them in the air now that the bag lost more and more buoyancy.

"I'm so sorry. So sorry," Timas said to Itotia. He'd tried to make his own way, make people pay, and now he'd caught his mother up in the damage he'd done.

"Don't apologize. I'm the one who let you down. I let this man into our house." She gripped his hand, and he squeezed back.

"Okay," the captain murmured over the speakers in the cabin. "The oncoming ships are popping up fast and calling for us to heave-to. Make sure you're strapped in, we're going to be dropping really quickly any second now."

Timas grabbed Katerina's hand. She looked confused for a second.

The engines swung back to their normal orientation with a thud. The pilot pitched the nose of the airship down and dove. Timas's stomach hit the back of his throat, but not in the normal queasy manner he knew all too well.

Despite a well-snugged belt, he rose off the padded seat. That changed as the pilot angled the nose of the airship down even farther and Timas pressed into the back of the chair.

Looking ahead at the long sets of chairs and over the back of the pilot's large chair, he could see through the pilot's windows. The familiar orange clouds lurked below them.

"Five thousand," Katerina whispered.

"What?" Timas looked over at her. She had closed her eyes tight.

"Feet. The ones chasing us are just seconds below us at this dive rate."

The propellers wailed, trying to help them as they

gained enough speed to hopefully flash past the attackers underneath them.

"Captain says that they've stopped ascending now," Katerina reported. "They figured his tactic out." The previous announcements had just been for Timas and his mother. Now the pilot was too caught up in his world to remember to voice this out loud.

Katerina grabbed Timas and pointed ahead. He could see five shiny darts in a loose pentagon. They grew larger as the pilot dove right at them. A bold move.

Tiny bits of dust twinkled in the air between the approaching airships and Timas.

"They're firing on us!" Katerina gasped. At the same time three Aeolians broke out of their chairs and jumped in front of everyone. They threw their cloaks wide open.

Small smacking sounds filled the cabin. The cloaks protected them, a shield that flared and rippled as if stones had hit calm water, dissipating the impact of weapons fire.

"Small caliber warning fire with tracers," the captain said. "They're repeating surrender demands."

"They need him alive," the woman Aeolian said. "They know we're armored. They won't do anything much more serious, but it will force us out of the cabin."

Acrid sulfur-tinged atmosphere leaked in through the bullet holes. They'd dropped far enough down that Chilo's atmosphere pushed in through the tiny punctures. Timas started coughing. Masks dropped from the ceiling with oxygen, and Timas grabbed the first one and took a deep breath. Itotia had hers on, and Katerina did, too.

The sounds quit, but as one all the Aeolians looked

at the ceiling and airbag. All three of them chorused "shit."

Distant popping sounds and one minor explosion, the sound of rigging shaking and slapping, made Timas shrink farther down into his chair. The airship struggled to maneuver.

"We're through them." Katerina sounded muffled through the emergency oxygen mask. The acidic air made her eyes tear up.

The Aeolians behind them leaped up, cloaks spread out, covering them from the rear.

More popping made Timas jump, but no more shots hit the cabin—they all hit the airbag above. The other ships were trying to get them to lose enough buoyancy to surrender and be taken off, but not enough to send them plummeting into Chilo's unsurvivable depths.

Katerina, Itotia, and Timas scrunched down, trying to keep a low profile. Timas heard a chuckle from Pepper in the chair in front of him.

Gravity hit Timas and shoved him deep into his chair. The airship had leveled and straightened out. "Twenty thousand feet lower now." Katerina looked out the porthole. "The pilot found some cloud cover."

"Go go go." The Aeolian behind Timas unbuckled his straps and then wrenched him up. "We need to get out of the cabin."

Timas took a deep final breath from the mask and scrambled out with Itotia to follow. The ladder had been pulled down again. He was picked up and handed to a pair of hands that yanked him up into the airlock.

"We stay here, the cabin's damaged and won't survive the next trick," said the soldier who pulled him up.

Itotia came next, then Pepper, and finally Katerina. Pepper slumped in the corner of the tiny airlock.

Timas looked through the porthole in the upper door. Overhead three large round balloons hung, cradled by catwalks and rigging, pipes and hoses that threaded all throughout. Several large generators sat mounted on bellows like suspension rigs between each balloon.

"Coming through." The Aeolians pushed through the lock and past them up the ladder. They fanned out into the interior of the airship's giant bag.

In the cabin they'd been lined up in the chairs and cramped. Now among the trembling catwalks, it felt like just a handful of them were up there, lost in the airship's innards.

The pilot shouldered his way up last. His data goggles trailed cables that he'd slung over his shoulder. "Come on come on," he hissed as he shoved past. The airship still dove, but not as rapidly.

Pepper needed to be pulled through, which the two Aeolians left in the lock did. Once Pepper was up, Timas, Itotia, and Katerina joined everyone.

"There aren't any seats." One of the Aeolians tossed straps and rope at them. "Find a railing, bind yourself to it."

The pilot ran toward the nose cone where he sat down on a tiny jumpseat, strapped himself in, and plugged his goggles in.

Without the insulation of the cabin everything sounded louder, more mechanical. Everything echoed several times inside, bouncing off the sides of the giant balloon. The drone of the propellers outside permeated the air and reached into the back of Timas's throat.

"It's weird," Katerina said as the three of them huddled around Pepper. His guards lashed themselves to the railings as best they could.

"That we're being attacked?" Timas saw that she

stared down at the catwalk, and at the airlock they'd just come through.

"I've never been cut off for this long. From everything Aeolian."

Timas stared at her. They might both be teenagers, but their worlds were so far apart. She had her perfectly engineered body, modifications available for the right money, and the constant babble in her head that linked her to the ghosts of her entire city and the Consensus it belonged to.

What a strange thing to be.

The airship leaned to the right. The catwalk shifted and twisted underneath them. Smacking sounds made Timas jump. "We're being shot at again?"

Itotia looked up. "I don't see any new holes."

"No, it's the pressure, we're still dropping a bit," Katerina said. "We're deep in the clouds now. But this airship isn't made for it."

The skin of the airbag looked like it was being sucked inward. It strained against the metal skeleton. Tiny jets of Chilo's atmosphere seeped in through bullet holes in the outer fabric. Eventually that would affect the air in here, making it dense, and less able to lift them.

A distant explosion thudded. The shock wave shook them. Another random pop from even farther away made them all jump. For a few moments the distant explosions continued in rapid fashion, then stopped.

"Balloon charges," Timas said. "They're under us."

The pirate ships were tougher than this airship. They were designed to drop into the clouds as they hid and smuggled their goods. That was why they'd gleamed silver when Timas had spotted them. Their hulls had been stripped clean by flying through clouds laden with sulfuric acid.

Another balloon charge exploded, closer, and the entire airbag rippled. To the rear a pipe exploded. Acidic steam shrieked out into the catwalks.

The pilot glanced back and a pair of Aeolians converged on the pipe at his silent order. They used a wrench to close a valve, and the steam subsided.

But the next explosion Timas felt in his chest. Three pipes exploded, and shrapnel bounced, clattering to the floor.

After ten more minutes of balloon charges even Timas could see the inevitable. The air around them was filling quickly with Chilo's own substitute. They all coughed constantly and struggled to breathe. The skeleton of the ship creaked, stresses ready to snap it, and the pipes providing air and managing the airship's lift abilities leaked all throughout.

This was a dying airship.

The pilot confirmed it. "I have the fans revved up at full throttle to keep us in the clouds. But when I run out of fuel we'll start falling if we have to depend on just lift. I have enough to limp us to the Yatapek rescue party if we give our guy up, or to just surrender. Either way, I don't intend on committing suicide for you people, risk bonuses only go so far." He looked over at the Aeolian woman leading the group. "And, Renata, I'm sure your bonus pay doesn't extend out that far either."

She had a name. Timas guessed he could have asked Katerina. The Aeolians wouldn't think to introduce themselves, it was true. They assumed if you wanted to know, you would be able to find out.

Renata nodded at the pilot and walked back to Pepper. "I guess you're going to have to meet some new friends."

She tapped the loops around his neck and wrist. As

they fell away Pepper stretched. "You're going to offer no resistance?"

"From what we saw before we took you, your information about this threat is needed. No doubt my fellow citizens will front the ransom money the pirates want for you. As far as the Consensus is concerned, it's just the price and people who bring you to them that has changed. Ultimately the will of the people doesn't care how you get to the cities."

Pepper smiled. "I hope the pirates are as accommodating as you expect." The fans howled as the pilot tried to climb out of the clouds.

"I have no idea what to expect right now," Renata said. She walked away as if washing her hands of it all, leaving them alone to wonder what came next.

Itotia leaned against Timas. "And what does Yatapek have to give for us? Nothing like what the Aeolians have."

Timas didn't answer. He didn't even want to think about what the pirates would do.

The airship shuddered and turned.

"They're docking with us." Katerina looked down at the airlock where the pirates would appear soon.

Timas moved closer to Pepper. "My mother is right. We are nothing to the Aeolians or the pirates."

Pepper's dreadlocks twisted with his head as he looked over at Timas. "And?"

"Heutzin saw the aliens under the storm so many years ago. Can he remember where it was? Will our records be easy to find, the date easy to backtrack?"

Pepper grinned, a sudden flash of perfect teeth. "You bargaining with me, Timas?"

"Yes. You put me on the surface, I'll find where I saw that alien in relation to where the cuatetl is on the surface. I'll take days off your search. Days you claim we can't afford."

"So what do you want me to do?"

Timas stared at him. "You're quick, you're dangerous, you're a soldier. You fight."

"You think I'm going to be able to do much with one arm and one leg?"

"Are you saying you have no plan, that you are going to let these pirates take you? I don't believe that of you. No, you say you don't have time, time for all this, time for ransoms and negotiations. But I look at you, and I think you're free to move again, and you want to make things happen." Timas stared at him.

Pepper grabbed his shoulder, one-armed, and pulled Timas's face close to his. "Are you willing to help? If I put a gun in your hands, will you be willing to take someone's life? Because the easier route is the Aeolians' right now."

He *was* up to something. Timas trembled slightly. He felt like he'd stepped off a cliff, moving to help someone like Pepper. This would be dangerous. "Yes. I think."

The grip Pepper had on his shoulder increased, squeezing until Timas bit his lip. "You think? This isn't 'think' time. This is yes or no time."

"Yes."

Itotia looked at them, not close enough to hear the whispering. But she suspected something. She unstrapped herself and shuffled over. "Timas!"

Someone rapped on the cover of the airlock down to the cab. Pepper used his one good hand to push himself back.

"Open it," he told Timas. "They're being cautious and want to see a face first to make sure it isn't a trap.

So open it, peek over the edge, and make sure you end up standing behind them."

Itotia shook her head. "Timas, no. Don't get involved with him."

"But we already are," Timas said, and turned to let the pirates in.

CHAPTER TWENTY-THREE

Pepper waited for the pirates to come through as Timas leaned forward. The boy offered a friendly, if somewhat nervous face to whomever came up the ladder.

The rage bubbled just underneath, but now Pepper wondered if it controlled him too much.

He'd been pent up, prevented from acting, and forced to use people around him as resources.

Pepper hated that. It wasn't him. He was never the man who sat there and schemed, and convinced, and maneuvered. Being . . . sly . . . that didn't fit him.

Timas had just offered him his life in the hope that Pepper had a careful plan.

And the truth was, Pepper didn't have a plan. Just an aching desire to hurt back, right now. Plans came when one had options, not when events forced themselves down one's throat.

For some reason events always forced themselves down Pepper's throat.

He liked it that way, he thought, as the spiked, armored head of the first pirate poked through and regarded them. Clean, simple. An arrow of action.

The pirate wore night-black armor. A fashion statement.

So did the next.

But at least the third had chosen red.

"Who's in charge?" The voice boomed out from amplified surfaces on the suit's chest and bounced all around the balloons, catwalks, pipes, and surfaces of the airship's bag.

Pepper looked at Timas, who jumped slightly, then stepped carefully behind the men. As he did so Renata leaned over one of the catwalks above them and removed her helmet. "I am."

The man in the suit on the left shot her. The other two men quickly took out five of the other Aeolians. Renata swore and dropped to the grillwork, and while the pirate lined up another shot at her, Pepper launched himself.

They didn't expect a man with only one arm and one leg to cross the distance that fast. He'd counted on that.

They didn't expect that same man to snag the fired weapon so quickly. Or for him to shoot the gun out of the second black-suited man's hand, and then for him to kick that man back down into the airlock.

Pepper turned and grappled the red-suited man. It took a second of squirming, grunting chaos as the second pirate with a now-ruined hand jumped on his back to rip him off, but Pepper found the release catch on the crimson helmet and ripped it off. The pirate's curly hair had been pulled back with a band.

"Hello," Pepper said, jamming the gun against the stubbly beard in the man's neck. "Both of you freeze. Aeolians, do *not* shoot!" He could hear seven of them moving through the shadows to pick a good position to begin shooting.

The man on his back let go.

"I don't know what you're thinking you'll do," the man Pepper held spat. "You still are surrounded in the air."

"Yes, but now we get play the game of hostage chess. And you are clearly not very trustworthy, are you? Hand your gun very carefully over to that young man standing by you."

Timas took the gun.

"Now point that at the man by you," Pepper said. "The safety is off, you pull the trigger, he dies. So don't get jumpy. But if he does move, squeeze."

"If they hadn't shot me, Pepper," Renata yelled down through the catwalk, "I'd be shooting you."

"They were going to kill you all and take me alone. Be grateful you're alive."

"So what now?" the red-suited man grunted.

"Good question. Pepper, what's your plan?" Renata asked. He could hear the pain in her voice. She'd been quick, literally realizing they were going to be shot and twisting enough to get shot somewhere survivable. Her companions, not so quick.

Pepper whispered to the pirate, "She thinks I have a plan. I had only thought ahead to enjoying killing you. The problem is, I've had hundreds of years of trying to die in a blaze of glory that takes everyone who's pissing me off with me, and for some damn reason people keep getting in the way with plans. It's strange."

"Look," the red-suited man said quickly. "People like me and you, we understand each other. We can work something out."

"Me and you?" Pepper grinned.

"Yes." The man nodded. "Yes."

"How important are you to the ships outside?"

"Important enough."

"There's not much honor among thieves, or command structure. Sure you won't just get written off?"

"It cost a lot of fuel to get out here on an intercept this quick. We had a tip that the Aeolians were transporting someone very important back to their cities. Look, we're all almost broke. We need to make money. If I can offer them money, they'll consider almost anything."

The man begged for his life in calm, rational terms. He kept his cool.

He was part of this group's leadership. "Next time you board a ship," Pepper said, "you shouldn't lead the rush in."

"And that would lead to respect from these men how?"

Pepper let go. "Captain . . . ?"

"Yes." Pepper got a somewhat hangdog look from him. Not often one stared down a sheepish pirate captain. "Scarlett Riviera."

Scarlett was having a bad day, and that made Pepper feel much, much better.

"Scarlett, you stay with me." Pepper pulled himself up to stand using the railing. "Together, we're going back with the crew of this little airship to meet the rescue ships from Yatapek."

"To be handed over?" Scarlett shook his head. "I don't think so."

"I know: you'll die before that happens, and so on. Here's what I'm offering. You'll pick three of your crew. They'll fly this airship back after it gets refueled and you're set loose."

The pilot from the front of the airship objected. "This is *my* ship you're giving away."

"A second ago you were wondering if you would live," Pepper snapped. "Shut up."

"But that still doesn't give *me* anything." Scarlett glanced around.

"We're not done playing 'trade the hostage' yet." Pepper leaned forward. Negotiation annoyed him. Everyone kept popping up objections even before the final lay of it had been set out. If they'd all shut up and wait it would go quicker.

"That takes care of you getting back out of this. What do we get?" Scarlett folded his arms.

"Money." Pepper named a sum. Scarlett shook his head. Pepper doubled it several more times.

"That's nice, if you ever come through with it."

"You'll take all them with you." Pepper waved at the Aeolians. It would do him good to get rid of them.

"That gives us more money in the form of ransom from the Aeolians, yeah. But if you pull a stunt when you get out of here, it leaves us still pretty dry. I'd be crazy to bring that back to my crew."

"You can't throw us to them like that," Renata said.

Pepper laughed. "Oh, who cares how you get home? Whether it's through your own efforts or escorted by these gentlemen for some escrowed money, as you said not too long ago, what difference does it make?"

"Go to hell," Renata grunted.

She didn't sound too convinced. She probably knew this was the best option. She didn't seem clueless. Pepper handing them over as hostages probably meant they'd live.

Back to the trade-offs. "If the Aeolian mercenaries aren't enough, then consider this." Pepper moved over to Katerina, using the railing to hold himself up. "An Aeolian avatar."

He grabbed her chin to twist her head and show the captain the silvered eye. She had quite a glare on her, but kept quiet. Scarlett nodded. "Okay, now we're getting somewhere, she's a symbol, important, they'll pay well for her. We had no idea she was aboard." He looked relieved. "I'm willing to play."

"Good." Pepper glanced at Timas, still holding the gun. He looked upset, but somewhat relieved.

Welcome to the world of compromises, Pepper thought. The world of things you'll regret, if you didn't keep your eyes on the bigger picture: that Chilo needed saving, that they were all on the brink of destruction.

Everything was weighed against that.

"Then let's do this." Pepper hobbled toward the airlock.

Scarlett grimaced. "One small thing."

Pepper stopped. "Yes?"

"The boy." Scarlett jutted his chin at Timas. "The boy comes with us."

"Why?" he growled.

"He was promised."

"Unpromise it. I can pay you." Pepper looked at Timas. The boy's hand trembled, the gun visibly shaking.

"I wouldn't look like a man of my word. He at least stays with the hostages until you make good on your ransom. Then we send him back, with the Aeolians and the girl-avatar."

Pepper looked at Scarlett. The man was quite serious. "Timas, hand me the gun."

Timas backed up. "You promised me that if I helped, you'd take us with you." He glanced at his mother. He gained some sort of inner resolve, straightening the gun. "You promised."

With a quick hop Pepper covered the distance and snatched the gun away. "Don't make this harder."

"You promised."

"I can only do what I can do. Now"—Pepper leaned in close and dropped his voice to a whisper—"tell me where you saw the alien, in relation to the mining machine."

"And then I am useless to you," Timas said.

"I'm offering to save your mother and your planet. I will try to come back for you. I will try to get the money for you. But now you need to step up and think about what is really important and what you care about. Do you love your city? Is that why you make yourself throw up, to fit a groundsuit, and risk your life on the surface? Or is it your family you live for? Is that your responsibility? If so, Timas, do the right thing, right now."

Timas closed his eyes, shaking, and then whispered the direction and distance. "Tell my father everything I did."

"I will." Pepper smacked Timas on the head with the stock of the gun and the kid dropped to the grating, out cold.

Itotia ran forward, but Pepper put his hand around her with the gun, hopping with her to pull her back. "He's brave, your son, leave it be. Listen," he hissed, "Yatapek is in the way of the invasion. Timas will be out of the way where he is going. If we live, we can get him back. If we don't, then at least he's alive. Trust me on this. It's better to live to fight again. Don't die needlessly for some cause. If you really believe in it, harbor your energy, and bring it to bear when you can do the most damage. Later."

She pushed him off. He let her. It refocused her on him and kept her away from Timas. "You can*not* just hand his life away," she said. "You can't do this."

Pepper looked at Scarlett. "His mother remains with me. You take him. But if he's seriously harmed, disfigured, or anything of the sort, you will pay. I will be back for him."

Scarlett nodded. "I'll pass that on."

Pepper looked down the airlock. "Then let's get moving, this airship doesn't have long."

The pirates in the cabin retreated, taking their Aeolian prisoners, a dour-looking Katerina, and the unconscious Timas. They left Scarlett, whom Pepper tied to the railing.

Itotia walked to the far side of the catwalk and curled up into a small ball by herself as the pilot got them underway again.

The pilot kept them in the air, barely, as sulfuric acid bit in the air around them. The airbag whistled and distended, the engines chopped away at full throttle, using the airship's minimal aerodynamic properties to keep it aloft.

It was a coin flip, Pepper thought, whether they'd make it before the whole damn airship just gave up.

CHAPTER TWENTY-FOUR

A sharp smell shocked Timas awake. One of the Aeolian soldiers, a slender man with green eyes and close-shaved head, waved a pill of noxious smoke under his nose.

They'd been stripped of their armor, capes, and weapons. Renata sat next to Timas. They were all crammed into a small hold along with crates on a subfloor of a large airship car. Brown light streamed up through tiny glass slits in the floor, giving everyone ghastly, underlit expressions.

Timas rubbed his forehead. "He knocked me out."

"Then they dragged us over to this airship and dropped us through the floor." Renata pointed up at the hatch above them. "We're still in place, they're shifting crew around. Maybe arguing about whether Pepper's deal will hold or whether just to do whatever they want with us and ditch their old leader."

"Then what happens to us?" Timas looked at her.

"It's tricky right now."

Timas stood up, wobbly on his feet. He could feel the swaying of the airship under him. It trembled and bucked about in the air.

He made his way, leaning against the wooden crates, to the prow where Katerina sat in a ball, hugging her knees.

"Katerina."

"Go away." She didn't look up. Her hair hid her face.

"I'm sorry about all this." He felt horribly guilty, knowing that for a moment he had condemned her to this while hoping to avoid it himself. It felt slightly right that he'd been hit and dumped here.

She pushed her hair aside. Tears dripped around the edge of the silver eye. "I had a *life*. I had a life. And I got unlucky enough to be thrown in with you in this primitive mess. I'm a damn hostage, Timas. And everything I know and love has disappeared. There is nowhere else to go. No lower."

"We'll all get through this."

"It's all lost. That man, he just gave me away like I was *property*. Take her, she's an avatar, he said. But I'm not anyone's *property*. That's what you people out in these ramshackle cities are like, maybe, but I'm an individual with rights."

She covered her face again.

"Besides, who can trust you?" she murmured at her knees. "I saw you bargaining with Pepper. Didn't work out the way you had planned, did it? And now who trusts you. Not me."

Timas turned around. She was right. He'd not earned her trust.

The hatch opened, a thick shaft of light spearing out from it. A ladder rolled down, and several armed pirates climbed down with it. They pointed at Timas. "You, come with us."

Timas looked at Renata, who shrugged. Nothing she could do.

The men hauled Timas up onto the next floor of the airship, a long corridor with rooms off to every side. The airship had once been a large passenger ship.

"Hello, Timas," said Luc.

Timas turned around. Luc stood there, wrapping a thick, heavy strap of leather around his right fist. Several pirates stood around him with big grins.

"Luc . . ."

"I said I'd make you pay." Luc stepped forward as the hatch dropped shut. The pirates who'd pulled him out stepped back, giving both boys plenty of room.

"They were real." Timas held his hands up. "We saw aliens. Pepper proved it, they're hiding on the surface somewhere."

Luc hit him in the stomach. Timas folded to the ground, the breath punched right out of him. "You tore me away from everything, Timas. My brother, and then my family."

Timas gasped for air as the next punch came. The pirates laughed as Luc continued hitting him. Timas fended it off as best he could, but each punch bruised his arms and shoved him to the ground.

He kept his head protected and curled into a ball. The pirates laughed. "Get up, fight back."

Timas didn't give them that; they'd crowded around hoping for a spectacle. He didn't have the strength to fight Luc, they were mismatched in every sense of the word.

But if he could survive this beating, maybe he could find something down below to carry on him for the next one.

The pirates got bored and pulled Luc off Timas. "He's still worth something." One of them pushed Timas back to the hatch. "You'll get your fun, Luc, just take it a piece at a time."

Luc stood, blood from Timas's busted lips and cuts staining the leather strap. His hair hung disheveled around his eyes. "You had me banished," Luc spat. "But I still had friends in the upper layers. I came to the smugglers sniffing around and told them Pepper would be transported out as soon as I heard. When I found out you came with them, that became my price for helping out."

Timas let them lower him back among the Aeolians. Renata looked up at them. "Is this what we can all expect from you, beatings?"

"So far it's just him," the pirate shouted back. "But keep making noise, I'm sure we can come up with something for you."

Timas flopped to the floor. "Don't antagonize them," he whispered.

Renata stood over him. "This is unacceptable."

Timas crawled away from them, ashamed of seeming so weak. His ribs ached, his arms hurt from the punches and kicks, and his face was cut up.

He found a corner between the curved wall and two crates and curled up there.

In the dark, time passed swiftly. Renata came to him with a bowl of meat and potato soup. Timas swallowed the whole bowl's contents and gave it back.

Half an hour later he looked around and crawled behind a crate near what looked like a drain. He was too nervous, his stomach roiled, and he found himself using a finger to provoke the response he craved.

He saw Katerina moving around to stare at him from the front of the storage space. He looked away.

Listless after throwing up, he just lay staring at the ribbed ceiling, listening to the footsteps of their captors and distant laughter.

At least his mother had left with Pepper.

That was a small thing.

And they would all know he had been right, about the aliens. There was a small measure of satisfaction in being proved right.

CHAPTER TWENTY-FIVE

Pepper sat on the docked rescue ship, Jaguar scouts guarding him. Ollin had taken Itotia to meet the pipiltin. No doubt a meeting to discuss what to do about the current situation.

Itotia returned through the docking tube after a good hour. She'd not talked to him for the entire flight. "The pipiltin want to turn you back over to the Aeolians, for goodwill. They've confiscated Heutzin's gold and the credit you gave him. They're trying to use it to get Aeolian help to repair the cuatetl."

Pepper shook his head. "They're too focused on the micro."

"They won't consider paying for Timas's ransom with your own money." Each word cracked out from Itotia's thin lips. "The welfare of Yatapek comes first, they say."

"Politicians," Pepper muttered, disgusted. "The mining machine is unimportant."

"Even the pipiltin know things are getting crazy out there." She sat on the seat next to Pepper. "The Aeolians aren't responding. The pipiltin are getting ready to take an airship to one of the nearest Aeolian cities. They want to send an envoy."

"I'm sorry," Pepper said.

Scarlett looked at them both. "Not as sorry as your son will be. I want my damn money."

Itotia stood up. Pepper would have expected a slap, but Itotia punched the pirate captain in the stomach. It caught him off guard. He staggered back, winded. Itotia turned and grabbed Pepper's shoulder. "What can you do?"

Kill the pipiltin. Destroy the envoy's airship. Instigate a coup. Kill everyone who kept annoying him. Pepper rubbed his forehead. "Get me Heutzin and the spare groundsuit parts."

If he could get properly mobile, all of those options opened up. Including going to the surface and leaving this circus behind. Finding the aliens would give him a better handle on what exactly the Swarm was looking for.

He looked back up at her.

"And then what?" she asked.

"Then I can do something about it all. No more dicking around dealing with people, but something serious." He locked eyes with her.

"And my son . . ."

"Getting me a groundsuit is the best thing you can do for your son." In the big picture of things. Pepper had no idea what the pirates wanted with a particular young boy like Timas, but it couldn't be good.

But he wasn't lying to her, not in the big-picture sense.

"Then you'll get groundsuits. But you know you can't fit in one, what limbs you have are too muscular." She stared at him, and Pepper stared back. He'd revved his body's metabolism up. Already his temparature burned. Sweat trickled down his back and stomach as his body literally began eating and destroying the weight and tone he'd been putting back on. He'd fit. If it meant mobility, he'd walk into the room tomorrow looking like a scarecrow.

Usually he only burned himself up like that for energy. In desperate combat. But now, Pepper only warred with himself to become xocoyotzin.

The staring contest ended. Itotia folded her arms. "I'll make Ollin delay the flight a full day. You have twenty-four hours. Heutzin will come pick you up and get you to the parts."

She walked back out, sweeping past Scarlett without a second glance. Four Jaguar scouts came in after her, but they surrounded the pirate captain instead of Pepper.

Itotia came later in the night to Heutzin's workshop. She stood in the doorway. "You look sick," she said.

"I'm burning my body up"—Pepper raised a hand up—"to fit the suits."

She looked around. "You could have the house, on the upper deck."

Metallic air, dingy light, grease, and oil hung heavy throughout the workshop. Pepper gestured at the hundreds of pieces of groundsuit scattered across the tables set against the cramped walls. "I'm happy enough."

"Do you have everything you need?"

"I have all I need, plus more tools." He used his leg to push the wheeled stool he sat on over. "What are you doing down here?"

"Checking up on you."

Pepper picked up a helmet visor and peered into it. He plugged it into the thick, rusty collar of a chassis. It lit up, green diagnostics scrolling over Itotia as he looked through it at her.

"You know, even if I get this thing working, you'll need to prepare for the Swarm." Over the last few hours the silent cities had come back to life. They broadcast a bewildering array of claims throughout Aeolian information space. Everywhere Aeolians gathered a new element of confusion brewed. The cities sent out information saying Pepper was a League agent, trying to undermine the cities. Others claimed a Ragamuffin invasion neared. Or a League invasion neared. People talked to odd-sounding, stiff, and familiar faces of old family members or friends who told them that everything was okay aboard these cities and the Aeolians could return.

Some Aeolians believed them, enough to confuse the matter further when the Swarm began to add its votes to the Consensus. Aeolians agonized over how to withdraw the right to vote from its own physical citizens on suspicion of being part of the Swarm.

All this visitors relayed to Pepper in snippets. If the Consensus kept falling apart, invaded physically and democratically, Pepper realized Yatapek soon stood alone.

"How do we prepare for the Swarm?" Itotia snapped. "You failed against them. The Aeolians are failing against them. What can Yatapek do?"

Pepper set the visor down and picked up a piece of paper. "You have metal and wood. You can make these."

She took the diagram from him. "What is it?"

"It's called a billhook. An ancient polearm, used very successfully in several battles on Earth. The edged bit on the end should let you form up formations with a good reach against the Swarm. Eight, ten feet, you can lop heads quite nicely if it lets us get close enough for hand-to-hand combat. I assume you don't have too many personal firearms in the city?" And the

Swarm couldn't arm every one of its members. The clumsiness of individual Swarm units suggested to Pepper that fast, effective marksmanship from their side wouldn't be something Yatapek would have to worry about.

Itotia shook her head. "Rifles for the Jaguar scouts, but there are, maybe a few hundred of them."

"You'll need to arm everyone: women, children."

"You think it will come to this?" She leaned against the door frame.

Pepper nodded.

"The pipiltin will not allow it," Itotia said. "They think we will remain safe by obscurity."

"I gave you the design. If you choose to build them, or use them, that is your decision. If you choose to wait and see what will happen, that is also yours. I just know that if it were me, I would at least like to die doing something to face my killer."

Pepper blinked away sleep. He had a long night ahead of him. When he'd rubbed his eyes and looked back up, Itotia had left.

Heutzin arrived just after she left, carrying two large boxes full of spare bits, electronics he'd scavenged from all over. He dumped them onto the table.

"Good." Pepper knew the suit models. Somewhere deep in his past he'd used similar enough designs. "You'll be glad to hear that one of the units still has a lot of juice, it was disconnected in an accident. It's working again."

Heutzin glanced at the half-assembled mechanical torso on the bench. "Just like that."

"Don't think lower of yourself. I have centuries of battlefield experience, including stripping and reusing crap like this. Get some of your assistants in here. This needs to be reassembled by dawn. In the meantime,

I need you to help me to a communications center. I need to see if I can talk to any Ragamuffins in orbit."

Heutzin still stared at the groundsuit pieces. "Are there any units that will fully power up?"

"No." Pepper shook his head. "We have about four hours power on the one that is working."

"That's not a lot."

Pepper agreed. But four hours of mobility would be better than none. And with some tweaking of the suit's design tolerances, four hours could be a lot of havoc.

"Get me that communications setup, Heutzin."

Heutzin shifted his belt. "I could get in trouble."

"You'll get in more trouble if you don't help."

"Again, you threaten."

"I just need things to move, Heutzin. We're still sitting around, waiting for fate to decide for us, when we need to be forcing fate's hand."

Without the strange avatar, Katerina, to help him figure out what was going on in the outside world, Pepper felt a bit nervous about timetables. The Swarm could be on its way already.

Most of the dilapidated cities near the Great Storm, like Yatapek, settled by Azteca immigrants from New Anegada, used shortwave radio to communicate back and forth. An ancient standby.

Through the crackle and hiss Pepper found that four of those cities still remained online.

A third of the Aeolian cities remained online and chatty, but they were buried deep in planning how to repel the Swarm and keep its infection contained.

Too little too late.

It took three hours to get things set up to scan orbit and call out, but eventually Pepper found a Ragamuffin ship. A few moments were spent exchanging prompts and codes, and then the familiar dialect of someone from New Anegada came through the tiny speaker.

"This the *Midas Special,* Jack Richardson speaking. Pepper, you all the way down there for real? We been hearing all kinds of reports about you getting move about, jailed. What the hell going on?"

He caught them up. The Ragamuffins had picked on some of what was happening, biological warfare of some sort. But they weren't sure if a League threat had arrived.

Pepper wanted to know about the Ragamuffin response. "Is the Dread high council moving any big ships closer?" They would have been hearing cities go silent, and picking up on some of the chatter. Anything suspicious usually prompted the Dreads to get some military might close to the problem in case things went sour.

"Moving slowly, but moving, man," Jack replied. "This still the DMZ, seen? They don't want provoke no war with the League. But all the merchant ship up here, fifteen standing to."

"Doing what?"

"Keeping it lockdown. No traffic allowed between habitats up here, no traffic allowed into orbit. You move, we fire."

"That violates the DMZ also." Cautious leaders everywhere, on Yatapek, throughout the floating cities, and back home.

"Only because we trying help Chilo. The other problem, ain't a single League ship here in orbit. They all hiding. We think they getting mass up for a big push, we seeing ghost images, that kind of thing."

So a fleet was building itself up out there. No doubt

the League used their merchant ships to house military elements as well, camouflaging intent. Now it waited.

The Swarm would destroy Chilo, and the League would mop up.

"Nothing entering, nothing leaving," Jack said from orbit. "We waiting. Worse comes to worst, we clean from up high after we figure out what the League trying. You on your own for a good while if you staying down there."

Pepper could only think about the images of the sterilized planet the crew aboard the *Shiek Professional* had seen.

And on this open channel, he couldn't talk any further specifics. He faced the Swarm alone if he didn't leave.

And then Jack added, "You get youself high enough and hail, we pick you up. We be around."

Pepper squeezed the old transceiver in his fist and left the pieces on the bench by the radio and had Heutzin take him back to the workshop.

Time to see about getting him to the surface to contact these aliens. If he could figure out exactly what the Swarm was after that would help. And he would have to see about recruiting these secretive aliens into the fight.

CHAPTER TWENTY-SIX

Another beating. Timas again offered no resistance, choosing to protect his head as best he could while Luc exacted his revenge before a laughing crowd of pirates.

This time Timas woke up on the bottom of the storage space when the Aeolians splashed water on his face to revive him. One of the men had a large bruise across his face.

He didn't want to talk to them. He took his soup and scuttled off into another hiding spot.

Timas found himself unable to keep down yet another meal, though. He found the drain again and jammed his index finger down his throat. It came easily.

Katerina, instead of pretending to ignore him, got up from her own corner of despair in the gloom. "What the hell are you doing? Are you sick?"

He held up a hand. "No, I'm not sick." He felt good. Light, ready to fight, and in control. That's how he felt. He might be locked up in the storage area of the airship, headed who knew where, but Timas never felt freer.

None of this was on his shoulders anymore.

"Are you doing this to yourself?" Katerina grabbed his hand and pulled him away.

"You don't understand. It's expected." And he couldn't stop. He pulled his hand from her. "We're not like you: rich, brimming with technology. I can't take a pill and thin my waist, I can't ask for a bigger chest for my birthday and," he snapped his fingers, "make it so."

Katerina put a defensive arm over her breasts. "You're being crude, Timas."

"I'm being true. We don't have your advantages, and as we got poorer we couldn't fit in the suits when they got handed down. Used items that our grandparents got, not even realizing we'd be *normal*." He hissed the last word. "So we do this to fit."

"There are other ways."

"Maybe, but this is being xocoyotzin and what we do. Leave me alone."

"You don't need to fit in a groundsuit, Timas, we're

prisoners right now. You need your strength." Katerina sat next to him.

Timas leaned back against the wall. The sour smell of half-digested food made him feel queasier. "It's not that easy. Doesn't just turn off."

"Listen, there can't be that much food around here. They'll stop feeding you if they find out you're doing this."

"I'm sorry."

Katerina grabbed his hand. "Don't be sorry. Just please stop it for now." She pulled him to his feet. "Now come."

"What are we doing?"

"This can't continue, what they're doing to us. I asked us all to take a vote. We can't check back into the Consensus, but we can certainly run one of our own. We don't think this treatment should continue."

"What can you do about it?" Timas asked. They had no weapons and were cut off and outnumbered. "And what do you mean, 'us'?"

"They wanted to grab Renata and take her upstairs," the Aeolian with the black eye said.

"And risk their payments?" Timas didn't understand. But he felt his mouth go dry. They lived at the mercy of these people up there. What if they stopped caring, and let Luc kill him?

"They're having trouble getting a Consensus focus, the cities are distracted by the Swarm. There's jamming, and their captain, Scarlett, hasn't called back. They're starting to think Pepper double-crossed them." Renata, Timas saw now, had a long and bloody tear running up her forearm.

"I think Pepper's right," one of the men said. "We're all on our own now. The Swarm is sweeping through everything."

"We'll need your help, though, to do anything," Renata said to Timas.

He looked at all of them and felt the heaviness settle on his shoulders. He always helped. It was what he did.

"What do I need to do?"

"Fight back." Renata folded her arms. "We need ten minutes the next time you get dragged away to get ready to jump them."

"Ten minutes." Timas stared at them. That was an eternity.

"Can you do it?" Katerina looked at him hopefully.

Timas looked down, scared to meet their eyes. "Yes." He hadn't started out hating Luc. He'd felt sorry for him. Now Cen's brother had distorted himself and lost all self-control. Timas couldn't afford that pity anymore. It had been beaten out of him.

Renata showed him several long planks of wood they'd pulled off the crates. "Just last ten minutes. When they come to throw you back in, we'll have the crates stacked to reach the hatch."

"Okay." Timas nodded. "I understand." He sat crosslegged under the hatch with them and waited for the next round.

The hours passed. Eventually shouting from above startled him. Feet pounded about.

"Come look at this." Katerina had her face stuck against one of the slits in the belly of the airship.

They all joined her. Timas cupped his hands around his eyes and looked down at the whipped, rusted-out clouds below them.

A ponderous creature flew below them, made of canvas and spars, an airbag at its center, a spiked nose, and large finned sails stretched out around its circular core.

The wings flapped, pulling the contraption up closer in jerking motions. Timas could see thousands of gears, and equally as many articulated joints pumping and shuddering.

"Strandbeests," Renata said. "I've never seen one this close, they usually make a run for it if they notice an airship."

Timas had never seen, or heard of one. "I didn't know there were living creatures in the clouds," he breathed.

"They're not alive, they're all gears and pulleys and joints." Katerina stood back up. "Analog machines, but they self-replicate. Or so we think, they're pretty hermitlike."

A cluster of them beat their canvas wings away from the airship. They wheeled about each other, flocking in a weird, grouplike pattern.

Eventually they dwindled away.

Timas had moved back to the end window in their compartment, pressing his face at an angle to try and see the last one, when the hatch opened.

Luc stood in the light of the square opening. He tapped the button that dropped the ladder down.

"Get up here, you little shit. We aren't done. Now that we've gone this long without Scarlett calling in, they're not as concerned about what happens to you."

Timas walked, step by careful step, to the ladder. His ribs ached, his face felt puffed up, and he hurt all over.

"Ten," Renata mouthed silently to him.

Ten.

Timas pulled himself up toward the decking.

CHAPTER TWENTY-SEVEN

Luc wasted no time in kicking Timas. The moment the hatch slammed shut with a metallic clank and a bounce he had knocked Timas over.

Timas covered his head, but scrabbled backward like a crab. He groaned as he stood back up.

"You're going to stand up to me now?" Luc shook his head. "Maybe you should have stood up for Cen!"

Timas glared at him. "He was my best friend. You know what it's like to lose your best friend?" He balled his hands up into shaking fists.

"Is it anything like losing a brother?" Luc wiped away tears. "We were close, too. Cen dragged himself up to xocoyotzin, running every night since he was four. Four. Already at that age he knew what he wanted to do, and how he wanted to save us from the city's depths."

Luc attacked, smacking a fist into Timas's nose. Timas wheeled back, bouncing off a door, then staggered around until one of the four pirates now watching grabbed him.

They shoved him forward.

"I know what it's like," Timas said. "I do know what it's like for him. Always with your family on your back. Feeling like everything is your responsibility. I knew Cen better than you. We were the same."

Now Timas ran forward and hit Luc. Luc absorbed the body blow easily enough. He twisted and threw Timas to the floor. The deck burned his hands as he fell again.

"You didn't know Cen, you just worked with him."

Timas struggled up. "You know why you're mad?"

He looked through Luc like he didn't even exist. "You're like all the others, the parasites around the xocoyotzin. The parents forcing them to stay thin in the hope that they'll remain on the top level. The distant family that feeds off them, depends on them. All of you crushing him as you stand on his shoulders."

"What the hell are you talking about?"

"You're angry because you lost your free meals," Timas spat. "Your undeserved status by just being his brother and nothing more."

Luc's eyes widened. Timas smiled. He'd struck way too close, and Luc ran him down.

The previous beatings had been nothing, Luc screamed his rage out while the pirates laughed and bet on how long Timas would remain conscious.

Timas wriggled, trapped beneath Luc's bulk, but suddenly full of fear as the desire to flee and the need to breathe took over his entire world as he was crushed.

A pair of mismatched wrestlers, the awkward contest of wills continued, Timas dragging it out for as long as he could.

At the ten-minute mark, with Luc still hitting him from a kneeling position, Timas rolled toward the hatch. "Please."

"Please what?"

"I'm done, I can't take any more," Timas said with bruised lips, a bloody nose, and throbbing body.

"Damn right." Luc leaned down and yanked the hatch open.

Renata reared up from under the edge, standing on a set of crates stacked and laid out like stairs. She grabbed Luc by the collar of his shirt and yanked him down into the hold headfirst.

Just as quickly two of her men crawled up the boxes past her onto the deck and sprinted at the pirates.

Caught off guard, they jumped back. The Aeolians raised their slender wooden stakes. Timas looked away as they impaled all four of the pirates.

The pirates thrashed about on the floor, slowly dying as they bled out and gasped for air that wasn't coming.

Timas climbed down past Renata to Luc's side. But Cen's brother didn't stir. Timas looked back up at Renata, and she shook her head.

For her, a minor regret. For Timas, he now had gotten both his best friend and his best friend's brother killed. He sat next to Luc, fighting the sick feeling deep in his stomach.

Katerina walked over. "You're hurt badly."

"We'll never get them back." Timas took the piece of shirt she offered him and dabbed at his face.

"He wanted you dead. This isn't your fault."

Timas put the bloodied cloth over Luc's face. He'd been to many xocoyotzin funerals and watched the families of distant friends collapsing. Everyone carried the burden that pervaded the top level, the fear of constantly wondering if their children would return to the surface alive after every trip.

Timas could only accept the responsibility of others' burdens for so long. Was it not also the responsibility of the creature he'd seen in the mist, for getting caught out when the aliens had stayed hidden for so long? Or the fault of his grandparents for making bad choices that led to their citywide poverty?

Didn't the League, all those wormhole junctions away, bear the blame for the aliens' persecution, the only thing that would drive aliens to hide here?

Katerina was right. It was time to let it all go, Timas thought, lest it eat him up like it ate Luc up.

"Come on." Katerina stood. "They may need our help."

Timas followed her up the crates. They'd bury Luc in the clouds with his brother later.

Timas and Katerina found the other six crewmen already tied with rope to chairs in the galley, taken by surprise. Pots of rice and stew still sat on the table that the chairs ringed, half-eaten bowls steaming in front of them.

Timas felt his stomach rumble.

"Let us go," one pirate begged. Timas hadn't seen him before, but bits of moss grew all over him. He looked dark green instead of brown. Bits of chapped moss flaked off as he pulled against the ropes keeping him trapped.

This happened to people who worked outside cities or on the outside of ships. Tiny particles in Chilo's atmosphere in the clouds would grow on you.

Gross.

"We'll pay you well," another promised.

Katerina snorted, and they brushed through a bulkhead and past sweaty-smelling unkept beds bunked up three high against the wall. Small canvas lace-up flaps hung down to prevent sleepers from being tossed out of the beds when turbulence hit.

After that, the chart room, where Renata sat looking down at several sheafs of paper with pencil marks all over them. She used a pair of rulers joined together to mark out lines in rapid strokes of the pencil. "The pilot spotted us before we got to the cockpit." She pointed forward.

Timas leaned out of the nook the chart table was in to look forward. Down past the next bulkhead where two of her men were, the pilot lay dead, sprawled face-down.

One of the Aeolians turned back and waved. "Renata! We're ready."

Renata grabbed Katerina. "We're making a run for it." They banked hard right, the small cluster of pirate airships in front of them sliding away to their side. "But they'll be able to keep pace. It'll be dicey. You're an avatar, randomly picked for this. As for us, we chose this. Because of that we feel you should have a choice now in what comes next for you."

Katerina frowned. "What do you mean?"

"We have guns to shoot back, charges to fire, and this is an attack airship. My men are up in the airbag to man guns there and on the airship's car. Things are falling apart all across Chilo, that much is obvious. We're in a good position to fight the pirates here, and maybe, maybe get back and help our cities. But we may get shot down.

"You can stay with us, or, we can get you aboard an emergency bubble. Three days air, food, and an emergency beacon." Renata shoved the map toward them. "After we drop you out the lock, which we'll do at cloud level, we chaff the area. We're headed back toward the strandbeests, between them and the chaff, the pirates will be hard pressed to stop and hunt for you. After we pass through, you increase the air and heat in your bubble, expand it a bit, and pop up five thousand feet. There's a strong air current that feeds into the Great Storm. That takes you back toward Yatapek. Fire off your emergency beacon after fifteen hours."

"I want that option," Timas said. "Whether she goes or not."

"I figured." Renata rolled the chart up. "But we here owe her that choice. She made a big sacrifice to serve the Consensus."

Katerina looked down at the rolled-up wind map in Renata's hand. "I'm not sure what to do. No friend polls here, huh?"

Renata laughed. "No. We're all cut out. I guess you've never had that happen, have you?"

"No." Katerina shook her head. "I miss everyone."

"You'll have about fifteen minutes before we get near the strandbeests again, we're gunning the engines here. Make up your mind by then. I'll leave you some quiet time."

Katerina glanced at Timas and then back to Renata. "I want the bubble. I think Timas saw something important. I think I'll best serve Consensus by getting back to Yatapek."

"Okay." Renata stood up, her arm around Katerina's shoulder. "Let's get you ready."

She led them down to the bunks, to another hatch Timas had not noticed on the way up. They clambered down the ladder into the bowels of the airship's car once again.

A small airlock jutted out of the bottom of this compartment, though. And inside of it would be their escape bubble. After a quick delay, Renata came down the stairs with a tightly wrapped box. "Food and water. There are . . . expandable bags for both of you in the bubble already."

"Expandable?" Katerina frowned.

"If it takes much longer than fifteen hours, you'll need to use the bathroom. It'll be uncomfortable in such close quarters, but many others have survived it."

Timas blushed as Katerina nodded.

"One of you in first, then the next. It's tight right now."

"I'll go." Timas took the lead and spun the hatch open. He dropped his legs through and then crouched in the tiny lock. He pushed his back up against the wall.

It crinkled. He was inside the bubble lining, hanging from the insides of the airlock.

Katerina's long legs slid through, and then she dropped in. They were pressed up close to each other. Embarrassingly close, hips brushing.

Renata leaned in, her puffy hair bobbing against the metallic rim. "Okay, usually these drop, wait, then shoot straight up. But you're trying to avoid that and lay low. So I pulled the climb sensor. You have to yank on this ripcord to initiate the climb."

Timas looked at the red cord nestled inside four dials, and several gauges mounted on the solid plastic floor under his feet. "Okay."

"This dial here adds air pressure from the tank under your feet. The walls are pretty flexible, just watch the pressure dial and don't go into red." Then there was the heater, which added lift, a vent to drop, the ripcord for the emergency beacon, and the tiny cupboard/trash can for waste. Including human waste. Ballast weights on the bottom, little bags of lead that could be dropped by another switch if needed, but the balloon would unbalance and tumble. Those were only for a desperation climb.

"We got it all," Katerina said.

"If you inflate the ball out hard, there's room for some five or six people, it should be comfortable." Renata pointed out the webbing on the edges of the plastic floor. They'd have room to lay out and sleep as it stretched out fully. "Now zip up your top. I'll fire you guys off when I hear we're in position."

She slapped the rim, and Timas stretched up and zipped the clear plastic around the edge of the rim.

They sat on the floor, knees knocking, facing each other in the tiny space.

"Are you scared?" Katerina asked.

Timas considered lying. He decided against it. "I'm terrified."

She laughed. "Me too."

Renata slammed the hatch shut and dogged it. They were truly alone. "But it's easier, with someone else." Timas bit his lip.

"Yeah."

The wait dragged on. Timas felt his mouth go dry. It ranged from seconds to an eternity, just sitting there waiting, his heart hammering.

"It's been a few minutes."

Timas nodded. As he did so the bubble lurched and then dropped out of the bottom of the aircar. He glanced up, reaching out to grab the sides instinctively, and saw the airship shoot up away from them.

Several thousands of tiny twirling bits of chaff exploded at random points in the sky.

They tumbled slightly as they fell, the grungy brown clouds swirling around them. Timas caught a glimpse of the pirate fleet far overhead.

The bubble stopped tumbling, inflating slightly with a hiss from under their feet, popping their ears. Then dropped through cloud wisps as the bubble slowed down, shook, and then steadied.

A glance at the altimeter gauge confirmed that they had stopped falling.

"We made it out!" Katerina smiled. Timas stood up, the edges of the floor stretched with webbing around it. He could even walk around Katerina a bit if he wanted.

He walked over and leaned against the edge, looking into the murk. "I wonder how long these walls can handle the acid in the clouds." Acid beaded up on the outside already. The clouds dripped with it, and the beads of acid started congealing into rivulets that dripped off the large balloon.

"We'll give it fifteen minutes," Timas said, watching the tiny rivers of acid. "I'll watch the balloon, you let me know when time's up."

She counted down, minute by minute, as he walked the edge of the platform, poking the skin with his finger to figure out if the sections in contact with acid were weakening.

By ten minutes he could tell that there were differences in give.

"Let's ascend." Timas poked at one part near the zipped top where acid had sat and weakened the skin enough so that his finger left an indentation when he poked hard enough.

"Timas? I think I see something."

He turned. Something *was* moving through the gloom at them, a large shadow.

Timas scrambled for the ripcord. A fast enough ascent to get over it, and maybe whatever it was wouldn't notice them in this muck.

But he paused at the last second as the shadow became a giant strandbeest, dwarfing their tiny bubble with its slow-moving canvas wings and slow trailing tail.

The giant spiked nose gently turned toward them and bumped them.

Katerina jumped back. "Can it poke through?"

"I hope not."

"It's like it's curious. The acid in the clouds can't be good for it."

The mechanical monster tapped the ball like a toy, nudging it along up out of the clouds. A second construction pushed through the clouds and joined it.

Timas grabbed the webbing as they jostled the balloon around.

"What are they doing?" Katerina asked.

"I don't know," Timas snapped, scared that they might break the balloon with their giant nudges. "Pull the ripcord for a few seconds, let's see if we can get higher and left alone."

Katerina gave the ripcord a long tug and the balloon filled out more. They rose, lifting out of the clouds, and the strandbeests followed.

Timas looked up, and to his dismay saw several more descending on them. He stood up.

"What are you doing?" Katerina asked.

"Trying to see if maybe someone is controlling it."

"There's nothing there but gears and arms," she said. "It's a giant clockwork toy."

Another insistent nudge spun the balloon upside down and threw him off the walls. Katerina smacked her nose against his knee. As the balloon righted itself, she clutched it. "It hurts."

"Quit moving about, lock your arms in the straps," Timas said. Looking up he could see more strandbeests surrounding them.

The flock of giant machines closed in, completely blocking out the entire world. A creaking, whirring, gigantic mass of strangely articulated parts, airbags, and motion that had decided to take them . . . somewhere.

PART FIVE

CHAPTER TWENTY-EIGHT

Heutzin held true to his word. Pepper found an al-most knightly suit of armor waiting when he re-turned to the workshop. He set his crutch up against the door and flopped down on the wheeled chair to scoot his way up to it. They'd even mounted a helmet on it.

Pepper checked it over, and then plugged the visor in to boot it up and run it through diagnostics. And damn if it didn't keep failing its integrity tests. Leaks. All the different parts and the adjustments to make them fit Pepper, even with him being so thin, and they still didn't have a proper groundsuit for him.

"These are the best seals we can get?" Pepper looked at Heutzin.

"You took all the spare part suits down yourself. It still isn't sealing?"

Pepper leaned in close at the suit. The seals could be replaced, but the low-tech crap Yatapek made didn't self-lubricate, so the suit's mobility would be nil. He'd break the new seals trying to move around. He needed the nanoscale frictionless seals, but they were letting air in after decades of use.

That wouldn't work for getting down to the surface.

Another Aeolian city had broadcast images of the Swarm invading. Bloodied corpses stumbling toward people with blind, rabid purpose. In the video Pepper saw that the Aeolians who kept shooting back at them could hardly keep a line in the chaos. The Swarm moved implacably closer now, city by city.

He considered stealing a working suit. But looking at the extensions Heutzin and he had also grafted on to fit his height, he doubted any of them would work. He would have to be thankful for mobility.

"Let's suit up anyway," he growled. "See how she moves."

The assistants moved around him, like squires from the days of old, and started taking the groundsuit apart.

They began with getting his leg in, and then the stump of his other leg. He stood on his own in the heavy device for the first time as they encased his trunk in the next sections. Pepper raised his arm out, and they started strapping the upper section on.

He smiled.

Segmented gauntlets on, and then the familiar prickle of contact via his lower spine as the suit asked permission to meld itself to his body's own information systems.

Pepper nodded, and he no longer needed the visor. The suit's diagnostics appeared over his own vision. Boot-up went smoothly with the suit's designer logo splashing over his entire visual cortex and then fading after some brief pyrotechnics.

As the workshop's interior faded back into view Pepper gave the command to conform, and the suit snipped and snapped as currents gave the metallo-ceramics commands to shrink, stretch, and flex until the suit felt fitted: a bulky second skin.

"This brings back memories." Pepper he clenched his good fist, flesh and metal acting as one.

Now for the moment of truth. He clenched his other fist, and the empty metal curled up.

Heutzin grinned as Pepper reached out and tapped

his shoulder with the nonexistent arm. "Not bad." The movement jerked a little. It'd take some practice to get used to it, but it would work.

Pepper took a few tentative steps forward, then back. As each footstep hit the grated floor, tools jumped off the benches.

He hopped into the air. This time he dented the floor when he hit, and knocked boxes of parts onto the floor.

Four hours of freedom.

Pepper walked out of the workshop, then jogged down the catwalk outside toward the edges of the docks. The walkways shivered and shook underneath him, and people going about their business stopped and stared.

He threaded his way out, holding his breath as he broke out into the open areas. The acidic air bit at his face and made his skin crawl. His dreadlocks slapped the collar ring of the suit.

Back inside, he cycled through a set of doors into air. He walked over to an observation window. The giant body of a docked airship wallowed at the end of a twisting tube, and far below, the dreary clouds mocked him.

The surface of Chilo was just as far away from him right now as when he'd started working on the suit.

He bent the rail in front of the window as he clenched his hands. Heutzin and his assistant mechanics burst through into the room, air masks held over their faces.

Heutzin panted. "What now?"

Pepper was still thinking about it, reaching for some plan. He enjoyed the surprised faces as he stormed down the walkways, and then he thudded over to a mechanic. He snatched an air mask from him. "Let's go say hello to the pipiltin."

Maybe this time he could shake them into doing what he needed.

CHAPTER TWENTY-NINE

After the first hour of being shoved along by the machines, Timas and Katerina relaxed. As the strandbeests rose, the lower ones bumped the balloon from below, and Timas or Katerina would yank on the ripcord to add air and stretch their balloon out further and rise with the flock.

By the second hour the great bumps of the clouds receded into tiny crenulations. They'd discussed triggering the beacon, but it was too early. They didn't want the pirates getting a strong signal, and the strandbeests hadn't hurt the balloon.

"This about as high as we can go," Timas said, looking at the altimeter.

"Look, they're thinning." Katerina pointed up above them.

The strandbeests fell away to reveal a great raftlike triangle, festooned with platforms and canvas wings, cranes and antennae and all sorts of junk. Half of a strandbeest hung suspended from the center of the triangle by a web of ropes and pulleys.

A large net dropped out and enveloped them, then pulled them up into the structure next to the desiccated strandbeest. The net fell away, and a thin man in plastic coveralls and an air mask with round goggles scrambled his way across ropes, nets, and walkways toward them.

He pressed his mask against the bubble and looked in at them, then pulled a pair of masks out of a pouch dangling off his waist.

"Take a deep breath, then," Timas said. He waited

until Katerina did, and then he grabbed the zipper at the top and ripped it open.

He closed his eyes as the balloon deflated and fell around them. Their host shoved a mask in his hand, and Timas pulled it on.

Then the man gestured for them to follow him. Timas kept a hand on the various lines that were draped everywhere.

From below, with the strandbeest trapped in its center, the triangular floating platform hadn't looked too large. But Timas realized the strandbeests were just as big, and the platform could have housed fifty people.

Inside an airlock leading into the nearest pontoon the thin man pulled his mask down. His skin cracked like leather left out to cure too long, with a strong ebony tinge.

"Hello, hello." He ran a hand over his shaved head, then changed his mind and pulled at a scraggly beard. "Van VerMeer's me name, and you two, look at you, you just kids. You're lucky I'm not hiding in the clouds today. They sting. They rot the canvas wings, even with my protective paints, so they don't like it. But we've never liked the big cities."

Katerina stepped forward and introduced herself and Timas, and explained that they were fleeing pirates as Timas looked around.

There was little rhyme or reason to the chaos. Machined parts, light tubing, rubber, canvas: all the basic elements of the strandbeests cluttered walls, floors, and any available counterspace.

The old man wobbled over to a bench. "I am deeply sorry, I don't get many visitors."

"We're not visitors, we were dragged here, by the

machines." Timas moved over to Van's side, trying to distract him from the parts he fingered.

Van cocked his head to regard Timas. "Machines? Machines?"

"The strandbeests," Katerina said.

A big smile. "Strandbeests. They're good-hearted." He looked wistful.

Katerina and Timas glanced at each other. "Why did they bring us here?" Katerina took the man's leathery hands in hers.

"You were spare parts." Van switched to looking at her. "You were in a bubble. They look for spare parts, they scavenge from whatever they find out there. Bits and pieces off cities, old dead airships, passing through airships. I barter for what I can here. Not a lot of flotsam anymore, they're all slowly dying from lack of parts. One day soon there won't be any."

"Well, thank you for letting us come aboard." Timas said each word carefully. "Can we use your radio, or whatever you have, to call for help?"

"Help? No . . ." Van shook his head. "No outsiders. Not now, not until that last one is repaired. See the trick is that no one knows I maintain them, and maybe they'll be able to do it for themselves, some day, but for now, they still need me."

"And how long will that be before the repairs are done?" Katerina asked.

A shrug. "A month?" Van smiled. "There are new things to put in its brain." He held up a complicated series of tiny cogs and wheels.

"A month!" Timas looked at Katerina, but she was moving through the benches, eyes narrowed, taking everything in. "We need to call for help sooner."

"Maybe more!" Van pulled in close. "You know how to program in analog-varient-viscous?"

"Viscous?" Timas shook his head.

"V.I.S.C.O.U.S." Van sighed. "A lost art. Used to be a popular hobby among academic artificial intelligence researchers. Using gears to model more precise neural decisions, not just ones and zeros, right? Babbage machines. The most complex behaviors can be modeled by a series of simple sets. Oh, what do you care, you're a regular, outsider, boring."

He meandered back through his bits and pieces, and Timas walked down toward Katerina. "He's been on the platform by himself too long."

"Yeah, longer than you think." She pulled a small paper brochure off the wall and waved it at him. "This shows him building similar things in orbital habitats. A hundred years ago. He's one of those spacers with alien technology in him. He's probably hundreds of years old."

Timas looked back at the doddering, odd man with a bit of awe. "And he's been building these things all that time?"

"I have." Van looked sideways at them with a grin. "The machines, they were first built by Theo Jansen."

Katerina walked forward. "I'm sorry, I've never heard of the man."

Van grinned. He looked sharp now, not so dreamy and focused on the work. "He lived on Earth, a very long time ago. Before Earth shut itself away and hid, destroying the wormhole there. Bit of a drag that. It stranded me. I was a traveling performance artist, resurrecting the greatest of the old Earth peculiarities for my alien owners."

"He built these things?" Timas asked.

"Machines that took the wind and converted it. They would walk across the beaches. Beach machines. Strandbeests. He did those. The Satraps kept me in an artist's zoo, had me build them strandbeests for their beaches. When the Raga freed the habitat I was in, I flew here. Now I build them around floaters, let the wind hit their wings and power their coils inside, and release the energy when they need it. They float and fly around, seeking spare parts. You see: I freed them." His eyes got wet and shiny.

"You did free them." Katerina folded her arms. "Congratulations."

Van gathered up an armful of parts, still teared up. "Thank you, sister." He passed them both on his way deeper into the pontoon.

"He's lost it," Timas whispered to her.

"Come on." Katerina grabbed his sleeve and whispered back, "I know he's a bit out of it, but he has moments of clarity, and he's harmless."

"I wonder if it's just because of so much time and his being alone for so long?" They followed the old man, hanging back to continue their hushed exchange without him hearing. The old man flipped on lights as he went along.

"Maybe, but if aliens held him for a long time, and gave him life-extension technology, I can't imagine his life was too great before he came to Chilo. The Satraps were wicked."

Timas nodded. He didn't have much schooling, but one thing almost all humanity knew, it was that. And then it hit him. "That's how we get him to let us use his radio."

"What?"

"Tell him aliens are attacking."

"Good idea." Katerina grabbed him as Van ran back at them, spilling nuts, bolts, and slender shafts to the ground. They clattered about at their feet.

"Aliens? Where?" His eyes bugged out.

Timas stood still, nervous. "The cities. There's an infection, it's . . ."

Van grabbed his shirt and pulled him close. "An *alien* infection?"

Timas nodded. Katerina had her hand on a pipe. "It turns people into something else. It's called the Swarm. And now they're attacking. Haven't you been listening in on the airwaves?"

"I'm a hermit," Van said. "I don't listen to *people*. I don't *care* what they're doing. I'm my own empire, my own thing. I'm not even supposed to be paying attention to you. You're wasting my time and making it longer to do this. I can't even think the programming straight. How can I concentrate with all this crap going on around me?"

He let go of Timas, and Timas took the opportunity. "We want to get out of your way so you can continue. The best way is for us to get off the platform. Can we use your radio to call for help?"

"You don't need to call for help." Van shook his head. "Come, we'll get you the hell out. You'll go with the miners. They'll know what to do with you. Yes."

Timas looked at Katerina, but she was just as mystified as he was.

CHAPTER THIRTY

It turned out that even an eccentric hermit like Van needed contact. Food, parts, medicine. He refused to allow people to venture aboard his domain, but he did venture out. In a disguise. "You have to understand"—he slapped the side of his head—"it's sideways up there, after the aliens were done crawling around in it. Don't want them around again."

He donned an air mask with silvered lenses, grabbed a wig of frizzy hemp, and shrugged on a giant, heavy leather coat that dropped to his ankles. He looked like a tiny child, lost in the coat's weight.

Railings, mounted haphazardly all over the place, let him hang on as he walked. Timas followed suit. The platform occasionally *leaned* when a very strong gust hit it.

Maybe that explained the messiness.

"Hey." Van popped his mask up off his mouth to speak. "Get masks, let's go. What are you waiting for? We have a schedule to keep."

Right. Timas fumbled about for the masks he'd given them when they boarded.

Back outside, with acrid Chilo air forcing itself around the edges of the mask, Timas followed the old man across the surface of the pontoons to a tiny hangar.

Inside, revealed by the doors Van swung aside, hung a small airship. It was just large enough for the three of them to cram into.

The envelope, a dull metal globe, lay nestled between four very large rockets strapped to it.

"That can't be safe," Katerina said.

"Fast." Van walked up to the tiny cab underneath. "That way no one is sure where I came from."

Timas looked at Katerina. This was their only way back. She seemed to think so as well. They both climbed in the one door into the small cab.

The tiny bench seat inside forced them all together, elbows and knees touching, facing forward to look out several industrial-looking portholes at Chilo's cloudy yellow-orange horizon. Timas was the last in. He shut the door, spinning the wheel to seal it until he couldn't force it any farther.

Pumps forced Chilo air out and filled the cab with breathable air. They removed their masks.

Katerina's skin was dry. Timas was very conscious of her arm touching his. He did his best not to move and draw attention to the fact. He liked it.

Van slapped a switch and the platform fell away from them as they shot up. Timas bit his lip and pushed his face against the tiny window to his right and looked at the triangular platform get smaller and smaller.

"Okay," Van said.

He flipped a series of switches. Pumps whined, and then a steady roar developed. Timas was shoved back into his seat. The strange contraption thundered its way along for a good hour, with their eccentric pilot making curving wiggles, crescents, and loops. The entire contraption shook to a steady rhythm of pings and creaks as the rockets slammed the large sphere through the thick atmosphere.

Several chirps from the instrument panel got his attention, and he flipped the rockets off. "Back in my day these things were always one shot. You turned them on and they just kept going until they ran out of fuel." He slapped the dashboard. "These ones, they're slicker."

More switches, Van even consulted with a small check board, and then finally he got the sequence right after some grinding sounds came from the sphere above them.

They dropped toward the clouds. Timas felt his ears pop.

After passing through the clouds, scattering wisps, Van snapped off switches with cool efficiency until they slowed, stopped, and hung just below the cloud layer.

"There." Van pointed at a distant chunk of black cloud. They coasted toward it.

It grew larger, massive smokestacks pumping out black smoke, cables rising up to extra balloons hanging above it.

"What is it?" Timas could see that underneath, clouds of fine dust showered out of several chutes, slowly dissipating in the air under the hulking, industrial complex.

"Ore processor," Katerina said.

"The *Triple-Two*," Van said. They slowly drifted into a giant floating net hung around the processor like a skirt. It rippled, and that produced a reaction. A tube festooned with airbags disengaged and snaked its way toward them, tiny puffs of propellant from the mouth-like dock steering it precisely to the cab.

Van's airship shuddered as it attached. It whistled as it blew out Chilo air from between it and the hull to make a seal.

Timas looked over at Van, who jabbed in the direction of the door. "Yes, open her up."

He did so. On the other side stood a man by a control panel. Covered in black soot, wearing blue coveralls, he looked at Van suspiciously. "What the hell, man, you know we are at the end of this rotation. No food, nothing to barter." He frowned at Timas and Katerina. "Who're they?"

Van shrugged. "Rescued them. They were in an escape bubble."

Katerina leaned over Timas. "I'm an avatar for the Consensus."

Something passed through the air between them, invisible to Timas. It changed the man's posture. Katerina might talk about democracy and Consensus, but apparently even the Aeolians had some sort of respect for special people in their strange government, like avatars.

The man nodded and stepped forward. "Let me help you out. We're in the final thirty-hour rush before the carrier comes for the ore. You can stay here until it swings by and ride back to the cities on it."

Timas scrambled out. Katerina followed, back in her element.

Van waved and then slammed the door shut between them.

"Come on," the man said. "Let's retract the dock tube before he fires off those damned rockets to head back wherever the hell it is he hides out."

Timas looked out the tiny porthole as they pulled back from the nets. He blinked when the rockets fired. The strange artist-hermit disappeared up into the clouds riding a fiery trail of smoke.

He turned around. "I'm sorry, what is your name?"

Katerina and the man exchanged quick glances, then he nodded at Timas. "She's right. You're certainly not from one of the Aeolian cities."

"No." Timas shook his head.

"I'll let the crew know to verbalize more around you." He reached out for a handshake. "I'm Achmed, the foreman of this sorry little operation. Sounds like you're both lucky to be alive. Certainly you're the weirdest thing Van's ever dropped off here."

Timas was just grateful to be somewhere safe.

"I'll show you around quickly, then get some food and drink in you. After that, it's back to work. We're on a tight schedule."

Food sounded like a wonderful idea, Timas thought.

CHAPTER THIRTY-ONE

Pepper thudded his way off the dock elevator and cycled through the airlocks onto the lower decks.

He removed his air mask, and looked out at a crowd of Yatapek dwellers. Many carried guns, others machetes.

Near the front, a pair of Jaguar scouts in baggy pants and vests trained their rifles on him.

"What's this?" Pepper stood still, running a rough count. This part of the city resembled a warren, and the atrium and elevators stood on the other side of the crowd.

A hundred angry people stood between him and the way up.

"Make him pay!"

"Pay!"

"Pay."

A bottle hit his suit and broke. Pepper reached under his chin and pulled out a sliver of glass.

He should have brought the helmet along. He'd have to consider how to protect his head. Plowing through the crowd, it could be ugly.

Another bottle shattered against his suit, and a pair of scruffy-looking guys moved forward, machetes off to the side.

"Stop!"

The voice came from behind the crowd, by an elevator that had just opened. People back there stirred and shifted, turning to face the voice.

"Stop it!" Ollin forced his way through the crowd. Out of breath, he grabbed Pepper's armored shoulder and turned to face the crowd. "None of this. Not now, not ever."

The old pipiltin followed him, three of them in boldly colored clothes.

"Go home, get out of here," the pipiltin yelled. One of them used a cane to smack several nearby bystanders. "You ignore your elders?"

Several Jaguar scouts arrived. They moved through the crowd and pushed people to head back down corridors or get in line for an elevator.

Pepper listened to the grumbling and swearing.

"I gather I'm not popular."

Ollin turned to him. "Things haven't gone well for anyone since you arrived. Can you blame them?"

Pepper brushed glass out of his locks. "Not really."

"We've lost people, as well as the cuatetl. Now all over the city people are getting radio reports from Aeolian cities about the madness that's spreading. No one knows what to think, but they do know you're involved. Some think you're maybe even responsible for it."

A handful of people remained now.

Ollin gathered the three pipiltin around. "Eztli and Necalli here, they stand with me."

Eztli nodded. "We've been listening to the radio reports, what the airships passing near the Aeolian cities are saying. Already our docks are crammed with ships paying us extra fees to just sit and wait. They want to see what happens. But I don't think they'll have cities to return to. This Swarm, we think it's what you say it is. We're convinced."

The other pipiltin nodded agreement.

"Good." Pepper leaned in with them. "We need to get your xocoyotzin on the ground right away then.

I have a rough map, thanks to your son." He looked at Ollin.

Ollin grimaced. "We have trouble, though."

"The other pipiltin refuse. It is their three against our two. That was why there have always been five." Necalli spread his arms.

"But you can at least get xocoyotzin on the surface." Pepper folded his arms.

"Not without one more," Ollin said. "There is no more surface travel allowed. Since you talked about aliens, people have been seeing them everywhere on the station. In shadows, in dreams. It's hysteria and it's spreading. It's heresy, so the pipiltin want a cooling-off period. The xocoyotzin can be impressionable. We can't afford them disappearing off into the storm or fog just because they think they saw an alien."

Pepper sucked his teeth in frustration. "Then why are you standing here teasing me? If we can find the aliens, bring one back, we have a turning point. I can promise you serious Ragamuffin support."

Ollin licked his lips, glanced at the two pipiltin. "We think you are right. And we need your help to get these things you need."

"My help?" Pepper looked at the two, and then he shook his head slowly. "You know what you're asking?"

Ollin looked him right in the eye. "Yes. Will you help back us against the other three pipiltin? We know you were once called the god-killer, back on New Anegada, and that you're revered among the Ragamuffins. We know that you're hundreds of years old. You will serve as a fellow pipiltin, and we'll be able to save the city."

"You sure that's what this is about?" Pepper arched an eyebrow.

Ollin flushed hot in infrared. They all fidgeted, distressed, worried.

"It's all for the city," Ollin said. "If we don't act to save it we'll fall silent, just like the Aeolians."

Pepper smiled.

There would be a price paid to get control, but here they were, finally coming to their senses and handing him what he needed.

The house of cards was falling in his direction.

"We'll need guns." Pepper pivoted the suit and looked at the warriors standing around them. "I think I left a sword up in your house. I would like that as well."

CHAPTER THIRTY-TWO

Achmed whipped them through a whirlwind tour. "We sit under the cloud layer, usually a lot deeper than this, but we heard Van's pip and came up higher for him."

The bulky ore processor was a long cylindrical tube at the core, nestled in the center of six hydrogen-filled pontoons that helped hold it up. Achmed took them through a series of air-filled corridors inside the pontoons and then through another airlock leading into the central facility.

They walked past windows looking over giant belts moving crushed rock toward giant automated foundries. The gaping mouths belched fire and hot gases.

"We rip up the ground using dredges, drag it back, process it, and then the carriers come take the product. We have one last dredge we're pulling up right now. The *Triple-Two* is a solid performer, my boys make good money during their rotations. And we're all fractional owners." Achmed was proud of his operation. "We should be able to get that last lot processed before the carrier gets here. So as much as we'd like to be courteous hosts, we're going to be rather too busy."

Achmed took them to rooms near the center of the processor. He cracked open a door and led both of them into one. Near the top of the cylinder the rooms featured skylights that they could look up through. Several larger balloons hung above them, and the undercloud layer above that.

It was always weird looking up to see an unbroken layer of cloud, Timas thought.

"We have a room for the two of you in this spare room. You'll have to share, it's all we have. Katerina will know when meals are. Sounds like you've both been through a lot, so rest up, though you're free to roam wherever. Danger areas won't open to your request, Katerina. You can only open the door if you're allowed to be in there."

Timas crawled onto the small pullout next to the bed. Someone had already been in the room to get it ready for them. The Aeolians and their almost-telepathic technology. Creepy.

"By the way," Achmed paused at the door, "you're in rough shape, kid. Pretty bruised. You might want to take a spin in our medical pod, get yourself checked over."

"I just need rest," Timas said. The soft bed felt incredibly luxurious. It conformed to his back perfectly.

"Okay." Achmed walked off.

Something occurred to Timas. "You didn't tell them about the Swarm."

Katerina sat down on the bed. "I did. The crew took a vote and decided to keep going. They're not sure what to make of all I sent them—the whole story— over the lamina here, but they noted that when the carrier arrives they'll get a data dump of all the latest news from it. They keep pretty quiet, they don't want any pirates finding them floating around, and under the clouds is hard to contact anyone."

"Oh."

"How are you doing?" She leaned over and propped her head up on a hand.

Timas linked his hands together underneath the back of his head. "I feel guilty, leaving Luc dead in the hold. I'm tired. I want to get back to my city."

"At least you have one to return to," Katerina said softly.

Timas bit his lip. "I'm sorry. I wasn't thinking."

"Not your fault. It's not like you invaded the city." She sighed. "I never gave a lot of thought to the worlds out there. You grow up hearing about how the Satraps used to rule all the worlds, how dangerous they were and how we all once lived under their thumb except the Ragamuffins. Now this new alien thing is invading us. I used to think all I had to worry about was my city."

"Me too."

Timas closed his eyes. His entire body throbbed. Bruised. Adrenaline had kept him from noticing it before. But now that he knew he was safe his body seemed determined to catalogue its hurts.

His eyelids scratched over his eyes when he closed them, and sleep lurked right around the edges of mind. But it never came.

"I'm just lying here, going over everything I did and whether I screwed anything up," Katerina said. The bed creaked as she sat back up. "I don't want to think about it all anymore. Come on, let's go."

"Where?" Timas sat up and looked at her.

"Anywhere. Let's wander. Let's just do something. I don't want to sit here and think about what happened over and over again. Lunch is coming soon, why fall asleep just to wake up again?"

Timas groaned. He couldn't get to sleep. And he didn't want to sit in the room alone. "Okay. I'll follow."

"Great."

Katerina followed a mental map he couldn't see. She looped them around through the galley, where a pair of pale-skinned Aeolians sat. One of them napped, his face cradled in his arms on the table. The other nodded as they passed, then returned to sipping whatever was in his steaming mug. There were bags under his eyes. The crew had been pulling a long shift.

After they passed through the galley Timas looked back. "Are there a lot of foojies in your cities?"

She didn't answer for a while, just pursed her lips and kept walking ahead. Finally, near another door, she paused. "Please don't use that word."

"Which one?"

"Foojies."

He looked at her, confused. "I don't understand. What did I do wrong?"

Katerina sighed. "Timas, it's a pejorative. My father's a 'foojie.' My mother's from New Anegada. They settled here. Dad was a refugee, he came from Astragalai. He fled both the League and the Gahe."

"Gahe?" Timas asked.

"Aliens. With tentacled tongues." She shuddered and made a face. "They use the tongues to pick things up and build things. Nasty."

"But he's seen them?" Timas wanted to know. That sounded similar to the alien he saw on the surface. He wanted to know more. It was almost a forbidden topic on Yatapek. The scars of their history still ran too close to the surface. But he'd seen one, and he wanted to know more about them. His whole life had been turned upside down by that glimpse. And his world was threatened by another.

"Gahe, yes. His family used to be owned by a prominent household on the planet. After emancipation he spent time in a human reservation, one that was liberated by Ragamuffin forces during the uprising."

Timas didn't see why the word irritated her so much. It was commonly used. Just like calling Aeolians zombies. "What do you call us?"

"What do you mean?"

"We call Aeolians 'zombies' sometimes. What do you call us?"

"Poor." Katerina waved her hand and the door opened. Timas didn't have time to snap back, they stood at the entry to the control center.

Seven miners sat at real control panels, complete with multiple screens set into the wooden-looking surfaces. "Can't they just use their minds, like you do?" Timas wanted to know.

"They could," Katerina said. "The build date on the facility is recent enough, it crawls with overlaid information. But I think the crew here uses the backups. Just in case."

"She's right." Achmed sat in the center of the room, monitoring everything. "It's a quirk of mine, mainly. I used to be a shiphand aboard a Ragamuffin merchantship doing the upstream run from New Anegada through the DMZ to Bujantjor. Raga don't trust lamina a hundred percent."

"Why not?" Timas asked. He'd thought they all pretty much lived in their heads, computers handing them visions of the world around them. This was the first Aeolian he'd met who said otherwise.

"The Satraps used to be able to take it over, used it to crawl up into your head."

"But they're all gone now. Suicided, killed, or disappeared," Timas said.

"Doesn't mean the risk is gone." Achmed shrugged. "Call me old fashioned. Traditional." He grinned.

Katerina walked over to a man who was using a pair of joysticks. "Really?" She was answering a question he'd asked her. "Sure, I'd love to."

The man stood up and waved at the joysticks. "It's the last run."

"What's she doing?" Timas asked Achmed.

"Here." He tapped a screen and dragged the edge larger so that it took up the better part of the control panel surface between them.

They looked down at the surface of Chilo. Timas looked up, and Katerina had closed her eyes, accessing information on how to operate the device. She grabbed the joysticks and the surface jumped toward them.

A giant, serrated revolving band drilled into the ground and the whole picture vibrated as rock and debris rolled into the mouth of the hopper.

"The crew thought that someone honored by chance to be an avatar should also get honored with the chance to bring up the last load. She's safe. It's easy enough to operate." Achmed grinned. "Just needs a human nudge and oversight."

Five minutes later the crew broke out into applause as the dredge pulled the band back itself, like a giant tongue, and the ground dropped away. It began its slow climb back up.

Katerina let go of the joysticks and shook the controller's hand. "Thank you."

"Our pleasure."

Achmed cocked his head. "Well, it's going to be a few minutes while it rises. Lunch."

Katerina walked past Timas, and he hurried up to catch her. "Are you ignoring me?"

She walked faster. "You asked if we used any nasty words to describe you. As if that somehow might excuse your using similar words. That's deflecting the issue, Timas."

"I'm sorry!"

She ignored the apology.

Timas sat at the table with the crew, but he was an outsider. Katerina laughed at unspoken jokes shared between them in the silent air, and spoke to them about cities and places he'd never been.

At least the small boxes of tasty orange-flavored chicken and rice with fried vegetables filled him.

Achmed must have noticed the weary look Timas had, because he leaned over. "The carrier will be here in the morning. You'll be home soon enough. It's all okay."

But Timas wasn't so sure. Not after what he'd been through.

CHAPTER THIRTY-THREE

The two pipiltin and their escorts, warriors, Ollin, and Pepper had all gathered by the elevator exit to the topmost layer of Yatapek. Pepper figured that two hundred stood ready. The beginnings of the coup, all ready to move out.

"Pepper!" Itotia pushed her way through the crowd. "You can't do this. Where's Ollin?"

"On the elevator, coming up." The groundsuit whined as it restarted and walked to meet her halfway through the loose crowd.

"I told him to wait," Itotia muttered. "But maybe he was right, and we should have tried sooner."

"What?" Pepper saw that some of the warriors paid very close attention to their conversation.

"We can't do this anymore. It would split the city, and we need to remain whole. We can't afford a coup, and more importantly, we simply have no time for something like this."

"What happened?"

"The Swarm is moving out in an armada of airships. We're getting radio reports from private airships passing by. It's coming toward us."

"When will it get here?"

"Between twenty-four and forty hours. They're staying together, but the ships that spotted them say it looks like hundreds of airships are flying in formation, maybe thousands. We're offering refuge for noninfected ships and people."

Everyone nearby muttered. Pepper ignored the word spreading through the crowd. "You *have* to get xocoyotzin on the ground, now, if you all want to live. That was my reason for following your husband. We have to confront your leaders. There's a chance the Swarm may go straight to trying to find the aliens and leave your city alone, but it's not likely."

"I can do that. Let me talk to Camaxtli. I'm like a daughter to him, and Ollin really rubs him the wrong way."

"And then we need real battle plans for their attack." Pepper raised his voice for all to hear. "Every person in this city needs to be armed. Every nook and cranny has to be a place to kill the infected. Fallback points, zones, you name it. The Swarm must pay such a high cost, it decides you are not worth it."

"You think we stand a chance against it?" a warrior asked.

"If you throw yourselves into it." Pepper looked at them all. "When I faced the Swarm in orbit, it asked for a truce from me. It was scared of the price a direct fight would be. I say you force it to make the same offer again."

The warriors nodded. "Yes. Make it pay for every inch."

"We need to start getting weapons made." He wanted people armed with the billhooks he'd shown them how to make. "And women and children armed. We have little time to prepare."

Itotia nodded. "We start spreading the word. And Pepper, I promise we'll get xocoyotzin on the ground now, just as soon as the weather lets us drop the elevator and anchor. We've circled around the Great Storm to the point that we're close to where the cuatetl is. It is doable."

She left, and Pepper looked around at his new army. And smiled.

CHAPTER THIRTY-FOUR

Timas woke up to the sound of thunder, and then a series of thuds. He shot up out of his bunk and stood up, swaying to the motion of the carrier.

"It's okay." Katerina held on to the side of the bed. "They're adjusting height."

The carrier was about an hour away and had hailed them, Katerina said. "We should eat breakfast, and then go meet it. And you should put your shirt back on."

He'd been too hot last night, and only she knew how to change the room's temperature. Timas pulled his shirt on. She was still angry with him.

Several scrambled eggs and bacon strips tasted heavenly. And there were sticky buns, sugar-crusted. As well as biscuits, which he piled with butter and honey.

The crew crammed in the galley, in good spirits, talking about what they'd do with their money as they rotated out and the next group came in.

"We save some of the good stuff for the last big meal," one of them grinned through his eggs. "A celebration."

They talked about pools and beaches in bubbles floating near their cities. A few said they wanted to take trips up elevator strings to space.

These hardworking, dust-covered men, were rich beyond Timas's imagination. And they were hardly at the apex of Aeolian life.

They called his people poor.

Katerina hadn't even been trying to be cruel, it was just a fact, he thought.

He left his last biscuit uneaten and returned to the room while Katerina was distracted and laughing with one of the crew. He closed the bathroom door behind him.

Things seemed normal. The madness of the pirates, of Pepper and his crazy stories, aliens on the surface, that all felt distant, like it had hardly happened when he thought about it now here in the strange calm of the giant processor. Maybe the Aeolians had contained the Swarm with their advanced technologies.

If so, maybe xocoyotzin would be needed again.

All those sweets.

He had overeaten, and he needed to take care of it.

Katerina kicked the door in and grabbed his collar. "No you don't."

Timas squirmed and slapped her hands away. Light from the room glinted off her silvered eye as she reached back in and pulled him out. "You need to stop doing that."

"First you're angry with me, now you're here dragging me out of the bathroom. Suppose I wasn't just standing there . . ."

"About to throw up again? I had a feeling."

"Leave me alone. You don't understand."

"That you need to be thin to fit in those suits? I understand. But you're damaging yourself, Timas. You can't do this."

"I have responsibilities to the city."

She hadn't let go of his collar. "When we get to the city, on the carrier, we're going to get you to see a doctor. There are things that we can do for you."

"Oh sure. And do those things come free of charge?" Timas twisted free. "I am, as you pointed out, poor. We can't pay to have technology injected into us that turns our bodies into perfect figures."

"Be a dick about it, Timas. Just keep at it. I can't fix everyone at Yatapek, but I *do* have enough to help you."

Timas walked out of the room. "I don't need your pity."

"You never had it." The hull shuddered. Katerina paused to look up into the air. "The carrier is here."

They dropped the argument to leave the room. As they walked down the corridor Katerina frowned.

"What's wrong?" Timas asked.

"It's weird. The carrier isn't talking to us, usually by now their crew would be part of the immediate Consensus. Or at least all over the lamina."

Katerina raised a hand.

"It's the Swarm, isn't it?" Timas said.

"I don't know, but let's go to the control room."

"Good idea."

They detoured. Katerina led the way, as Timas had only figured out the relatively straight route from the galley to their room. Achmed, alone in the control room, didn't even look up when they entered.

He slapped the console and swore.

"Swarm." Katerina grabbed Timas by the elbow and pulled him over to a screen.

One of the pale-skinned Aeolians lay on the floor near the middle of the docking tube. He held on to his arm and groaned. Four men shuffled down the dock, chasing the miners who retreated.

"Shut the airlock," Timas said.

One of the miners stepped forward with a pipe wrench. He hit the first one of the Swarm, but the other three piled on him.

The entryway slammed shut. Or at least, partially shut. One of the Swarm had shoved the pipe wrench taken from the miner in between the door and the frame.

"Shit." Achmed spotted it as well. He ran out into the corridor. Smashed glass tinkled to the floor, and Achmed peered back in, ax in hand. "I'm going down to help force them back, then unconnect the dock."

Katerina nodded as Achmed ran down.

"Tell them not to get bit," Timas shouted after him. On the screen the Swarm members were forcing the door open now, one of them breaking its arm from the effort.

"There are more of them." Katerina pointed to a monitor showing the other end of the dock by the carrier. Fifteen Swarm shoved their way down the tube.

"Not good. Not good." Timas watched them join the effort to force their way into the processor. "Why isn't Achmed disconnecting the tube?"

"The tube is open on the carrier's end *and* ours. The

safety programs won't allow it to be disengaged." Katerina stared at the screen. "He needs to shut the door. Then they can manually disconnect."

More bodies piled up, the Swarm mass trying to get into the ore carrier. Timas took a deep breath. What would Pepper do?

Kill them all, somehow. That seemed his sort of thing.

Timas looked over at the joysticks. "Katerina. You need to destroy the docking tube."

"What?"

"Use the dredge. Now. It's us or them."

Her eyes widened. She ran over to the control panel and grabbed them. "Achmed says you've got the right idea. It's got control jets on it, hydrogen peroxide thrusters."

The screen by the joysticks lit up. The dredge looked down into the clouds below. Katerina closed her eyes and the camera position jumped to facing forward, then dissected into views facing up, sideways, and to the rear.

"Come on, come on," Timas muttered.

The dredge came about slowly, dragging hoses and belts with it. Katerina winced. "I'm causing lots of damage."

"There's no time to worry about that. We're under attack!"

She dropped the giant rock-eating belt out in front of the dredge and turned it on. The vicious teeth blurred as they spun past the camera. The dredge lumbered out from under the shadow of the processor and rose up into the space between it and the carrier. It twisted slightly in the turbulent space between the two craft.

"Here we go." Katerina tapped the console, and the dredge slipped forward and struck the docking tube.

It pierced it, sending shards of metal flying. Air puffed out in a spreading cloud.

A faint mist of red covered the camera and Timas winced. Katerina groaned, probably seeing something similar in her internal world.

As the dock collapsed, Timas saw bodies tumbling out and falling slowly down toward the clouds. Ruddy Chilo air burst inside through the half-open airlock door. The miners struggled to force the nearest Swarm back through the door, and Achmed showed up, swinging the ax and using it to help them.

Katerina's hands shook. She let go of the joysticks. "I don't feel so well."

"You did it." Timas looked at the screens. The miners had shut the airlock door now, although several of them looked hurt.

Achmed ran through the door of the control room, out of breath, his shirt covered in blood. He didn't have any bite marks, though. "This is insane," he said to both of them. "Tony's dead! Tony was on the docking tube, they *bit* him and left him in the tube, whatever they were."

Katerina pursed her lips. "Tony was dead the moment those things bit him."

On the screen the crew cursed and nursed their wounds, breathing fresh air out of a pair of emergency oxygen masks they passed back and forth.

"We told you," Timas said to Achmed. "This's happening all over the planet. Now some of your crew's infected, and there might not be any cities for you to return to."

"He's right." Katerina stared at the screens. She put her elbows on the edge of the panel and pushed her face into her hands.

"The carrier is moving." Achmed looked around at the screens. "And there's a second airship, off in the distance, not talking to us."

"More Swarm," Katerina predicted.

The carrier lumbered at them. "They're going to ram us." Achmed blinked. "They're actually going to ram us."

"Do something," Timas said. "Drop the ore."

Achmed looked startled. "You're talking about bankrupting us."

"It's the ore, or your lives." Timas leaned across the panel to stare at Achmed. "They'll ram us, then throw more of them through. You've seen these things face to face. They've taken whole *cities*. Do they look human to you?"

"You've got to do it now." Katerina walked over. "The cities will understand later, they'll work something out. But time it well, you don't want them trying to rise over us. You dump half your load now, then half when they pass underneath us. As an avatar, I beg you."

Achmed stared at her, then nodded. "You're right, that kind of load, all at once. We'll shoot right up." He turned back and stared at the screen as the carrier, long and tapered, grew larger.

Timas thought he was waiting too long, but then Achmed tapped the screen several times, and hatches along the underside banged open. On the screens Timas could see that they rose, the carrier falling below them.

"He's under us," Achmed said.

The rest of the hatches on the underside swung open. Metal and metal-rich rock, slurry, and ingots tumbled out and hit the carrier, now several hundred feet below them.

Parts of the skin crumpled and the entire carrier shook with the impact of the sudden weight. It fell hard as the *Triple-Two* continued to ascend. Not too fast, however. Achmed tapped away, dumping air.

The carrier folded at the center now, and then began to spin. Air vented with occasional bursts of fire that extinguished the moment Chilo's atmosphere snuffed it out, giving it no oxygen to burn.

"The other ship's coming," Katerina said.

Achmed strapped himself into the seat by his consoles. Now he wasn't tapping commands out manually: his eyes rolled back up into his head, concentrating. He looked posessed. "We've got a jump on it."

"What are you going to do?" Timas asked.

"We're a processor. This thing's built like a tank, ready to get down to fifty thousand feet easy, forty maybe. We dive low, gain us speed, and keep ahead of him."

"They might have bombs to drop, or missiles," Katerina said.

"Not that ship. It's a passenger ship. I don't see anything mounted on it that looks like that." Achmed had his confidence back, Timas noticed. For a while there Achmed had been trying to process what was happening and he had looked dazed.

But then if Timas hadn't heard Pepper's story, what would *he* have done? Timas grabbed the control panel as the floor shifted, the entire ore processor angling down until Timas felt like his feet would slide out from under him.

"We're diving. But where should we go?" Achmed looked at Katerina.

"Yatapek," Katerina and Timas said at the same time.

"Yes." Katerina stumbled back across the floor to the chair by the panel with joysticks. She snapped herself into it. "Timas, get in."

"What about the crew?"

"They're safe in the room, it's small. . . ." Achmed stopped and locked eyes with Timas.

Timas swallowed. "It takes four hours, Pepper said. They start off with a heavy fever, then pass out. They awake as part of the Swarm. There are bitten people down there. What are you going to do to protect us from them?"

A long moment passed in the control center, and then Achmed tapped his throat for an announcement.

"Would everyone bitten hold up your hand?" he said.

Everyone in the hold raised their hands. Only Achmed, with his ax, had held the infected away from him.

Achmed sighed. "I have to ask you all a favor," he said, voice catching. "Please get in the airlock, because you're all infected. In four hours, you'll be like . . . the things that attacked us."

Confusion bubbled out, and then anger, and then finally, after a series of silent, fast arguments, they all moved into the airlock. Three of them walked to corners, arms gesturing as they talked into the air.

"What are they doing?" Timas asked.

"Last messages for loved ones." Achmed turned the screen off. "We'll give them their privacy."

"They went in there so easily." Timas still couldn't believe it.

Katerina looked at Timas. "They voted. Consensus said it was the best thing to do, giving us three a chance to live."

"And you voted?" Timas let go of the console and slid his way toward an edge of the room for a chair of his own.

"We abstained."

"I know you want to give them their privacy, but we should keep an eye on them." Timas buckled himself in. "When they change, they might try and figure out how to get back in using manual access."

"We'll leave them alone for three hours," Achmed said. His voice sounded firm. It was final.

The entire bulk of the processor shook. Turbulence? It shook again and Timas turned his chair around to look at Achmed. "That didn't feel quite like turbulence."

"It wasn't. We're pulling away, but they dropped an explosive, hoping to rattle us. This is as close as they'll get, distance-wise, until we stop our dive."

"And then they catch up?"

"Then they catch up," Achmed confirmed and nodded his head.

"I thought," Timas said, "that you said there weren't any weapons on that ship."

Achmed held on to the edges of his panel. "I was wrong. At least they don't seem to have missiles."

It was a small comfort.

CHAPTER THIRTY-FIVE

Pepper walked the ranks of Yatapek's citizens among the fields of the upper level of the city, outside the circle of buildings that clustered around the atrium. The long, edged blades of billhooks smacked against each other all around him, and the crack of practice fire echoed from the top of the city.

Up there Yatapek had mounted more anti-pirate batteries, pulling the long-barrelled guns out of storage from somewhere deep in the city.

All around the upper area residencies, where the few

elite lived clustered around the atrium, the corn and wheat had been cut back to give fighters a good zone of fire.

When trying to arm a whole populace in the space of a couple days one realized that guns weren't realistic. There just weren't enough lying around in a city to arm everyone. And not enough time to build any. The billhook was a throwback. Nothing but a chunky, slightly curved bit of steel fastened to a pole nine feet long. But, Pepper hoped, it would let Yatapek's volunteers keep their distance and thrust at the necks of the Swarm.

Quite a few had armed themselves with pikes, hammering iron spikes onto poles, but Pepper doubted those would be effective.

The traditional macuahuitl of Yatapek, an iron or stone-studded club, would be good for skull-crushing.

Pepper clambered up and sat on the roof of one of the last houses on the edge of the cleared land. He watched a group of twenty teenagers struggling to keep themselves in a tight square, imitating a phalanx.

A wall of them with shields and swords made the first line, and then rows of billhooks followed, the bristling formation struggling to keep their long weapons steady in front of them. A clumsy hedgehog.

They couldn't turn quickly, but stumbled apart as they tried to attack a set of scarecrows.

Pepper had a secret. Now that he had mobility, late in the night he'd gone hunting. A little bit more clumsy in this metal skin, but he'd found an emergency balloon that could hold the weight of him in his new incarnation.

He'd made his way to a spot near the rim of the upper level, by a set of airlocks leading out. These were service ways to let people get out on the city's skin for repairs. And a useful exit for him.

He wasn't sure how long the city would hold when the Swarm came. It had only cost him a half hour's worth of power to make sure he had a backup plan. Pepper had moved quickly, in bursts. Three hours and thirty minutes of continuous power remained in the suit's batteries.

Maybe, if the ten xocoyotzin now on the surface found anything, got contact with the aliens, then they'd be in a different place. With the aliens found, the Dread Council would have to move to take Chilo under its protection to gain access to their technology and re-sources, and protect them from the League. And the aliens might offer a hand in the fighting. Either way, if that didn't happen soon, Pepper would need to move on. Yatapek, as he saw it, was doomed.

"Pepper." Itotia walked to the wall and looked up at him. "I just got a call. There's a ship full of Swarm at the docks."

He jumped off the roof, enjoying the flight, his dread-locks flying behind him, the suit a second skin around him, weightless.

The ground dented and threw up dust when he hit with a grin.

"How bad?"

"Some of ours are wounded. We forced them back into the ship."

"Let's see it."

Smoke roiled in the docks, and fifteen dour-looking warriors with rifles guarded one of the docking tubes.

Four dockworkers lay curled up on the grating, bleed-ing. A doctor crouched between them, bandaging their wounds.

"We've shut the docking tube down and forced them back," Necalli told Pepper, falling in beside him as he thudded his way from the elevator through the docks. "We can fire on the airship with our guns, if we aim just right. We can rip it apart where it sits."

"But it hasn't moved?" Pepper stared at the door. Why the hell hadn't they had the docking tubes closed? Had they just been letting people aboard?

Necalli must have guessed what he was thinking. "It won't happen again. Not everyone was taking the new policy too seriously. Now we are. And no, the ship remains docked."

Pepper walked up to the wounded. "Get them in a cage, hang it over a drop hatch with a rope."

Itotia tapped his shoulder. "These are fellow friends, neighbors, coworkers, family."

"For the next few hours. After that, they're Swarm."

"You push us. First, you arm women and children. The traditional among the city are outraged. Now this."

"There will be less outrage when the Swarm pours over us and people realize that they at least have a weapon in their hand to face this with."

There was a reason the ship had come early. The Swarm, with cities full of people, was now sending out emisarries. Was it arrogant, Pepper wondered, to assume that there was a message from the Swarm here?

A cage was found and dragged down, and the four feverish men bundled into it. The men were too far gone in the process to notice what was happening, but someone slipped food and water into the cage anyway.

The hours slipped by as Pepper waited. Itotia stayed with him, watching the men pass out in the cage from the fever.

Eventually the still forms stirred, and then stood up

as one. They grabbed the bars of the cage and looked at Pepper. "We again come to offer you something."

Pepper stepped forward and looked at the vacant-eyed faces of the Swarm. "Talk."

"Surrender," said the first.

"Stand your city down."

"We will only take one in three of you for our needs to replace what is lost to attrition and time."

Pepper leaned forward toward the bars, and the moment the nearest Swarm lunged for him, Pepper grabbed its hand. He snapped its finger back, then tore it off with a ripping pop.

He walked over and slapped the button to open the hatch below them. Acrid Chilo air roiled in, forcing everyone to grab their air masks. He walked over to the rope holding the cage and cut it loose with a knife.

None of the four Swarm made a sound. They calmly stood by the bar as the cage fell down through the hatch, whipping the rope with it.

Pepper looked over the edge as it silently dwindled down to a dot. He pulled out a small vial and massaged blood out of the finger into it, then tossed the finger down after the cage. He capped the vial and tucked it into a niche under the suit's collar.

"You should have taken the offer to the pipiltin," Itotia said. "They are the ones responsible for this city. Not you."

Some deals one just didn't take. Still. "Do you think that offer would have come if I wasn't here?"

Itotia didn't respond, she gave a command, and someone closed the hatches. "We won't know now."

Necalli strode across to them. "I gave the order to destroy the airship. It's not worth the risk trying to board it."

A few minutes later the heavy repeated thud of an antiship gun filled the docks. The Swarm airship crumpled and ripped off the end of the docking tube, taking several dock lines with it as it fell.

"What kind of people are we," Pepper said, "if we just hand it all over and accept the price the Swarm wanted?"

He left them on the docks, but Itotia cornered him in Heutzin's workshop. "Why don't the Ragamuffins just come to protect us all?"

"This is the DMZ," Pepper said. "It was expensive enough to fight the League to agree to leave this area alone, and that the Raga should be allowed to be independent, separate. And now, they don't want another war with the League. We'll break ourselves, on both sides."

"But why the aliens?"

"The Satraps destroyed most of their refineries, and we're clever monkeys, but not clever enough to get deep down in those black box machines to figure out what makes them tick. We have no idea how to use most Satrapic technologies. And when we rose up, we killed many of the Satraps, and many of the rest either committed suicide, or just disappeared.

"The problem is that we're like a bunch of tribesmen. We stole the guns from the invaders, and we can use them, but we don't know how to make them, or the replacement gunpowder. And we're running out. Some of these aliens are going to ground, they know more about Satrapic technology than we do. They may even be hiding a Satrap."

Itotia shook her head, disgusted. "Our lives are weighed against fuel and technology."

"Of course." Pepper looked at her. "Civilizations live and die by power and technology. If New Anegada throws its best, uses all its resources, to fight here, they leave that whole planet open and undefended. There would have to be an incredible payoff to risk the home planet."

She sighed. "So it's just us versus the Swarm."

Pepper nodded.

CHAPTER THIRTY-SIX

An hour passed before Achmed pulled the ore carrier out of the dive. The airship chasing them flew far overhead, but far enough behind them that it couldn't drop any more charges.

The infected crew's fevers had passed. Timas and Katerina walked down to watch as they stirred through the thick glass of the airlock. Their movements were jerky, as if their bodies were being controlled by strings.

The nearest two staggered to their feet and flung themselves at the glass, beating it with loose and awkward fists.

Timas jumped back. "They look possessed."

"They are." Katerina stepped forward and looked. "It's just like Pepper described."

"But maybe there is still something deep down, human. Maybe they can be fixed."

As an answer, Katerina tapped the airlock's control panel. Through the window they could see the outer lock door slide open. The Swarm inside threw themselves against the door and silently continued pounding against the glass. "They've destroyed entire cities, millions of people, and have almost taken all Chilo for their own. Our world, Timas. And they've done it in a timespan of days. We have to act quickly. You were right up there, when you said it was us or them."

The air inside had become a muddy brown. The infected finally dropped to their knees, gasping for air that had fled, replaced by Chilo's own poisonous mix.

"At least they don't change to breathe Chilo's air," Timas said, finally looking away.

"If they did, there wouldn't even be a chance for us."

Katerina walked over to a small locker on the other side of the antechamber and dug around in it. "Here." She handed him a small earpiece the size of a seed. He slipped it into his ear.

"Hi." Katerina's lips didn't move, but her voice came through in his ear.

"Welcome to the public channel," Achmed said.

"Thanks. Do you hear me?" Timas wasn't sure.

"Yeah, if you can hear yourself we can, too." Katerina's lips still didn't move. Creepy. "Achmed, is there any way to tilt the processor to its side?"

"Yes."

"Let's dump the infected out like that and make sure we don't get any surprises. I'd hate to open the door and find out they can hibernate or something."

Timas agreed, and they both found corners to press against as the entire ore processor tilted over.

Once on their side, Katerina nodded. "They're all out."

The processor slowly righted itself again.

"We have another problem," Achmed reported. "That airship is catching up. It's also dropping down."

"How much lower can it get?" Timas asked.

"Not too much lower before it starts getting crushed."

"And if it keeps going, it'll overtake us soon?" They

were level again. Timas looked out of the airlock and into the haze.

"Half an hour. Then they can drop more charges."

"Buy why? What do we have that it wants?" Timas asked. "Now that we're escaping, it should just leave. We're just a few extra bodies for it."

"If it plans on spreading and taking the whole planet, the fewer humans in airships running about, the better," Achmed replied. "There's another cloud layer, it's at thirty-five thousand feet. We can lose them there for sure."

Katerina looked up, alarmed. "You said forty thousand feet was the edge of the processor's limit."

"At best, yes." Achmed cleared his throat. "I think it's our best option. And there's another issue. We can't do it too quickly. We can drop fast initially, but we'll need to start adding buoyancy back as we get lower, or we'll drop even faster. We could overshoot, or stress the hull."

"How long?" Katerina asked.

"Slightly less than thirty minutes. It'll be close. I wouldn't ask you two to try for it without a Consensus here."

"But this is your ship, and you're the oldest." Timas shook his head.

Katerina made a sour face. "We have the right to decide how to risk our lives. They're every bit as important as his, don't you think? What is age but some demarcation? Today you are twenty years and can have input on something that impacts your life, but yesterday you were nineteen and couldn't?"

"Do you people sit around and vote on everything? Sometimes something just needs done." Timas started walking back to the control center of the processor.

"With the right technology, it's second nature and takes almost no time. We're just being polite to you."

Timas swallowed. "But he knows more."

"Which means we should pay close attention to his advice." Katerina looked out the airlock window. "I say we run deep and risk it."

Achmed agreed. Now they both waited on Timas, even though they had the majority. "Okay, sure. Let's drop."

Katerina shut the outer door to the airlock. "We should probably be in the control room."

"Why is that?"

"More bulkheads between us and the outside, more sealed doors."

Timas followed. They closed thick doors and dogged them tight behind them as they went. It took five minutes to get to the control center, and by the time they did Timas noticed that he had started to sweat. "It's getting hot."

"The heat exchangers are getting overloaded," Achmed said. "It's pretty nasty outside. We've done most of the drop already."

"We're at the edge. From now on, it gets dangerous."

"Slow and steady." Achmed grimaced. "And with much prayer on my part."

For Timas, that sounded like a good idea.

The entire processor creaked, and in the distance, echoing down corridors, pings and snaps made both Katerina and Timas jump.

Achmed closed his eyes, sweat rolling down his forehead. He was focusing on safely taking them into the clouds once again. The heat got unbearable, even the consoles got too hot to touch.

Timas kept swallowing. His clothes were drenched. His exposed skin stuck to the chair.

"Six thousand to go."

An explosion shook the ship. Timas jumped. "What was that?"

"The balloons just burst. We're falling a bit fast, but I'm dumping ballast, I anticipated this happening. Just falling a bit fast."

Another explosion jarred the processor. Timas wiped sweat away from his eyes and gripped the chair. They weren't going to make it. If the balloons kept bursting like that what would keep the processor up? Its natural air inside?

Achmed looked up. "Without the balloons we can keep altitude at this height: the *Triple-Two* is built to level on its own air at fifty thousand. We're dropping below, that's a risk, yes, but as long as our hull doesn't break, we should be able to climb back up with our safety balloons. Just shoot them up ten thousand feet or so with lines attached and inflate."

"But then the Swarm airship sees us." Timas gripped the chair even harder as they lurched again.

"So we run low until we're sure we dodged them." Achmed clutched his panel as they fell again. "That should be the last of them."

"The Swarm airship, something's wrong with it." Katerina tapped and a screen by Timas lit up. The tiny dot of an airship jumped, zoomed in, and resolved to show the cigar-shaped pursuer.

The pressure had shoved the skin so hard inward Timas could see the understructure of the airship. Then he saw the cabin, shattered and destroyed. "The windows all broke."

"I think so. They must all be in the airbag, if they survived." Katerina shook her head.

Then, as they watched, a hole appeared, widened, and, as if being crushed by a hand, the entire airship folded in on itself.

"They just committed suicide trying to follow us

down." Katerina put her hand on the console, as if trying to reach the dying airship as it fell.

"It's not suicide to the Swarm." Timas kept watching the airship fall. "It was like losing a fingertip, maybe. Not people, just pieces."

An explosion rocked them, this one louder and closer than any other.

"Hull breach!" Achmed ignored the plight of the falling Swarm airship and closed his eyes.

"Is it bad?" Timas felt his stomach flip. This was it. They'd come this far, and the hull had finally given out just as he'd gotten hope back.

"It's a hull breach, what do you mean 'is it bad'?" Katerina snapped.

The processor began to fall as air fell prey to Chilo's heavy atmosphere rushing in, weighing the processor down, boiling it, trying to drag it down to its surface.

Timas felt that he'd always known he would die on the surface, he'd imagined it countless times at night in his bed. He'd never counted on falling out of the sky onto the surface to die, however.

CHAPTER THIRTY-SEVEN

Just walking around the docks Pepper counted a hundred airships. A bedraggled armada. Straggling airships from all around Chilo clustered around Yatapek in holding patterns, drifting with the city. Many of the Aeolian Consensus's finest had fled aboard anything they could as the Swarm fixed its hold throughout the floating cities.

They came to Yatapek with its promise of being Swarm-free. And because Yatapek had prepared itself for the battle.

At least here, many reasoned over ship-to-ship radio, they had knowledge of what approached. And they had time to prepare, as well as a place to catch their breath.

But it also gave the Swarm time to plan, time to consolidate itself in the cities and root out any survivors or resistance, and time to slip a ship of its own into Yatapek's armada to keep an eye on the resistance.

Pepper stopped thudding around the docks and gripped a railing. He needed to stop pacing.

Heutzin found him there, half an hour later, still gripping the railing and looking down into the loading bays where dockworkers prepped food for transport to airships full of quarantined Aeolians.

"They're telling me the Aeolians are getting their Consensus going again, right here around us," Heutzin said. "Zombies are zombies."

"As long as the quarantine holds who cares what they do." Pepper looked over at him. "What do you need?"

"The xocoyotzin are back."

"And?"

He already knew Heutzin's answer, or Heutzin would not hesitantly be standing there with an apologetic, and somewhat desperate, look on his face. "Nothing."

Pepper bent the railing. "And has the importance of finding something been really, really impressed upon them?"

"They're as desperate as any of us."

"Give them the map, have them fill in where they searched for me." A formality.

So that was that, then. He'd armed them with bill-hooks, given them the best warning he could, and figured out why the Swarm was here. And he'd done it with minimal violence.

What more could anyone have asked of him?

It was time to confirm his escape route. He had three hours of continuous power in the suit left. What could he really offer these people here? Not much.

Pepper had Heutzin take him back to the communications room. Operators packed the tiny space, taking messages from airships. A small board hung in the center of the room with airship names, designations, crew numbers, and quarantine status.

Pepper took his seat at the old radio, with a new mic. He found the right frequency using the old-fashioned dial.

The *Midas Special* still waited up there for him. "Got a lot of people worried for you."

"How much time you giving me, Jack?"

"Ten hours."

Pepper signed off. Ten hours before he needed to get into the emergency ball and head for the sky, giving up on all this.

The phone rang. It got handed to Heutzin, who stood. He hung it up and walked over. "Timas and the Aeolian avatar are back."

Pepper was intrigued. "The pirates returned?" They had Scarlett jailed here, much to his annoyance. But what was the sense in worrying about negotiating with pirates when the Swarm approached? Scarlett was the last thing on anyone's mind.

Maybe the pirates would prove a valuable ally.

"No. They escaped. They returned aboard an Aeolian ore processor."

Itotia had a very plucky son. With a slight grin Pepper turned to Heutzin. "Take me there. I want to talk to Timas."

Heutzin raised an eyebrow. "What for?"

"Either you and he saw aliens on the surface, and I'm right, or Yatapek is going to die for no particular reason. I want to talk to him."

Heutzin nodded. "Okay. Let's go."

Pepper walked through the room, which at the word *aliens* had gone near silent.

Just the idea still spooked them all.

Timas was tired, wired, dehydrated, and elated to be alive, Pepper saw. He sat on a box inside an airlock, alone, waiting for four hours to pass and his quarantine to lift.

He'd arrived in an ore carrier that limped its way to the city, radioing requests for help that many had ignored. It could have been a Swarm ship, another trick. But Timas had demanded to speak to his parents. It didn't take long for everyone to realize it was really him.

Itotia and Ollin also stood by the airlock, their smiles almost infectious.

"He's alive!" Itotia grinned.

"I'm impressed." Pepper stepped back from the door. "Let me in."

"He's under quarantine."

"What can he do against me, even if he is infected?" Pepper walked up to the airlock door. "I want in."

"What for?" Itotia asked.

"More questions about what he saw on the ground."

"We aren't sending more xocoyotzin," Ollin said.

Pepper remained where he was. "Open it or I force it open myself."

Heutzin worked the controls, earning a nasty glance from Itotia. The door opened, and Pepper thundered in, almost clipping his head on the top of the metal rim.

The door shut behind him.

Pepper looked down at the young man with the bags under his eyes. "I'm going to have ask you to go back down to the surface, because I can't, and none of the other xocoyotzin found the aliens. And you have to succeed, because if you don't, this city dies when the Swarm arrives."

The words seemed to force Timas farther down onto the box, Pepper thought. Just one last time into the muck, one last time to try and save the city.

It was Yatapek's last chance.

CHAPTER THIRTY-EIGHT

Pepper dominated the airlock in his groundsuit. He'd gotten it powered up, although all the old parts still had stains and rusted bits on them. He creaked, sometimes hissed, but mainly thudded as he moved around. A machine-man, Timas thought. Though, given that Pepper was as much machine inside under his skin, it was nothing new for the strange warrior.

Katerina would have been impressed, even. But she'd remained aboard the *Triple-Two*. All the Aeolian ships around Yatapek were up to their weird political games, voting on what kind of army and defense to create. She wanted to play a part in the new Consensus, just as he'd wanted to reunite with his family.

He guessed the armada out there, and Achmed, was the closest thing she had to a family for right now.

But instead of a reunification with his family, Pepper was here, and he wanted Timas to bear another great burden. He crouched in front of Timas. "Timas, the future of humanity depends on our ability to move. We know our old enemy, the Satraps, exist out past New Anegada. The creatures your priests called gods, the Teotl—"

"That was a heresy, they were not gods. The real gods were not worshipped, and we suffered." Timas responded by rote, and automatically. He was tired.

"Okay, but those aliens, whatever heresies they plied on us, fled the Satraps and passed through here. We even found them a nice cometary belt that suited their needs, far, far away from noise and intrusion." Pepper sat now, his back against the wall.

"You helped them?" Timas couldn't believe it. "Ragamuffins helped them after the war?"

"They helped, in the end, fight the Satraps."

"They were the Great Liars."

"We didn't have much in the way of allies." Pepper folded his giant metal arms. "The Satraps controlled our technology. Even in defeat, they took with them most of their secrets. They suicided and took their minds with them. They destroyed almost all the factories that made antimatter, leaving us limping along from wormhole to wormhole out there. And now we know there are greater dangers out there, waiting for us, ready to prey on us. We are at a disadvantage. We need these technologies, and we need alien allies. The Satraps in the Forty-Eight worlds are all gone. And the other aliens . . .

"The problem is, they're disappearing, too, hiding, going to ground. Scared we'll pay them back, and rightly so. And now we've found them, but the Swarm is ready to wipe them out, and you in the process."

Timas thought about Van. "We need them that badly, the aliens? After all they did to us in the past?"

"Without these things they can give us, we are lost in the dark, Timas. And if you can get down there we have allies: the aliens will want to fight to protect themselves, and the Ragamuffins will help us out."

"That's a lot to be responsible for," Timas said. Again, he could feel a weight shoving down on his shoulders. That sensation again.

"It is." Pepper leaned forward. "But look, think about it like this: Bring me back an alien and you save your city."

"Haven't you sent xocoyotzin down already?"

"Two waves, they didn't find a thing. They also didn't stay down as long as I had hoped, the weather's been unpredictable."

Now Timas frowned. "Where did they look?"

Pepper smiled and stood up. He gave the order for Heutzin to bring back the map the xocoyotzin had updated with their search patterns.

It was back in fifteen minutes, and as Timas looked at the markings, Pepper pulled out a small glass tube.

"What's that?" Timas twisted the map around.

"Blood." Pepper gave it to him. "Infected blood. For the aliens to analyze. In case they might be able to find something to fight the Swarm with. They may know more about it than we do."

Timas pocketed it, and then folded the map up and pocketed that as well. "Okay." For the city. For Cen. For himself. What other choice did he have? How could he not try to save his own city and people?

"You're in?"

"Just one question." Timas patted his pocket. "How am I going to speak to an alien?"

"That's the least of your worries. They'll have translators and technology for that. You just worry about finding them. And use this next three hours in quarantine to get some rest."

"Okay." It wasn't hard to agree. He wanted to find

the aliens and prove that he was right, even if Pepper had convinced everyone else that he was right.

Timas had noticed on the map that the xocoyotzin had been moving away from the storm, in the direction he'd seen the alien. But why would the aliens hide in the open when there was the storm to hide in? Maybe Timas had seen an alien returning to its hiding place.

He'd head into the storm when he returned.

He also noticed the xocoytozin ventured out only as far as half their breathable air. If he was going to head deep into the storm to find aliens that were hidden, he was going to have to risk using all of it.

CHAPTER THIRTY-NINE

Itotia had them wait before lowering Timas. "You should give him the power pack in your suit. He'll have a better chance down there."

Pepper shook his head. "No." He needed it. In case Timas didn't return.

"You're a selfish creature," she said.

"Or maybe turning on a suit he never learned how to control would be more dangerous than letting him use it the way he knows how."

"But either way, he isn't getting it."

Pepper looked down into the clouds and wondered just how hellish it really was.

He looked over at Timas, waiting patiently in the open cage.

"We're losing time. Lower him."

Itotia stood by Pepper as the cage began its descent toward the ground. Timas stood stiffly inside in his great, buglike suit, next to a second xocoyotzin, Momotzli, also in full groundsuit. Timas waved on his way down.

The giant spool spun and whirred as the cage grew smaller, and then finally dipped into the muck of the cloud layer underneath the city.

"Once again, you've sent my son away from me." Itotia stepped back, holding an air mask to her mouth. Her eyes watered. Crying, or from the acid-tinged air?

Pepper wasn't sure which.

He also didn't reply. The universe was tough on humans. Young and old. And unfair. But why burden Itotia with that. It was better to let her keep her anger directed at him. Anger was useful, Pepper thought, and always appropriate.

"So when will you be leaving us?" Itotia asked.

Startled, Pepper stepped back. "What do you mean?"

"I remember something you said, back aboard the airship when you gave Timas to be beaten by Luc over and over again."

"And that was?"

"Don't die for a cause when you can come back later and inflict more damage. You know you'll be able to do more with the Ragamuffins than here, with us. You won't be sacrificing yourself for this cause; you have an out, don't you?"

"The mongoose-men, I formed them, centuries ago." She was right. "They're damn effective. I'd like to bring them back."

"We're in the DMZ, you said they won't come

without the aliens. What if Timas comes back by himself, like all the other xocoyotzin?"

"We cross that bridge when we come to it," Pepper said.

"I thought you hated politicians, now you give me their excuses."

Her words hit sharp and hard. Calculatingly effective. "I bet a lot of people underestimate you." Pepper thudded toward her. "I wonder if Ollin's jockeying for power is really you behind him?"

Itotia stepped forward, eyes narrowed. "I love my son. So does Ollin. I see Timas in the middle of the night crying, and when he doesn't tell us why, we're not stupid. We know the weight on his shoulders. A whole city? Look at how tired he looks, how old that boy's eyes are. We love our son, both of us. We do everything in our power to make sure that when he no longer fits in that suit and serves, that he will be taken care of. Wouldn't you do the same?"

Would he? Pepper thought about it. He'd been relieved to see Timas alive. But was that because he had a chance to find the aliens again, or was it because he'd been impressed, and glad to see the kid return?

"I don't know."

She backed off and deflated slightly, the tension gone. "How long before you leave?"

"Six hours."

"And he has five hours of air." Itotia brushed her bangs aside. "Can you take him with you when he returns?"

"The bubble can carry me in my armor. If there is time for me to shuck it and get in with him, yes. If there isn't, I can't."

Itotia swallowed. "I guess that's as fair as I can hope for."

"Fairer than most will get on this city."

"Just do one thing?" she asked.

"What is that?"

"*Make* sure you have the time to get him aboard." She tapped the metal collar with her hand, then turned and left Pepper by the hatch.

PART SIX

CHAPTER FORTY

At the surface the elevator's screws dug in and the cage's lip bit into the ground. Timas opened the lift door and stepped off. He looked around at the heat-rippled landscape, gaining his bearings. Momotzli stumbled after him.

Timas turned around. He'd never buddied with Mo before. When Heutzin had asked who the second xocoyotzin on the ground would be, Mo's intense father had pushed Mo forward.

One didn't go alone to the surface.

Timas got the impression, though he couldn't say for sure, that Mo was not excited about being volunteered. He hadn't spoken at all, just accepted his father's orders and walked to the nearest groundsuit like a prisoner receiving his sentence.

Now the two of them stood in the murk.

Timas tapped Mo's faceplate and took the lead. He could see the dim form of the cuatetl, and steered them step by heavy step toward it. The wind kicked wickedly today. It scoured up the muck and struck hard enough with the occasional gust that Timas worried about falling over.

Mo stayed behind him. Using him as a windbreak, and also close enough behind to try and catch him if he fell.

The sound of wind against the suit filled his ears as Timas moved on. Sweat dripped down his forehead.

During the long drop to the surface, he'd gotten used to the body odor of the suit again.

At the cuatetl Timas took his bearings again, remembering the incident. The thing he'd seen had been 30 degrees off from where the cuatetl pointed, as he'd told Pepper. That was the direction to strike out in. It seemed.

But that was not in the direction of the storm.

Timas checked to make sure Mo followed, and then started the hike.

A small windup timer hanging around his neck inside the suit ticked. It would sound two alarms. The first, at the halfway point, warned him to turn around and get back to the city.

The second told him when to expect his air to run out.

Rock rubble crunched under his feet, and he had to stop several times to let the suit catch up to his heavy breathing and dehumidify the interior. Water droplets and condensation covered his visor, making it next to impossible to see out.

Behind him, Mo struggled. Timas occasionally paused to let Mo catch his breath for a few minutes before starting up again. When he glanced back during these breaks, Mo looked frightened and tired through his faceplate.

The wind increased noticeably an hour into the brutal trek. And with visibility this low, the distant strobelights on the lift had disappeared long ago. Timas checked the small radio compass frequently to keep them on track.

And the march continued. Every ten minutes the wind seemed to increase. Timas now bent forward to counter it, and occasionally a small piece of dust would smack the suit loud enough to startle him.

It got better in the second hour as the land rose to their right, creating a windbreak. The wind and dust flowed just over their heads, although now they had rocks and boulders to climb and worry about tripping over.

Timas skirted the hill for the next hour, and at fifteen minutes before the two-hour mark they both stopped, huddling against the bottom of the hill. Timas pressed his visor against Mo's.

Mo dripped sweat as he yelled, the faint words almost drowned out by the ever-present roar of wind overhead. "We are almost at the turn-back point."

Timas yelled back. "I know. I'm going to keep going."

"You'll get us killed."

"I'm not asking you to go with me." He and Mo blinked. But he knew that he had to continue on, and he'd been wondering how he was going to say it to Mo. It was a terrible burden to put on Mo, too similar to the burden Timas had gotten thrust on him when Cen died, and he'd had to face Cen's relatives. "I want you to turn back. I'm going to keep going in."

"I will wait here then."

"Momotzli, I'm not going to be back in half an hour. You should start back now."

Mo shook his head sadly. "My dad believes the heresy. That's why he sent me. If his son were the one to help welcome the true gods, the incarnate gods, back to our society, what honor he'd bring. Now you'll throw your life down for this as well?"

"No." Timas shook his head. "It's something different. Just, trust me, I don't believe the heresy."

Mo didn't believe him. "I would try and drag you back, but I would kill us both trying, and I'm tired. What am I to tell your parents?"

"If I don't come back, that I'm sorry. I tried to do the right thing."

Timas pulled back. Mo stood there in his giant groundsuit, framed by a pair of boulders, as Timas turned around and continued on.

He hadn't paid attention to the ticking on his chest for a long period, too focused on getting around boulders and moving forward. When the alarm buzzed Timas jumped, and then laughed nervously to himself.

It didn't feel like he was killing himself, he thought, as he continued walking toward the storm. But he certainly felt all alone in the dim, brown light.

CHAPTER FORTY-ONE

Timas pushed on, reminding himself to keep checking the radio compass. It would be easy to lose track of time, or start wandering in the wrong direction.

He couldn't tell how many miles he'd walked, or how deep he was into the storm, but it felt like the winds weren't getting worse.

The steady rattle of debris against his groundsuit became a comfortable static. The limited visibility kept him focused on just getting from where he was to the next spot just ahead.

Muscle spasms hit. Knots of fire building deep in the tissue, trying to force him to stop. Signs of heat exhaustion. But if he stopped, he was just sitting still breathing, not getting closer to the goal.

Timas dealt with the dizziness and exhaustion by taking it one heavy step at a time. He blinked sweat out of his eyes, and scrunched them tight when the world around him skewed and spun.

It was a spell of dizziness that saved his life. Staggering his way up a slope he paused, swallowing several times to try and stop the nausea. Timas collapsed to his knees. The world spun and washed past him, and his vision blurred as he unsteadily moved forward.

When he looked back up he realized that he had crawled his way to the edge of a lip.

He inched forward and looked down over a precipice that didn't seem to end. A valley.

This was a landscape he had no map for. He couldn't cross that.

But what if the aliens were on the other side?

Timas followed the edge for several feet, looking for a way down. He didn't find one. A strong gust of wind blew a hail of pebbles at him. Timas held his hands up as they struck, trying to ward them off, and as he did so he fell over.

He heard the crunch from the rear. A radiator fin, or several. He had minutes to live before he cooked to death like Cen had.

Already he felt the edges of the suit warming up. Timas blinked tears from his eyes. He tried to move, but the effort was beyond him, the heat had beaten him.

There was nowhere to go, nothing more he could do but lie down and wait for the heat to take him.

CHAPTER FORTY-TWO

For a brief second, Timas thought he was hallucinating. Humans, not aliens, in sleek, form-fitting suits had surrounded him.

They picked him up and dragged him quickly along with them. He knew it wasn't a hallucination when his fingers burned against the suit's gloves as they jostled him. That was too real.

Timas wanted to be grateful, but he was too confused. He hadn't found aliens. But he had found people?

The figures dragged Timas into an airlock with a boulder that rolled aside as its door. Inside, once pressure was reduced to normal, heat normal, they skinned out of their suits, leaving just their gloves on to manhandle Timas's cherry-red and smoking groundsuit.

They cracked his helmet and ripped it off. Timas tasted brutal, cold air through his cracked lips.

"Stupid, stupid child," the nearest figure snapped. It looked like a woman with her black, silky hair cut short but with long bangs. They tickled Timas under the nose as she leaned forward. "Look at the light."

A bright light made Timas flinch.

"Okay, he's responsive. Let's get the rest of the suit off him and some liquids in him."

They had Timas out of the suit and on a stretcher. He felt the prick of a needle, and when he opened his eyes saw a bag of fluid swinging over him.

The woman saw him looking around. "You are a very lucky person."

Timas coughed. "You're people. . . ."

"Yes." A tight-lipped grin. "And I even have a name. Claire. And you were you looking for gods? We get those, wandering out in the storm from your cities, convinced they'll find that."

"No." Timas waited as she dabbed ointment on his lips. "I'm here to talk to the aliens. It's important."

"It's always important." Claire rolled up the sleeve of his shirt and put a patch on his shoulder.

"I was sent by the city because they know there are aliens hiding down here. I was sent to warn them that the invasion coming this way is coming for the aliens. It's an attack, and you're included. I'm not here for gods. After I warn you, I need to go back, to help defend the city."

Claire looked up at the others. "Well, that's a variant on the usual." She used a cloth to wipe his face off. "But you don't get to leave Hulbach. You're here for good, now."

"What do you mean?" Timas struggled to sit up. He wore his single white undersuit, and they'd left the timer around his neck, still ticking away.

"This is a place of refuge. A hideout. The stragglers we rescue from the surface stay, or choose to have this entire experience wiped from their mind before being returned. We're not cruel, but we do have our own survival to worry about."

Timas shook his head. "But I need to talk to the aliens, they need to know what is happening."

They moved him into a wheelchair as the doors opened. Timas had been lying in an elevator descending from the airlock. They wheeled Timas out into an antechamber with seven different corridors, all well lit, leading off like spokes from the elevator.

The two men that had helped pull Timas in remained behind at the elevator, like guards.

As the corridor continued it widened, and a strong, sweet breeze rushed down it. The sound of rustling reached Timas. The corridor ended in doors. Trees blocked his view from there.

The doors opened to let them through and under a large pair of palms that framed them. A set of gardens, deep underground?

Timas leaned back and looked far, far up to the top of a giant cavern, hundreds of feet over his head. Artificial lights blazed down at him.

He looked back, and as far as he could see were trees, grounds, and domed buildings. The walls all had windows and balconies looked out into this massive space. He felt like a speck. Cultivated gardens, park, roads: an entire world had been injected into this massive two-mile-long bubble under Chilo's surface.

At the center of the cavern hung a giant, round surface, surrounded by gently flashing lights.

"Welcome to Hulbach Cavern. Our refuge, our home. Right now, humans are rampaging across worlds. Sure, some hold to their home worlds and maintain their dominance, but humanity attempts to consume everything else, like a plague of locusts."

Timas twisted and looked back at Claire. "I'm sorry?" He wasn't sure what a locust was.

"Even now, in the air, the destruction continues that your species so loves. It's what we came here to avoid. Before humanity there was a three-hundred-year peace under the Benevolent Satrapy. But your species is still hungry, and thinks real estate and expansion equals success. We lost our wariness, our edge and distrust, and we paid the price."

Timas looked at her. "You keep saying 'we.' You don't consider yourself human?"

"You came looking for aliens. Here we are." She had walked out in front of him. Now she turned and smiled.

"I don't understand."

"This is a drone, I am talking through it to you. I am the Satrap Amminapses."

Timas stared at her. "You don't completely take over another's mind, you pop in and out as you please?"

"Some find it a compelling arrangement with the payment I offer. My examination of you is done. I am also done speaking with you."

It was like the Swarm, in many ways. Claire's face relaxed, and then reanimated. She shook her hair and smiled at him.

"Are you okay?" she asked. Then blinked. "I gave over, didn't I? Well, it looks like you got your audience with aliens after all."

She walked around and started pushing him toward a nearby building, curvy and low to the ground. "You still need some tests and further checking over."

"But what about the coming invasion? Your entire cavern is at risk!"

"The Satrap has decided not to interfere with this new war among the outsiders. Any war puts us at risk, but revealing ourselves? No, that is not going to happen. No matter how savage they all get out there." Even though she wasn't being used by the Satrap, she still sounded like she didn't consider herself human.

"You sit while danger gets ready to rain on you," Timas muttered.

"We have a way out." She pointed off over the treetops toward the center of the cavern at the top half of a circular void, encased in girders and beacons. "That's how we got here. A wormhole. Right now it's tied on the other side to an asteroid in the middle of a nowhere system."

"So you can just leave anytime? Why are you still here?"

"We can't use it right now. The wormhole is buried in the asteroid to hide it."

The path turned, hiding the wormhole behind trees. They approached a wrought-iron arch. Under it stood what looked like a large bird with razored spikes instead of feathers. It had flattened arms, with sharp, pointed hands holding a small ball. It sped toward him and ducked aside at the last second.

Timas didn't have time to turn to keep the alien in view, but the creature's flattened face slid over his right shoulder, the neck snaking around so it could look directly at Timas, face to face, an inch away. It smelled sharp, like a cheese gone bad.

Eyes the size of his fist regarded him without blinking.

Timas froze, looked over at Claire. "What is it? What does it want?"

"It's a Nesaru."

"And my name is Skizzit. I wanted nothing more than to tag you." The words came from a band on the alien's neck. A speaker. It was just like when Katerina had spoken to him without moving her lips. It pinched his shoulder, and then put the ball away in a red purse that hung near its breast.

"What was that for?"

"A tag. It will let me know where you are in Hulbach." Skizzit moved back to stand next to Claire.

"Skizzit is part of Hulbach security," she explained.

"I rolled the dice and was unlucky enough to get this assignment." It looked over at a set of bushes and trilled loudly. "Now that that's done, you'll rest and then get acquinted with Hulbach rules and regulations so you don't do anything stupid. We'll also need to find you a job."

"You don't understand, I'm here to warn you about

what's coming." Timas pulled out the vial of blood Pepper gave him back on Yatapek. "I have proof that this is not just a human issue. The attacker is alien, it's an infection that gets transmitted by bite and blood. It creates mindless bodies. And it's coming for your cavern."

Claire's eyes rolled back up into her head, and she staggered, then leaped back. She looked at Skizzit. "Was the human not unarmed and vaccinated upon arrival?"

The alien waved its arms. "It had no weapons. It received shots on the elevator down. Apparently the humans bringing it down did not bother to properly search it." It stomped the ground. Anger? Or frustration? Timas didn't know which.

Amminapses, or so Timas assumed, turned back to Timas. "Are you threatening us, bringing that bioweapon in here?"

"I'm not threatening." Timas glanced around, hearing bodies moving through the grass to surround them. Ten, then twenty, then thirty Nesaru slowly formed a circle around them. Suddenly those barbed quills didn't look so harmless. Even more worrisome were the black guns they had aimed at him. "We think you're the target of the Swarm. And we're caught in it as it comes here."

The inhabited Claire held out her hand. "Let's see it."

Timas hesitated for a second, and then gave it to her.

It was bagged and handed off to a human who had appeared in a clear plastic protective suit. Then Claire bent over and started pushing him quickly along. "You've upset the Satrap."

"You have only been here minutes," Skizzit said. "Already you are an incredible inconvenience."

The circle melted away.

"What's going on?" Timas asked.

"Quarantine. And thanks to your little stunt, I'm going to be stuck in there with you. So is Skizzit."

"I'm sorry."

"You're a fool, antagonizing the Satrap. You need to know your place." Claire led them into the nearest building, where the staff hustled them, from a respectful distance, into a small room with chairs. "It's dangerous to challenge it. It is the Satrap, you understand?"

When the door locked, it did so with a solid thud.

Timas wasn't going anywhere for a while.

CHAPTER FORTY-THREE

Momotzli returned in the cage, alone. Pepper watched Itotia crumple, losing that stiff posture as Heutzin ran to her side and helped her stay on her feet.

Pepper helped unsuit Momotzli. He leaned in close when the sweaty, exhausted teenager stumbled on his own toward a bench. "What happened?"

Momotzli had his forehead in his arms, panting. "He took me toward the storm. And then at the turnback point, he made me leave him and return on my own. He kept going."

Itotia left with Heutzin helping her along. Momotzli's chastened-looking father dragged him away.

They left Pepper alone on the docks facing the empty and still-steaming-hot groundsuit.

Heading into the depths of the storm made sense.

Risking his life for his city, that was admirable.

Pepper rubbed his face, tired. Beneath the weariness was a small trickle of anger.

Tough universe.

Yet, Pepper thought as he turned away from the groundsuit, he wanted that death to balance out somehow. And the only person that could guarantee to remember to tip the scales for Timas was him. Itotia, Ollin, everything would be gone soon. Yatapek couldn't resist the Swarm.

Even with him helping.

Pepper checked the power level. He had two and a half hours of constant use left.

It was time to get to that escape bubble and leave Yatapek. Then he would return and destroy the Swarm from above.

CHAPTER FORTY-FOUR

This is all so typically human." Skizzit stood in a corner of the room, while Claire folded her arms and sat in a chair with an annoyed look on her face.

"What do you mean?" Timas asked.

The birdlike Nesaru waved a quilled hand at him. "Your kind. Barging in, causing drama. No finesse. No civilization."

"My kind? We didn't create the threat that's coming," Timas snapped back.

"Well was it Nesaru who did it? I doubt it. Besides, who's creating chaos right now?" Skizzit shook its quills and ducked its face in them, cleaning them with its beak. "Your wars are spilling over again. Your violence and darker impulses come to light once more."

"It was the Satrapy and your kind that enslaved humanity. Would we be fighting so much if we hadn't been reduced to so little? You took us off the mother planet and scattered us across the Forty-Eight worlds. And you did worse." He thought back to Van's scars and behavior.

Skizzit puffed out its quills, doubling in size. "Your own kind sold you to the stars from your mother planet happily. Your kind starved in the millions on its own planet. We developed your other planets. We brought technology and civilization. Without us, you would *never* have gotten this far. You should be grateful to us for the lives you now live."

"You took advantage of us, exploited us, and now you pay for your sins." Aliens everywhere ran to hide from humans now. That made Timas feel good.

"My sins? My sins?" Skizzit stepped forward, and Timas stared at the needle-sharp tips of his quills. "I've never had any of you for a pet, nor taken any of you from Earth. Those things were done hundreds of years ago, human."

Claire watched the argument with a bored expression, but Timas turned to her next. The more he understood about these people, the more he might be able to get them to realize that the Swarm threat to them was real. "And what about you? How can you work for creatures that have done the things to us that these have?"

She smiled. "We have an agreement."

"What kind of agreement could be worth doing what you do?"

"How old do you think I look?"

She had small lines around her mouth, a hint of crow's-feet by the eyes. "Maybe thirty-five."

"I'm ninety-nine." Claire looked at Skizzit. "The prize is a life measured in the centuries, for one century of service."

That was the price it took for this woman to turn her back on her own kind and identify with the aliens, then. A tempting price. Without the city to return to, if they kept him here, what would he choose to do?

"Do a lot of people that you rescue on the surface stay here and take that prize?"

Claire nodded. "Wouldn't you?"

Timas changed the subject. "I was on the surface not too long ago. I saw one of you. And my friend died down there, when his suit got damaged. Why didn't you help us?"

"There was debris. It was too dangerous, or we would have. We do keep an eye on your surface activities. If you get too close with your mining machine or your people, we act to stop discovery." Claire stood up and looked out the door.

Another thought occurred to him. "If the wormhole is closed up, is that why one of you gave Heutzin a box to deliver?"

Claire looked off at the wall. "We are self-sufficient. There is no need to send anything. The ones who try to make outside contact . . . pay a dear price for breaking the rules."

Timas wanted to ask more, but the ticking from the timer stopped. It buzzed until Timas turned it off.

"What was that?" Skizzit asked.

"My air timer. As of now, the people who sent me think I'm dead." Timas sat down with his back against the wall with the timer's chain wrapped around his forearm. He dangled it just above the floor. His parents would be grieving, just like Cen's, for his death now. What a depressing thought.

Claire took a deep breath and squatted in front of him. "It is I, Amminapses."

"Yes?"

"You brought a dangerous thing here. Tell us exactly where you got this and what is happening."

Timas repeated everything he knew. Pepper's original encounter, the spread of the Swarm throughout the Aeolian cities, the attack on the processor, and then the news that a massive fleet, thousands of airships, now moved on this location.

"And there are people up there who suspect, strongly, that we exist down here. Not just the Swarm?"

Timas nodded. "Yes."

"Yatapek readies for this invasion. Pepper thinks the League of Human Affairs will come and clean up," Amminapses said. "But alone you will not be able to face it. Pepper is right, you need my help."

Skizzit jumped toward them. "No, you cannot do that! We have achieved stasis here again."

Amminapses held up a hand. Claire's face contorted into a strange and frozen expression of anger. "That is *not* for you to say. You will be quiet."

The words had the crack of authority, and anger at being challenged. Timas flinched at them, as did Skizzit, who folded its arms and backed away.

"This weapon you delivered, it's an extraordinary measure. An emergency tool. It is used to destroy civilizations and races."

"You made it?" Timas asked.

"Others made it, we are familiar with it. Organic DNA-based computing that uses clustering to achieve computational power at an exponential spread, with a goal-oriented artificial intelligence laid over the top. There's been a safety modification: a four-hour incubation period. As well as the new target. Us here."

"But can you help stop it?" Timas asked.

"We have worked in the past on a counter-infection. I will use drones and a ship to get you back to Yatapek. We need to at least slow this attack, yes."

Timas hated to do this, but he had to ask. "What do you mean, at least slow it?"

"It may be impossible to stop. It gets more intelligent as it grows. By now it is a formidable foe. As we infect it, it may be able to study what is happening and it may withdraw to find a cure. Our best ally is time, the virus is coded to let its host starve. It is designed to rage through a people, engage them in war, and then when it has spread all throughout, let them starve and whither away so that in time, the universe will hardly have known that the infected race even existed." Amminapses stood Claire up. "It's beautiful, elegant, and brutally effective. When the Satrapy ruled the Forty-Eight worlds, we never had the courage to deploy it. Our loss."

"We are released," Skizzit said. The door had unlocked itself. The alien held it open, and Claire walked through.

Timas got up and followed them out of the building. He gawked again at the giant arch of rock far over his head, lights blazing away from its apex, as well as the twinkling from the hundreds of thousands of windows in the rock's sides. Dwellings for humans, aliens, all living here.

But now the quiet of the gardens and the cavern had lifted. Activity spread all throughout. Timas looked at the sight of thousands of people, mostly human, moving crates and ferrying aliens in small electric carts toward the center of the cavern.

Timas saw the kind of alien he'd first spotted on the surface. A four-footed creature with a bulky chest, thick neck, and massive mouth. It opened its mouth wide to reveal tongues with multiple ends that would pick things up, or flick buttons and levers.

"Stop staring at the Gahe," Skizzit said. "They get annoyed, it's a challenge for them."

Timas stopped. "What's going on?" Everyone had exploded into action.

Skizzit pointed at the giant dark spot at the center of the cavern. "They're getting ready to leave. They'll fire the nuclear charges in the asteroid to clear it free of the other side of the wormhole, reopening it. Then we evacuate."

Amminapses added, "The threat of the Swarm is very serious. We need to delay it long enough to get off this planet."

Everyone here ran for safety, while Chilo's humans laid their lives down to slow the Swarm. He wouldn't forget this. Timas looked at Claire. He was really looking at the enemy of his enemy, he felt. A creature that had helped enslave mankind, and still thought of its fiefdom here as its own world.

Allies for now, but a friend, no. Claire, and the intelligence behind her, was something else. Dangerous. Like the ancient heresies: monsters manipulating humans and their fate. He was, Timas thought, facing a kind of devil. And making a deal with it.

CHAPTER FORTY-FIVE

Amminapses remained in control of Claire. It led Skizzit and Timas across the long width of the cavern into a new corridor, up a flight of grand sweeping stairs, and into a subchamber with heavy-looking, thick spheres. "Our transport back to your city."

"You have the cure already?"

Another Nesaru waited for them. It stepped forward and handed a black briefcase to Amminapses, who tapped it. "We adapted a counter-infection for your genome a while back, it just required synthesizing. It does not have a four-hour block."

"And you're going to give it to us merely to slow it down, while you run away? You expect nothing out of us?"

Amminapses looked at him, contorting Claire's face into some emotion that Timas couldn't identify. "You will be fighting it, correct?"

"Yes."

"That's all we need."

Skizzit tapped a five-number sequence on a translucent pad on the pod's shell. Timas paid close attention, trying to memorize the numbers. Just in case.

The hatch opened up and Claire stepped into the vehicle. She picked one of the five seats facing one another in a circle deep inside the armored sphere. They angled slightly up.

The seat reacted to her weight, shifting and adjusting its headrest to cradle her neck and head. Then padded arms reached out to hug her body into itself.

Skizzit went next, and the seat it chose radically reconfigured itself to accept Skizzit's anatomy.

"You're going with us?" Timas couldn't believe that he would be showing back up to the city with an alien in tow.

No one could deny he'd seen an alien on the surface now, could they?

Timas chose his chair and let it wrap around him.

"Ready?" Skizzit asked.

"As I can be." Timas tried to shift, but didn't budge. "Clear."

The interior of the sphere fell dark. A small screen

revealed the rocky roof a hundred feet above them. The sphere rumbled and rose toward it. Timas flinched as they appeared to dash themselves against it, but at the last second a pinprick of a hole grew into a large opening.

They shot through the tube in the rock until a point of brown light appeared, grew, and then they popped out into the heart of the Great Storm.

Instead of climbing, the sphere moved slowly near the surface.

"It's tough to keep a good connection to the cavern," Amminapses explained. "We keep the clouds of this planet well seeded with metal-consuming spores. That makes it hard to catch any leakage from Hulbach, or for radar to hit the surface. We can't afford discovery. We're keeping close to the surface to use a laser link to keep communications while in the storm."

Timas stared at the familiar murkiness as the sphere bumped and trembled along.

Amminapses released the chair restraints and sat up. "Among us, there are conflicting memories, early traces of a group story. Call it legend, creation myth, or maybe it is memories of our distant past."

"Okay." Timas sat up, and the chair let go of him.

"You should not tell them these things," Skizzit said. "You will give them leverage over you."

"I'm the last Satrap of the Forty-Eight worlds, but I am still a Satrap. I will do as I please, and you will be *quiet* now, Nesaru." Amminapses didn't believe in using the names of those who worked for it, it appeared. Claire's face turned back to Timas. "We are a created species, we understand this by examining our genetic heritage. We are massive so we cannot depend on rapid mobility like most species. We are forced to be symbiotic. Our tendrils can penetrate a conscious mind, adapting to the species after several attempts, and now with technology, we have extended these abilities and our range. We hunger for interesting new thoughts. And why would something like that be created? you ask. It is important, now that we face a new threat that may undo us both, that we understand this.

"You humans believe we are the enemy, out to destroy you, or at least inhibit you. That is true, but . . ."

Amminapses stopped, mouth open, and Claire shook her head. "Where are we?"

"Interruption," Skizzit said. "Lost a laser link."

Claire froze. Amminapses returned. "Among ourselves, we see that intelligence breaks out, flourishes, spreads, and eventually, inevitably, it comes to war with itself in its various forms. It fights, consumes, destroys, and upsets the balance of the universe.

"Farther out into the universe where you have yet to venture, this has played itself out with repetitive regularity. And the universe, whether as some larger organism, or whether via creatures that regard themselves as its stewards, has developed mechanisms to combat the ill effects of intelligent life. They seek out and destroy it, balance it, and through evolutionary pressures, force the creation of races that are better equipped to know their limits and cease their natural instincts.

"We don't know what created us. The counterforce, using us as a limiting mechanism to protect the universe? Or a mightier intelligence that wanted us to slow the spread of intelligents, to limit them to an area and give them more time to develop an awareness, a chance. Both stories had their adherents among my peers."

Amminapses folded Claire's arms carefully on her lap. Timas waited several beats before speaking. "The League of Human Affairs, the revolution, the Ragamuffins, and our history on Yatapek all agree that your kind set out to eradicate humanity from the Forty-Eight worlds. How can you defend that? That is not the work of stewards."

A raised finger. "But it was. You think our methods were harsh, but remember, humanity had several worlds to itself. Earth had been granted emancipation, and it had shut itself behind a wormhole. The birthplace of your species knew the universe was dangerous, and regarded expansion dimly. Chimson remained behind its own wormhole, and for a while, so did New Anegada, until the Ragamuffins colluded with another subject race to reopen the wormhole using very, very illicit technology. It was not an extinction attempt. It was a controlled burn. There are other Satraps, far out there beyond the Forty-Eight worlds. They have chosen more brutal methods. They alter races, change their genetics to make them docile."

The sphere cleared the storm. They rose now, headed toward Yatapek. How much time remained before the great Swarm fleet hit?

"It was hard to be so lenient, understand. These impulses are designed into us by the creators. When the revolution swept through humanity we felt our failure down to the DNA. We destroyed technology and factories that produced the tools you'd need to spread faster. We committed suicide, or we ran.

"But this weapon you bring now, it is not Satrapic. It's a weapon that those forces destroying intelligent life use. It's made by our creators, who we either worship or fear, we aren't sure which.

"It is strange to you, maybe, that we do not know what we are. It is strange to us. But understand that I remained the last living Satrap in the Forty-Eight worlds out of a hidden drive, put in me by something outside of my will, to salvage what I could out of the Forty-Eight worlds. This was to be the base on which I planned the repacification of humanity, creating warrens under the surface of Chilo until this planet was all mine. I had a hundred-year plan, and now I've seen it crumble in front of me and I realize it is time to let it go. I only ever have acted for the good of all species in the Forty-Eight. This agent, released, will not stop with humanity, it will adapt and set out to destroy all intelligent life here until the creators encounter its spread and deactivate it."

Timas stared at the alien before him, and it smiled back.

Skizzit broke the moment. "Yatapek is asking who we are, threatening to shoot."

"Tell them it's Timas, son of Ollin."

Once again, Timas had made it home. But how long that home would exist, he didn't know.

PART SEVEN

CHAPTER FORTY-SIX

Itotia stood alone in front of the airlock leading out to the rim of Yatapek, her arms folded, dress dirty from dragging through the dirt and corn. She'd run through the fire line that had been set up: a ring of ethanol-drenched ground and dried hay and cornstalks. The smell of the accelerant rolled off her.

Pepper had walked his way across the upper deck slowly, conserving power, muddying himself up as he passed by rows of armed people. The upper deck had a ring of older fighters with their billhooks standing in front of the fire line. After the fire line were the prime fighters, and then in the streets and rooftops, the children. Spears and guns, to cover the others if they fell back into the houses.

"You're really leaving us." Itotia's eyes were red. "I know you are a cold and soulless creature, but I didn't really think you would flee."

"I am a man of my word. I can do more, later, with the mongoose-men at my side." Pepper stopped in front of her.

"Are you even human anymore?"

"You work so hard to keep on my good side, all of you." Pepper pulled her aside. "But I forgive your grief."

"Wait."

"For what?"

"Don't you wonder how the gods will judge you?"

"Let them come get me," Pepper said.

Itotia stepped forward. "You have half an hour, still, before you said you'd leave."

"Is there a point in waiting? I saw you give up down there as well." Pepper looked down.

"And I was wrong." Itotia smiled. "Because we just heard that Timas is coming back up. He's in an alien airship of some make. It's asking permission to dock. I ran here the moment I got the call."

Pepper looked past her at the airlock. "What do we know?"

"I don't know anything yet. But you have a choice in front of you, don't you?"

He looked back down. "What do you mean?"

"You have thirty minutes left. It's close. Do you run off in your escape bubble, or do you throw your lot in with us? Instead of waiting for some vengeance in the far future with your mongoose-men, stand firm with us." She walked around him, leaving the way to the airlock open. "You talked about making the Swarm pay so hard it would choose to leave us alone. Why don't you give it the hurting that you wanted to when you were aboard the *Sheikh Professional*. Or, you can leave us, just like you left those people aboard that ship to deal with the Swarm."

She started to walk away, and Pepper grabbed the edge of the frame to the airlock.

"Just remember," she said. "You were wrong to give up hope an hour ago. You might be cold and soulless, but you still make errors of judgment. Think about it."

Errors of judgment. Like jumping out of a spaceship without a parachute? Pepper tapped the airlock door open and stood at the threshold.

CHAPTER FORTY-SEVEN

Timas jumped down out of the alien airship onto the metal grating of the docks. The ship had floated up through one of the large docking doors easily, small enough to fit through and land inside the docks, instead of tethering itself to the outside.

No one suggested he be quarantined. Dockhands and passersby, warriors with guns, and citizens with long curved blades mounted on long poles all lined the walls. And outside the city airships held their positions, getting ready to stand with Yatapek against the Swarm.

Behind Timas, Skizzit and Claire clambered down. Surprise rippled through the crowd as they spotted Skizzit.

Heutzin stepped forward with a massive grin. "You did it, Timas."

The grin was infectious. Timas grinned back. Before he could reply to Heutzin, though, Itotia and Ollin shoved past the crowds in the large hangar and ran to him.

Itotia crushed him to her, and Ollin grabbed both of them in a giant hug. Timas pulled away, embarrassed and feeling awkward in front of the crowd. "Mom, Dad, this is Skizzit, and this is Amminapses."

No sense in confusing everyone by bringing Claire's name in just yet.

"We are pleased to meet you," Ollin said.

"The pipiltin will be here soon to meet you," Itotia added. "We have to hurry, the Swarm is already engaging outlying Aeolian airships, it will be an hour or two before they reach us."

The floor beneath his feet shivered. Timas looked over and saw Pepper in his powered groundsuit move quickly through the crowd until he stopped in front of Timas.

"Well done." Pepper shook his hand. "Very well done."

"It's good to see you," Itotia said to Pepper. Timas recognized the triumphant look on her face, as if she'd won an argument.

Pepper brushed one of his dreadlocks aside. "I will help. But I can always steal that alien airship if things get too bad. Don't assume I don't have my own reasons."

He pointed at Skizzit. "So, we know at least the Nesaru have hidden down there, who else is dug in?"

Amminapses stepped Claire forward. "I am Amminapses."

Pepper cocked his head and raised an eyebrow. "Oh really?"

"You know of me?"

"I know the name that each Satrap called itself to humans," Pepper said. Pipiltin arrived on the docks now. "You disappeared, although I do know the League claimed to have captured you at some point."

"They lied."

Ohtli, Tenoch, Eztli, and Necalli joined them. "Camaxtli is unwell, the stress has left him bedridden," Ohtli said. "But he promises to abstain on any decisions."

"Okay. But it's too late to get Ragamuffins involved, two hours before the Swarm hits. They won't arrive in time." Pepper pointed at the two behind Timas. "What resources do the aliens bring to the table?"

"Amminapses has something that can attack the Swarm back," Timas said.

Amminapses held up the case. "I have a counteragent that will infect and nullify it. But there is the small matter of delivery."

Timas, as well as everyone in the tight crowd in front of the possessed human, listened.

"There is little time to mass produce it. This is enough to inoculate one human, and then that human will need to have contact with the Swarm to infect it. This poses a few problems."

"The first one is, who do we inoculate?" Necalli said. "We will need to find a volunteer. Or hold a lottery."

"No need." Amminapses carefully handed the case to Necalli, who held it gingerly, as if it might infect him. "This drone is human, and can serve for the purpose."

The pipiltin didn't understand, but Timas saw that Pepper did.

Timas shook his head. "No." It was a firm command. "Claire is the real owner of this body. You just rent it. She should have the right to decide her own fate in this matter. She is not just a receptacle for you to use."

"The boy is right." Pepper backed him up.

"I don't ask for your input," Amminapses said. "This method contains fewer flaws. This body I am controlling will not feel fear, or pain, or change its mind. It will go where I command it. You quibble over one life when so many are at stake?"

The Satrap had a point. Yet it felt wrong, and Timas couldn't help that gut feeling. Maybe humans were ruled by their instincts as much as the Satraps by their artificial instincts, laid into them to look at a larger, stranger picture.

Pepper took the case. If Amminapses thought he would get it from Pepper, the Satrap was mistaken. That Timas knew. "We will find a volunteer," Pepper grunted. "How long does the infection need to take hold?"

"Five minutes to drop the individual into a state.

Physiological changes take hours, but subject is infectious and no longer conscious as you know it at that point."

"Good, that's all I need."

That was that.

"The Aeolians will want to know about this," Itotia said. "We should include them, this might change our plans."

"The Aeolian avatar arrived and is in the communications room." Ollin grabbed Timas by the shoulder. "I'm sure she'll be relieved to hear that you made it back."

Katerina was back on Yatapek!

CHAPTER FORTY-EIGHT

Word had spread rapidly, because Katerina waited at the door with a big smile. "You made it back! It's good to see you. We were worried."

"She came over an hour ago, been in this room since." Itotia walked past Katerina and smiled. "Katerina asked to continue being the avatar so she could be here."

"My friends call me Kat." Then the relieved Katerina faded. The avatar facade returned. She walked over to a clear pane of plastic mounted in the center of the room. "It's crude, but it lets Yatapek see what's happening."

A crescent marked the mass of the Swarm and its location. An estimated time of contact had been scribbled at the top. Divisions of Aeolian and Ehactl airships similarly positioned themselves around the small circle at the center. Yatapek.

Katerina looked like she wanted to talk more, but with the aliens, pipiltin, and Pepper arriving, the room got even busier. The radio operators for Yatapek along the walls dropped their voices, but still passed on traffic and scribbled notes to give to the pipiltin or to commanders.

"We have two new things to add to our fight," Katerina told the group. "The first is Renata, who comes back with more of Captain Scarlett's friends. The Aeolian fleet is running a poll, but it looks like everyone is in favor of releasing Scarlett so he can lead the pirates. Their city was attacked, these are the survivors. We propose, if we all survive in any intact form, to give them participation in the Consensus."

"She made it." Timas had wondered whether Renata had outrun the pirates.

Katerina erased the crescent wave of the Swarm, and redrew it a bit closer to Yatapek. "Somewhat. After bubbling us off they got recaptured and their airship shredded. But as prisoners they witnessed the fall of Haven, the pirate city, to the Swarm. They decided to fly back to Yatapek. The pirates released Renata and her squad in the interest of mutual survival."

"Wow." It sounded like they had just as much an adventure getting back to Yatapek as Katerina and Timas had.

"The pirates also came back with this." Katerina waved her hand over a tiny box sitting near the center of the room. The air above the box danced and shimmered, then solidified to show the upper layer of a city. "Footage obtained from the attack on a nearby city."

It was packed with catwalks, tramlines, tube elevators, and a densely packed honeycomb of houses connected by latticework. It was like looking into a human hive. Some advanced materials, stretching with the city, but holding millions of people in that space where Yatapek had nothing but air and sun shining through the upper layer over its crops.

"At this point," Katerina said as an explosion rocked the side of the city, debris falling from the city's walls, "the citizenry knows what the Swarm is and how it works. The bites, the infection spreading, and so on. A standing security force is defending this city and the upper layer has just now been breached."

They watched as robed Aeolians advanced toward the fractured section of the city. The line hit the initial wave of Swarm pouring out onto a walkway just under the breach and high over the solid surface of the upper layer. And the Swarm fought back.

"Notice the initial line of the Swarm has weapons, but the second and third do not. We presume the Swarm does not have much in the way of personal firearms, most Aeolian cities have little if any, only its initial breachers are armed."

The initial swarm were not very accurate, either. But the Aeolians fell back, trying to avoid both gunshots and bites. But the Swarm did not rush as a whole, only the armed members moved forward at the Aeolians in the running gun-battle.

Defenseless Swarm jumped off the edge of the walkway, a waterfall of humanity.

Some smacked into tubes or catwalks. Others continued to fall until tiny white puffs of cloth opened up.

"Parachutes," Katerina said. "A Swarm airborne assault."

Down on the street level, a cloud of Swarm landed and moved with single-minded purpose toward citizens. From above, the footage demonstrated a fast pincer developing, herding the city's people into a large and tightly packed group.

And then the catwalk the Aeolian forces fought on exploded, three precise detonations in the middle of the Swarm.

As the long ribbons of metal failed, the Aeolian defenders fell out of the sky along with debris.

"There is more, but it's much the same. The Swarm is able to adapt to varying situations, as you just saw. It does not rely on infection and vectors anymore, it is using pincer movements, feints, weapons if it can get its hands on them. Obviously, since it waited for the parachuted Swarm to check in, it's using radios or equipment to communicate, not just the touch communication we've seen. That means it can spread out further and talk between itself faster. Which brings us to the next order of business."

Katerina addressed the pipiltin. "The Consensus has something else it would like permission to use. One of our defense airships has a nuclear device it managed to get off one of the cities. We include you in the discussion because your city is the dominant part of this action. We are not sure how to include your votes, so it was decided to let the pipiltin speak for all Yatapek."

"You have nukes?" Pepper was impressed. "I never heard that."

"Sometimes, even the Consensus can keep a low-level secret."

Amminapses looked distressed. "A nuclear device? Brutish, yet worthwhile. The Swarm uses touch for higher bandwidth, its effectiveness is reduced when separated. The electromagnetic pulse from a nuclear charge would prevent it from having high bandwidth communication. But it would also sever my ties to this drone. That is unacceptable. I need to be here to help coordinate against this threat."

"It would affect us as well," Katerina noted. "The

Consensus is held through this. We understand what we are asking. If it slows down the Swarm, then it's absolutely necessary."

"Still unacceptable." Amminapses shook Claire's head.

Pepper crouched down and opened the case and looked at the small vial with a tiny injection cap on it. He shut it again and addressed the Satrap. "We're not asking you, the pipiltin will decide. Unless you have a compelling force that can take to the air? I see just one Nesaru warrior with you, hardly a compelling force. We have the antidote, we'll deliver it."

He looked satisfied with what he held, and a large bit of the tension in Timas's posture dissolved. They had some sort of chance against the Swarm. Sure Amminapses believed that they were fighting to slow the Swarm down, but Pepper now held the tool that could defeat it.

"You all frustrate me," Amminapses said.

"You have less to lose," Timas said. "Right now you have a wormhole down in the underground chamber. You're getting ready to sneak back down it to safety somewhere else. We'll be the ones left up here."

"There is a second wormhole? On the surface?" Katerina was shocked. As was everyone else. It was news to everyone in the room.

"There is no way to evacuate you all." Amminapses saw what sprung into everyone's minds. "We don't have the capacity."

"Some of the Aeolians have craft that can get down there, some could be saved," Katerina said, her head cocked, listening to commands. "The Consensus sees this as an interesting development."

Amminapses backed up slightly. "I have hundreds of

thousands to get out to safety. They are my responsibility."

"There are children that deserve the right to escape this final showdown." Katerina's voice sounded gritty as she channelled the anger of the thousands of people in airships all around the city, the remnants of the once millions of the Aeolian Consensus. Timas watched as she stepped in front of Amminapses. "You are telling us you will leave us against the Swarm."

"You are ungrateful." Amminapses drew itself up, regal, arrogant, and sounding like they'd just confirmed a deep suspicion it had about humans.

"*We're* the ones dying." Katerina stood up just as straight to the Satrap.

"If you insist, then keep the counter-infection and fire your nuclear device. We will warn the cavern and I will take my drone and move back far enough that my equipment isn't hurt. I will return to observe."

Timas wondered why the Satrap was not as upset as Timas expected it would be at being defied. He'd seen it react down in Hulbach. Angry. Here it seemed to expect a script, almost.

Maybe Timas had been thinking wrong, assuming Yatapek was the most important section of this creature's plan to delay the enemy. They had been given the counteragent, but what if Amminapses had lied, and had made more?

Timas slowly backed out of the room as Katerina updated the clear screen to represent the Swarm's continued approach.

Outside Timas ran for the docks, sliding down rails and tearing across gantries until he got to the sphere.

Several Jaguar scouts had it surrounded, rifles slung at the ready. But they recognized him.

"I left my timer in there. It was a gift from my father when I became xocoyotzin," he said. A lie, he'd left the timer down in Hulbach. But they didn't know that, and let him through.

The hatch had shut, but Timas closed his eyes and mentally ran back the numbers he'd seen Skizzit tap to open the hatch.

It worked.

The hatch rolled open, and Timas pulled himself inside and let the hatch close. There were places under the seats to store things. Maybe Skizzit, or another drone, had hidden something there.

He slid doors open and checked under the seats, moving quickly.

The hatch opened and shut behind him.

Timas turned around to face Skizzit. The Nesaru's quills prickled up. It very deliberately blocked the way out. "What are you looking for?"

The hatch hadn't, Timas saw, shut all the way. If he could run, it would just pop open.

"My timer, I left it here. I had it on my neck, it had sentimental value."

Skizzit cocked its head. "You lie. You left it in Hulbach, and did not seem overly emotional about it. I repeat, what are you looking for?"

"Nothing." Timas tried to dart around the alien. It slapped him with the side of its flat arm, driving the edges of the quills into his shoulder.

Timas dropped to his knees. Blood dribbled down his chest and arm as Skizzit forced Timas to sit down. "I think," it said, "that you are up to no good. Again, what are you doing here?"

The hatch flung open and the entire craft rocked as a pair of giant metal hands grabbed Skizzit. Pepper hunched in the opening, not able to fit through to get inside. The Nesaru twisted, writhing to get away. It threw quill-backed punches at Pepper, who fended them off with his armored limbs.

Skizzit aimed higher, for Pepper's unprotected face. Pepper yanked the alien out, leaving Timas holding his shoulder alone inside the craft.

He stumbled forward to see Pepper and Skizzit face each other.

Skizzit pulled its gun free of the pouch and Pepper leaped into the air, higher than a person stood, and slammed both fists down on the alien's torso. He crushed the alien, stomping on it with metal boots, once, twice, and then one last time for good measure. Clear fluids and entrails burst across the grating and dripped down between the metal slots. A hand jerked, a foot splayed out at a right angle from the destroyed torso.

Pepper stood up, shaking goop off a metal hand.

Amminapses appeared at the edge of the dock. "You killed one of my vassals, why?" Its angry voice projected across the entire dock.

Pepper stepped backward to stop it from getting into the craft and near Timas. "Your pet Nesaru tried to shoot me."

"It probably had a good reason." Amminapses stepped over the corpse without a second glance and folded its arms in front of Pepper.

"Timas, you mind explaining why Skizzit just tried to kill us?" Pepper asked. Timas faced the back of the man's dreadlocks, and looked directly over at Amminapses.

"Why only one dose of counter-infection? I don't trust Amminapses. I wanted to see if there was more in this ship. Maybe it plans to use some of us, like Katerina, who can access lamina, to be its drones to go forward and infect the Swarm."

Pepper grabbed Amminapses. "Is there a second cure?"

Amminapses struggled to get free. "Let go."

"Where is it?"

"You think you accomplished anything, boy?" The Satrap froze. "I am, right now, launching three more craft into the sky, all loaded with counter-infected drones. The Swarm needs to be infected early, not late in this stand. Before it gets over the storm. You are being too tentative."

"We infect them once we get into hand-to-hand combat," Pepper said. "That way the Swarm can't blow the counter-infection out of the sky before it even reaches it."

"You still dream that you will all survive it. I doubt this will happen." Amminapses shrugged. "We have chosen our directions. I have maximized my chances of spreading the counter-infection, with you as backup. Yes, there are extras. Take them. It means little in the end."

Pepper waved at the nearest soldier. "Tie it up, put it in a cell, whatever you have, make sure the Satrap's 'representative' doesn't go anywhere."

"Is this how you treat an ambassador?" Amminapses snapped.

Pepper's dreadlocks fell forward as he leaned in. "I don't trust you being up and around. You have your own agenda, for now it's similar, but that is never a guarantee with the Satrapy, is it?"

"I work for the benefit of all."

Pepper saw to it that Amminapses was dragged off. Katerina, the pipiltin, and Timas's parents now stood staring at them.

"I think they're a bit unhappy with us," Pepper observed with a wry grin. He pointed at the warriors. "Tear the inside of this ship apart. We're looking for an extra vial."

They looked uncertain. Pepper strode forward, the grating jumping with each powerful step. "Now! Get moving."

Several scurried to the sphere. Timas followed Pepper. "What about Hulbach?"

"What?"

"The cavern under the Great Storm."

"Ah." Pepper waved Katerina over. "Tell any Aeolian with a craft to get to the surface, start seeing if they can get people in groundsuits to get into the cavern down there. At the very least, the cavern might be a better place to hide the youngest."

Katerina nodded. "We're already working on sending down some crack teams with them, whoever we can spare, in case they try and shut us out."

Timas moved closer to Pepper. "But how are we going to save the other three people that the Satrap is going to kill?"

"We don't. You want us to risk airships, lives, to try and intercept those three? No, they're already dead. And maybe they'll get lucky and get through. Or maybe they won't. Either way, kid, you saved one life. Be happy with that. When we fire off that nuke, when the Swarm gets close enough we're not wasting it, maybe she'll even thank you for it.

"Take what wins you can get, because they will be few and far between from this point on. Now, I'm off to get ready, we have a little over an hour before the main force hits."

Pepper walked away. As he passed the pipiltin he jerked his head in the direction of Timas. "Have someone clean the dead alien off the floor, too, when you get a chance."

The stunned leaders of the city just nodded.

CHAPTER FORTY-NINE

Back at the communication room Pepper looked at the board. The crescent of approaching Swarm on the clear status board had been updated. The radio handlers worked via instructions from Aeolians calling in the new guesses as to where the edge of the Swarm was. Katerina had left to see what happened on the docks.

Pepper took the radio. *Midas Special* was there, and Jack was upset. "We can't pick you up, we getting ready to break orbit. League ships coming in from all over."

"Peace, brother. I'm not bubbling up, and it's probably too risky for you to have tried to dip in and back out just for me." Pepper licked his lips. "How bad is it up there?"

"They doing the same thing as all we Raga, you know? They using merchantships, with armed crew. Look normal, but they been juggling schedules, hiding extra ships in the DMZ. Now here they all is."

"How many?"

"Over the air and in the clear?"

"We all know each other's cards now."

Static washed over the radio for a moment, an edge of jamming, but then *Midas Special* punched through. ". . . fourteen ships, all that into consideration. All light. Nothing coming through the wormhole yet, but we can expect it."

Fourteen. Pepper knew the Ragamuffins could spare four armed merchantships like the *Sheikh Professional*. And maybe two real attack ships, made for the expensive pursuit of war in space.

There'd been some serious clashes in establishing the DMZ, back in the days after the uprising. The League played for keeps, but once it started having trouble in its own backyard keeping down alien counter-revolutions and human breakoff movements, the DMZ became practical.

So how hard was the League playing now? This handful of merchantships hardly seemed like a vast attack force. The League had fought over the DMZ the first few rounds with much larger numbers.

Pepper toyed with the mic. If this was a feint, and they'd managed to hide League ships anywhere near New Anegada, he would risk an entire planet with his next request. The land of Aztlan and the land of Nanagada, all at risk.

Yet, to throw Chilo to the League . . .

"*Midas,* tell the Dread Council we have a Satrap on the surface. Tell them a whole nation of aliens is hiding under the Great Storm, it's what the Swarm is trying to get to, in addition to taking everyone else down for the League to mop up later. This isn't a feint against New Anegada, it's all about Chilo and the aliens here. It's worth the fight, tell them Pepper said so. Get clear of orbit, come back bristling, you hear?"

"Loud 'n' clear, transmitting it along the line now. We go respond back, we go take, maybe a half day. Burn some serious fuel. We'll be back."

And that was that.

The cavalry had been called. Ragamuffins scattered throughout the DMZ and New Anegadan space would be on the move. The special forces of the entire organization, the mongoose-men, soon would be descending up on Chilo. Help would arrive.

If they could last long enough.

And in doing this, he was requesting the Ragamuffins to burn most of their fuel reserves, putting them in a weak position to defend themselves and ply the spaceways in the near future.

CHAPTER FIFTY

Katerina intercepted Timas. "I have a gift for you."

"Okay." Timas followed her as she dragged him along the docks to a storage room filled with wooden crates stamped with barcodes. He'd just finished visiting his parents, both of them pressed for time. Itotia had helped organize the women's resistance, getting them billhooks, teaching them to use them. And Ollin, always the unofficial pipiltin, kept busy involving himself in everything the city's leaders did.

Itotia had told him about Pepper's escape plan, and the bubble, when he'd asked her why she'd been looking so triumphantly at him. "Be careful of him," she said. "He does have a weakness for getting involved in causes, I think, but there is a limit. I think he's liable to leave you for dead when it really comes down to it."

Timas filed the knowledge away.

Now he watched as Katerina zeroed in on one crate in particular, pressing her thumb on the keylock to open it. Inside sat a pair of thick machine guns.

"This is a Sharkov 9." She held it up, somewhat awkwardly. "The Consensus moved these over, and I requested some particularly for us. I've never fired anything before, but this one has very low recoil, which is good for amateurs like us, explosive rounds, and a grenade launcher. They're also very light." She was reading off a script.

She gave it to him, and Timas hefted it. It was indeed light. "I've never fired one either."

First she had him add his thumbprint by pressing it against the top of the stock. "If you lose it in battle, it can't be used against you." After that, seeing some hidden manual in the air that she'd called up but that he couldn't see, she showed him the basics. "Traditionally, this is illegal for me to hold. Consensus doesn't like teenagers handling this kind of weaponry. But we're rewriting Consensus law on the fly right now, and we have these to protect ourselves with."

There were five grenades already loaded in it, and one full clip with a hundred rounds. The safety, the built-in thumbprint on the stock, pulsed green slightly. "It's live."

They practiced holding the gun with their fingers to the side of the trigger, stock snug on their shoulders, the flip-up readout giving Timas information he couldn't interpret. "Don't worry about it," Katerina said.

It took fifteen minutes, and Timas felt somewhat confident that he could fire the weapon. "Thank you."

"You're welcome. I wanted you to have it. I wanted to come back. I was relieved when I heard you were safe. I worried about you down there, and when your mother came up to tell me you'd stayed . . ." She clipped a strap to the gun and looped it up over the back of his neck, hand brushing Timas's cheek as she did so, and then clipped it back around.

The Sharkov hung near Timas's stomach. The strap bit into the still bloody punctures from Skizzit, but Timas didn't complain. "Thank you," he repeated awkwardly.

"This all feels like a dream." She still held on to the strap.

"A nightmare."

"If I live, I don't think I'll ever be quite the same."

"I know."

She hugged him, tight and long. He hugged back, with a silly smile on his face. All the Aeolians in the new Consensus, hanging around their city, would probably be able to see him. Who knew how many thousands saw his silly grin right now? He didn't care anymore. "Where are you going to fight?"

"I should go with my parents, but I really want to be near Pepper. You've seen how dangerous he is. I think he's seen fights like this before, and I think anything I can do to help him is good."

Katerina let him go. "I think you're right. I'll see you there, then. The Consensus thinks my being near Pepper is important as well."

"Just be careful, okay?"

"You too."

Together they walked back out onto the docks, both carrying their machine guns, safeties thumbed back on.

CHAPTER FIFTY-ONE

Heutzin stopped Pepper outside the communications room with a quiet, almost bashful manner. He held a long wooden box out to Pepper. "For you."

Pepper took it, accidentally crushing a corner with his grip. Inside lay his sword. "Heutzin . . ."

"You'd mentioned wanting it back earlier."

A big grin. Things were coming together, Pepper thought. Heutzin handed him the scabbard as well.

Pepper fastened it to his metal waist. "Thank you. Now what do you want?"

Heutzin grinned. "Yes, I do have an odd favor."

"Let's hear it. Walk with me." They advanced toward the atrium. They dodged crates, walked past barriers of wire spun so fine it cut off limbs, and zigzagged around spikes welded to the floor.

And everywhere stood armed citizens and warriors.

"I have no family, Pepper. I never had children. I have no legacies to pass on, other than teaching my skills as a mechanic."

Pepper sighed. He saw what was coming. And he liked Heutzin; the man had helped him out and stood by him. It was going to be hard to hear what came next. "And?"

"I used to be xocoyotzin. A proud position in this city. I fell from everyone's favor, though. But still I love my people, Pepper. I love my city, that is why I was always happy to serve on the docks, fixing the suits, helping the boys as best I could.

"I'm getting old, Pepper, and I'm facing death here, defending my city. And I see a chance to do something noble, grand, that will take my name and make sure no one in this city ever forgets it . . . if it survives." Heutzin stopped and looked up at him.

The pipiltin would be relieved, no doubt, not to have to figure out how to get someone to volunteer to do the deed. Pepper nodded. He tapped his chest. Underneath, safe in a pocket, was the vial. "Stay close. The counter-infection will be quick once I inject you with it, so we'll have to wade out into the thick of it. You fight until you drop, so that the Swarm doesn't suspect anything. And you stay close behind me, until this happens. We don't want you getting hit by something random."

Heutzin let a long breath. "Thank you."

Pepper shook his head. "It is the others who should be thanking you, Heutzin. Come, I'll tell the pipiltin, and then let's go to the top layer. It'll be the best target for a landing on this city by the Swarm."

CHAPTER FIFTY-TWO

Heutzin had joined Pepper where Katerina and Timas already stood with him near the lip of the upper level. It gave a great view of everything happening outside the city.

According to Katerina, the horde's forces would hit Yatapek within the hour. It was a long hour. Long enough for Timas to realize how much the entire city had changed in just the days since he'd been gone. Pepper had been busy.

From Yatapek's atrium all the way out toward the rim of the city, Jaguar scouts, Aeolian soldiers, and civilians all lined the streets with weapons and body armor made out of whatever they could find.

Over the stately upper-city buildings where only the elite once lived, large mounted weapons waited to unleash hell on anything that penetrated the city's transparent walls. Mothballed anti-pirate guns had been taken out of retirement, transported through the city, and bolted in here.

The air vibrated with tension, and so did Timas.

Everyone had seen what the Swarm would do. No one had any doubt that this was a fight to the last one standing.

Ollin would be burning incense to the family gods while Iotatia waited in the courtyard. Timas felt he should have been there. But he also felt, as he looked out over the brown and red clouds below the city as if standing on the prow of a mighty ship, that the gods would understand his indiscretion.

Let his father offer something for his son.

Timas looked at Katerina. "Anything?"

Katerina looked up into the sky. Overhead the rag-tag fleet of Aeolian airships moved around the giant orb of Yatapek. Many of their hulls glinted. The paint had been stripped clean from flying in the protection of Chilo's acidic clouds to get to Yatapek. Mingled among them were the dun-colored cigar shapes of airships from Yatapek's sister cities, their noses painted with fierce teeth or feathers. They bore names like *Bloody Retaliator,* and *Sun God's Strike.* And among them, large spotter and barrage balloons painted with red and brown camouflage.

"Do you need to be shifted?" Katerina asked. Pepper had hardly moved the entire time. He'd been stood near the balcony on the level's edge for the last half hour, saving power. The mottled and rusted-out suit held him in its grip, both man and machine looking like not much more than an old metallic statue.

A statue holding a very large gun at one side, and a wickedly sharp sword of some sort strapped to the other. The recently polished edge glinted.

His dreadlocks shifted as he shook his head to Katerina's question. "I only get two and half hours when I power this up."

Pepper looked intently down at the clouds. "I wasted

enough clumping around the last day." A bead of sweat dripped down his forehead to his nose, balanced there, and then dropped to hit the breastplate.

Katerina twisted her head, listening. "They're spotting outriders. Scouting airships, just under the cloud layer."

But none of them could see anything in the murk below.

"There." Katerina pointed. "The Swarm's coming."

It looked like a cloud of gnats in the far distance against the haze and sharp sunlight, just skimming over the rust-colored clouds.

Timas felt numbness spreading over him as he realized the sheer immensity of what he was seeing. "There must be thousands of them."

Pepper snapped his fingers. "Tell your friends now is as good a time as any."

"Are you sure we're ready for this?" Katerina reached up and unconsciously rubbed the filigree of her silvered eye. She was about to be plunged into a form of personal darkness, Timas knew. Like standing in a dark closet, she'd said.

"We slow them down." Pepper looked around. "Now is the time."

"Then close your eyes," she said.

The very back of Timas's eyelids flared with actinic light, purple and yellow and hot.

When he opened them again, the giant fireball of the nuclear explosion burst out a cloud in the far distance, vaporizing the leading edge of the Swarm's armada. Tiny midges of airships slowly fell out of the sky, burning the whole way down.

Now there were just hundreds that had been lagging behind, regrouping.

"Now they know we're fucking serious," Pepper shouted.

Katerina shivered, cut off from her entire world now. She was no longer the Aeolian avatar, she was just Katerina. "Feels like chopping off our own arms just to hurt them."

"No. More like chopping off your arm to buy yourself a couple hours."

"Here are the scouts."

Pepper grunted and strained to move the suit unpowered. He leaned closer to look farther over the city's edge through the transparent aluminum shell.

Like lean sharks, ten jet-powered dirigibles shot out of the cloud layer toward the city. Twelve Aeolian airships dropped from around Yatapek toward them, and the dockside anti-pirate batteries began a steady thump.

Anti-airship fire blossomed, black puffs carpeting the sky below the city.

One of the airships crumpled as it caught a good shot and then continued to limp forward until the batteries zeroed in on it and destroyed it.

Now the Aeolian airships engaged, tracer fire creating a matrix of brightly colored lines all throughout the space under the city.

"We're holding them," Timas said. The Aeolians kept the scouts away from Yatapek, chewing up the attacking airships with well-aimed fire.

This might be a winnable fight.

Timas was about to open his mouth to say that when two scouts swung around and raced straight at the nearest Aeolian. All three of them watched as the first one burst apart before reaching its target, but the second struck nose-cone on.

Both airships crumpled, then slowly started to sink toward the clouds.

"We told the pipiltin and the Consensus they're suicidal." Timas shook his head. "They did that trying to get at us when we escaped in the ore processor."

"Any individual, any ship, is merely a small appendage. It's a group mind. It's one thing to hear it, another to see it." Pepper looked down as the wreckage caught flame, then disappeared into the clouds. "A bad way to die."

Slowly sinking down through the acid-soaked clouds, waiting for the heat and pressure to build to lethal levels.

The Aeolians reacted to the Swarm's suicide run by moving back and coordinating their gunfire attack via radios and the anti-pirate battery guns.

By the end of the first hour the first wave of scouts had been destroyed, and the second as well.

Now the entire city watched the full invasion fleet grow, details emerging as the midges turned into larger and larger cigar-shaped airships.

Timas wished they'd had more nuclear weapons as he looked back out up toward the approaching cloud of airships. The sun behind them glowed strong yellow, the rays twinkling and flashing throughout the fleet.

"Here comes the real battle." As if on Pepper's cue, the Aeolian fleet moved forward.

The entire air filled with explosions, smoke, tracer fire, and flashes as the hundreds of airships intermingled, creating random paths around each other, swarming through the air.

Wreckage dropped, spars, flaming stretches of cloth, and occasionally flailing bodies as airships scored precise hits. Anti-pirate fire constantly shook the ground on the top layer of Yatapek. The large ones mounted inside the city remained quiet, reminding Timas that the battle still had a long way to go. They would need those before the fight wrapped up.

The chaotic mass continued moving closer. A mile, a quarter of a mile, and then one lone Swarm airship burst through. All the defending airships had targets of their own. And this one flew too close to the city now to get targeted by antiship fire.

"Gods have mercy on us," Timas whispered.

The tip of the airship grew, bearing down on the city, but off to their right. Spars and rigging became discernible. The reinforced nose cone had been sheathed with metal, and a long spike on the end had been added by the Swarm. The spike ripped through the city's shell just above the rows of corn.

More airships broke through, smacking into the city. Each one pierced its way in. Different ships into different levels. Yatapek must look like a pincushion from a distance, Timas thought.

Air slowly leaked from the edges of the tears. Katerina glanced over at Timas, who reassured her. "We're high enough, the outside air pressure's the same. It'll leak, but slowly."

"And your bulkheads?"

"They'll be shutting them. Just like during any emergency holing." Although who could hear the breach klaxons over all this?

"Are you going to help them now?" Katerina asked Pepper.

He shook his head. The guns mounted on top of the buildings near the atrium started firing at the Swarm ships. These didn't thud, but chattered and howled as tracer fire lit up the inside of Yatapek.

From each ship ropes dropped, and figures crawled clumsily down, many slipping and falling to the ground.

Beside Timas Pepper now stepped forward, his whole suit whining and thudding forward with a snap-quick jerky motion as heavy gunfire hit the nose cones of the zombie airships.

"Do you see that?" Pepper asked, pointing down at the clouds.

The interior of Yatapek strobed with green and white tracers from the interior guns. The red flames of burning airships stuck to its hull reflected off polished surfaces and windows all around.

Pepper pointed down again. Something glinted in the clouds beneath Yatapek. A large shadow moved underneath them.

Timas's mouth dried as an Aeolian city laced with metal spars slowly burst from beneath the clouds, its entire skin scoured shining and bright.

"A whole city?"

Rockets glared as the entire structure adjusted course.

"There'll be millions of infected in there," Katerina whispered. They'd be simply overrun.

"Run." Pepper grunted at them as the last wisps of cloud fell away from the approaching city. "It's going to ram us."

CHAPTER FIFTY-THREE

The Aeolian city struck as Pepper ripped straight through the cornfields, leaving a swathe behind him that Heutzin, Katerina, and Timas followed through.

He could feel the shuddering underfoot, and the thuds, cracks from overhead. And a horrible, long, screeching and shrieking of superstructure: the impact twisted and broke the shell around Yatapek where the two cities collided.

When Pepper finally slowed and looked behind him the edges of the two cities were still combining in a mix of tangled girders, shattered outer layer, and inter-leaved decks.

Brown, noxious Chilo air ever so slowly seeped in between the two cities. The city wouldn't lose buoyancy right away, but the striking city had crippled them. Yatapek's layers and bulkheads could only hold so much air against a crushing blow like this, Pepper thought. They were going to have to cut loose the docks, or find some other way to radically lighten the city. While fighting back the Swarm.

Pepper didn't see Yatapek winning here.

"You okay?" He looked at his small group. They were shaken, but unharmed. They stood well clear of the impact zone, deep into the ranks of defenders get-ting ready to repel the Swarm. People had died from falling debris near the impact point, but since most had hung back behind the fire zone, away from the lip, Yatapek still stood ready to fight.

A runner sped toward them with a note in his hand. He gave it to Pepper and then wobbled in place, hands on his knees, hyperventilating.

From the pipiltin. Amminapses had, before collaps-ing when the nuke went off, gotten quite agitated. Apparently during their check of the getaway worm-hole, before setting off the nuclear charge to unbury the wormhole from the depths of its asteroid, they'd detected League ships.

A lot of League ships.

Pepper started laughing. Everyone stared at him, and he crumpled the note up. "Good news. Ammi-napses is just as screwed as we are. The League set a trap on the other side of the wormhole for the Satrap, no one in Hulbach is going anywhere, they're not setting off the charge, they're leaving the wormhole buried in the center of their asteroid."

They didn't have much time to celebrate, though. Already the older defenders at the far edge of the corn, armed with their billhooks, had engaged the Swarm dropping down out of the airships.

Now gangplanks and rope ladders were tossed out of the adjoining city into Yatapek. Hundreds of infected swarmed between the wreckage, and hundreds more lurked behind them. The river of stumbling bodies just didn't stop pouring in.

"Okay, Heutzin, let's roll."

Timas stepped forward with them, but Pepper shook his head. "You stay here. Katerina, too." He pointed out several warriors with rifles, waved them to him, and then checked the weapon the Aeolians had given him.

Sharkov 9. Nothing truly unique about it. Standard fare. He had extra rounds on his waist, the sword, and the suit still worked.

Pepper thumbed the safety, and the gun streamed information to him via the direct skin contact. He ignored the information laid over his vision and willed it to go away.

"Heutzin, it's been an honor." He shook the man's hand. Then louder. "Let's haul ass!"

The five men ran with him. Their heads down, whipping through the corn, they passed the fire line quickly enough, leaving the houses and barricades behind them.

And then it was into the men trying to hold the line with billhooks. The first line held up shields and wore thick, makeshift padding so that the infected couldn't bite through to their skin. Behind them, three rows deep, the long billhooks lashed out, trying to decapitate the infected before they even got close enough to hit the shields.

Looming over them all was the ruined mess of the contact point, girders tortured into strange and surreal shapes, layers visible with their edges cracked, warped, and sagging.

And the Swarm stretched out before them, a crowd of corrupted humanity acting as one.

"Coming in!" Pepper yelled. Shooting the approaching Swarm to give them space, they slipped in right behind the shields, as if part of the defensive structure.

The Aeolians had to have guns, but so far the Swarm didn't seem armed. It might be holding those back, or saving them for the attack on Hulbach, not thinking that this city would be such a tough nut to crack.

Pepper reached under his chest plate and pulled out the vial. He flicked the tab off the top and jabbed Heutzin. "We fight. In a few minutes, you will start feeling it. You don't run out there, you let me handle our fallback."

Heutzin nodded, eyes wide.

Pepper tapped the soldiers to the right after four minutes. "I need you to fall back, as if tired and wanting to exchange places with others, fumble about. We're going to lull them in."

He didn't tell them what was about to happen to Heutzin, he wanted their surprise, their natural reactions.

They did exactly what he asked, and as they fumbled, the wall broke, Swarm dashed forward. Heutzin moved to stop them, getting out in front of the shields.

For a moment the gunfire Pepper laid down, along with the other warriors, kept the bodies dropping.

But then the first one got Heutzin, biting his arm.

A second piled on, and then Heutzin was dragged into the crowd. After knocking him out they left him alone.

Pepper moved back, trying to find a higher spot of ground for a better vantage point, but several of the Swarm paused, looking at him together. They stood at attention, and started shouting.

"You!"

"You are the one."

"The one known as Pepper."

"We wish to speak to you."

"We will keep a zone free, we will cease our attack here."

"For now."

And just like that, the line in front of him froze. The empty eyes all locked on Pepper. Like sand, behind that front line, the others started moving sideways, heading off toward other areas to attack as they streamed in.

"What do you want?" Pepper asked over the sound of steady marching.

"An offer."

"This city is well prepared, and will cost us."

"Not too much that we cannot reach the aliens below."

"But enough that we make an offer."

"It is only certain aspects of your consciousness that are dangerous."

"We can offer you an infection that does not degrade your individuality."

"We will only blunt your baser instincts for progress and expansion, and you will be allowed to keep your individuality."

"Imagine, how fulfilling it will be to maintain your sense of self, but not feel compelled to consistently war, struggle against new environments, and dash yourselves against the universe."

"We offer you true and total peace. Many of the remaining people aboard these cities in the middle layers have taken this option."

Pepper saw Heutzin stirring, slowly sitting up, a vacant look in his eyes. "I have a philosophical offer of similar import for you," Pepper shouted back.

They waited expectantly.

Pepper, with a straight face, looked out at the entire crowd of the Swarm and said, "Bite me."

The crowd surged forward, but he could see Heutzin muscle over to one of them and bite it right in the neck, then turn for another. Bits of the Swarm noticed that something was wrong, but Heutzin attacked them as well.

"Take their heads off," Pepper yelled. "Press them." Add some confusion to the mix.

As he walked away, Heutzin ran off, biting everything he could. Already fifteen Swarm were counter-infected, but still standing up, so they turned back to their duties.

By the time Pepper passed the fire line at a slow amble, the fifteen Heutzin infected had turned and started biting other Swarm nearby.

Consciousness might be a liability, but right now it was coming in handy, Pepper thought.

CHAPTER FIFTY-FOUR

From their vantage point Timas and Katerina could see Pepper coming back through the corn, leaving a long trail of broken stalks behind him. The first line of billhook fighters slowly retreated back as well, and then as they hit the fire line they ran.

The Swarm didn't take the bait; the crowd paused at the edge of the soaked corn and slushy mud. Behind them, where the two cities remained locked together, more Swarm slowly laid down more gangplanks and ropes. A road of makeshift bridges zigzagged its way through the debris from city to city. Swarm marched along it toward Yatapek's fields.

"Damn," someone by Timas muttered.

Katerina had been listening to a small handset, hardened against electromagnetic pulses. It was what was left of Aeolian communication. She grabbed Timas by the shoulder. "Timas, Yatapek is losing altitude."

They both glanced back to the crushed mess where the two cities remained joined. "Too much Chilo air getting in."

She nodded. "It's going to slowly get worse."

Pepper broke out of the corn and walked past the defenses onto the street below, then hopped one story up to land on the edge of the wall near them, crouching on the edge. "Trouble?"

"Yatapek is losing buoyancy," Katerina told him.

"Shit. I'll be back." Pepper dropped off the edge and took off at a run.

Timas looked out over to the city that had hit them. They hadn't been thinking on the same scale as the enemy, where a city could be a weapon. What other mistakes where they going to make?

He squinted. There seemed to be more chaos in the Swarm's ranks. Zombies bit other zombies. The counterinfection slowly spread.

But still, there were tens of thousands darkening the better part of the rim that Timas could see.

Katerina tapped his arm. "Strandbeests!"

Five of the massive creatures, or constructions, had moved swiftly in on one of the Swarm's ships attached to the hull of Yatapek. One of the Strandbeest's spiked tips pierced the airship's gasbag. As it deflated other Strandbeests swept in, pulling lose rope, rigging, fabric, and anything else they could tear free of the dying airship.

"Van said he hated aliens," Timas said. "He's helping us."

"Or they're scavenging." Katerina pointed out a pair of strandbeests swerving at a damaged Aeolian airship dead in the air.

"Who cares? They're helping pick at the Swarm airships that made it through to the hull." They'd take any help they could get at this point.

CHAPTER FIFTY-FIVE

Pepper found the pipiltin gathered with engineers, looking at old, yellowed copies of the city's blueprints. Someone used an orange to hold an edge of the paper down. "You heard?"

"We're falling."

They were trying to figure out the best way of sealing off the upper level. But it wasn't going to help, other levels struggled with airships penetrating the shell, and the upper layer was a very buoyant section. "We're going to have to seal it, or start throwing whole buildings off the side somehow," Necalli said.

"Another problem." Ohtli stood behind Pepper, who turned to see that the pipiltin, sweaty and breathing heavily, had pulled a stretcher along with him. "Look at this."

He ripped the sheet off the corpse to reveal one of the Swarm's victims, but it hardly looked human. The face looked stony, and the skin abnormally thick.

Pepper rapped the thick skin. It was skeletal. "Serious gene tweaking going on there. The Swarm's adapting them for high-pressure environments, they're going to be dropped to the surface."

The new type had a secondary eyelid grown into a thick, glasslike enclosure over the eye. The shoulder structures Pepper had seen in orbit had grown into heat-dissipating fans.

"We can't lose to this," Necalli said.

"We've started to order dockworkers to ferry out on Aeolian airships docked at the city." Tenoch now stepped forward from his fellow pipiltin. "We can ferry them to other ships, but we can't evacuate Yatapek, there's nowhere for us to go. And the farther we drop, the more Chilo's air will be forced in and replace ours. We'll fall faster and faster."

Between facing the hundreds of gangplanks between the two cities and Swarm boiling into the upper layer through that gap, as well as the impending fall, the pipiltin realized that they faced the death of everyone in the city.

The orange rolled slightly, and Necalli grabbed it absentmindedly.

Pepper frowned and took the orange from Necalli, and set it back on the center of the table. He let go of it. It rolled, very slowly across the table until Necalli caught it again.

"I think I have a solution," Pepper said. "What's holding that side of Yatapek up?"

They didn't get it at first, and then Ohtli did. "The city that hit us."

"Aegae, I'm told, is its name," Pepper said. "Obviously it isn't as damaged: better bulkheads, design, whatever. It's pulling that side of Yatapek up. We know if you hole a city it doesn't lose too much air to Chilo at this height, the air pressure is similar enough inside and outside, so that city is just in better shape than ours. We storm it, we take it."

"The Swarm must have millions aboard," Necalli protested.

"Maybe," Pepper said. "Or maybe not. The Swarm tried to offer me a truce again. It offered us the opportunity to be cattle. We could feed a fraction of our population to it, in exchange for living. It said Aegae had people in the middle layers who took that deal.

"There might be millions. Or we might be already facing most of the Swarm. Look, we can face them right here in a while, when we could be well choking on Chilo's air all around us. But I'd prefer to fight them with good air, buoyancy, and a city under my feet."

The pipiltin started to argue with Pepper, much to his annoyance. They yelled at him for turning down the truce without consulting them, but then agreed that they wouldn't want to live as brain-dead pawns to the Swarm.

"This is our home," Ohtli finally said, stating the biggest objection.

"Not anymore." Pepper tapped the table and the blueprints. "It's a failed battleground. We need to, quite literally, take the high ground."

They stared at him. Pepper realized that they agreed, and were looking for him to lead.

"And the sooner the better." He clapped his hands.

"What about the elderly. . . ."

"Get them down to the docks as best we can, give them the choice to stay with guns and snipe at the Swarm or take a final shot. Get as many children into the center of the attacking force or down here to get aboard fleeing ships as you can. Everyone else, spread the word. Use loudspeakers in the lower layers, word of mouth in the upper so that the Swarm doesn't get wind of this. You have an emergency system, klaxons of some sort? Good, tell everyone when they sound off, they rush for the other city."

"We'll lose so many. . . ." Necalli said.

"We'll lose everyone if we don't," Pepper replied.

There was a shocked silence as everyone surrounding the pipiltin reset. They'd been planning a long dug-in defense on their home territory. Now they were invading the enemy.

But the alternative was to stay here and die. They realized Pepper was right.

Pepper clapped his hands again. "Let's get moving."

He would hold back, helping the stragglers, fighting the rearguard action. He had the most protection, speed, accuracy, and strength.

CHAPTER FIFTY-SIX

The fire line went up in one giant whumph that Timas felt from a hundred yards away. The blaze leaped high into the air, hiding the Swarm from them. Everyone got to work, pulling the barriers aside and lining up in the streets. The elevators had been working overtime, and people packed every inch of the houses of the upper layer.

Over the last hours of fighting people had been evacuating by the docks as fast as possible. Thousands more had moved up to the upper layer. They packed the streets outside the atrium, waiting for the signal. Below the roof Timas stood on he could have walked on people's heads all the way to the elevators were it not for the forest of billhooks people carried.

Katerina grabbed Timas by the hand. "Good luck."

"You too."

They walked down the stairs together to the street level, and then looked toward the fire. Soon the alarm would sound, and at the moment they would open up full fire.

Then they would rush the Swarm, not even trying to stop it, but just get to safety. It had to be waiting. It had to know that Yatapek was losing altitude.

Timas felt his stomach flip-flop.

He was going to run straight to his death, and he trembled slightly.

He'd faced death on the surface. But this was less academic, and more real. The Swarm waited over there, out in the open.

The fire danced high, mesmerizing him as he stood in the jostling crowd.

"Have you seen Pepper?" he asked.

Katerina shook her head just as the klaxons sounded. The crowd surged forward. On the road in front of them several grenades exploded, blowing the fire out.

They moved out in the thousands, and on the other side of the fire line the Swarm milled, waiting. But it was confused, riddled with the counter-infection, parts of it jostling, wheeling about, and trying to cordon off the biting recipients of Heutzin's blood.

Someone at the front started a loud scream, a war cry, and it rippled down the ranks, until it reached Timas, and he found himself caught up in it. He was a part of the group, running in rhythm, a primal rage directed out as they ran toward their enemy.

The mass of humanity struck the Swarm. Billhooks out, shields raised by anyone on the edges, they scythed their way through, momentum and edged weaponry carrying the tide on.

Timas spotted the vacant face of one of the Swarm shoving through, but a billhook hit its neck, blood spurted, and it dropped down where it was trampled.

People fell, to the sides, yanked away. The front lines folded as Swarm threw themselves at people's knees. But those following stampeded right over them.

The herd of humanity continued, forcing the Swarm out from in front of it, until it hit the tortured mess between the two cities.

This was where people toward the back came in, carrying large planks over their heads to reinforce the rickety bridges the Swarm had already laid between the two cities. These were passed forward, as well as rope. Yatapek stormed into the space between the cities.

Swarm threw themselves at the sides of this river of humanity, and billhooks lashed out in response. Blood flowed, bitten, slashed, shot, from all sides. And for every human that fell, another showed up from behind. Timas could see all this from farther in the back.

Anyone bitten rushed into the midst of the Swarm, trying to cause as much chaos and death as they could, trying to die fighting.

Swarm waited on the other side as Yatapek took bridges and approached Aegae.

"Ahead!"

"Take a deep breath if you don't have an air mask," someone yelled. "Then make a run for it. Those of you that have air masks, take a breath, then pass it back."

Timas reached the planks, slowly now, moving over the wreckage around the worst of the gap. Some moved too quickly and fell off the planking. They fell between the cities, screaming on their way down, bouncing off parts, impaling on others, or just falling down toward the clouds.

Timas slowed even more. He climbed up a large spar that stuck up into the air at a gentle angle. Katerina followed him as he walked up it, bent forward. Now he looked out over the thousands of faces determinedly thundering their way through the wreckage toward Aegae.

"Do you see Pepper anywhere?"

Katerina scanned the masses. "There. In the far back."

Pepper fought at the tail of the invasion, trying to slow the Swarm down from their attempt to dissolve it. The suited figure leaped into the air and twisted, a constant flash of muzzle fire from his gun as he sped from spot to spot.

From a distance, it was like watching a hummingbird. Pepper moved so fast one couldn't see the individual movements.

But then Timas saw it happen: the Swarm moved like a pincer to cut off the stream of humanity between

Pepper and Timas. Pepper and the people he stood with made a large ring that faced outward. They were being forced away from the bridge between the cities.

Timas couldn't stand and watch. "Please, don't follow me," he told Katerina as he ran past here. "I have an idea."

The airlock where Itotia said Pepper stored his escape bubble was out along the nearby rim, and Pepper was being forced away from that one as well. Pepper tried to break free, but the Swarm piled bodies deep to stop him. It clearly regarded Pepper as the most important target.

There was another airlock, even farther down. Timas started shouting for an air mask, loudly and while fighting the people storming past him.

Someone finally shoved one in his arms.

Timas moved to the edge of the crowd and began climbing down through the wreckage. His machine gun hung crooked, and he almost lost it a couple times.

There were no Swarm in the nooks and crannies, and when he finally got down to the outside lip, one of the seams that ran around the outside of Yatapek, he pulled the air mask on.

He had no safety lines, and the seam jutted out only a foot. He'd felt safer when he walked over the wreckage between the cities.

Timas leaned against the city wall and carefully made his way along to the airlock. His exposed skin tingled, exposed to the wicked air without protection. As they had dropped closer to the clouds, the sulfuric acid in the air had increased.

Now it burned a bit.

He got to the outside of the airlock with only one turbulent, lurching moment where the city shook and almost bounced him right off.

Once safely in, Timas hunted around until he found the large package. Pepper's escape bubble.

He opened the inside door to Yatapek carefully, thumbing the gun's safety off.

The Swarm all had moved through the fields toward the elevators.

Timas held the package up and fired his gun into the air. He saw Pepper, in mid-leap, in a ring of much fewer surviving fighters, spot him. Timas held the package up, and then pointed at the next airlock.

Pepper nodded.

Timas cycled back outside, but this time he snagged a run-line and snapped into a track on the lip's surface. This time he ran.

To one side: a long fall to the clouds which now lay just a thousand feet below the city. Yatapek's hull would kiss them soon.

The airmask started to run out of air by the time he got into the next airlock. He swapped it out for another. As he did so, a heavy vibration hit and the entire city tilted up even higher. Timas pressed his face to the airlock's porthole in time to see the Aeolian city rip free, debris falling clear as the two massive structures separated.

The door opened, Timas swung around, his gun up, ready to shoot, and stopped himself as Pepper leaned in. "What the hell do you think you're doing?"

"Helping you."

"You got clear with everyone else. At least ten thousand people got into Aegae, but you're still down here trying to get yourself killed." Pepper pulled a clip out of his gun, slapped a new one in, and looked behind him.

Swarm gathered several hundred feet away, getting numbers together, moving against each other in odd, swirling patterns with their hands held up.

Pepper held the gun up with just one hand and fired in careful, single-shot bursts. Five heads exploded. The Swarm retreated another hundred feet.

"I have your escape bubble," Timas said. "It's a multiple-person one. If we strip you out of armor and get in, we can get out of here."

"You assumed I needed help, Timas. I was trying to save those people back there. I wasn't trapped. Don't think that I can't handle myself. What you're asking me to do now is render myself defenseless. I won't be doing that."

"Then what are we going to do?" Timas looked back out at the door. He couldn't try and get back to the other city now.

"Give me that." Pepper snatched the escape bubble away from him and tucked it under an arm. "And come on."

Shots kicked up dirt. Timas jumped back into the airlock. "They're shooting! Why now? They haven't done that before."

Pepper shot back, and ducked into the lock himself. "The Swarm aboard Yatapek realizes it won't be growing itself or taking the city, so now it just wants to kill as many of us off as possible. There are maybe a couple thousand left, thanks to the counter-infection."

Timas saw the world outside the airlock turn a thick brown. They'd fallen into the clouds. His ears hurt as the air pressure increased. "What do we do?"

"We're going for the docks. Do me a favor, be careful with that gun and don't shoot me in the back."

Of course, Timas thought. The alien airship was down there. Pepper lived among that level of technology; he would be able to fly it.

They burst clear of the airlock, and Pepper sprinted ahead, shooting at the Swarm off into the distance. The ones with guns. He dropped them with deadly accuracy, and the ones nearby, he kicked back to clear the path.

Timas fired his machine gun in small bursts as he saw figures jump at him. They fell back, but he could see them crawling along, still alive. You really had to hit them exactly in the head.

One of them got close, really close, biting the hem of his ragged trousers. A strip of cloth tore off in its mouth as Timas kicked it in the head and kept running up the street. Up, it seemed, because Yatapek hadn't quite recovered. It still tilted, losing more air, and thus buoyancy, from the rent where the other city hit. Looking over at it, Timas could see more brown Chilo air pushing in like a malevolent brown fog. The thick clouds dispersed throughout the entire upper layer, making the whole dome hazy. And it grew worse with each passing minute.

Everything cast shadows in the gloomy, deep brown twilight now that the entire city was wrapped in the clouds. Sulfuric acid rivulets dripped from the great gaping wound in the shell.

They burst into the empty streets. Timas could feel his mouth getting dry, and he gasped. Pepper slowed to a fast walk, occasionally shooting stray Swarm in the head as they stumbled out from between alleyways. The air had grown almost too thin. Survivors who hadn't made the escape to Aegae choked as they tried to hold the Swarm back from the atrium. Fortunately most of the Swarm choked as well, vulnerable to the same problem.

"Falling back into door-to-door fighting is good," Pepper said. He didn't sound affected by it at all. "Touch seems to be the way they communicate fastest, so the open fields were dangerous. Here we break them down into individual units with basic instructions." He fired again as another one stumbled down a set of stairs.

It dropped back minus a head, blood geysering out from its throat. Timas jerked his eyes back down the street, but it felt like the image had seared itself onto the back of his head.

"Keep moving," Pepper said.

They hurried through the streets, retreating with the surviving hundreds that converged on the elevators and emergency stairwells.

Timas looked around, astounded as the survivors lined up quietly. No pushing, no noise. They all rode the city down to its bitter end, fighting the Swarm for every last inch. And they didn't see the need to panic, they just maintained their determination. It took ten overly long minutes to wait in line, trusting people near the back to keep the Swarm at bay.

The Swarm had gotten within a couple hundred feet when they stepped into the elevator and headed down.

Far overhead the city groaned. The layers were exerting heavier loads on the parts of the shell that were undamaged. As they slowly descended through the atrium Timas saw fires burning among buildings, gardens, and avenues. They passed opposite the other side where a tiny figure of a single person with a billhook held off seven Swarm advancing on him. The man climbed up onto the balcony after one of them bit him. He plummeted down the atrium's shaft, hitting some of the spars on his way down.

Pepper watched the body fall, but made no comment.

The air got better. Here it was trapped behind street bulkheads, in between layers, and in the atrium. Timas stopped wheezing.

When the elevator got to the docks Pepper ducked

out first, checked the area, then waved Timas on. Before he stepped out of the elevator, the brown murky light washed out into a general dimness. Timas looked up through the elevator's transparent top, up the long shaft all the way to the top of the city. He could see the undersides of the clouds. They'd passed through.

He ran out after Pepper.

Down here, it was like the exodus in all the other layers hadn't happened. Grim-looking Jaguar scouts manned the same defenses Timas had passed on the upper layer to get to the atrium.

Pepper and Timas used call and response passwords to pass through. Several men had large jugs of pulque and big smiles. They were dead men, finding liquid courage.

Timas couldn't blame them.

Others sat with their guns cradled, business as usual, waiting for some threat to attack them.

"We didn't have time to assemble," they told Pepper. "We were to be the second wave, but the cities separated, so we retreated down here so we could at least die with dignity."

Several of them had come down, layer by layer. "We found some children in the houses in the mid-layers," they reported. "Their parents couldn't get them up to the upper layer or down here to the airships that were leaving."

They took Pepper and Timas to the alien airship, where the hatch had been shut. "Do you know how to fly it?"

Some of these people had drawn straws to fly out on the last airship that had risked docking with the city. And those that had found escape bubbles stocked in the docks had already since bubbled out.

A little less than half the city had escaped, they all guessed, comparing notes. Although what the thousands who crossed into Aegae would find, no one knew for sure.

The mid-layer children had missed both chances. They stood huddled together in a small group, grim, tired faces regarding Pepper with a faint flicker of hope.

"I can't fly it," Pepper said. "I have no idea. But it is designed to survive the surface, and inside it will have anti-crash mechanisms. There's a good chance they'll survive the impact. The city has enough air in its buildings and inner structures that even as it drops down, with remaining buoyancy, heated air, and the thicker atmosphere, terminal velocity will be fairly low. Leave them in there."

But there was no more room for Timas once the children were herded into the alien machine.

Timas turned to Pepper, who looked at the mechanical hand in front of him. The hand that Pepper didn't have.

CHAPTER FIFTY-SEVEN

Pepper made a fist. "Timas, I'm not going to risk being infected. If I bubble off and get picked up by them, I'm an easy capture. There are things I know that the Swarm could use."

"You're Pepper, damn it!" Timas looked slightly panicked, certainly trapped.

"I can't risk it." Pepper grabbed him by the elbow and forced him to march along.

The damn kid had complicated it all. All he had to

do was to follow what he'd been told and invade the other city with everyone else. It had been a bold gesture, trying to save Pepper's life. But sadly, one with consequences. Whether fair or not.

Pepper led him into the prep rooms for the groundsuits and pushed Timas toward the nearest, a bulky yellow one. "Let's suit you up."

Timas didn't get it for a long second.

"Move," Pepper snapped. They didn't have much time. Timas jumped into motion. Pepper helped him get into the insectlike contraption. "You have almost the same chance as the kids in that craft back there, in your suit. The heat, the pressure, they won't kill you. The impact, that won't kill you as long as you find a solid place to hide with some cushioning. What might kill you is the structural collapse."

Timas stared as Pepper snapped the torso together. "Collapse?"

"When the damn city hits the ground and starts breaking up. I recommend not going to the upper layer, as parts of the city's wall will break off and fall onto it. Get a couple layers beneath that, but as close to the atrium as possible—it's stronger."

"You're leaving me here to die."

"We're both at extremely high risk for dying; don't assume the bubble will work. We could get picked up by the Swarm."

"You're leaving me here to die," Timas repeated.

"I have *responsibilities*," Pepper said. "One of them is to destroy this threat. The last is revenge. You're panicking right now, but you're not dead. You need to keep yourself pulled together. You made a mistake, I'm trying to help you save your life."

Pepper grabbed the collar of the groundsuit. "I would go down if my suit didn't leak. I would have gone for the aliens. I would ride the city down to the surface with you. You understand. I'm not asking you to do anything I wouldn't, if I had the right equipment. Understand?"

Timas swallowed. "But we're falling out of the sky."

"When they drop probes on planets like Chilo they don't include parachutes." Pepper tapped Timas on the cheek. "They let them drop out of the sky. If you want cloud data, you use the parachute to hang out up here for a while. But if you're headed for ground, you jettison it. How fast does the probe, filled with delicate instruments, hit the surface in soupy air like this?"

"I don't know."

"Timas, look me in the eye and guess." Pepper again tapped the collar of the suit, getting him to look forward.

"A hundred miles an hour?"

"Fifteen."

"Fifteen?"

"Fifteen miles an hour. The thickness of the atmosphere that deep changes terminal velocity. The city will still have air, compressed into odd spots, but still helping buoyancy. The heat will also add buoyancy. It's why your suit filled with air gets easier for you to use down on the surface than up here."

"Fifteen." Timas looked down.

"The atrium is the core of the city, made out of nanofilament, as are the layers. They'll flex, but hold at those speeds." Well, near the atrium they should, the edges would snap for sure. But Timas didn't need to know that. "You keep your cool. Find a place that's soft and safe where I just told you, and then your job is to get to Hulbach so that they can go rescue those kids from the craft down in the docks. Here, this is a beacon, you hang it from your neck. Use your chin to trigger it. Even Hulbach will hear it. It's pretty powerful. Raga from orbit will hear it, okay?"

That got his attention. "Okay."

"You stay here, though, until the heat starts cooking the Swarm. You don't want to get attacked."

Pepper latched the helmet on to Timas and slapped it. Timas gave a thumbs-up, and then Pepper left him.

Already acrid Chilo air had started to seep in everywhere. In the distance Pepper heard coughing as people struggled to breathe.

He had thirty minutes of continuous power left in his suit. Less than he'd wanted, jumping around so much. Had that been worth risking Timas's life for, even with all the assurances Pepper had given him?

Pepper couldn't be sure as he sprinted out of the docks and up through the city, headed for the airlocks. It took too many minutes to get up there. There was also a risk that the escape bubble would not be able to work in the pressure they'd descended to. Pepper had been adjusting his ears all along.

Swarm waited for him as the elevator opened. It only took Pepper a couple minutes to empty the clips in his gun as he tried to clear a path to run down. The air almost choked him, thick with acid and carbon dioxide.

Even altering his lungs in anticipation wasn't helping. Most of Yatapek's breathable air had been mixed with Chilo's up here.

The doors shut, hit his elbows, opened again.

Pepper pulled out his sword. The empty-eyed people crushed inward, and he walked out into the middle of them, step by deliberate step.

"You're just lining up for me now," Pepper said. "Aren't you?"

Each step was accompanied by the death of another

piece of the Swarm trying to stop him. It was clear what it was trying to do: slow him down to trap him here on the doomed city. It just threw bodies at him, regardless of the cost. The counter-infection had reduced its numbers, but what hundreds it had, all moved to block Pepper's route out of the streets.

"A brutish solution." Pepper swung, time after time again. He created a charnel house of blood and severed heads. He stopped only to dip into houses, seeking pockets of fully breathable air where he would gasp and listen to the Swarm batter at the doors.

Then he'd break back out into the street to force his way to the next house. Blood dripped down his arms via the sword and stained his boots where he crushed in heads.

A strange peace washed over him. He'd always anticipated dying in battle. This stand would not be forgotten: slaying the Swarm while standing on the deck of a doomed city falling down toward a hellish ground.

It fit.

The Swarm would win. And that pissed him off enough to pick up his pace, slowly pushing the carnage along, aware that Swarm blood ran in the gutters of Yatapek's streets. He'd moved from the elevator through the central street, almost to the last houses, when the Swarm stopped.

The bodies, their strange communicative waves of fronds shifting, moved out away from him.

He tensed, expecting weaponry. A grenade, a distant sniper shot . . . anything. He staggered, alone in the street, in front of a faceless enemy, that looked back at him with hundreds of faces that had once been people.

The Swarm spoke to him again. Parts of the entire crowd spoke each phrase.

"We are no longer effective."

"The battle is over."

"We offer you the freedom to pass, if you will give this message to our otherself."

"Our nature has been betrayed, and it undid us."

"We trust you will keep your word."

Pepper looked at the line of speakers. Then nodded as he coughed. "Is that it, or should you tell me something more detailed?"

"Our otherparts may already know about it."

"If not, it can determine what we mean by pondering."

Okay. Why not? "I'll pass it on. I give my word."

And then like some bizarre honor guard, a lane opened. The Swarm stood side by side along the road. Pepper staggered through it.

Minutes later, shooting up toward the clouds, looking down at the city far below slowly plunging down toward Chilo, Pepper crossed his legs.

Betrayed?

What could betray the Swarm?

It was a question he had to shelve as he rose above the clouds and into the still explosive air battle. A strong wind current would take him toward the Aeolian city.

If he didn't get shot out of the sky by any number of airships and crossfire on his way there.

CHAPTER FIFTY-EIGHT

People died not too far from Timas. They collapsed against the wall, bent over, sucking in deep lungfuls of air and then coughing and choking. One of the soldiers dropped his gun and the bottle in his other hand and staggered past Timas. His reddened eyes darted around the room. He fell forward and balled up, gasping, wheezing, and sucking at air that only betrayed him.

Timas could hear the screams, distantly, through his helmet. He wished he could block them out, but he couldn't. Could he go out there, and see what was happening to the people who couldn't escape?

Not yet.

He sat on the bench in his suit, staring straight ahead at the lockers until one of the posters began to curl and blacken.

Too long.

Timas staggered up and walked out.

All throughout the docks people lay sprawled in tortured poses. He stumbled past them, trying not to look.

He had no idea how much time he had left. Or if the elevators would even work. He had gotten too scared and he'd frozen up. He might die yet.

Halfway to the elevator something moved. A strange-looking member of the Swarm with extra-thick skin, like nothing Timas had seen, staggered forward. It was adapted for the deep, he realized. Thick, almost skeletal skin. Glassy eyes. It struggled to breathe, but it still lived, unlike anything human in Yatapek now.

When it saw Timas it changed course, stumbling for him. Timas patted his waist. His gloves clanged against the groundsuit. His gun remained left behind. Not that he could have used it, but he felt naked.

The creature hit, and Timas grabbed its throat. He struggled, off balance, scared of falling on his back and damaging the radiator fans on the back of the suit. It pushed him, but weakly. Timas leaned forward, thinking about the choking soldier, and squeezed. He kept pushing and tightening his grip, screaming, until he fell forward with its dead body limp in his hands.

Shaken, he pushed himself back up to his feet.

Heat rippled off everything, and just as Timas reached the elevators the power shut off to the entire city.

Darkness reigned. Light spilled in from the atrium, and in the distance through the layers via the edge of the city. But everywhere else, night.

Timas ran toward the edge of the city where he could see what path to take.

Each layer had grand steps leading up to the next at the edge by the city's shell, like at the mezzanine. He began to clamber up them, struggling his way foot by foot. Condensation dripped from his visor as he panted. He sprinted as best he could in the heavy suit for his life.

He wasn't going to get as high up the layers of the city as Pepper recommended. He stopped at one point, looking out of the city and realizing that the city wall wasn't bulging inward like the airships he'd seen fall.

Because it was already holed.

As he realized that, the city broke through the last cloud layer and Timas saw the surface.

Now he ran inward, into the dark, toward the atrium. With every heavy step he scanned for more modified Swarm. Fortunately, no more came. He cut through alleyways, homes, and kept going until he found a garden.

There was a fresh pile of dirt near a half-finished flowerbed.

Timas lay down face-first on it as the entire city started to shake violently. They had hit ground.

He could twist himself to look out the side of his large helmet and see the city, all askew from his perspective on the ground. At first, it shook, like on a heavy turbulence day. But then nearby buildings collapsed, facades falling forward. It was worse than any heavy weather he'd ever been through.

Layers trembled, visibly curving, and roaring filled the air, thudding through his chest.

Pieces of the upper structures started breaking off and raining down around the city's edges. The walls exploded, compressed as waves rippled through them.

Then the real shock hit. The ground underneath Timas kicked him up into the air. He fell back onto the dirt face-first and smacked his head against his faceplate.

Dizzy, lip bleeding, Timas waited as the world came to a stop. Girders, large chunks of plating, and then a mountain of dirt rained down on his layer's edges, but the atrium held firm.

The rest of the city was a mess and he was trapped in its maze with hardly any light. But he was alive, and on the surface of Chilo.

Timas fumbled about with his chin and triggered the beacon Pepper had given him. In the sweaty darkness, still feeling rumbles outside, he wondered what to do next.

PART EIGHT

CHAPTER FIFTY-NINE

Pepper sat in one of the round airships that Hulbach Cavern had given to the Ragamuffins so that they could ship people from Aegae down. He hadn't had time to visit a medical pod; others needed assistance more than he did. But he had scrounged up a fully powered pack for his groundsuit.

He filled out the bulk of the craft's interior on one side. Someone had removed three chairs for him to sit on the floor, back against the curved wall. Claire rode with him on the other side, free for now of Amminapses's control. She sat in her chair, staring ahead, deep in thought.

"How's Aegae?" Pepper didn't want to sit alone with his thoughts for the whole length of the trip to the surface.

"You were there," Claire muttered.

"I left the moment the Ragamuffins arrived. I haven't been back. We just picked you up: talk to me."

Her eyes darted around the cabin. "The Swarm's been shoved back into the lower three layers. The survivors there were using an environmental control to vent the air, level by level, then repressurize. They think within a week, between the Heutzin cure, starvation, and brute force, that the Aeolians will have a city of their own again. One that they'll be sharing with Yatapek's survivors."

In orbit Ragamuffin ships clustered, a show of force.

Every day more of them arrived. The League had pulled back. No one was interested in a full-scale space war, and the League could ill afford to lose all its ships.

They claimed to have been coming to offer aid.

"There are other cities the Ragamuffins are taking?" Claire said.

"Yes." From orbit the Raga coordinated a careful action against the Aeolian cities. Any Aeolian cities with tethers to orbit saw them cut, the counterweights deorbited. "Anything in orbit's mapped by control ships, anything capable of holding a human, destroyed. We have the high ground again."

And of course, Heutzin's cure, as it was being called—hopefully to Amminapses's annoyance—was spreading to counter the original infection.

"Our luck," Pepper said, "is that this wasn't released on a normal planet, with cities and air and roads and land. Here, with each city its own world, it slowed down, and once you have the high ground, it's somewhat controllable."

"Are you going down to be involved in the talks?" Claire asked.

The League had always been a threat, but not on this level. Now the talk was on about creating a counterentity to the League, formalizing the process of getting Chilo defended, and turning the DMZ into something else.

So delegates with the authority to make things happen had arrived. Cousins to the people in Yatapek came from Aztlan on New Anegada and made their way down to Hulbach. From Capitol City in Nanagada more Ragamuffins arrived. Pipiltin from Yatapek's few sister cities that swirled around the Great Storm joined as well. Though poor and low in population the Aeolians aboard the airships wanted to settle in these safe Azteca cities. Avatars from the Aeolian fleets flew down to Hulbach as well.

"No. The last thing you'll ever see me do is get involved in that."

Pepper had heard rumors of the various aliens within Hulbach secretly sending representatives of their own, without the Satrap's knowledge, to join the conversation. All of them needed to unite against the League and pool their resources, they said.

The League had thought loosing the Swarm on Chilo would break the Ragamuffins and whoever survived on Chilo, and make the ready to be pulled into the greater human umbrella for an undivided front.

Instead, it had prompted something else.

The Ragamuffins had called it a commonwealth, but after the Nesaru and Gahe formally came to the table and asked for representation, one annoyed negotiator, not interested in having aliens at the table, wondered if it shouldn't be called a *xenowealth*.

The term stuck.

The Xenowealth sprung into creation, born in the high-pressure muck of Chilo's surface.

"Then what are you coming down here for?" Claire asked.

"Visiting someone."

She pulled her knees up. "They thought I was insane to come back down. The Aeolians offered me citizenship in the Consensus."

"You turned it down."

"Amminapses offers extended life in exchange for a hundred years of service. I have one year left."

"You could die tomorrow," Pepper said.

"Big rewards take big gambles." Claire let go of her

knees. "My parents were owned by Gahe, content to parade behind glass for visitors. They were pets. They got fed, they were safe, they were happy. I wanted more. And since then, I got it. I've seen so much more than they could have imagined. I've seen the three suns of Midhaven set. The crumbling reservation walls of Astragalai. The Dawn Pillars, with suns peeking through the dust."

"And what are you going to do when you get free? Other than act like a tourist and see more amazing sights throughout the worlds."

"Undo the damage I may have done these past hundred years. Sometimes I've been released, standing in front of people whose lives are ruined. These hands have killed. I didn't do it, but the blood has been left on them anyway. After that, maybe, I will be truly free. Judging by what I know, I will have two, maybe three hundred years of life after that to see the worlds, and everything else."

Pepper nodded. "You think it will take a hundred years. I've found that redemption drags out longer, because there's always someone else who needs help, some consequence of something you were involved in that keeps perpetuating."

Claire's eyes widened. "You're one, too?"

"No. But I know blood is never a simple equation. You have to fix the things that cascade from the problems you cause, and sometimes, you cause even more problems doing that. I also know that once you make a compromise of the kind you made, other compromises come just as easily later on."

The craft fell through the crust of Chilo's surface down into Hulbach.

Katerina waited for him when the hatch opened. But Pepper had one more question. "Those worlds you've seen, what was the most recent one, before Hulbach?"

"Midhaven."

Interesting, Pepper thought. Very interesting.

"Claire," he leaned forward. "I would beg you to leave the Satrap. It cannot end well."

It never did.

CHAPTER SIXTY

Timas wasn't sure if he wanted to see Pepper. It still felt like the man had condemned him back on Yatapek. Or at least tried to kill him.

But here he stood in the small medical room. The hulking groundsuit Pepper inhabitated was now polished and buffed, gleaming in the cold hospital lights.

By the time he'd been saved, the suit had started to fail and he'd been gasping for air, about to pass out. But all that seemed worlds away, waiting to die inside the ruins of his old city.

So Timas said nothing at first, but took the carefully offered metal guantlet that Pepper still now called a hand, and shook it. "You survived in one piece," Pepper said.

"So did you. Though people won't stop talking about what you did." Pepper had punctured the escape bubble with a sword to fall a hundred feet and land on the airbag of a ship filled with the Swarm. He'd taken it over to land on Aegae.

"You rode a dying city down to the ground," Pepper said. "They're talking about you as well. Trust me."

Timas was embarrassed. "I was lucky."

"That's the spirit." Pepper smiled. "We're all lucky. Enjoy the gift of life, and love the moments that come next."

"I will."

"I wanted to give you my condolences, for your father."

Timas glanced down and held himself together, gripping a pillow. "Thank you." He didn't want to face that right now. So far it had felt like Ollin had gone away on a long trip, and his absence wasn't an absence, but a temporary hole. Like a blind spot.

"I wanted you to know, if you ever want it, you have a position with the Raga. You could work on a ship, see what worlds they see."

"Thank you. I'll consider it." He didn't tell Pepper he had made other plans.

Pepper nodded, and then he looked uncomfortable, not knowing what else to say. "Well, I'll be on my way. I've found some new business on the way down that has my attention."

When he was gone, Katerina sat on the bed by his side. "Somehow, thinking about him just wandering around, looking for something to do without the Ragamuffins directing him, makes me nervous."

Timas agreed. "It's the age."

"Age?"

"He's like Van, with those creatures he made. Only Pepper's project is us."

Katerina shivered. "That's just creepy."

"So." Timas struggled to sit up straight. "You said you need to talk to me."

"I'm now speaking as an avatar of the Consensus, do you understand?"

Timas bit his lip. "Yes, I understand."

"Your application has achieved sponsorship and a successful vote. You are now a citizen of the Consensus, with all the rights and protections that entails." Katerina shook his hand, her face a frozen mask of formality, her words intoned like a judge's.

Then she broke into a great big smile and hugged him. "Congratulations."

Timas grinned back. "Thank you."

"Why didn't you tell me?" She punched his shoulder.

"I wasn't sure I would get in." He'd filled out the paperwork, and since he didn't want to fail in front of Katerina, had asked Itotia to take it to any Aeolian she could find.

His mom had kept herself busy, as if trying to work the memory of Ollin away. She'd even taken his spot hovering around the edge of the pipiltin, getting involved in the politics of the survivors, and the newly developing Xenowealth, as it was called.

"Are you sure you want this?" Itotia had asked.

"We need to be involved, and to understand them," Timas said. "And I'm tired of Kat seeing things that I can't, or talking about things she is learning as she reads them on the spot while talking to me."

"But to become Aeolian . . ." Itotia shook her head. "A zombie . . ."

He had always thought the Aeolians were weak, rich, and foppish. But Katerina had been through all the same things he had, and faced them just as fiercely. "They face the same enemy we do: the League. Besides, we're all foojies now, Mom, you and me, everyone from our city. Foojies no matter whether we go to our sister cities, or back to Aztlan on New Anegada. Or any new Aeolian city. And they're not zombies; we've seen real zombies, I don't think I can ever call the Aeolians that again."

"But my own son, with a metal eye."

"I'm told not everyone has to wear it. It's something you do to let outsiders know you're a citizen. Like wearing a badge, or something."

Itotia had assented, but didn't look thrilled.

Katerina leaned back, and got serious again, snatching Timas away from memories. "You are also aware, that as part of the Consensus, you have rights, but you also have responsibilities."

Timas nodded, nervous. "Yes."

"Your name has been drawn from a limited pool, an unfair civic assignment, but one deemed needed by vote. You are to be avatar to Hulbach."

"I'm not even a part of the Consensus yet," Timas protested.

Katerina grabbed his hand. "I know. We're just letting you know what's in store. We're going to get you wired up for citizenship tomorrow, that's why you're still in the medical center."

"Oh."

"But, since you can leave for now, do you want to go get something to eat together?" Katerina asked.

"Yes." Timas felt like he could leap out of the bed, but she still had to help him. He had been badly burned by the inside of his white-hot suit, and the new skin regrown by Hulbach's advanced medics here still felt stiff.

Eventually it felt okay to walk on his own, and they stood in the park by a wrought-iron arch, looking out toward the wormhole. They found a small place serving stews and soups, not too far from a large green space where small tents camped, full of refugees.

"Our little secret," Katerina said, when she handed him a bowl of steaming stew that smelled divine. They'd been giving Timas packets of warm goop in the other building, all made to help him and full of medicines. But tasteless.

"Our secret." When the tiny robot that probed and investigated his injuries fell out of the ceiling, it had complained about damage to his teeth, throat, and body.

The human doctor, an Aeolian, had come in and

talked to him about fixing all that, and also about preventing it from happening again.

Now there were pills to take that would help his mind readapt, things to read. His bulemia wouldn't go away overnight, but he had tools to fight it. One was knowing what Yatapek, and his parents, had unconsciously forced on him.

Half the battle, the doctor said, was realizing that it would hurt him to continue, and that he had a problem that needed addressing.

Timas sat with Katerina, listening to her talk about what being an avatar was like, and ate his entire bowl of soup and savored every drop. With her to help, it would all be okay, he thought. He would get past this, the death of his father would ache less, and he would find a new home again.

CHAPTER SIXTY-ONE

Pepper found Itotia not too far away from Timas and Katerina. "Spying?"

She jumped, and turned to look back at him. "Just curious; they called to say he'd left the medical building."

"They make a cute couple."

"They've been through a lot together."

Itotia had the red eyes of someone in a great deal of private grief. Timas, he'd seemed somewhat still in shock. But the young always bounced back faster, and Timas was still doped up to the eyeballs.

"Will she move on after things settle? Is he trying to impress her by turning . . . Aeolian? How much will she hurt him if she leaves for other things?"

Pepper looked at them chatting in the distance. "We only ever have now."

"I know. I know." She pushed her newly cut bangs out of her eyes.

"I didn't come to talk about Timas, though."

Itotia looked at Pepper. "What, then?"

"There are delegates down here. It seems like everything not to do with the League has journeyed to Hulbach. And somehow, you've found your niche." Itotia, not being allowed to become pipiltin in the more patriarchal Yatapek, had nonetheless been all over the cavern, talking to representatives in long sessions about what to do next.

"You know what some of the talks have been about. I have yet to meet them, but I know the Dread Council of your Ragamuffins has met to figure out how much fuel it would take for one last attack against the League. We know a great deal of their force is on the other side of this wormhole, which means a lot of their worlds are vulnerable."

Pepper leaned against the tree. "We have. Many want to attack."

"Like you."

A slow grin. "I only wish for the party responsible for all this to pay."

Itotia sighed. "It will be a disaster. We'll kill each other off, and bankrupt each other. The cost in human life will be immense, and the aliens will be the winners, as it will be the League against the Ragamuffins."

"And I agree with you." Pepper waited for the shocked look to fade. "As a founding member, a standing chair of the Dread Council, I think it would be suicide for us to face off against the League."

Pepper took her toward the wormhole, and didn't stop until they were in front of it. "The Dread Council

cannot afford anymore to fly ships back and forth between New Anegada and Chilo. We're almost dry, Itotia,
but we're forming a cordon around the wormhole that
leads out toward Ys and Nebler. That's the new DMZ."

And a lot of captains had protested bitterly at leaving New Anegada to protect Chilo. Even though half
the Raga fleet still remained at New Anegada, they'd
all fought so hard for the planet that it was hard to do
something like this.

With little antimatter left, they'd be limping slowly
from wormhole to wormhole, using tethers to throw
ships out toward their destinations, and using chemi-
cal rockets. Things were changing.

Pepper continued, "The League backed off upstream
through the wormholes. Now we have to decide what
to do here. You're right. We need something unified.
We *need* the Xenowealth. We need to figure out how
to coexist, because when we get the technology to get
out past the Forty-Eight worlds, there will be other
aliens out there. They'll have even scarier weapons,
and if we can't figure out how to fold them in, it will
always be xenocide. Us or them, constantly. And one
day, one group that's stronger will come across us and
wipe us out because we'll have a reputation, and be a
threat."

"So you're with the Xenowealth?"

"The Dread Council agrees with you." Pepper nodded. "Good luck putting your new political entity together. It sounds messy."

She looked relieved.

He saw it in her eyes. She would help create it. She had
the skills, honed from working with Ollin and on Yatapek. And she was like her son. Give them a cause, something larger than themselves, and they both responded:
taking it on their shoulders and soldiering on.

"Just one last thing," Pepper said. "Where's the Satrap?"

"It's gone silent ever since it heard that League diplomats would be coming to offer up a peace agreement, signing the DMZ over to the Xenowealth formally if we all agree to pretend that they didn't try this."

"Ah." He was, Pepper thought in a self-congratulatory moment, becoming better at this . . . lack of brute force. He'd helped usher in something new in this world, but for only as long as the Ragamuffin ships could hold that upstream wormhole against the League. But he was getting better at doing these things.

Being a sly bastard.

But of course, there was still the case of revenge for the millions dead and the loss of his two limbs. He'd mislead Itotia a bit.

What Pepper had planned next was not going to be sly at all. It would be a return to some very old habits.

CHAPTER SIXTY-TWO

The den lay deep in Hulbach in an area few knew how to get to. It was an area filled with deadfalls, poisonous air traps, and airlocks camouflaged to be indistinguishable from the rock wall around them.

The Satrap lurched even deeper through its defenses into its most private chamber. Over the millennia it had grown massive, three hundred feet long, but unlike some of its former brethren, it had always prided itself on being able to move through its own warrens.

Through the eyes of the fourteen drones walking solemnly next to it, armed and alert, it could see what it looked like. Giant, pale, sometimes the humans compared it to a massive trilobite, but without any natural armor.

Hundreds of filaments roiled from its front end, fine enough to plunge deep into any conscious being's brain. They tapered all the way down to points so fine they could caress and fire individual neurons.

The drones around it—Gahe, Nesaru, and human— had brains wired to the local computing environment, as did the Satrap. It used this modern device to control them, although sometimes it missed the physical feeling of taking direct control.

As it entered it took care to utilize every feature of its indentured army to scan its private den: a full view of every crevice, shadow, smell, and sound from three different species.

So it completely felt the stab of panic when all that disappeared right out from under it and all its resources fell away.

Something was attacking its personal den.

The League had come for it!

The Satrap's tendrils whipped out and found the nearest head and plunged deep in, taking control and regaining its sight.

Another couple stabs. It had three viewpoints, Gahe, and two human, scanning the tunnel it had just come through.

"Prepare to defend the den," Amminapses ordered its drones through the voices of the three it controlled. The others blinked as their own personalities came to the fore. They were confused and out of sync with where they were.

None of them had seen the den before.

They reacted, though, fanning out and getting their weapons up and ready to protect it.

Something thudded quickly from shadow to shadow and one of the drones fired at it. Sparks flew, a few shots hitting something.

Then it was gone.

But the Satrap, through the Gahe drone that it controlled, could hear heavy breathing. It flicked the Gahe's ears about, trying to find the source.

"Who's there?" Amminapses finally asked. The assassin had to be human. None of the client races that held the Satrap in such high regard would ever dare think of something like this.

"I'm death." The voice echoed all around. "I have an offer to your drones not under your control. My issue isn't with them: leave and live. Stay and die. You have ten seconds."

It was human.

Two human drones looked around, then took off at a sprint.

Amminapses was disgusted. Disloyal, disgusting . . . humans. They couldn't be used unless under its thrall. The Nesaru, however, now they were a credit to their race. They backed in closer to the Satrap, chirping quickly back and forth to each other, trying to determine where the intruder was.

The Nesaru chirped at the walls, using the sound to echolocate the intruder.

Something dropped from the roof, and Amminapses struggled to spot it with its drones. They lit it up with flashlights, revealing a hulking suit of metal.

"You!"

Pepper shot the first two human drones in the head. Deadly accurate. Deadly fast. The Satrap wondered who gave him those skills and upgrades as it watched the deadly performance. The Satrap's initial defenders dropped without even firing and Pepper leaped away.

Three Nesaru exploded out after him. Cracking gunshots filled and reverberated throughout the den, deafening everyone.

One Nesaru dropped from return fire. The second, Pepper closed the distance on, as bullets sparked and dented the powered suit and the armored hands Pepper held up in front of his face.

He hit it straight on and didn't stop. Amminapses saw in horror that Pepper had destroyed the drone much like he'd done back on Yatapek. The Nesaru spoiled for a fight, but were light. Unless they got their quills in their prey, they were toys.

Pepper threw the third one at the nearest Gahe. The Gahe screamed as it was speared in the face.

Five Gahe ran off as a herd, veering away from Pepper toward the tunnel.

Amminapses would have shot them in frustration, but Pepper turned on the remaining three drones that Amminapses controlled. Shot number one dropped the Gahe, number two, one of the humans.

Then Pepper walked forward. "Did you, for a moment, think that your actions would not have consequences, Amminapses?"

"What are you talking about?" At least this drone had a bead on Pepper with its gun. The closer he got, the better the chance of the headshot working.

"I thought, when you had the counter-infection ready so quickly, that it was awfully useful to have that just lying around." Pepper fired, the movement too quick for the Satrap to anticipate, and the drone dropped to a knee, wounded.

Despite total control, the drone almost dropped the gun. As it bled, the Satrap had to force it with all its mental might to hold the gun up. "That was judiciousness," Amminapses said.

"I didn't think about it much," Pepper said. "I was just grateful to have an ally. Not until I met one of your drones, and she said she'd seen the sunset on Midhaven recently, did I suspect anything."

"My drones have been to many worlds."

"A visit to the heart of the League? A strange place. It got me wondering, and then Itotia told me about your odd reaction to hearing the League was coming."

"Defeat is written into my fabric of being. It is time for me to retreat and give up dreams of reestablishing the Satrapy. I can offer you technologies."

"Yes! Yes, you can." Pepper shot the drone's hand again, and when it dropped the gun he crossed the distance and kicked the weapon away into the shadows. "But you've made that offer before, haven't you? I asked myself, why bury yourself here to hide, and why have an antidote? You told Timas you wanted to gain control, and what better way than with a clean sweep. You gave the League this weapon, a final solution. You told them where to find it, how to alter it.

"Of course, you knew what it was for, and that it would probably even evolve itself to hunt for all intelligent life in this area. That's what it does, it's part of those counterintelligent defenses you claim the universe has made. But we're clever monkeys, and the League, after setting you free in exchange for your transmitting these things to them from a safe location, they decided to hunt you down anyway." Pepper laughed.

But he was close enough. The Satrap whipped tendrils at him.

Pepper had another surprise: a sword. He tossed the gun aside and sliced and twirled his way through the sudden forest of tendrils Amminapses threw his way, trying to get in through his scything to take his mind.

But it couldn't. Bit by bit Pepper kept hacking away

until the Satrap felt dizzy. It was losing fluids from cuts. Its ability had almost been shorn off.

"Stop," it begged through the drone.

Pepper kept at it, using the sword now until only one tendril remained out of the hundreds, the ground littered with their limp remains.

Amminapses felt several stabs to its forehead. It began to bleed out ichor. "I can give you more life," it pleaded.

"What's that?"

"You're already centuries old, I saw that, but how many more centuries are left for you? I can extend that. I have the technology."

"It's not worth it." Pepper stabbed it again, getting close to areas that wouldn't stop bleeding. "Who are you to kill on such scales?"

"And you're different? Look at you now, committing xenocide."

"I'm a scalpel," Pepper whispered. "You're a bomb. Twice now you have all tried to destroy us all. It's time to get you out of the picture. Besides, you said your kind exists out there still. So I'm just killing the last Satrap in the Forty-Eight worlds."

"Let me go and I'll head for deep space and never return."

"You are too full of guile and lies. I can't afford to risk it. You almost wiped us out again. Amminapses, your actions have caught up to you. I'm your consequences, here to settle it all up."

"You are no jury," Amminapses screamed. "You need me to face what is out there in the greater universe."

"You *are* the greater universe out there." As the drone staggered Pepper stepped forward and caught it. He slowly let it fall down and whispered, "I'm sorry, Claire."

Amminapses couldn't even get the drone to attack his face, it was useless, drained of energy. Dead.

Then Pepper said, "Good-bye, Amminapses," and cut the last tendril.

Blind, it listened to Pepper thud closer, and felt the sword bite into its head, carving a long, jagged tear across its front.

"There were millions up there that died, and billions you threatened with your ploy, and I swore I'd find who was responsible and make them pay," Pepper whispered into its earhole. It could only buck slightly, it was so weak. "Maybe you were right, maybe among the lurking threats out there in the universe you were the safest of them."

The voice left the earhole, fading as it walked away, leaving the Satrap to die.

"But whatever else comes for us, we'll be waiting, us and the other aliens, standing together. We'll be stronger as our own people, rather than as subjects to you. Even if you were protecting us.

"And I'll be there with them, just in case."

The door to the den shut with a loud clang.

The Satrap struggled to breathe, sitting alone in the dark, dying. A sad end for one that had ruled all, it thought. Its final attempt to fix the human problem had failed.

Pepper was right. It could no longer help or protect the races it had once ruled. They had been born into the universe, and they would face it all on their own with their childish enthusiasm. It was no longer Amminapses's burden, or that of any other Satrap.

That era, in the next few minutes as the Satrap slumped in its own oozing life fluids, a decorative sword jutting out of its side, was over.

The humans, and their alien allies, were on their own.

ACKNOWLEDGMENTS

A couple of years ago I attended a fascinating lecture about Venus by NASA scientist, author, and good friend, Geoff Landis. He began by saying, "Except for the crushing pressure, acid rain, and melting heat, Venus may well be the next most habitable planet in the solar system, because at 100,000 feet over the ground a lot of this changes completely. The temperature is bearable, the pressure is normal, and you can get above the cloud layers." I listened as Geoff went on to mention that air in a Venus-like atmosphere also provided lift, which meant if you filled a large enough object with normal breathable air it would float.

There was a scientific rationale for a cloud city! But in a very noxious and dangerous setting. This, of course, sparked my imagination. Within ten minutes of Geoff's presentation I had sketched out the outline for *Sly Mongoose*.

After the presentation, I approached Geoff and asked if I could use this setting idea in a novel, and Geoff said "of course." He also burned me a disc of all his research on the matter. So, anything well-thought-through is thanks to him; I bear responsibility for all the mistakes.

I also owe a debt of gratitude to the writers at the 2007 Blue Heaven workshop. My thanks go out to Charles Coleman Finlay, Sandra McDonald, Greg Van Eekhout, Heather Shaw, Ian Tregillis, Paul Melko, Holly McDowell, Rae Carson, Sarah Prineas, William Shunn, and Paolo Bacigalupi for reading portions of the manuscript. Extra special thanks go to Charles Coleman Finlay and Paolo Bacigalupi for reading extended parts of the manuscript and the outline.

I also want to thank my wife, Emily. She patiently deals with my mentally disappearing for long weeks at a time, when the last stretch of writing the novel infects my mind and turns me into something rather resembling a zombie.

Thanks, also, to John Scalzi and Glenn Reynolds. Your links to my work and Web site have gained me a much larger audience than I ever expected with my first novels. Thanks, also, to everyone else who's taken the time to link and spread the word. I'm amazed and always humbled by your charity.

The United States has an amazing library system and such dedicated librarians; my thanks to the libraries and librarians that purchase my books for communities and schools. I'm always pleased when I encounter younger readers who've discovered me in the stacks.

And lastly, my thanks to my readers for continuing to buy my books. You all make it possible. You all rock.

Turn the page for a preview of

ARCTIC RISING

TOBIAS S. BUCKELL

Available now
from Tom Doherty Associates

TOR® A TOR BOOK

CHAPTER ONE

Centuries ago, the fifty-mile-wide mouth of the Lancaster Sound imprisoned ships in its icy bite. But today, the choppy polar waters between Baffin Island to the south of the sound, and Devon Island on the north, twinkled in the perpetual sunlight of the Arctic's summer months, and tons of merchant traffic constantly sailed through the once impossible-to-pass Northwest Passage over the top of Canada.

A thousand feet over the frigid, but no longer freezing and ice-choked waters, the seventy-five-meter-long United Nations Polar Guard airship *Plover* hung in a slow-moving air current. The turboprop engines growled to life as the fat, cigar-shaped vehicle adjusted course, then fell silent.

Inside the cabin of the airship, Anika Duncan checked her readings, then leaned over the matte-screened displays in the cockpit to look out the front windows.

The airship's cabin had once held twelve passengers, but was now retrofitted with a bunk, a small kitchen area, supply closets, and a cramped navigation station. Tourists had once sat in the cabin underneath the giant gasbag as the airship glided over New York's tallest buildings. After that tour of duty, the United Nations Polar Guard purchased it well used and very cheap.

Airships didn't use much fuel. They could put observers into the air to monitor ship traffic for days at a time, wafting from position to position with air currents.

It saved money. And Anika knew the UNPG was always struggling with a lean budget. It showed on her paycheck, too.

"Which ship should we take a closer look at, Tom?" Anika asked.

She'd unzipped her bright red cold-sea survival suit and rolled it down to her waist, as it was too hot for her to wear fully zipped up as regulations required. She had her frizzy hair pulled back in a bouncy ponytail: a week without relaxant meant it had a mind of its own right now. She'd consider letting it turn to dreads if she could, but the UNPG didn't approve. And yet, she thought to herself, they expected her to sit up in the air for a week without a real shower.

Someone once told her to just shave it. But she *liked* her hair. Why hide it? As long as it was tied up, regs said she could have longer hair.

Now Thomas Hutton, her copilot, was all about the regs and then some. He had his blond hair millimeter short. Shorter than required. But even *he* wore his survival suit halfsies.

It was one of those balancing acts: if they kept it cold enough in the airship's cabin to wear the suits zipped up, using the tiny, cramped toilet was torture.

Particularly, Tom said, for the guys.

"Tom?" she prompted.

"Yeah, I'm looking, I'm looking." He walked back from the nav station, the top half of his suit floppily smacking along behind him as he peered down through the windows along the way.

Four ships were funneling their way into the Lancaster Sound from the east, where Greenland lurked beneath the curve of the horizon. The ships looked like bath toys from up at this height. Three of the ships had large wing-shaped parafoils hanging in the sky overhead.

The parafoils, connected to the ships by cables, reached up to where the strong winds were blowing to drag the ships through the water.

"I want to take a closer look at that oil burner," Tom finally announced.

"You are getting predictable," Anika said as he slid into the copilot's seat. Though one of the things she liked about Tom was his easy predictability. Her own life had been chaotic enough before coming so far north. It was a different pace up here. A different chapter of her life. And she liked it. "It *is* supposed to be a random check?"

He pointed at the black plume of smoke trailing from the stacks of the fourth ship in the distance. "That one sticks out like a sore thumb. Hard to say no to."

Anika tapped the scratched and well-worn touch screens around her. She pulled up video from one of the telephoto-lens cameras mounted on the prow of the cabin and zoomed in on the fourth ship.

Thirty meters long with a bulbous-prowed hull, flaking rust, and colored industrial gray, the ship was pushing fifteen knots in its rush to pass through the sound.

"They seem to be in a hurry."

Tom glanced over. "Fifteen knots? She hits a berg at that speed she'll Titanic herself quickly enough."

The Arctic still had an island of ice floating around the actual Pole. It was kept alive by a fusion of conservationists, tourism, and the creation of a semi-country and series of ports that sprang up called Thule. They'd used refrigerator cables down off platforms to keep the ice congealed around themselves despite the warmed-up modern Arctic, a trick learned from old polar oil riggers who'd done that to create temporary ice islands back at the turn of the century.

It was an old trick that didn't really work anywhere

else but near the Pole now. But even the carefully artificial polar ice island that was Thule still calved chunks, some of which would get as far south as Lancaster.

Hit one at the speed this ship was going, they'd sink easily enough.

"Shall we get closer to him and sniff him over?" Anika asked. "Remind him to slow down."

Tom grinned. "Yeah, their credentials should come through shortly. The scatter camera's up. Let's see if this ship's radioactive."

The neutron scatter camera, mounted on a gimbaled platform right next to the telephoto cameras, hunted for radioactive signatures. Port authorities had been using them to hunt for potential terrorist bombs for decades. But what they found, over time, was a secondary use for the scatter cameras: catching nuclear waste dumpers.

At the turn of the century, after the tsunami that washed over East Asia, UN monitors found themselves contacted by East African countries about industrial pollutants washing up on the beaches. People had been falling sick after approaching large, well-insulated drums washed up from deep in the ocean. People had also been showing statistically high rates of cancer near coastlines throughout countries where standing navies and coast guards just didn't exist.

Toxic waste, including spent nuclear fuel, was clearly getting dumped off non-monitored coasts by commercial shipping.

The gig started when a shady company got the lowest bid for safely storing fuel or industrial waste. Ostensibly, they were transporting it out of country to another location.

In reality, once offshore of some struggling African country with no navy, they'd dump it.

Even so-called "first world" countries weren't immune. A statistical study of waste-transporting merchant ships thirty years ago showed a higher number of merchant ships "sinking" in the deeper Mediterranean.

Charter an old leaker, stuff it with barrels full of whatever the host country and its businesses didn't want. Take the big payout, head out to sea, and then experience difficulties. Instant massive profit.

The African and Mediterranean dumping had faded with the EU and East African naval buildups and public outrage. More dumping was going on off Arabic coasts these days. The post-oil-boom nations were too busy trying to destroy each other for what little black gold was left to have the capability to worry about what was going on off their coastlines.

But now the Arctic was also seeing dumping. With the whole Northwest Passage open and free of ice, merchant ships could cross from Russia to Greenland, on through Canadian polar ports, and then to Alaska. Which also meant they crossed over some very deep Arctic water.

As nuclear power boomed across Eurasia and the Americas, with smaller corporations offering small pebble-bed nuclear reactors to energy-hungry towns and small cities demanding an alternative to oils needed in the plastics industries, the waste had to go somewhere.

Somewhere was more often than not . . . out here where Anika patrolled.

Hence the old, repurposed UNPG spotter airships with scatter cameras. Anika and her fellow pilots hung above the Northwest Passage helping monitor ship traffic that came from the world over. But mainly, they were hunting for ships with radioactive signatures.

The program had proven effective enough. Word had gotten out, thanks in part to a major UNPG advertising campaign online. For the past seven months Anika's job had become rather routine.

Maybe even a little boring.

Which is why, for a moment, she didn't notice the sound of the scatter camera alarm going off.

CHAPTER TWO

Anika gunned the turboprop engines to shove the airship down toward the choppy ocean.

"Do you have an ID on the ship?" she asked. The ship could be nuclear powered, she guessed. There were plenty of bulk carriers that were. But this one felt way too small for that.

Tom had a tablet in his lap and was paging through documentation.

"The transponder onboard claims it's the *Kosatka*, registered out of Liberia. Papers are in order. She cleared herself in Nord Harbor." He looked across at her. "She's already been cleared by Greenland Polar Guard. We shouldn't even be paying attention to her. If we hadn't left the camera on, we would have just pinged the transponder and let them through."

They'd dropped a couple hundred feet, and the *Plover* picked up speed in the still air as the four engines strained away.

"Is there anything about radioactive cargo when she cleared Greenland?"

Tom shook his head. "She's clean on here. Do you still want to get in closer?"

That was Tom, following the letter of the law. The rules said the ship was cleared, that someone had checked it over in Greenland. They didn't need to run a second check.

"Someone in Greenland could have slipped up," Anika said. Or, she thought silently, been bribed. She picked up the VHF radio transmitter and held it to the side of her mouth. This was weird enough to warrant a closer look, either way. "*Kosatka, Kosatka, Kosatka,* this is UNPG 4975, *Plover,* over."

Nothing but a faint crackle came from the channel.

Tom waved his tablet. "Says here it's a private research vessel operating out of Arkhangel'sk."

"So they are registered in Liberia for convenience," Anika said. "But operating out of Russia. And they're studying what?"

"It doesn't say."

"Search around online, see if you can find anything."

"Already on it."

Anika piloted them down through the black plume of smoke in the air behind the Russian vessel. They were catching up to it.

Once abreast, she would run the scatter camera again. This would get them better data for Baffin Island. This way whoever was doing this couldn't then claim the camera flagged a false reading. Even if the ship dumped its waste, Anika could prove it had been carrying something obviously radioactive.

Then the gunships would get involved. And boarding parties.

But that wouldn't be her problem. Which was why Anika liked flying. Back in the Sahara, after she'd put Lagos well behind her, she'd flown as a spotter for the miles of DESERTEC solar stations out in the middle of nowhere. High over the baking sand, she'd run patrols looking for trouble.

Like a god looking down from the clouds, she'd

directed guards out to the perimeter to make sure Berber tribesmen weren't really disguised terrorists looking to blow up the solar mirrors that ran most of North Africa and Europe.

Anika throttled back as she matched speed with the *Kosatka* and glanced portside, down at the ship. It was a few hundred feet away. She could see the silhouettes of figures behind the glass panes of the cockpit windows looking over the ship's decks. The gasbag of the *Plover* had blocked the sun out for *Kosatka*. Surely the bridge crew had noticed her by now.

They had. Two men opened a rusty door on the side of the bridge and looked at her, shading their eyes as they did so.

They ran back inside.

"Well, they're paying attention now," she laughed.

Kosatka was a beater. Rust showed everywhere, and where it didn't, it had been sanded away and covered in gray primer. Patches of the stuff blotched the entire ship.

"*Kosatka, Kosatka, Kosatka,* this is UNPG *Plover* off your starboard side, over."

"Case of beer says they're dumping," Tom said, standing up and looking over her to the ship.

"What kind of beer are we talking about?" Anika asked as she fired up the scatter camera again. She backed the readings up to a chip and slipped them into a pocket on her shoulder. Old habits. Hard copy trumped all. Half the equipment on the airship broke down, and she didn't want to lose the data. Dumpers deserved nothing more than to rot in jail, she figured. And she'd be really annoyed if some slipup of hers let one of them slip through. "If it is that cheap 'lite' beer you had at your barbecue last month, I don't want to win a bet with you."

Tom looked wounded. "Jenny picked that out, not

me. I was stuck in the air with you all that week, re-member?"

"I remember." Anika looked over at the radio. Still static.

"What kind of good Nigerian beer should I bet, then?" Tom asked, sitting back down and looking up his results for the search on the ship.

"Guinness will do."

"Guinness?"

"Number one in the mother country," Anika said. "Someone told me they sell more of it back home than in Ireland." She tapped the picture of her and her father sitting on a blanket on Lekki Beach just outside Lagos. Each was wearing a crisp white shirt, holding a pint. Big smiles. Hot sun. Cool ocean.

"No shit?"

"None at all." Anika grabbed the mic. "Let's see if we can raise them and get them to heave to, okay? Next step: we call in the nearest cutter and get this over with. The camera still thinks they are hot."

Before she could call again, a heavy Russian voice crackled over the radio. "Yes, yes, hello. You are United Nations Polar Guard. Correct?"

Anika sighed. "The crew doesn't know how to re-spond to us on the radio properly." She keyed the mic. "*Kosatka,* switch to channel forty-five, repeat, four-five. Over."

She waited for confirmation, but none came. She was considering switching to channel forty-five when Tom tapped her shoulder. "What's that?" He sounded as if he knew, though, but just couldn't believe what he was seeing and wanted confirmation.

Anika glanced over. The two men had pulled a small crate out onto the metal deck around the bridge. Anika squinted at the contents, but spotted the distinctive and familiar long tube of a shoulder-held rocket-propelled grenade launcher.

No time to react, no time to think. She yanked on the joystick and gunned the turboprop engines to maximum. The massive, lighter-than-air machine banked hard to the left as she flew just fifty feet over the old ship's superstructure.

Crossing to the other side of the ship would force those men to move the RPG over, Anika thought. That'd give her a minute. And it would get them further away as the airship struggled to accelerate toward its top speed of seventy miles an hour.

This was bad, Anika thought. Probably worse than Nairobi.

Definitely worse than Nairobi.

"Is that what I think it is?" Tom shouted at her over the roar of the engines.

"RPG." Anika yanked her survival suit up over her shoulders and zipped it up.

"Jesus Christ," Tom said. "Jesus Christ."

Anika snapped her fingers to get him to look at her instead of back at the ship. "Hey. Stay calm. Zip up your survival suit. And grab the controls."

He fumbled at his suit with one hand and held the joystick loosely with the other. She left him to hold their course and raced back down the cabin.

She kicked a large plastic chest open with one booted foot and pulled out an old Diemaco C11 assault rifle packed inside. She slapped a clip in it, shouldered it, and stood up in front of the rear window.

Some small part of her wanted to join Tom's mantra of "Jesus Christ," over and over again, but she knew that was the sort of useless shit that got you killed. You needed to take action.

She flicked the safety off.

They'd pulled clear of the ship by several hundred feet. The two men had moved to this side of the bridge, and one of them got the RPG launcher up onto his shoulder and was aiming at the *Plover*.

Anika's heart raced as she yanked the rear window down. She could hardly focus as she aimed and fired a burst from the Diemaco, hoping she was in time. The ear-bursting chatter shocked her. It drowned out the engines.

A flare of light burst on the *Kosatka*'s bridge as the RPG launched and flew right at her. Anika scrunched low and winced. This was it.

The entire airbag over the cabin shivered, but didn't explode.

"Did they hit us?" Tom shouted back at her.

"I think it punched through the bag but didn't explode. It just kept going. Check the bag's pressure."

"We're losing gas and lift," Tom yelled.

Anika propped the Diemaco up on the windowsill and tried to get a better shot at the men on the ship, forcing them to take cover in the bridge with their launcher. Waste-dumping *bastards*. An RPG? This was the Northwest Passage. They were just north of Canada, not in some war zone.

The *Plover* slipped slowly out of the sky as the *Kosatka* churned on past.

Up front, Tom got on the radio. Over her quick bursts of fire, Anika could hear him calling for assistance, his voice suddenly sounding pilot-calm as he followed a routine. "Nanisivik Base, Nanisivik Base, Base this is *Plover,* we've been hit by an RPG. We're under fire. Repeat, under fire. We need assistance by *anything* in the area."

Anika kept the men pinned inside the bridge with her rifle. But now another man with a launcher appeared down on a lower deck. Anika swiveled to shoot at him, but he fired first.

She kept firing just ahead of that flash of fire, trying to intercept the insanely fast blur of the rocket leaping at her airship.

The rocket struck the bag and this one exploded as it hit a structural spar inside. Melting fabric rained down around the cabin. Alarms whooped from up front in the cockpit. "We're going down!" Tom screamed.

Anika could feel it: her stomach lifted toward her chest. The *Plover* dropped out of the last fifty feet of air in a dignified, fluttering spiral that gave Anika enough time to make sure her survival suit was zipped and to make sure that she had braced herself against the corner of the cabin.

Outside, the waves became choppier and more defined with each split second as they rose to meet the airship.

The *Plover* smacked into the Arctic Ocean with an explosion of spray and flaming debris as the burning gasbag overhead collapsed and draped itself over them with a fluttering sigh.